ALSO BY PATRICIA STEELE

Living with Cystic Fibrosis
Shoot the Moon
A Roundabout Passage to Venice
Cooking DRUNK, a cookbook
Goodbye Balloon, a children's book

BY PATRICIA RUIZ STEELE

Spanish Pearls Series:
The Girl Immigrant
Silván Leaves – Out on a Limb
Ruiz Legacies – in progress

TANGLED LIKE MUSIC
More than a love story

Patricia Steele

Author's Note

Thank you so much for taking the time to read Tangled like Music. Lark Point is not real and the story you just read, is, for the most part, fiction. Any resemblance to actual persons, living or dead, or actual events is purely coincidental. If there are mistakes in the story, they are my mistakes totally. However, the life lessons and values are real. I learned them from many people who have graced my life. Some, I still miss every day. Others are still touching my life with a smile.

Plumeria Press
Printed in the United States of America

ISBN: 978-0-9890013-2-8
@ 2014 by Patricia Steele
First Edition

ACKNOWLEDGEMENTS

This story was written twenty years before publication. The manuscript was in pieces; notes inside files were so convoluted, I doubted I could ever finish it. In those days, people smoked in offices, restaurants and on every street corner. Ash trays overflowed and smoke lingered in dusky offices. In those days, in an emergency, people used phone booths; cell phones were rare…no camera and no texting. Google was on a desk computer if they were lucky enough to have a computer at all. In those days, my friends took time out of their San Francisco holiday to be my ears, nose, and eyes; they scribbled notes as they traversed the streets and in the restaurant to use in this story. Their vivid notes filled three pages, their accompanying photographs perfect. Today, I Googled the restaurant; it is still in business, larger and successful. I smiled when I compared the sign of today with that of twenty years earlier from the photographs my friends gave to me. Thank you, **Clyde Earl** and **Nancy Donofrio Earl** for your support, believing I might someday write this story. I have filled the trek through Chinatown with your thoughts and my characters eat their meal from your table. You two are the best!

I would also like to thank my friend, **Jeannette Rhodes**. At a time when I was burned out from writing two out of my three books in a genealogy series, she suggested I write something for fun. When I told her I had three manuscripts packed in boxes, she asked what they were. When I mentioned this story, she said, "Do it. I know you love writing fiction." I pulled out the box of files the next morning. Gathering all the notes, finding mismatched chapters, struggling through the maze of papers, I wrote for six weeks before copy editing began. And, I thank you, Jeannette because you were right. It was great fun!

And I couldn't have written it without my copy editor, **Lucie**. She asked me thought-provoking questions through each chapter, helped me fill in the holes and center myself over the crux of the story.

Music can make a heart sing
If your life has lost the music..............
Stop a moment.
Listen until you hear it again.
Follow the feelings.
Make changes

In this world, one can twist in the wind and become tangled in relationships. But there is always the music to activate and stimulate the entire brain. Without music to whisper through our memories with instant recollections of times past, how can we savor the present and look forward to the future? There is classical, jazz, pop, easy listening, country, Strauss, Elvis and Andrea Bocelli. And the beautiful "sweet music" of France or the flamenco guitar sounds of Spain.....

TANGLED LIKE MUSIC

PROLOGUE

He wanted to rip his senior partner's head off. "Darrin Lucas is really a piece of work," he muttered.

Gut clenched, Cole tried to curb his raging thoughts when screeching brakes and the blare of a horn stopped his angry mind chatter. Jamming his brakes, he narrowly missed the white Volkswagen; the other driver answered with a stiff finger, a sure sign his waving-hand apology wasn't accepted. Cole's knuckles gripped the wooden steering wheel. Shaking his head fiercely couldn't dislodge memories of the last hour; a headache inched toward his temples. Still grimacing when the light changed, he pointed his navy BMW through the intersection.

What was it level-headed partner, Steve, mutters? *Breathe in with the good, breathe out with the bad.* He inhaled deeply, thinking it would take a hell of a lot of breaths to make the day right. He focused on his cozy den ready to welcome him. He must balance his partner's duplicity against the scrambled puzzle pieces. Cole was mad as hell and couldn't remember the last time he'd left a court room so bewildered. Driving steadily through the streets of Lark Point, California, he still simmered with the boiling cauldron of questions.

Cole Nites loved his small town with its own art museum, Repertory Theater, television station and small shops that brought a stream of year-round visitors. He enjoyed the small-town-social gatherings that usually helped disguise the personal dissatisfaction living in the fringes of his mind. But no socializing today. He sighed heavily, stretched his fingers from their death grip and loosened his tie.

Today, he didn't see the trees or lush landscapes that typically eased his court-day stress. His mind slipped back to Darrin Lucas again, the principal law partner in his firm, Lucas, Mapes, and Nites. Cole clenched his jaw as he drove the familiar streets, dodged cars, cats and bikes winding his way home. Historically, the three partners respected one another, intertwining their business lives with valuable connections.

For Darrin, it was just business. His legal acumen in the courtroom had always impressed Cole Nites and he learned the importance of connections. Darrin had major links to not only the judges but the staff that dealt in the background. Cole had learned to follow his partner's lead despite his quirky, grumpy exterior. Cole had become a top-notch criminal attorney in Lark Point under the man's gruff, tenacious tutelage.

Cole laughed suddenly and his eyes narrowed a moment before turning his thoughts to the beginning of his law career. Twenty years earlier, he'd begun practicing law in San Francisco. He'd worked harder than many of his classmates, graduating with honors and top of his class besides being the editor for the Stanford Law Review. With diploma in hand, he'd passed the Bar with a burning desire to become the best damn lawyer he could be. He hated the derogatory lawyer jokes. He aimed to prove them wrong. In San Francisco, he'd acquired a host of clients from all over the city. Besides his legal acumen, he was interested in everything; politics, charity, the arts, socializing. He didn't like the word, schmoozer, but he was that too.

He thought back to those days in San Francisco and the sly German who mentored him. As a fresh new attorney at Kent and Heinz, he'd become a shrewd criminal attorney at ease in anyone's company. How he got his polish was a miracle based on his country upbringing but he was in demand at parties, a good conversationalist. He dated but he'd been heartbroken in college and vowed never to fall in love again or get married. The pain just wasn't worth it.

But Manfred Heinz had other ideas. He was devoted to his beautiful daughter, Lauraine, but nervous about some aspects of her life. Her bohemian life bothered him. Manfred wanted to find a strong man to rein her in, but to his frustration, she rejected every man he'd brought home. So, he took an interest at young Cole Nites for more than his law degree. He liked him, thought he might be who Rainy needed and became Cole's mentor. The old man was sly alright.

Cole's thoughts automatically shifted from his late father in law to his wife. A paper thin, fragmented relationship had developed. He hadn't swooned over her and she liked that. He made her laugh and she considered the advantages of becoming a lawyer's wife. She knew it would make her father happy and he'd stop questioning her every move. The old man maneuvered the young couple together. Cole knew he didn't love her. They both knew she didn't love him. But a partnership? It could work.

Cole had learned over the years that slyness ran in the Heinz family but he shook away the dark thoughts. His lips thinned and his eyes grew troubled again. His other partner, Steven Lucas, was a good friend who agreed Darrin's ruthlessness made him a worthy adversary in court.

Today the man had been merciless. Yes, he was dynamic. Yes, he was articulate. But his fairness had always kept Cole's skepticism nibbling at bay. Until today. Today, Darrin's actions warred with ethics.

"He used me to browbeat our own witness!" Cole drummed his fingers on the steering wheel. "Dammit! I won't let this go......." His stomach muscles tightened and his gold watchband gouged his wrist when he jerked the little car into the driveway beside his two-story brownstone. The sodden sky looked ominous while oak trees swayed in a sudden turbulent wind. Cole smiled wryly. The sky matched his thoughts; dark, grey and heavy.

He sighed loudly and closed his eyes as he remembered the date. *Oh, God, Rainy has another event tonight.* How he hated the thought of smiling through another event, but to avoid arguments he didn't usually beg off. But maybe tonight he would.

Blaring music welcomed him when he pushed through the leaded-glass front door making his headache spike a notch. "Ah... how can Rainy enjoy that music so flippin' loud?" he muttered into the empty room. He slouched out of his grey-striped suit jacket and rolled his eyes toward the stereo behind the wet bar. He'd imagined soft music when the Bose player found a home on his bar shelf, not piercing opera or classical.

His shoulders slumped. His neck muscles tightened, hot and stringent, from neck to butt. Mentally dredging up relaxing techniques in his head, he dropped the volume down a couple of notches and sighed with relief. Cole leaned his 5' 10" frame against the small mahogany bar and braced his elbows against it before lifting a bottle of Malbec wine toward his stemmed glass.

After taking a long sip, he looked at the monstrous mirror in the corner of the room where his reflection was caught in the tiny diamond-shaped pieces of glass to bounce back at him. A taut bearded jaw, well-shaped nose and a froth of dark hair fell casually over his forehead. He called it fly away. His mother called it wavy. He glanced at his reflection, studied his face, noticed a bit of grey. The slight indentation of a half-moon scar beneath his left eye squinted. Then, it was lost in the laugh lines at the corners of his grey eyes, luminous, almost too delicate to belong to a man. At fifty, he decided he'd pass inspection. He straightened up and tossed back the wine, running his tongue around the rim trying to catch the last drops, still working away his anger. *Now, another damned event.* He grunted. "I know I've lost cases before......but not often." He chuckled slightly before placing the glass on the bar, hoping a semblance of humor could remove the crustiness he'd carried into the house.

His fingers itched to replace Rainy's CD with George Winston or maybe Joe Sample. Wiping the grimace off his face, he wished for the hundredth time that his wife enjoyed soft music. He resisted the impulse to punch the stop button before retracing his steps. As he pulled off his wrinkled tie, he stretched his neck loose from its confining knot. Slowly climbing the steps, the creamy carpet silenced his weary approach. He heard Rainy's soft murmuring as he turned from the landing where her words flowed softly like feathers in the wind.

"Darling, you *know* I'd love to meet you but tonight is curtains up on the Waverly Home Benefit, remember? I need to hurry. Cole's due home any minute." She laughed intimately in response to the person on the other end of the phone said to her. "Mmmmmm, you *know* I think of you all the time. God, yes! Okay...1:30, I'll see you then...." Rainy laughed quietly again.

Her words penetrated through his headache. Momentarily reeling for the second time that day, he felt like an intruder in his own home. His head swam as he continued to eavesdrop. He knew he should jerk the door open. Confront her. But he did neither.

"No," he heard Rainy whisper, her voice teeming with emotion. "You know I need Cole. We are a good team.....No, darling, not *that* way, you must know that."

Cole arched dark eyebrows before turning on his heel but stopped with his hand on the railing, poised to get away. Anger seeped in to replace shock. Disappointment stepped in second and lastly, to his surprise, studied indifference. Furious but not heartbroken, he called out, "Rainy...I'm home. I'll grab a shower."

His voice hit Rainy like a splash of frigid water. Her red lacquered nails gripped the phone. Blue eyes panicked and then cleared. Full lips puckered before saying loudly, "Yes, Mrs. Peterson, the 24th is fine. I'll call you tomorrow." Rainy gently returned the receiver to its cradle, knowing the listener would understand and placed a hand on her chest.

"Yes, dear, go ahead. I'll shower after you. I'm running a bit behind…."

She heard the firm click of the shower door.

Cole stood in the steaming shower as hot water pelted his tired body. With hair plastered to his head, he lifted his arms and braced his soapy hands against the tiled wall. Now he had two puzzles to solve. One mattered. Did the other?

Later, as Rainy showered, he thought of her large teak box. She'd told him years ago that everyone needed a few secrets. *Strange woman.* Secrets in the box? She was in the shower. He didn't have much time. Secret be damned. As the water continued to run, he lifted the smooth, wooden box from the closet and placed it on her dressing table. It was beautiful. He'd always thought so. The clasp was antique brass and it flipped open with a finger, its hinges worked perfectly. *So much for secrets, it should have been locked, right?*

Inside, he found several letters. M and a miniature butterfly sat in a circle where the return address should be. His fingers stalled over them. Peeking from underneath a scribbled note that read, *I won't forget our first time together* lay red, lace panties. Another letter. Another M and butterfly. He felt sick as he stuffed everything back in the box and snapped the door shut and pushed it back into the closet.

As Cole shrugged into his shirt, he realized he actually didn't give a damn. Sex with Rainy had never been passionate and this was probably why. *Oh hell.* Words flew around in his head. He admitted they rarely enjoyed sex and for some time, they rarely shared the same bed. As the years accumulated, along with a thick layer of indifference, was it any wonder she sought comfort in the arms of another man who undoubtedly looked upon her with affection? Cole was more troubled by his lackadaisical attitude than her unfaithfulness. They'd allowed their marriage to crumble like a dead piece of wood.

Now fully dressed and in control of his random thoughts, he looked steadily at Rainy as she sat before her dressing table. She was staring at her reflection dejectedly to study the wrinkles around her eyes, her mouth. "Oh, God, I'm getting old, old, old." Her hair was draped casually around her shoulders, giving her a sleeker, more mysterious air. Her forehead was high and proud, her cheekbones a model's envy. Her eyes were rimmed in charcoal-gray mascara and she wore a turquoise one-piece gown. The diamond bracelet he had given her several anniversaries ago sparkled brilliantly on her wrist. She stared at him in the mirror and wondered why she never saw fire in his features. She surmised he might be having an affair as she dabbed blush on each cheek, watching him from the corner of her eye.

Cole came up behind her and pulled a tight curl into his fingers. "You are lovely, Rainy. Too bad looks are only skin deep," he said, quietly. He picked up his jacket and walked away.

She stared after him, her blush brush slowing as pink powder drifted onto her table. Her forehead creased and her hands shook. Rainy wasn't surprised at his words, wondered at his strange manner a moment, but hoped he'd get himself together for the evening's event. She lifted an eye shadow brush to her lid and pursed her lips with dispassion.

ONE
Six months later

A brisk breeze tossed strands of dark curls into Anna Berg's face as her Audi wove in and around other cars. They all seemed to be heading in one direction. Hers. Smiling, she turned up the radio and sang along with the Beatles. "All our troubles seem so far away……….."

"Push back the clock with KLOK," the radio announcer's voice echoed around her when the song ended.

"Pleeeeeease…..Mom, must we?"

"Yes, we *must*," Anna said with a grin. "Now tell me about your day, Tessie." She turned to glance at the young woman sitting next to her and marveled again that her little girl wasn't little anymore.

"My Forensic Psychology class is really getting interesting and I aced my English Essay, the one you read on Sunday, remember? Things are really heating up….And the guys are so cute, especially one." Tess grinned impishly. "Mom, wait until you meet Nicholas Alonzo. He has a beautiful face, a cute butt, gorgeous black hair and eyes that burn the soul…." She purred the last toward her mother and hugged her books close to her breasts.

"Tessie, you're only twenty one. Remember, looks are not everything. Look inside the guy for some brains, please."

Atesha Berg, more commonly known as Tess, rolled her eyes skyward. "But, Mom, I have plenty of time to look inside. Nicholas is sexy *and* very smart," the pert young woman whispered with a secretive smile and laughed at her mother's expression.

Anna groaned exaggeratedly.

Tess stretched out her small hand and tapped Anna's shoulder, her bright grape-colored nails glistening. "Get a grip, Mom."

They both laughed.

Anna was forty six. Her skin was soft and remarkably smooth; a delicate olive complexion that suggested southern European descent, which was typical of her French bloodline. Her thick, curly hair was still dark with wispy curls mixed with silver that hung just shy of her shoulders. Snappy, cinnamon-colored eyes smiled beneath faintly arched brows. She thought laughing was good for everyone; it felt like an instant vacation.

Sharing time with her only child was her number one pastime. Her second was her passion for words and writing. She spent time at her beach cottage, *Mirafleures*, to fulfill that need often. It was her haven for writing. Tess was her haven for life. Today she was greedy for girl-time even though it was only driving her to college classes during a busy day.

Tess glanced over at her mother.

The light changed and Anna headed toward LSU along Lake Alminor Highway, weaving in between cars well past the speed limit. Anna kept glancing in the rear-view mirror and singing along with the radio as several songs triggered chords of sweet memories.

"Hey, this is Friday...don't you and dad have that fancy party event tonight?" Tess, looking at her mother's profile, thought again how young Anna looked.

"Yes. It's a benefit for the Park Blocks Association to bring local artists to Bell Towers Auditorium. Tonight's event is at the University Club. It should be *very* elegant," Anna drawled in exaggeration. "Our invitation arrived through the television station for Dad, of course. I heard that all the events Rainy Nites coordinates are spectacular. It appears she organizes events all over town. I've only been to the University Club one time. Now that women are allowed to grace the place, I feel decadent walking through those tall doors......" Anna's voice trailed.

"Rainy Nites? THE Rainy Nites in the society columns?" Tess squealed.

Anna laughed. "Yes, *that* Rainy Nites. She looks so glamorous with all those blonde curls tied up like a halo around her head. I'm anxious to see her up close. I'm told she's a classy woman and not a snob like one might imagine. You know how I dislike people who think they are more important than others based on what they do, who they know or how much money they have...."

"Is she married?" Tess couldn't remember reading anything about a husband.

"Mmmmm, I don't know. The photos usually have her in a group of women...always lots of glitter and jewels with that blonde, curly hair."

Anna was thoughtful a moment before stopping near a grassy incline near a beautiful block of buildings that encompassed the college campus.

"He must be neat too," Tess said through another bubble of laughter. "I can just picture him, Mom....old, rich and bald."

"Really, Tess, what a vivid imagination you have."

"God, Mom, you never know...people marry for money all the time. And besides, imaginations run in our family, right?"

"Okay, okay.....well, we're here, honey."

"Mom, have lunch with me?"

"Can't sweet pea, I have to hit the cleaners and then stop at the library for some research that I can't find on the internet. I'm into juicy tidbits about the rich and famous in this chapter and....."

"....Jeez, don't you have enough yet? You are always doing research or writing," she said, half pouting.

"I need to finish this last bit and then find a murder trial to sit in on. Then I'm set, Tess."

"I know. I don't mean to sound pissed. What are you wearing tonight?" she asked as she half turned toward her mother and reached for the door handle.

"My blue. The fancy one."

"Oh, mother, the sexy one dad likes so much?"

"Sexy one?"

"You know, because part of your boobs spill?"

"Tess, must you bring sex into so many of our conversations?"

"I don't," Tess replied, clearly hurt. "What's so bad about liking sex, Mom?"

"Tess, my darling daughter, nothing is wrong with it. It just seems to be on your mind a lot," Anna said quietly as she closed her hand around her daughter's outstretched fingers on the seat beside them.

"Mom, do you realize you clam up every time sex is mentioned? I don't see you and dad hug much anymore and you hate jokes about sex....and sometimes it seems like you shy away from dad.... you've been married so long, I just don't understand...Does it just disappear?"

"Hey, my girl, leave my sex life out of this," Anna replied quickly, her eyes wide and sparkling. "We are talking about YOU."

"Well, didn't you have sex on your mind even a little at my age?" Tess cried, eyes suddenly angry.

"Yes, I thought about sex a lot then…." Anna stated quietly.

"And you don't now?" Tess asked bluntly.

Anna glared at her daughter.

"Okay, okay." Tess blew air out of the side of her mouth and stared at the campus. Huge fir trees lined the lake; elite houses along the shoreline spoke money across the street. Then Tess smiled.

"Mom, what does Laura think about the book so far? I know she loved the first three chapters. Have you sent her more? What's she say now? Can I still go to New York with you when it's finished? And did you figure out the final title yet?"

Anna's face cleared. "She loves it, yes you can and yes I have." She was happy Tess wasn't still angry but still simmered slightly and wondered why. This child could jump from one mood and subject quicker than popcorn in a hot skillet.

Tess reached for the door handle again but pulled back to ask, "Mom, can you go around the other way just this once? I can run into the west entrance. It's faster and I'll eat there. Maybe Nicholas will come around. Oh, Mom, he is *really* wonderful. When he smiles at me, I melt down to my toes. He kissed me under the tree the other day when we sat out on the grass to study together and I felt filled up, clear up to here," she held her hand up to her chin and grinned. "I'll bring him to dinner one night and show him off, what do you say?"

"Tess, tell me when so I can prepare. You know, linen table cloth, candles, soft music, Taco Bell," she teased, relaxing again.

Tess jumped out of the car, crossed her eyes and struck a pose. "You're crazy, Mom. Love you," she yelled as she slammed the door.

"Love you too," Anna whispered as she watched her daughter nearly gallop across the lawn. Twenty one and still running. Where was I when my baby grew up?

With her wide blue eyes, oval face, high forehead and sculpted features, Tess was a beautiful child and the image of her father except in height. She stood five feet, four inches tall and it looked as if she'd reached her peak. Black leggings and a long yellow top covered her size eight figure and daisies splashed from neck to hem. Her long black hair flew behind her as she ran.

Anna shook her head, looked down at herself and tried to remember when she was a size eight. Did she really care? She pulled away from the college and drove to the cleaners, picked up the infamous blue dress with a vague ache of discontent and moist eyes. Shaking away the sadness her conversation with Tess invoked, she grabbed her notebook and tablet before slowly trudging inside the library.

Her husband, Sam, was waiting outside the library a few hours later. "Want a ride?" He grinned. "I saw your note and thought I'd see if I could catch you here."

Surprised, she slid in beside him. "My car's here, Sam," she said simply. "I just finished another two chapters. Sometimes I can write better there with hundreds of books whispering around me." She looked at him. "Sounds nuts, right?"

Sam only smiled. "I have about an hour before I need to be back at the television station. How about a glass of wine or a quick beer at the pub, then I'll bring you back to your car?"

She contemplated her husband. Dear, sweet Sam. Big, dark and handsome, a man who loved her. And she loved Sam too, loved his patience, his calm, his goodness even though he depended on her to give him strength. She'd always tried to be a good wife and mother and write, write, write until the cows came home. It was the way they'd planned their life together so long ago. But now they weren't in sync and hadn't been for awhile. Maybe if she could get him away from his job awhile?

"France in June," she murmured. "remember?"

"Anna, I don't think I can go this year. Take Tess, honey."

Her eyebrows rose, "Why? You deserve a vacation. I can work on my book just a little and you can have a break," she cried, exasperated. Going to France every year made her soul sing and she would not give up her annual pilgrimage. Postpone until fall maybe, but no longer.

"Anna, Brock said he's talking to Elliott about a new show he might set up at the station. I had the idea and he liked it. It may go through and there may be an anchor spot later." He waited.

"And you want it, don't you?"

"My God, of course I do," he said with a laugh as he coaxed a cigarette out of the Marlboro package. "You know it's what I've dreamed about for too long to remember. It's in my blood and with Elliott pushing my idea and the possibility of actually creating something of my own at the station makes my heart beat so fast, I have to run to catch up with it."

"Yes, I know....." She thought a minute before continuing, "Tess plans to go to summer school so she can graduate sooner. She's ambitious just like we were at that age. She's going to work at the little stationery shop in the mall near the college. So, of course, she can't go to France with me, Sam. Did you forget so quickly that she is tied up for the summer? Maybe I'm being selfish but dammit, I think you and I need time away together. You and I both know something is brewing and we don't like it," Anna said pointedly, feeling miserable.

"Time away, Annie? Will time away change anything? You know I'll always be here for you but I have to grab my chance. I've worked like a slob to get Brock to see my potential as a news star!" He puffed wildly on the slim cigarette and blew curling smoke out his window.

Anna stared at the glowing end as he inhaled. "Come on, Sam, a star?" Anna laughed. "Ok, stay and be a star," she said derisively. "You deserve it. Let's go back for my car. I don't think I can gag down a beer right now after all." She snapped off the words like frozen twigs.

"Anna, don't do that! Honey, this is my big deal. My dream," he countered. I created something here that could take off. My idea could resolve these burglary cases. I can't leave town now," he finished.

She stared at him sharply. "*You* created it? What about Elliott and the crew who put the shows together? You're taking a king's bow? See, Sam? That's what I mean...you are so wrapped up in yourself and the job, your ego is manipulating our lives. You're rarely home anymore; your god damned sleeping bag should be down at the station. That way I won't expect you home!" Tears formed in her eyes.

Sam slowed and stopped the car beside her Audi. He searched for words to make her understand his uneasy feeling about taking even one day off. "I love you, Annie," he mumbled into her dark curls after reaching across the cabin of the Jeep to pull her face toward his.

Anna's anger cooled. Poor Sam. She would make everything all right like she always did. She returned his kiss and pushed the door open while sighing inwardly. "Your tuxedo is pressed and we need to leave tonight about seven thirty for the University Club. It's your invitation, not mine......I'll be ready. Please don't be late, Sam."

He nodded, agreed and gunned the Jeep quickly away from her.

By six thirty, the electric-blue dress lay spread out across the creamy coverlet and Anna stood beside the bed in her lace half-slip. With reluctant curiosity, she studied the cocktail dress that generated the little argument with Tess. The sleeveless bodice was gently gathered at each shoulder, then all the soft fabric was pulled together at the waist with a diamond-shaped, blue sequined appliqué gently swirling above one hip. It was knee length and fit Anna perfectly.

"Sexy?" she asked aloud to the empty room. "Tess was right. That's why I was angry." She grimaced. "What's happened to me? Yes, I used to think about sex. And I enjoyed it. Am I worn out? Am I frigid? Now, just thinking of sex unnerved her; her mind rambled and reeled with self inspection. "I don't want it. Are we just too old or is it something else?" The words jerked out of her soul, her fingers clutched her throat.

She sat on the bed beside the beautiful dress and trailed her fingers along its softness, remembering the time when Sam's touch electrified her with an aching need. She could not remember when the warmth had begun to fade. Maybe it faded for all couples?

Shaking her head, she squeezed her wet eyes closed. Sniffing deeply, she headed to the shower and glanced at the clock for the third time since arriving home. "Where is that man?" she asked aloud again.

Naked, she stepped behind the glass-block wall and braced against the hot water beating at her skin like a thousand diamonds tossed across a room. She reveled in the heat, the solitude and her own space.

"It's me," she whispered as she pulled her hands over her face and pushed it upward into the rush of water. "Sam is such a good guy. Good looking, ambitious, clever, a good friend. But I am a fraud. He deserves to have someone who is truly in love with him, not a woman who pretends, pretends, and pretends!" She twisted around and leaned against the tile, raising her face into the steaming water, and sensitive to the lulling patter that echoed around her.

Her mind raced. *When did I stop enjoying sex? What does Sam think...really? I know he's confused, sometimes angry. If he just didn't want it so often! Dammit. He doesn't demand it, for God's sake. I always say yes. I don't reject him, not physically. It's just...well....*She forced her mind to go blank.

She stepped out of the shower. "Friendly rape," Anna whispered as she walked into the bedroom and gazed at her naked reflection in the vanity mirror. *Yes*, she thought, *that's all it is now. Friendly rape... when you have sex because you don't want to hurt your mate's feelings. Friendly rape is when you pretend you are somewhere else when he touches you. And you mostly pretend he is also someone else.* Just because she wasn't happy in her marriage didn't mean she just needed a man. She wanted to love Sam! Her large dark eyes stared back at her, sad, anxious, and heartsick. She dried her body slowly, feeling the nap crush against her soft skin, a bubble of panic bursting into her chest.

Frustrated to tears, Anna yanked the dress over her head, unmindful of hair or fabric. Reaching behind her back, struggling with the zipper, she walked over to her dressing table and looked into the mirror once again. Her head ached and her brain was filled with a barrage of questions that crashed around inside her mind like marbles.

Leaving her neck bare, she slipped on dangling, blue earrings. Her dark hair fluffed around her face in loose ringlets and her golden tan lent an exotic look to her already lovely face. *Now stop it*, she argued, swiping wet cheeks.

Anna closed her deep brown eyes and pushed her thoughts inward, deeply where she could not analyze them. She applied powder, blush, mascara, blue eye shadow and lip color to complete the look with a quick brow pencil to frame her face. She glanced again at the bedside clock. Seven thirty. We should be leaving now. Where is he?! His tuxedo hung in the closet waiting for him. Her uneasiness mounted. When the clanging telephone shattered the silence to break her moody introspection, she jumped and held her hand over her thumping chest. *Sam.* "Hello?"

"Anna, honey, can't talk long. A big story broke about 5:30 and I got it. We're almost done. Would you mind taking a taxi to the party? I'll drive us home. Sorry about the tux...they'll have to take me as I am. I should be no later than 8:30 or so. They're wrapping it up....'ok, Sal, I'm coming!' he yelled. "Sorry, honey, have to run. I love you." Sam finished, breathlessly.

"Yes, I know. See you there," Anna said, clearly disappointed.

Sam stared at the receiver a moment before replacing it and ran his fingers through his greying black hair. His deep blue eyes looked confused. "I know?" he repeated. He glanced at the phone for a beat before nervous energy enveloped him and he pushed Anna's cryptic response to the back of his mind. He realized he did that more often than he cared to contemplate as he joined his crew with his television-smile.

"Hey, Sam, it's ready," yelled a small man rounding the corner screaming directions to four other people who were milling around the doorway. Everyone, including Sam, jammed into the small viewing room.

"QUIET!" yelled Elliott Barrios, the producer of Channel 14. He had been the producer for nearly twenty years and everyone admired his leadership and ingenuity. He offered Sam a bit story several years earlier allowing him the opportunity to learn the political ropes that invariably ran rampant through a television station.

Tonight's show was a clincher. Elliott was sure of it. The past few months had been a good change. Nobody doubted it. This time, their brainstorm might put Sam in the driver's seat. Channel 14 would be on the map; Sam's own time slot; fifteen minutes every week day. Elliott was so wired nobody in the station could have held him down with anything but a two-ton truck. His sudden movements made Sam tired but he was too excited to do anything but drift along in the producer's wake.

Despite being a short man, five feet seven, no one in the station thought of him as any less than six feet tall. Their awed estimation of him was a given; he felt it, enjoyed it and knew he'd earned it. His bushy grey eyebrows danced spasmodically with each word he uttered. Now his eyes darted around the room, assuring himself that everyone was ready to do his bidding upon command. The technicians watched him for the go ahead. Sam watched the monitors.

"Go!" yelled Elliott as he pulled Sam into the chair beside him.

Lights blinked out. The machine purred and Elliott flipped the remote control button. Sam sat erect and poised, as a fuzzy picture met fourteen pairs of anxious eyes, suddenly clearing as the video rolled.

"Good Evening. This is Sam Berg reporting to you from Channel 14 standing in front of Mayor Sterling's home where…….." Sam watched himself as everyone stared at the monitor, listening intently to Sam discuss the recent theft of the Sterling home. "…..a recent theft has joined a list of others overtaking Lark Point…." Sam's voice continued, his image filling the screen. "…….even down to his wine cellar, his most exotic bottles stolen, which left the Mayor's shelves ghostly and empty.….."

Sam's greying black hair was thick and waved gently in the late afternoon breeze. His intense blue eyes pierced the audience. His six foot frame dwarfed most of his co-workers, although at 200 pounds, his body filled his dark suit coat smartly. His good looks gave women pause and fed their fantasies. Sam was flattered but he loved his wife and his marriage.

Biltmore County had a population of 22,000 in the 415 square miles that surrounded the city of Lark Point, and stretched toward the beach highway. One quarter of the total land mass included artists, professionals and active social communities less than a day's drive from San Francisco.

The artistic growth of ballet, repertory and music hall entertainment satisfied the social demands of the small community by self involvement. The art community grew as more events filled the Lark Point Community Calendar, its Main Street Manager constantly feeding the artistically-thirsty community with events, posters and media blitz.

Hence, the outrage stifling the Lark Point citizenry knew no bounds; its police force fought to contain their fears, answering calls faster than they could investigate the unsolved thefts. The lieutenant on the LPPD was a friend of Sam's and shared as much information as he could without upsetting his police chief, Sebastian Grant. Their office was disgruntled; they disliked having private citizens work unsolved cases. However, they were forced to agree that Sam rattled enough cages that oftentimes, he led them up the right alley. Some said they should hire Sam as their private police consultant. Some laughed, others didn't.

Sam watched the end of the sequence, "…..cleaning up Lark Point is important. We want to encourage our community to relax again. We are a moral people living in a moral community. Thieves will make a mistake. They always do. We'll stop these thefts. There must be many people involved, a very calculated and organized gang. The LPPD is working diligently to stop the pillaging in our businesses, our neighborhoods and our homes. These thugs will regret locking horns with the Lark Point Police Department, Channel 14 and our community. Whatever it takes to run you down, whomever and wherever you are, we will use your conviction as a springboard to make Lark Point the best it can be." He stared into the camera, took a neat breath and smiled. "Sam Berg. Channel 14. Good Evening."

The light went off.

Wild jubilance exploded in the room as the applause wiped out any post-conversations. Sam stood, placed his right hand on his stomach, his left behind his back and bowed to the crowd in mock exaggeration. "Thank you. Thank you my friends and accomplices," he said solemnly and winked at Elliott.

"You were great!" Elliott said excitedly as he squeezed Sam's shoulder. "You should get an award; it's one of the best pieces of reporting I've seen in awhile."

Everyone agreed and started talking at once. More conversation and brainstorming ideas filled the room and hallway outside the viewing room. Minutes sped into an hour.

The craziness had begun earlier in the day when Sam slid into the newsreader's chair. His gut was tight as he clutched the sheaf of news announcements. Watching the floor manager count off the final five seconds on his fingers, he turned to the blinking red light over the camera's lens and the director cued him in. He began reading clear, clipped sentences, his eyes never straying from the camera, his mind on the dark area beyond as if he spoke to his friends.

As his confidence surged, he'd decided to take a risk. He laid down the shuffling papers and smiled into the camera, eyeing Brock Lane across the room. "We have someone special in the studio today," he'd said. "He is a man who comes to us from the realm of small businesses. Brock Lane is co-owner of Channel 14 and the Committee Chairman for FSBO, Fairness to Small Business Owners. He has given us some insight and ideas in connection with police involvement among small business crime." Sam waved him to the desk.

Brock smiled, although guarded, when Elliott found a chair and slid it beside Sam before placing a microphone in front of him.

Sam smiled again as he turned toward Brock, giving the camera his profile. "Thank you, Mr. Lane, for agreeing to share some of your expert opinions with us. In our latest community meeting you mentioned the importance of police backup and the need for aggressive involvement when any businesses are hit with crime activity. Can you expand on that please?"

Brock looked amused, listened to the buzz of anticipation amid the floor crew and acknowledged the professionalism of the man before him. Clearing his throat, he smiled at Sam before turning to the camera.

"Sam," Brock said smoothly, "first of all, our police are ramping up their investigation in order to stop the growing crisis hitting our city. Whether small or large businesses, we all pay taxes and expect a fair amount of police protection. However, our last meeting involved a new set of events as I'm sure the fine people of Lark Point heard recently. There have been systematic and well-planned burglaries randomly hitting our community. We have been assured by the LPPD they are addressing the crime wave and I, for one, trust in their ability to solve these crimes."

Sam nodded. "And, Mr. Lane, don't you agree that a bit of investigative reporting can add something positive to the police investigation following these crimes? You and I both know their team size is limited, barely keeping up with the enlarging case list. Lark Point undoubtedly needs a larger force but, of course, that takes money. Wouldn't you agree, using community volunteers to help canvass the neighborhoods or at least keep special attention focused on strange occurrences might be a disincentive for these thieves?" Sam pushed.

Brock sat nonplussed a moment before shaking Sam's hand across the space between them. "The LPPD can always use fresh information, Sam. I commend you for your offer to help and I invite you and the community to call the police department with any and all leads." Brock finished with a resigned sigh.

The director gave Sam the sign and counted down to close the show. "Our guest today has been Brock Lane. As you see, we are focused on putting the cuffs on crime," Sam said to the camera. "Thank you, sir, for your valuable thoughts and time. Sam Berg. Channel 14. Good evening."

As they cut the lights, Brock asked for a run through of the tape. They stood in the crowded control booth watching their brief interview. "That was good, Sam," Brock said when the tape was finished. "Very professional." He shook Sam's hand and glanced into his face. "Nervous just a little? Well, you hid it. Well done. I think we will want to keep you around....but don't *ever* put me on the spot again without my prior approval." He stared steadily at Sam.

Sam returned his stare, neither blinking.

"Let's talk next week over lunch. Set a date with my secretary. For now, you're our feature newsman, let's go with that." He paused just a beat before looking at the producer whose face was a roadmap of worry. "It leads the seven o'clock, El."

Elliott was startled.

Collective murmurs followed Brock and the smile on his face as he left the newsroom. Several clustered around Sam, some patting him on the back, others pumping his hand. He couldn't believe the difference between this month and last month. Most of the group knew that when a tip came in for a leading story; they scribbled notes for the script but remained faceless. Sam wanted more. As he was placed in front of the camera more often lately, he was repeatedly called a *crime stopper*. That day, Sam believed it.

His burning desire to succeed pushed his job into top priority status. Though stressful, he always tried to be first with the story. Fighting the competition of the local newspaper was a steady run against time. He knew both the newspaper readers and their television audience were a fickle bunch. Whichever media crew had the most breaking news story, that's where they swung.

Sam's thoughts switched gears. Anna used to be as close to journalism and the competition as he was when they both wrote for newspapers in the old days. Then she'd moved to magazines, a weekly column and feature articles before changing to novel writing. Now, she didn't understand or maybe she didn't have time to listen. She shied away from work-related conversations. So obviously irked, that when he found time to fit her into his fast-paced schedule, she turned a deaf ear. He also tried to share his excitement with his daughter, but Tess's world revolved around her college classes and a boy named Nicholas.

The thought of Brock's last words as he left the group made his mind feel like a tangled web of yarn that he didn't want to unravel. The seven o'clock lead! He'd done it. His mind raced. Would Brock offer him the lead again? Would Elliott think more seriously about the idea Sam handed him days earlier about a program geared to a specific audience at the same time every day? Would he get the idea past the decision makers now that Sam's interview with Brock would be the lead tonight? His head hurt and his heart beat to a faster drum than he'd heard for a long time. Or ever?

Elliott called him to go over the other video session and asked him to meet with the cameraman to confirm the interview sessions they'd set up for the next day.

"Hey, Sam, I know you have to get going to that big party, but can we go over a few things first? Brock is going so if anyone asks, he can tell them you had some important issues to take care of. I promise it will just be a few....."

"Sure, but I have to watch the clock, Elliott, don't let me forget I have to be at the party. Now that we have the seven o'clock, I want to watch it. Damn, but this is a love-hate relationship sometimes, huh?" He punched Elliott's shoulder lightly on the way out of his office and followed him to the brightly-lit room the producer headed for. The man didn't walk, he ran, and Sam would do his best to keep up.

Sam jerked in surprise when he looked at the large wall clock. Eight twenty five. He turned for the door. "God, I hate to leave this party ladies and gentlemen, but I'm out of here. Anna's going to castrate me if I'm any later even if I *am* a star....." he said with a chuckle. Throbbing with renewed excitement, Sam threw on his suit jacket and grabbed his Norelco shaver while he shoved Old Spice into his pocket.

Pulling out his car keys, he ran for the parking lot and whispered, "I was great. It feels so good to finally make it happen. God, I can barely stand it....I can't wait to tell Anna." He couldn't stop smiling or talking to himself all the way to his new black Jeep Grand Cherokee.

He shaved as he drove along the rain-washed streets and loosened his tie to splash on the aftershave. The storm of yesterday had left a bright sheen on the streets and pavement. He rolled down the window and took a deep calming breath, pulling to the curb because he needed both hands. "This should make Anna hot. God knows I've tried everything else...." he said aloud, suddenly serious. "There's such a thing as trying too hard," Sam whispered. "It causes constipation of the mind." He harbored the notion they nearly had a platonic relationship after twenty three years of marriage. "Okay, stop the negativity, stop making a mountain out of a god damned mole hill," he said through clenched teeth.

He tried to ignore the seeds of doubt.

Sam lit a Marlboro, drew on it rapturously by long, thoughtful inhalations, making it look like an extension of himself. His fingers squeezed themselves around the leather-wrapped steering wheel sporadically, gripping it as he raced across town to the University Club on the other side of Lark Point.

The Jeep wound its way into the lot and Sam dipped his head slightly after drawing into a parking space. "Oh, Anna...." He sat a moment before jumping out and heading toward the majestic brick building. Shrugging out of his erratically-bizarre mood, he tossed his cigarette into the street. He lifted his hand to loosen his collar, entered the imposing doorway and felt the knot of excitement return.

He needed a gin and tonic and the welcoming group he was sure awaited him. His black hair wasn't long but hung straight to his shirt collar. He was a member of the Confederated Tribes of Grand Ronde, which included twenty-seven bands of federally recognized Native American tribes. But as the face of Grand Ronde ancestry, Sam did not look the part. His Native American ancestry was easy to miss; blue-eyed and black-haired, Sam was a testament against stereotypes. And while his heritage was hard to guess at first glance, as soon as he began talking about his involvement in the Native American community, it became apparent. Somewhere down the line, his great grandfather had married a Quaker woman and the die was cast; his dark hair coloring against tan skin and blue eyes a devastating combination.

The University Club had been around for years; the building was built in 1930 and renovated in 1997, leaving the old intact, encasing the edges with a new façade that defied the old-line members' wishes who grumbled regularly. Many new, younger members pushed, won and the club moved with the times.

Sam's expensive membership gave him a step up in his much-needed confidence. He refused to delve into the conversation earlier with Anna. She could laugh if she wanted to, but he did feel like a star. Was it just an ego trip? Was he just pretending to be a better journalist than he really was? Was she justified in her thinking or should he ignore it? How could a person be a success if he didn't believe in himself? The membership was important and so was his status at the television station. One day she would see it and applaud his work a little louder than she'd done lately.

Once inside the building, his feet rushed up the carpeted stairs, avoiding the small elevator. He didn't want to waste another moment to find Anna, share his news. And of course, he was anxious to meet everyone who expected his arrival. There had been a personal note on the invitation from Rainy Nites, telling him how special his presence would make the event. He grinned.

Brock must be looking for him by now but he shuddered to imagine Anna's frustration when he'd promised to be there by eight thirty. He glanced at his watch and took the stairs two at a time. He arrived smiling but slightly out of breathe. The lights beckoned. The Champagne glittered in their flutes and he began looking for Anna. The room was crowded and he gently worked his way through the throng, needing a drink and looking for faces to light up in recognition. Where was Anna? She should be watching for him, ready to boost his excitement. He needed her strength, warmth and presence. Sharing his newest laurel with her was almost as important as the adulation he expected from the crowd.

He was a star, but a man nevertheless; a man with a dream that was finally coming to fruition all the way from obscurity into the bright lights.

TWO

By 8:00, Anna was strung so tight, her fingers nearly clutched a hole in her purse. Her revelations in the shower and afterward had her mind so nuts, she didn't realize they'd arrived at the University Club until the taxi driver stopped suddenly and jolted her forward. Despite her seat belt hugging her tightly, her head slammed against the headrest and surprised the breath out of her. And she dropped the purse.

"Sorry ma'am..," the young man apologized when he jumped out and rapped his knuckles onto the side of Anna's door before helping her out.

Anna suppressed a groan, paid him and stood on her own two feet, more than relieved. Hugging her ivory jacket around her shoulders, she whispered, "*Seigneur Jésus .... désolé, oui, je suis d'accord*," and realized she'd lapsed into French. "Sorry…yes, I am ok."

He smiled apologetically again before pocketing her money and drove away leaving her alone in front of the imposing building. She shivered, gazing upwards at the immense brick structure surrounded by gigantic oaks laced with tiny lights. Looking at the massive wooden doors, she entertained the notion that the old building was peering down at her. Tall, dimly lit windows beckoned as she walked forward slowly. Each bricked step seemed an unbearable width. As she reached the top, the doors suddenly burst outward, startling her. She prepared for a nasty fall that, thankfully, never came.

An older gentleman with overgrown brows grabbed her and smiled lopsidedly. "Sorry, young lady. I'm always in a hurry and I've never figured out why. Let me help you inside," he slurred amid the perceptible scent of brandy.

"Thank you," Anna said, recovering with a throaty laugh. "At least I'm not entering alone. I've been here before, but….. never alone."

The inebriated man was already gone when the huge doors whispered shut. Luxuriating in the warm interior, she exchanged her jacket for a round pellet that she tossed into her dangling handbag. The unmistakable sound of piano music brought her around abruptly into a large, dark paneled room scattered with chairs where old men sat chatting and smoking. It had been an exclusive men's club since 1867, every corner demanding an image of speculation, politics, dreams and money. Anna smiled slightly. *But times have changed haven't they, fellas? Now women are allowed in.* Her mind instantly conjured an army of stuffy arguments, the vote and finally acquiescence; the club's mystery turned to dust.

There were fresh, tall-stemmed lilies on a side table. When she headed toward the huge open stairway, dark wood reached out to her from every corner. The scent of the old men's cigar smoke lingered and she vaguely wondered why they were smoking inside the building. Turning away from them, she opted for carpeted steps and its oak balustrade in deference to the tiny elevator.

Other finely-dressed women walked next to her, speaking quietly, laughing slightly behind their hands. Anna wondered if they also felt the do-not-disturb feeling emanating through the University Club? She continued upward, pulling herself along the shiny oak railings, her new pumps sinking into the carpet.

A dreamy mood descended upon her as the lilting piano music wafted down the stairs to touch her soul. Smiling at the women ahead, her confidence returned as she entered the large room.

The club was alive with laughter. Murmuring conversations surrounded her. She saw guests wandering from room to room, clad in tuxedos or dresses straight from fashion magazines; the usual attire for a Rainy Nites' fund-raising event amidst diamonds, Champagne and sparkling chandeliers.

Suddenly a smiling waiter appeared holding a serving tray aloft with several flutes of sparkling Champagne. Smiling at the man, she tipped it to her lips and gazed over its rim at the crowd around her teeming with anticipation. She licked her lips, enjoying the taste. Glancing at the label, she was stunned to see it was the high-dollar French *Veuve Clicquot Ponsardin* from Reims. No wonder it went down like velvet.

Beside her, an admiring well-dressed man in a striped navy suit watched Anna's measurement of the crowd around her. Studying her curiously, he said, "Nice party. May I get you another and are you alone?"

Anna nodded toward the gathering. "I'm with them," she said and inched away. The man's gaze followed her lingeringly.

Strangers surrounded her like a human tide. The room was as she remembered, but more elaborate with a fancy face. It was a large room, possibly sixty feet in length. A long cherry wood bar could be seen through double glass doors with an art nouveau front off to her left. She saw the bartender wiping an already gleaming bar, nodding to a waiter while filling a short glass with liquor. There was standing-room only next to them and the group buzzed with chatter.

A long narrow table sat along one wall, an elegantly etched mirror above it. Large crystal chandeliers glowed; their light's gleam washing over the laughing, chatting crowd. Lighted tapers on small, round tables beside stuffed easy chairs reflected the soft glow of lamps beside them; acres of starched, white linen and gleaming silver covered the buffet table beyond.

Anna was pulled into conversations; some people she knew, most she didn't. Voices raised and lowered periodically in competition with the pianist ensconced at the shining baby grand in the far corner. The pianist's tails hung over the back of his bench as his tapered hands flew over the ivory keys. He played *As Time Goes By;* she chuckled while imagining he was Sam, the pianist from *Casablanca.* Drawn to the music, she started easing that way when a familiar voice caught her attention.

"Hello, Anna. I thought that was you," said a huge, burly man about fifty. His premature white hair didn't match his youthful face. "Where's Sam? Haven't seen him yet." He looked around absently, his sea blue eyes scanning the tallest men nearby.

"He's arriving late, Brock. A last minute news story, surely you heard about it?" Her dark curls roused and bounced as she spoke to him.

Brock Lane had known Sam since college. He'd read some of his columns and followed his career. When Sam Berg's daughter, Tess, began college classes two years earlier in Lark Point, he enlisted Sam and never imagined he would take him up on his offer to join Channel 14. As co-owner, he harbored a special fondness for the man and his family.

His eyes beamed at Anna. "Oh, yes. Jesus! The cameras were turning like wildfire when I left to go home and jump into this monkey suit," he said, touching his black tuxedo. His deep blue eyes looked over Anna appreciatively. "He interviewed me earlier, Anna. Great stuff," he continued, "our new star. You know, Sam --- our man with the news. Elliott told me…….."

"……..Yes, Brock, that's him, our man with the news," she said with a twinge of sarcasm she disliked hearing in her voice, "but don't expect him to arrive in *his* monkey suit. It's still hanging in the closet because he's still at the station…." She didn't try to hide her resentment.

Surprised at her tone, he looked at her intently. "Let me get you another drink, Anna love, yours is nearly empty." Brock steered her toward a large group of people beside the long, low mirror.

Anna glanced longingly at the piano but let him propel her along as he waved and nodded to others around them. "Yes, Brock, Champagne will do nicely," she answered softly, enjoying his companionship as she tried to shrug off her moodiness.

Brock placed her beside a slightly plump, but lovely woman in a black lace gown she instinctively recognized as Rainy Nites. He placed her hand in Rainy's and squeezed their hands together with both of his.

"Rainy, here's Anna Berg, the lovely woman I told you about. Treat her nice; she's Sam Berg's wife and a dear friend of mine too. Don't let her disappear. I'm off to find some drinks. Your party is stunning, as usual, darling," he said as he placed a quick kiss on the woman's cheek. Then he strode away through the crowd.

Anna disengaged her hand apprehensively.

Rainy studied Anna, while her eyes sparkled with mischief.

Anna liked the way her smile clearly reached her eyes.

"He's the usual darling and outrageous flirt," Rainy said, "but we love Brock. I'm so glad to finally meet you, Anna. I'm sorry I missed you when you came in. Where's our news hero?" she asked with raised eyebrows, her blue eyes glancing around her as Brock's had previously.

"Sam had an important news story to film and should arrive by 8:30 or so. It's now 8:10," Anna murmured, glancing at her gold watch.

Rainy sensed disquiet beneath the surface wondering about the French woman before her. "Oh, not to worry, Anna, let me introduce you to some of my friends."

Anna followed Rainy as the woman's charm flowed, touching everyone in her path. Her smile was magnetic, her eyes the color of morning glories. Anna tried to memorize everything about her to share with Tess later. The woman's shoulder length blonde hair hung in spirals, the color neatly covering any wispy grey tendrils at her temples. She was almost theatrical, but tastefully covered in a gown that gracefully fit her plump body. Nestled into her abundant cleavage hung a pearl and diamond necklace, its sparkle reflecting off the chandeliers.

Rainy led Anna through the throng and motioned the waiter to fill Anna's glass, wondering what happened to Brock.

Lauraine Nites was in her element as she led Sam Berg's wife to various acquaintances, showing off the newest member of Lark Point's society. Even though the Bergs had lived in her town for a couple of years, now was the time for introductions. He would soon be an important man in their midst and she wanted to be remembered as his launch pad into the community.

She knew Anna was a published author and their friendship would create a new spoke in Rainy's social wheel. Artfully dodging kisses from men like a butterfly dodging bees, she stayed focused and never stopped moving.

Anna wondered if she imagined the fleeting grimace when men reached to hug her before the woman's quick smile was back in place.

Coming to a sudden stop, Rainy introduced her to a group of women who stood in a clutch near the buffet table. "Anna, this is Marla Brie, my friend and the owner of the small boutique on Laurent Avenue called the *Galerie Chloe*."

Anna caught the slightly aloof expression on Marla's face. She cocked her head as if Rainy had interrupted a conversation between her and the Queen of England. She lifted a limp hand while the other women turned toward Anna and lifted their wine glasses in welcome.

"Marla, this is Anna Berg, Sam Berg's wife...you know on KILT TV. She's a published author living right here in Lark Point."

This tidbit wrought an instant change in Marla's demeanor and she murmured in delight. "Anna, you must come into my shop sometime. It's so lovely to meet you. We've just received the new fall line from New York and you would look wonderful in everything," Marla gushed.

Well, missy, I doubt I'll grace your door anytime soon. Anna cursed Sam's lateness again. Marla's slick attitude adjustment was so blatant that Anna seethed. She smiled thinly.

"I found you," Brock interrupted as he swished a glass toward Anna. His eyes dipped toward the women and he moved close to Rainy, but laughed when she danced quickly out of range and waved a finger at him. "You already have drinks, you clever girls."

Anna reached for the glass, smiled at Rainy and promised to see her later. She needed space to breathe. Anna mentally stored Marla's face in her head and grinned. *She can be the bitchy character in my next book.*

"I'm fine now, Brock, you don't have to babysit me, but you could point me to the restroom, like a dear."

"Oh, we're on top of it, dear," Brock whispered as he looked toward the long hallway beside them.

"Translated, that means what exactly……..?"

He pointed and she quickly placed her drink on a table and slipped away as she heard Brock being greeted by friends.

Rainy studied her reflection in the hall mirror beyond Marla's shoulder after Anna and Brock left. She touched a finger to the corner of her mouth, smoothing a tiny smudge of bright red lipstick and enjoyed the mirror's image of the successful event she had envisioned.

Pulling a few curls caught in the chain of her necklace, her eyes darted to the guests gathered in corners and smiled. Buoyed by the number of people who filled the room, she mentally counted the proceeds for the Park Blocks Fund and the artists it would support. Ever willing to use her organization skills for these events, she rarely forgot how she got to her place in life.

Marrying a prominent attorney gave her the prestige she was unwilling to lose. At times, she felt a seed of disharmony slip in when she was at her most vulnerable but she dodged it. She preferred her social life and played her way through that life to keep it intact. It was only in the darkest moments of the night or when she slipped into her other life that those seeds tried to germinate. Reaching down to press her lacy skirt folds into place, she lifted her head and surveyed the party. And then she smiled again.

Cole drifted up to Brock next to the bar a moment later.

"Hey, old friend, how are you? I haven't seen you in awhile."

"You're the one with his nose in law books, Cole Nites. Not me," Brock joked, enjoying the camaraderie with Cole, liking him.

"Well, I'm done for awhile now. In fact, I'm flying to San Francisco to speak before the American Bar Association Convention next month. I have to bone up for it; they want me to present the advantages and disadvantages of whether small business owners should keep their noses out of politics," Cole said, with a twinkle in his clear grey eyes.

"Was that a burn, Cole?" Brock shot back, slightly irritated, since it was well-known he hoped someday he'd have a career in politics.

"Of course not. You have to do what the hell you believe in, I never thought otherwise. The Bar gave me the topic, I didn't choose it with you in mind, Brock, and besides small business owners usually make the best politicians anyway because they know, from the ground up, what our country needs to stay on its toes."

They both laughed and lifted glasses in a silent toast.

"Say, Mr. Television, where's your news star? Rainy said she invited him and his lady. I would think the walls would be rattling with his excerpts by now and I don't see a loose beam," Cole said, his eyes half closed as he smiled across at his friend.

"Running late. You know the news must go on with a time all its own, but his gorgeous wife is here. I left her in the ladies room. Well, I wasn't in there with her...."

He stared. "God, I hope not. Rainy would frown if her party was scandalized," Cole said with laughter in his voice.

"Ha ha ha, very funny. You know what I mean. She's clever and strong and speaks her mind. She's an author, been writing since she was a child and she's good. Real good. Sam says she's working on a novel. He said she buries herself at home or at her cottage in Ashby...like she runs away to write...like it's her sanctuary. Her French grandparents left her a wonderful old cottage there named *Mirafleures* and she's managed to fix it up, added a computer, the whole bit. I'll find her for you in a minute. Isn't that Stu Burns over there...?" Brock pointed.

Cole turned. He saw the shining lights. The pianist offered a familiar musical interlude that filled him with pleasure and offered relief. He unexpectedly wished he was alone with only music for company so he bent in that direction and began to ease his way toward the piano.

"Hey, Cole, there's Anna now," Brock pointed slightly with his glass and touched Cole's elbow.

Cole swiveled toward Brock and stopped. His eyes slowed to a stand-still, gazing at a woman in blue. Blue sequins glittered from the mixture of candlelight and lamps to give Anna a soft ethereal look. He stood, mesmerized. His breath went out of him as he saw her throw back her head and laugh up at the waiter before carefully lifting a flute. For a moment, he was back in college when dreams lived in tandem with studies, when a woman's face knocked him flat. When his life hadn't been strung out with fund raising events by a woman who was bent on upping others in the community and he allowed himself to hope for more.

"Do you see her, Cole? She's in blue, black curly hair, nice legs, pretty smile," Brock's voice continued.

"Yes," Cole managed, feeling light suddenly, before shaking his head when he heard Rainy call his name. When he turned toward his wife in slow motion, he no longer heard Brock or the other men around him.

"Come on, dear; I want you to meet........" Rainy's voice drifted through the fog as she steered him to one person then another. He nodded, shook hands, smiled.

"Here you are, Miss."

Anna smiled up at the waiter, taking the beautiful fluted crystal glass. She had babied the last two, barely tasting them. She wasn't much of a drinker but enjoyed Champagne. Suddenly, however, she wanted to gulp this one quickly. Anna threw her head backward, laughing. "Now, that makes me feel welcome," she said, "I haven't been called miss in a very long time. Thank you."

The waiter smiled wide, considering the pretty woman in front of him. Rarely receiving a word from anyone attending these functions, he was warmed by it and served Champagne with a jauntier step to his walk.

A few moments later, Anna heard *Smoke Gets in Your Eyes* as she walked steadily toward the baby grand. The Champagne relaxed her mind. She would enjoy the music and pretend she was listening quietly all alone. There were a few people standing around the piano as she inched herself among them. Now past 8:30, she'd stopped watching for Sam's entrance some time ago. A large crystal globe, half filled with water, sat on top of the piano where a bed of clear marbles held long-stemmed lilies.

Anna watched the man beside her, noticing his long curling eyelashes that took her by surprise and hair that shone in the lights. She listened to him humming faintly along with the song. "That was nice," she murmured. "Do you sing here often?" she asked impishly.

Cole turned around, clearly startled. The blue dress. Snappy chocolate-brown eyes met clear grey. His words flew away.

"May I join in with another song?" she asked with a chuckle.

"You have a wonderful laugh," Cole said quietly.

She flashed a smile of thanks, surprised and pleased beyond proportion to the compliment. He had a nice face. That was the best way to describe it; a face that was open and honest. His hair was dark, peppered with gray, a tidy beard and he had the silver eyes of mystics, their expression gentle; his sensitive mouth was quick to smile.

Outside, twilight deepened into night. Inside, conversations escalated in volume in direct proportion to the liquor being consumed. Anna and Cole seemed lost for words, pleased when the pianist turned around to laugh and talk to his attentive audience.

"What shall I play… an Elvis tune, Mr. Nites? Do you think we could sneak it by her tonight?" he asked conspiratorially, throwing his dark hair back from his brow and watching Cole expectantly.

Their laughter broke the awkwardness. Cole's composure returned. Bantering resumed. He grinned when the man began to play "*My Way.*" Despite being a Frank Sinatra song by many people's standards, it was very Elvis to him, nevertheless. The man's fingers danced a ballet over the keys; music drifted through the room like soft waves circling from the drop of a pebble in a quiet, still pool.

"So, you're Rainy's husband," Anna said as she gazed at him steadily. Then, without warning, a burst of laughter slipped out. "Oh, my God, I'm sorry; I didn't mean to do that."

"Why is that funny?" he asked, suddenly curious.

"Well, it's my daughter...."

"Your daughter.......?" he stated with a question at the end.

"We've seen your wife's picture in the papers. She's always dressed beautifully and mostly surrounded by other women; not usually with men in the pictures of the social columns. We were sort of speculating if she had a husband and.....well, you were not what we imagined," Anna said lamely as she rolled her eyes and smiled thinking old and bald.

"That sounds a bit naughty," Cole said, chuckling.

"Sorry, truly. So, Mr. Nites if you aren't a singer," Anna said, lifting her bubbly drink to her lips to sip the golden liquid. "What do you really do for a living besides humming tunes and charming strange women?"

"Actually, I'm an attorney here in Lark Point. I have to admit I already know who you are." He bowed toward her, unable to take his eyes off hers.

"Oh?" she inquired, suddenly confused. There was a shadow in her rich, brown eyes, hovering for only an instant.

"Brock Lane pointed you out to me earlier. He mentioned that you are married to Sam Berg and that you are writing a novel."

"Yes, my first. It's a bold step away from magazine articles and newspaper columns because I needed something with grit for a change. When the story popped into my head, I just started tapping it out and loved it. Basically, I've nearly finished the story and I'm into the research phase. I don't suppose you might refer me to a criminal attorney?" she asked mischievously. "You see, it's a novel titled *Twisting in the Wind* and it includes a woman murdering someone in self-defense."

He smiled easily. "*Twisting in the Wind*? Sounds intriguing. What is it about?"

"It's about a broken romance with a twist of suspense woven into it." She smiled briefly and a shadow crossed her features for an instant.

Cole watched the expressions flit across her face. As she talked, her hands moved expressively, accentuating each word as she simultaneously swayed with the music. She was a puzzle and he was stunned by his reaction to her.

"Call me Cole. Mr. Nites was my dad."

"Cole. Forgive me for being bold, but can you help me?"

Cole laughed. "Yes, and yes, I know a criminal attorney you can use for your research. Me."

Anna's eyebrows arched. "How wonderful. Where? In the courtroom? Do you have a case now? Should I come to your office? Do you have time within the next few months?"

"Whoa. May I call you Anna?"

"Please do." She nodded absently while watching his eyes dance and the way his mouth lifted when he smiled. Her stomach clenched.

Brock suddenly appeared beside them. "Cole, I see you've met Anna. And Anna, you've met my friend, Cole Nites?"

Smiling, Cole reached out to shake her hand. "Hello Anna."

Anna placed her hand in his. "Hello, Cole." Anna noticed his eyes were so clear to look almost silver and his expression mirrored her own. Breathlessness. She removed her hand from his.

Brock watched them with a satisfied smile.

Cole reached into his tuxedo pocket and extracted a finely-printed, white business card and handed it to her.

She reached for it and their fingers touched again. The card landed near Anna's feet. She was disgusted with her reaction to this stranger, stunned, angry and breathless.

Neither moved for a beat.

"What is this, I'm a little late and my wife is already exchanging phone numbers with strange men?" Sam said, laughing as he bent to pick up Cole's card. He glanced at it and held it out toward them, unsure whether to return it to Anna or to Cole.

Cole recovered first, retrieved the card and reached out to shake Sam's hand. "Sam Berg. I recognize you from TV. How often do you hear *that* in a day?" Cole asked as he studied Anna's husband.

Sam nodded, a glint of curiosity framing his thoughts.

"Just offering to help Anna with some research on her novel," Cole said as he slipped the card into Anna's trembling hand.

She quickly placed it inside her purse and introduced the men properly before Brock could do so. As Anna watched the men, deep in conversation beside her, she considered Cole. He was good looking, a measured confidant quality about him with a full mouth that half smiled every so often. Something caused him to laugh then.

Unexpectedly, he lifted his face. Their eyes locked. Anna discovered she could not look away; the intensity of his gaze unnerved her and heat rushed to her face. She dropped her eyes and touched one dangling earring while listening to the men's quiet voices. Then, looking up again, she was pleased to see he'd measured her reaction and moved slightly away. Her breathing returned to normal.

Sam seemed unaware of the crackling atmosphere.

Cole's grey eyes were humorous when he smiled again and she felt stirrings that Sam had not generated for her in years. Something important was happening and she was loathe to stop it.

"Let me introduce you to Rainy, Sam. She has been chomping at the bit to get you to herself before everyone else grabs you. Brock has been singing your praises since I arrived," Cole said quickly.

Brock laughed and touched Sam on the back gently.

Sam enjoyed Cole's words and felt taller than his already six foot frame. He smiled at the people in the room as they welcomed him and held Anna's hand, enjoying the feel of it in his palm.

Anna watched Cole and Sam ahead of her. They were very different, yet alike, she mused. They were both business men and she felt a definite presence in both of them; each exuding a strength of his own. Sam had fought hard for the accolades of this night. She didn't know Cole's history. She found herself wanting to and frowned.

Sam chose that moment to look back at her as he pulled her along beside him and squeezed her fingers. "Anna?"

She raised her eyebrows, squeezed his hand in return and promised herself she'd enjoy the rest of the evening for Sam. She wanted him happy. She wondered for the hundredth time why…. She caught herself comparing him to Cole and her chest grew tight again.

The evening progressed. Sam canvassed the room, talking to so many people, that suddenly Anna saw a stranger; one who resembled all the politicians he abhorred. She tried to shake off the feeling but the evening had already drained her emotions. Anna, who had, all her life been able to hold her own with anyone thanks to her beloved grandparent's upbringing in France, found herself silent instead of spirited. Her truth meter told her it wasn't due to her disillusioned relationship with Sam. She'd been in denial for several years.

No, she admitted it was definitely Cole Nites.

He was tremendously attractive and yet a bystander might possibly disagree. She saw sensitivity but also a curious sadness belied by deep-throated laughter and sparkling silver eyes. The shock of feeling an electric jolt by touching a stranger's hand to grasp his card when her own husband had not ignited her so, made her heart ache.

Returning her thoughts to Sam as his voice filled the space behind her, she glanced at Cole again. A man to feed my fantasies she thought guiltily as sadness cloaked her mind. For some time, her sexual enjoyment with Sam was only managed after wine consumption or by pretending during sex that he was Russell Crowe, George Clooney......but this man was real. *Oh, dear God, what a mess.*

Cole surreptitiously watched Anna's face. Curiosity stirred his insides. It was hard to concentrate on the conversation swirling around him when he wanted to take her back to the piano and send everyone home.

The remaining evening flew by, the minutes ticked away. Champagne flowed. The buffet table was constantly filled to bursting, a plate never dwindling before being filled once again. While music entertained in the background, peaceful, smooth and haunting, the atmosphere was exciting, stimulating and crazy.

Anna began to really enjoy herself until Sam whispered, "Let's go, honey, you know that blue dress turns me on and I can't wait to get you alone. I had a sky-high day and I want to share it with you... I want you..."

Anna stumbled.

"You okay, Anna? It must be the Old Spice; you're falling all over me......," Sam whispered with a gleam in his eyes, challenging her.

"Yes, that's it," Anna said quickly, trying to tease in return. Saying their goodbyes, they edged toward the elegant staircase.

Cole's eyes followed the shimmering blue of Anna's dress as they inched their way out of the room. His breath held uncomfortably. He realized he wasn't old and used up after all. Laugh lines crinkled around half-closed eyes. *Pull yourself together, old man.*

Anna's skin prickled. She felt him watching her as Sam gently led her through the crowd. She twisted around and lifted her arm, pretending to wave at a woman near the piano.

Cole caught her gesture and memorized her smile.

Her face swung toward him. Their eyes met where no music played, no chatter continued, no others demanded.

I can feel. Oh, God help me. He's dangerous and I should run like hell right now. Anna turned quickly toward Sam, anxious to move, to leave. Each stair step danced beneath her feet as she counted them; slipping away from Cole like Cinderella leaving the prince at midnight. Only this prince was married and so was she. She smiled miserably when the pianist began playing *"You're the Wind beneath my Wings."*

Cole Nites was a man Anna would not forget quickly. But of course she would… and tried to shake the man from her mind. The way he moved, how he cocked his head to listen to people, making one feel important. Beautiful eyes and that smile… Anna sighed deeply. As Sam guided her into the Jeep, she guiltily winced at the mind chatter filling her head. As his car sped through traffic, she forced the brakes on her thoughts, refusing to allow Cole's charisma to follow them home. She didn't need another complication now.

Sam glanced at her and squeezed her hand, smiling. "What?" he said, feeling her remoteness.

"Nothing," she answered, wishing it were so. *Why do I always do this? Why can't we be honest with one another instead of fearing the other's response? We are not one anymore. We've skidded in opposite directions for so long, we each think this is normal. Neither of us wants to hurt the other, but aren't we doing worse by denying the changes?*

Tess's sweet face flitted across Anna's mind and she relaxed. *It's okay. I must make it all okay.* Tess's face helped Anna push Cole into the recesses of her consciousness. Admitting her marriage was over for all the reasons she'd hammered to exhaustion through her mind was one thing, doing it because of a fiery attraction to another man was quite another.

"I lie to myself to escape reality. I know that I pretend so I can make everyone happy. Anna hated confrontations. Over the years, she'd learned to master the art of hiding her feelings, her anxieties. She feared the imploding reactions that could change all their lives irrevocably if she vocalized her vulnerability, fought for her own peace, her own happiness.

But acting the martyr was nearing an end and rebellion began to build. *If a charming man can make me feel so volatile, I'm lost.* She began to think of ways to open a conversation, get them talking about their problems instead of....

"Anna, I wish you could have seen me today. It was as if I was hovering on that proverbial cloud nine. The words just came out so easily, my interview with Brock was impromptu. He wasn't happy I did it but he and I had a great conversation. Those burglaries are rotten for Lark Point but I have a feeling they are going to be my key to success. Do you have any idea how many homes have been burglarized? It is incredible. Wait until you see the news that I recorded from tonight's show."

Anna stared out the windshield. "I am happy for you, Sam, but I can't imagine using bad news to lift you up into success. I know that's not what you mean but it sounds a bit raw to me."

"You know what I mean, though, don't you, honey?"

She sighed quietly. "Yes, I do. I want you happy, Sam, but….."

"But? Didn't you enjoy yourself tonight? You seem so quiet. I always worry when you get quiet…" He chuckled.

"Ah, now I'm the big talker, right?" Anna tried to lighten the mood and patted his arm. "I'm ok. It's just that I have a lot on my mind."

He folded his hand over hers and twisted his head to kiss her fingers. "Anna, it's just going to get better and better. You just wait and see." The night folded in on them while they angled their way home. They were sitting close but their minds were a million miles apart. Neither could have guessed, nor would they admit, that their lives were at an incomprehensible crossroad.

That night, true to his word, Sam's urgent foreplay began the instant Anna slid beneath the covers, almost before her head hit the pillow. She surrendered to his seduction, they made love swiftly and he slept. She lay staring at the ceiling until she saw the first gray light of dawn. Snoring softly beside her, Sam was blithely unaware of her distress; emotions that were ragged, a mind jangled and frayed and her stomach in knots.

As the faint fingers of dawn crawled across the carpet, she squeezed her eyes closed to ward off the resentment and turned, instead, to thinking about her manuscript.

The chapters were not numbered, the timeline still cloudy and her characters needed spiffed up. She wanted her readers to know them, what they looked like, how they felt, how their surroundings smelled. She refused to shortcut through the story and lay there, moving words around in her mind. Maybe she should add ink drawings to each chapter page; was she an artist? No. Should she use photographs instead? No. Should she create the heroine to be less than perfect? Yes. Nobody is perfect, she argued. Even though she placed herself in her heroine's character, she tried to stay true. Maybe she should change her heroine to make those crazy choices she, Anna, would like to make if she had the fortitude to do so. Would her heroine turn to someone else when her own romance lay broken in pieces around her? Would she be mesmerized by silver eyes, salt and pepper hair, an easy smile? No. A broken romance in her story is one thing. Infidelity was quite another. But this was make believe, she thought, as she smoothed the blanket over her breasts and listened to Sam sleeping beside her.

My story is just make believe, just like my life. She slid from the covers and quietly closed the bedroom door heading for the shower, wishing she smelled coffee and thinking about the pages that waited for her on the computer.

THREE

Metro Assurance Company was the largest insurer in Lark Point. The offices were on the tenth floor of the Tower Building in the middle of Lark Point where it had been since the building was raised sixty years earlier. It had been renovated several times and gave the feeling of old-world charm and success. Transom windows of stained glass stood above mirror-polished marble flooring in the entrance hall in a quiet lobby.

Metro's offices were an offshoot from their home office in Chicago. It insured most of the commercial buildings and industry while still finding a place within its book of business to include nearly every homeowner in the city. Safeco and Chubb were their main competition but it did not concern Benjamin Russell since their clients more than paid his salary and made his Board and employees happy.

The company employed two insurance investigators when claims were made, such as the recent thefts in the community. Morris Leach was the president's son and barely made a dent in his adjustments. The other investigator, however, was the wife of a well-known local attorney who thrived more on the adventure than earning a percentage of the find. She was by far the best investigator of the two and she knew it.

Rainy Nites straightened her cream shrug as she stepped off the elevator on ten. She glanced at Ellen, the receptionist, who nodded in her direction. Offering a nod in return, her mind was already on the thefts in

Lark Point and the sketchy facts she had to work with. The other part of her mind was on the case Ben mentioned and the possibility of flying to Alaska. Her forehead wrinkled in concentration and a sly smile danced on her lips.

"Knock, knock, can I come in?" she called out while smiling at the large man behind the green, marble-topped desk. She marveled again at the marble and would have loved having it in her own office, say next to the window with a potted palm beside it and……."

"Hello, Rainy. Do come in. Ellen said you were on your way." Ben got up and came over to put an arm loosely around her shoulders to lead her to a deep-cushioned chair in front of his desk. A coffee carafe sat on the metal tray with two cups and creamer beside butter cookies..

Rainy stiffened an instant against his quick embrace before sitting in the chair facing the windows that visibly promised another clear summer day.

Benjamin Russell shrugged before smiling broadly at her. He'd been in charge of Lark Point's office for so many years, he felt like he owned the place. In his late 60s, he had a paunch that threatened to slide over his belt and a bald head that shone from the overhead lighting. He grabbed a file off the top of a stack of others and handed it to her. "This is all about the ferry system, Rainy," he stated, quickly drawing the meeting together. Their relationship was based on getting jobs done and he didn't waste time on extended pleasantries except coffee and a short chat. He knew she also liked it that way.

Rainy opened the blue file and quickly ran her fingertip through the papers inside before gently closing it again. She looked up at Ben, waiting for his usual summary.

"It's all there, but let me go over the main points for you. The Alaska Marine Highway or the Alaska Marine Highway System is a ferry service operated by the government of Alaska with headquarters in Ketchikan. It operates from the Aleutian Islands in the east and the Inside Passage of Alaska and British Columbia, Canada. The ferries serve communities in southeast Alaska without road access and vessels can transport people, freight and vehicles over 3,500 miles of routes as far south as Bellingham, Washington and as far west as Dutch Harbor. There are 32 terminals. They receive federal funding. The Alaska Marine

Highway System is a rare example in the U.S. of a shipping line offering regularly scheduled service for the primary purpose of transportation rather than leisure or entertainment. Voyages can last many days, but, in contrast to the luxury of a typical cruise line, cabins cost extra, and most food is served cafeteria style. The five largest vessels on southeast mainline routes are the Columbia, Kennicott, Malaspina, Matanuska and the Taku."

Rainy's interest was piqued but she knew it did no good to hurry Ben through the explanation, so she listened intently because she knew he always had a reason for the back story.

"The ferries that hold our interest are between Juneau and Skagway, Alaska and specifically the Malaspina ferry. The security people have struggled with the oddities for over two months and cannot clear up the mystery. That's where you come in, Rainy. I want you to go up there and act the tourist…camera around your neck, jeans, tennis shoes, the whole bit. If you can take your friend again, that would be even better…" Ben continued for several minutes.

Rainy would, of course, take her friend. She knew Cris would love Alaska and as she listened to Ben drone on, her mind was already on the lunch date following her meeting.

"You see what we are facing here, Rainy?"

"Ben, you do not have to tell me how to do my job. I do it very well and you know it, so let's just get on with it. I'll charge the airfare to Metro as usual, for two. I expect an all-expense paid trip, of course, and ten percent of the find as usual."

Ben stopped talking, took a quick breath and watched Rainy lick her lips, push her blonde hair back from her face and wait for him to respond. "Of course, as always," he said hurriedly, anxious to get on to the next file. "You'll need to leave on Friday. When you get to Juneau, you'll have ferry and hotel reservations waiting for you in an envelope at the terminal window. The security rep will have a letter waiting for you from the Captain of the Malaspina. Just follow his instructions but check in with me each day as usual. Agreed?"

Rainy nodded, her mind already flying ahead to the weekend. Of course they'd leave on Friday, it couldn't be soon enough for her. She grabbed her purse, lifted the folder and placed it into her slight briefcase for later reading and waved her hand. "See you when I get back and yes, I will call every day. Don't I always?" Then she was gone.

Ben sat down at his over-sized desk, deep in thought. Working with the woman was damned interesting but he always felt as if she was the one in control, not him. He didn't particularly like it but she got the job done and her name added prestige to Metro. They both knew she was there as long as she wanted to be.

He moved his thick body deeper into his padded chair, squirming to get comfortable. Then, he immediately wiped her from his thoughts and grabbed another file. The stack grew higher each week as the burglaries mounted and his patience was running thin. The insurance claims were highest from Thursday to Monday as if the weekend was a free for all. His Chicago people were screaming. He reached for the phone to call Mayor Sterling again. No news was not necessarily good news but he promised to get the police working with Berg and Ben meant to make sure it was happening.

María Crissman's flaming curly hair and freckled face exuded earthiness and glamour. Rainy, in contrast, was quietly poised and pretty, her smile sincere. Her mind was clear about what she wanted. Her life with Cole had always been sufficient, despite the inconvenience of intimacy but neither seemed to mind. It seemed unimportant; she was relieved on that point since her sexuality had left them flat and he'd accepted it years ago. That was before María walked onto that stage at the theater and into her life. Cris filled her with a fullness that no man ever had and she still marveled at their relationship. Rainy had Cole. Cris had Michael. But, Rainy wanted her. Michael wasn't important in Rainy's mind and she pushed a place for herself in Cris's life that went beyond all bounds.

Cris had to be wooed and Rainy won; a love she'd forever longed for. It was strong, good and whole even though it was new to Cris. Rainy had known since she was a child that she was attracted to girls more than to boys. Her father knew it, hated it and ignored it most of the time. With Cris, the strangeness gave way to a solidity that surprised each of them as they learned how loving another woman could make the difference in a life lived and a life one survives.

Wanting Cris to herself was the most important piece of her life. She hated it that Michael was there for Cris to depend on when Rainy was elsewhere. As resentment built between Rainy and Michael, Cris was sometimes caught in the crossfire. Realizing she was bisexual, Cris loved Michael a little, though she craved Rainy's love more than the other.

Despite Cris's confusion where her sexuality was concerned, she recognized that Rainy wielded the power of manipulation in her love life. They had been together as one for four years and managed to keep their love affair in the closet. Rainy's public façade in business was too important, never would the community accept a lesbian organizing the gala jobs she coveted; she refused to allow one part of her life to interfere or jeopardize the other.

Cris entered the restaurant and stood in the foyer a moment to search for Rainy before meandering between tables in her direction. She wore an orange sweater and black knit slacks. Her copper ringlets were tied back with a bold tiger print scarf and her green eyes were laughing and quick.

"Been waiting long, Rainy?" she asked with a warm smile.

"Only a few, but it was definitely worth it. My God, you look fabulous," she said as her eyes turned soft. Lauraine waved the waitress over for a glass of white wine. "I have a proposition for you," she whispered softly, her eyes holding the sweet promises that Cris loved.

"I'm relieved to hear it," she said with a wink at her companion, "so do I." She smiled a little and let the wine trickle down her throat, her red hair shining in the afternoon sun. "Tell me yours first."

"How about a weekend pretending we're tourists on a huge ferry boat floating up the glacier-filled waterways between Juneau and Skagway? It's just like a big cruise ship without all the bells and whistles. I need to catch another thief." Rainy teased.

"Just the two of us?" Cris raised her carrot-colored eyebrows. "To Alaska? I haven't been there since I acted in a theater years ago. What on earth would I do while you tracked the thief down?" She smiled impishly.

"We'll stay on the ferry. They're big --- a ship actually; we'll board in Juneau and ride it northward, sliding along beside snow-capped mountains. A cabin of our own….Just you and me. You'll be surprised at how much we can find to do," she gave her a look and licked the rim of her wine glass.

Cris glanced uneasily at the nearby tables. "I don't know Rainy. When would we go? You know the show runs until tomorrow night instead of the usual Thursday to Monday. Then we begin rehearsals for the new play and there's Michael to ….." She struggled to get her thoughts together and frowned at the look on Rainy's face.

"Come on, Cris. There's time. We'd leave Friday and stay three or four days max. Tell Michael you need to help me on a case. He'll believe you, he usually does, right? Light resentment laced her words.

Cris heard the crispness in Rainy's voice where there had been warmth a moment before. Her mind calculated the planned story for Michael and she smiled across the linen-covered table.

"Of course, I'll go. It's not as if Michael owns me but you know how he feels about our trips together….. Just give me time to pack jeans, sweaters, heavy socks…" Cris smiled, feeling warmth invade her chest and throat trying to ignore her remorse at lying to Michael. She swallowed tears, loving Rainy beyond reason and moistened her lips.

Rainy visibly relaxed and reached across the table to pat Cris's hand, lingering over her knuckles, enjoying the feel of her soft skin. She winked and sucked in her breath at the promise on Cris's face. "Just please don't give into his whining this time…..."

Cris's jaw tightened for a second before she turned her own hand and held Rainy's a moment, looking around covertly. She loved Rainy but they each avoided public demonstrations for several reasons. One being the possibility of open ridicule. Despite it being 2014, narrow-minded people lurked around every corner.

"Cris, we'll have four days…I want you."

Emotions throbbed with a familiar need, a hammering of hearts, between the women as they finished their wine and salads. Rainy's lips curled in satisfaction when she saw Cris's cheeks turn pink. They toasted their decision and resumed eating; each frantically creating lies for their men. Plans made, they headed back to separate lives and waited impatiently for Friday.

"Again?" Michael sat on the corner of Cris's bench in her dressing room. "You're always off somewhere with that woman. Can't she do her nosing around without you tagging along?" He couldn't hide his frustration and felt strung out every time they took off somewhere together.

"Oh, come on, Michael, you can't take me to those places and Rainy is amusing to spend time with. You like her and Cole. Don't be so wicked," Cris said, suddenly busy with her powder and blush. She watched him in the mirror and saw a frown burrow into his forehead like a trench.

"Why don't Cole and I go on this trip with you? I'd love to see those mountains covered in snow, the glaciers and….."

"….Are you out of your mind, Michael? Cole would never do that either. It is a business trip. Rainy will be investigating for Metro…there have been a lot of thefts on the ferry and she'll be busy….…."

"……Well, what will *you* be doing while she's sleuthing since her time will obviously be so tight?" he snorted.

Cris gripped her powder brush.

He didn't really want to go, but finished with, "…well, we'll have three days before you leave. After the play tonight, let's go out for a late dinner, just the two of us." For an instant, wistfulness stole into his expression as he watched her in the mirror.

Cris busied herself with lipstick, liner and more mascara. "Michael, you know we'll be too tired. You know what a dud I am after a play. It takes so much out of us…."

"I have a surprise for you…." He said, crooning, testing.

Cris opened her eyes wide, the dark blue shadow mingling with the purple as her eyebrows touched her curly bangs. Her bright red hair, always frizzy, made a halo around her small features. Green eyes, which astounded people, now instantly stared into Michael's face.

Michael wiped his hands on his pants and slicked the sweat off his forehead. He reached across the space for her, making sure they were alone. Cris smiled, her freckles hidden beneath a layer of liquid foundation. Touching her arm, he slid his hand toward her ample breast and smoothed the blouse over the mound, caressing the nipple until he felt it expand and meet his fingers.

Cris moved toward him, anxious suddenly to have him hold her close. Her mouth became dry as she arched toward him. Michael caressed her back, lowered his hands to find her bottom and pulled her toward him.

"What's the surprise?" she whispered.

Michael squeezed her buttocks and kissed her hard, feeling her fold around him. "You have to agree to dinner after the play to get it," he said as he backed toward the door and his mouth twitched in amusement.

Her green eyes snapped.

"Lily's coming to help you read your lines, Ms. Crissman. I'll see you about eleven o'clock." His voice belied the sexual antics moments earlier as a cast member drifted into her doorway. He winked and disappeared from view.

Cris was tempted to throw her hairbrush after him, spent with confused emotions, leaving her weak and ready to run. She plopped down again on the padded bench and looked at herself in the mirror. Pushing at her frizzy mop, she wrapped a hair band around the perimeter making her face look like a gift-wrapped Easter egg.

She was known as María Christina Crissman at the theater but close friends knew her as Cris. When she became Michael's roommate to save money, it made sense until Michael fell in love with her and their relationship moved from platonic to intimate. She liked him a lot, even loved him, but he wasn't Rainy. Rainy filled her. Michael only warmed her. Cris was frightened to think how Michael would react if he ever found out about her dual life with Rainy.

Her leg thumped against the dressing table and her eyes filled. It was times like these that she turned to Taekwon-Do. The martial art helped balance her confusion by giving her an outlet that made her feel whole. It was a Korean martial art using kicks, blocks, punches and open-handed strikes and sometimes various take-downs or sweeps and joint locks. Pressure points were used as well as grabbing self-defense techniques borrowed from other martial art forms. It was a combination of combat and self defense that Cris enjoyed, offering her strength, self-defense and self-control over energy and attitude. Cris had learned about Taekwon-Do from an old friend, a Grand Master of the art, several years before.

At first, she joined his class for the exercise and then gradually fell into the disciplined martial arts culture it was based upon. The daily workouts proved to be exactly what she needed. She found herself lying in bed at night, visualizing the forms until she would jump up and do them swiftly and quietly, then fall back into bed, exhausted. She moved from White Belt to Black Belt in just under four years. The belts hung on her wall as proof of her precious accomplishments. Grand Master Bettencourt proudly posted her photo in his dojang. As a Black Belt, Ms. Crissman became her new title. Juggling the theater schedule with Taekwon-Do soothed her spirit by keeping confusion at bay.

She taught Taekwon-Do at the YWCA in Lark Point every Tuesday, Thursday and Saturday. She loved the way her body felt after a workout and thrived on the challenges involved in teaching. She kept her body taut by jogging every morning too. Seeing children and adults confidence grow kept a healthy balance in Cris's life that neither Rainy nor Michael touched. Another Black Belt student filled in for her when she was unavailable. And Saturday, she'd need him, so she made a mental note to call him later.

Now, Cris leaned toward the mirror and watched Lily come in and walk toward her. "Hey, Cris, want to study lines? I know we go on in an hour but you know how nervous I always get....."

Cris wiped liner from beneath one eye and turned around. They could hear the crowds milling around, waiting expectantly while drinking wine or coffee and sampling fancy pastries. The taped piano and violin music was piped into their dressing rooms to give a soothing and shared aura of enchantment. The women immediately immersed themselves into their characters as the theater filled with guests.

The American flag hung in tandem with the flag of Korea. The room held eight students, all barefooted and dressed in white doboks, the uniform of Taekwon-Do, meaning foot-fist-way. Each student bowed reverently to the flags, then at Cris upon entrance to her dojang. She was intent on earning and sustaining the respect of each student by referring to the room and each level of achievement with Korean names. Her Black Belt status earned her the right to teach others and she was never referred to by her first name in the dojang, but instead as Ms Crissman, a designation earned by the rank of her belt.

Students lined up in twos before her as she led them through their typical stretching and warm up exercises before class began. 1-2-3-4-

5....everyone performed synchronized movements. Cris enjoyed their eagerness as much as the sense of wholeness teaching gave to her esteem and psych. "Chonji...." The class continued as she barked out each level of curriculum requirements and worked with each student. She discouraged contact during pre-sparring exercise since Taekwon-Do was favorably known as a non-contact art. She'd never used Taekwon-Do seriously and was thankful it had never been required of her. Michael refused to join her classes. His muscles could just atrophy, she'd told him and continued to teach others a skill she vitally applauded.

Sam Berg finished another news show, stepping out of the paradigm, pushing the envelope. He thought he could really get used to the way he felt after staring into the camera's eye and telling his town to stay tuned. He would be part of the investigation team whether the police wanted him in there or not. He hated stepping on Charlie's toes, since he was a good friend and a good cop, but would hate not being the man of the hour more.

When Sam got back to his office, there was a call waiting for him.

"Hey, Charlie, I was just thinking of you."

"I'll bet you were, old friend. Trying to do my job is the way I hear it. The sheriff just left my office, steaming for trouble. He is not happy about you trying to get a foot in his door. This is an active police investigation, Sam, and you know there are some things better kept here at the station rather than running into the community's living room from your desk. I know you are just doing your job, but you can't do ours too." Charlie was clearly unhappy, clearly kicking the cat and somebody had to take the brunt of it. It might as well be Sam since he was the cause of the friction in the first place.

"Ah, Charlie. People need to know what's going on. I can't let the Democrat upstage me, we need to get the news out first. The Democrat doesn't sign my paycheck and Brock......" Sam blustered a little.

"Bullshit." You are doing this just because you want to be a bigshot. I've known you a long time, Sam, and I don't like it." Charlie slammed down the phone.

When Sam looked up, Elliott was in the doorway, his bushy eyebrows framing eyes that asked the obvious question.

"Are we going to lose the story? You took a big chance, Sam. I like what you're doing but I don't like the way you're doing it. If it works, good...I'm prepared to put up with the grief. But we don't want to cause a rift between us and the police. We need them for the bits of information that flows in here. Remember that. Why not go home early tonight? I've asked Norman to do the news tonight. It will give us some breathing room with the police chief." With that, he was gone.

Sam sat back in his chair, lifted his hands behind his head and leaned back with a thoughtful smile on his rugged face. "Crime catchers, that's the new logo I should use. What is it the little gingerbread man says? Run, run as fast as you can... You can't catch me, I'm the gingerbread man." His laughter slid out the doorway into the noisy staff room too low for anyone to hear him except the girls closest to his door.

Tess slammed her book closed just when the doorbell rang. She was delighted to hear Cris's voice in the foyer but frowned when she saw her friend's serious face.

"Hey! What's wrong?"

"I just needed some good conversation and thought you could use some too."

"Stay for dinner. That's ok, isn't it Mom?"

Anna nodded before heading back into the kitchen. "You ladies sit in there and I'll bring those fat pretzels, dipping mustard and we can have a glass of something wicked. It appears we are all in need of some girl talk. Age knows no difference when it comes to that, right?" She was glad to see Cris because it would give Tess a reprieve from all the studying and give Anna a chance to spend time with them. Her mind could drift away from Sam and all the problems that shadowed them.

Cris grinned.

Tess led her into the living room, her voice echoing through the kitchen toward Anna. "I needed a break. Glad you came over. And Mom has been real quiet lately. Maybe we can cheer her up. Booze and pretzels will help...she has some pretzel dipping sauce you will love...."

Sam slipped in the back door and jogged upstairs, hoping the evening would not end in another argument. He was tired as he slipped off his tie. He didn't want to explain to anyone why Norman Chubb had taken over his news program that night. He just wanted some peace and needed time to think about it.

To say that Anna was surprised to see Sam so early in the day was an understatement. She'd wanted girl time but the last thing she wanted was a scene, especially with company, so she berated herself and shut up.

Throughout the meal, Tess and Cris both noticed Anna was unusually quiet while Sam was funny, telling stories about the TV station and the investigation he was currently involved in. His passion about solving the thefts spiked the emotion at the table.

Cris thought he was nice, reminding her of George Clooney in *Ocean's Eleven* when his eyes went soft and you weren't sure what he was thinking. He had a warm smile and soft voice. She liked listening to him. It was a nice change from Michael's incessant whining ever since she'd told him about the trip to Alaska with Rainy. Her face grew hot at the thought and she looked up quickly.

Tess was listening avidly to her father.

Anna was picking at her food and watching her husband.

Cris thought it was obvious something was amiss between them and they might want to talk alone, so she suggested going to the library to help Tess with the school's drama project.

Tess jumped at the idea.

Anna wanted to cry.

Sam studied her silently. He tried to dismiss the sense that their marriage was crumbling and couldn't seem to do a damn thing to stop it. Instead of talking to her, he quietly left the table as the girls drove away.

Anna put her head in her hands in the dimly lit room. It seemed that nothing made sense. Maybe she needed counseling. She thought how ironic it was that Tess was specializing in that profession and wondered if she should be her first patient.

FOUR

Alaska, the land of the midnight sun. Cris and Rainy were like children on the last day of school as they boarded an Alaska Airlines jet in Oakland to fly to Seattle and onto Juneau. They arrived late afternoon on Friday as instructed, found their reservations and a letter of instructions waiting for them at the terminal. The Malaspina was scheduled to leave the dock at 7:00 a.m. the following day. That meant they had the afternoon and evening to explore Juneau.

The snow-capped mountains met the edges of the little town as if Juneau was placed there as an afterthought. The wind was blowing as they were shuttled into the town, their bags stashed beside them. "Here long, ladies?" the driver asked as he glanced back towards them.

"Just the weekend," Rainy answered as she watched the mountainous scenery flutter by. The city was just shaking off its last significant snow of the season. Clouds hung low in spots and rain fell even though bits of blue sky peeked out in patches above them.

"You might want to fit in a helicopter ride to the spectacular Mendenhall Glacier at the end of the road. It's located about twelve miles from town in the Mendenhall Valley. The center offers a variety of walking paths that lead to amazing photo shots plus a trail all the way to the waterfall near the glacier." A grizzled, but earnest, face looked at them from the rear-view mirror, clearly proud of his town.

Cris looked at Rainy and they raised their eyebrows. "Sounds like fun, what do you think, will we have time?" Cris asked expectantly.

Rainy shrugged. "After reading Ben's notes from Metro, I have a feeling we'll find our answers on the Malaspina. The rep has done his homework well and I just need to confirm his suspicions. If I can do that, we can return Sunday afternoon, do the helicopter tour and fly home Monday morning. How does that plan sound?"

"Mmmmmmmmmmmmm, good." Cris murmured, smiling into Rainy's eyes, anxious for their time together.

Rainy reached for Cris's hand beneath the folds of her jacket. The airport/hotel shuttle wove its way to the seven-story Goldbelt Hotel above the downtown waterfront on the Gastineau Channel and surrounding mountains. They'd been told original, museum-quality Tlingit artwork was displayed throughout the hotel reflecting the pride and rich heritage of the native Alaskan culture.

The women scanned the skyline, enthralled to see the mountains meet the bay. The sky was blue as a robin's egg. Glancing downward toward the bay, a cruise ship sat anchored across from the entrance of their hotel, amid churning waters. Breathtaking was the only word that came to mind as they approached the doorway near a lounge with music flowing toward them.

Later, Cris was stunned when she walked out the sliding door of their room to stand on their wooden balcony. The water traffic was minimal although the huge ferry at anchor below them, just across the street in the bay, looked like a toy from their vantage point.

Across the bay, another group of houses slumbered at the base of the mountains accessed from a bridge that led from Juneau. She glanced at the brochure in her hand and saw the town was called Douglas. Far to her right, she twisted her head around as far as she could to see water and mountains going on forever. She didn't think she'd ever seen anything so beautiful. When she'd been in the Repertory Theater in her younger years, she'd never been to Juneau and turned to thank Rainy as she slipped out the doors to join her.

"Hey, Ben had the management leave us some Chardonnay in the fridge and Cabernet Sauvignon and fruit in a basket. He really wants this case closed and he's willing to pull out all the stops. I found an opener and poured us each a glass." She handed Cris the stemware and they sat down at the small table sure they must be on top of the world and clinked rims.

Cris stared into the wine a moment before looking up to quote Janice MacLeod, "A tiny chasm in her soul opened up and peace began to trickle in."

Rainy nodded, noting Cris's new haircut, the bountiful red curls shorn off into a rather unforgiving pixie cut, struck her with renewed warmth.

"Do you think we will ever have a real life, Rainy, instead of these fleeting moments, stealing time out of other people's lives to share time together? Don't you sometimes wish we could run away to a place like this where nobody knows us and just have our own life?" Cris throbbed with intensity and Rainy didn't miss the tears in her voice.

"Sometimes you really don't make any sense." She leaned over and kissed her gently on the lips. "But I love you anyway."

"Thank you, Rainy, but are you listening to what I'm saying? Why can't you give up the life you have with Cole when you tell me it's in limbo and you love me?"

Rainy sighed deeply and lifted the wineglass to her lips and nodded. "Cris. That's not fair. It's not about the life I want over you. I'm not naïve about reality. Homosexuals are still the fear of the world. We're the last group it's okay to hate. Are you willing to place us in a position that could undo all the beauty we share now?"

Cris didn't answer immediately. She looked across the bay, over to Douglas and across the city of Juneau, wondering how many gay couples lived below among the houses that littered the valley and marched slowly up the mountainsides.

"Cris?"

"Rainy, choices aren't always easy. I know that. I think you are using our homosexuality as a crutch. You are afraid to make a commitment that would change your lifestyle. You say you love me. Michael says he loves me. And I'd bet a mint that he'd put me first no matter what. And you don't," she finished sadly.

"Don't compare my feelings for you to Michael's. Your relationship with him is held together by shoelaces and bubblegum. Ours is real."

Cris looked at Rainy and did not reply.

The 408 foot ferry, Malaspina, colloquially known as the *Mal,* is a mainline ferry and the original Malaspina-class vessel for the Alaska Marine Highway System. The Malaspina is nearly identical to its sister ship, the Matanuska. Its namesake is the Malaspina Glacier located in Yakutat, Alaska. Designed by Philip F. Spaulding & Associates, constructed in 1963 by the Lockheed Shipbuilding Yards in Seattle, Washington and elongated in 1972 at the Willamette Iron and Steel Company in Portland, Oregon, the Malaspina has been in the ferry system for over forty years.

As a mainline ferry, it serves the larger of the inside passage communities (such as Ketchikan, Petersburg, and Sitka), its route spans the entirety of the inside passage, beginning runs in either Bellingham, Washington or Prince Rupert, British Columbia and running to the northernmost Alaskan Panhandle community of Skagway. Beginning in the late 1990s, the Malaspina has mostly operated during the summer months as a "day boat" in the upper Lynn Canal, making daily roundtrips between Juneau and Skagway with stops in Haines, Alaska. The Malaspina's amenities include a hot-food cafeteria; cocktail lounge and bar; solarium; forward, aft, movie, and business lounges; gift shop; 54 four-berth cabins; and 29 two-berth cabins.

Cris had been happy to stand at the railing to marvel at the view the next morning when Rainy left her to greet the captain, Lachlan O'Leary. They'd walked across the plank to board the ferry with other foot passengers, holding hats and scarves tightly. The wind was cold but the day was beautiful.

The Captain had steaming cups of coffee in his office waiting for them. After closing the door, he pulled out a large folder. "Call me Locky, Ms. Nites. Everyone does."

"And please call me Rainy." She shook his hand and busied with her iPad, prepared to put notes in her Penultimate App because she could write with her stylus and email the cursive notes to herself with a copy to Ben. It was quick and efficient. She looked up at Locky and saw him hesitate before beginning.

"Rainy." He nodded. "I know Metro Assurance is watching my boat closely and it frosts my onions that I can't find the culprit. I'll begin at the beginning, if I may?"

She laughed. "That's usually the best place to start, Locky."

He answered her grin, pulling papers out of his folder and placed them on the table in front of her. "This is a copy of the items that have been stolen. Cameras, jewelry…why travelers leave these items in their cabin is beyond me. They lock the doors, yes, but it hasn't stopped our thief. One man left his laptop and a small external hard drive. He was on his way to Skagway to meet with the town council. Gone, everything gone. And I don't believe in magicians around here!"

He was so angry; Rainy imagined he could spit nails out on the desk. She watched the man's passion for his boat and felt his sincere hope that she could find his answers.

"You see, this ferry has been in Portland, Oregon for months before she came back to us last spring. Deep in the heart of Swan Island's industrial sprawl, a rebirth took place at Portland's Vigor Shipyard. This was the first of the Alaska Marine Highway System's original ferries and it was her 50th birthday. It had an $8 million makeover. We're talking more than just fresh paint. From electronics to mechanics to murals and flooring, she got a thorough overhaul/refinish while retaining that vintage look of January 21, 1963, when she sailed north from Seattle's Lockheed Shipyard on her maiden voyage."

Rainy's eyebrows rose, looking around her with appreciation.

"In early April, the inside of the Malaspina was a glorious mess with reconditioned floors covered by plastic, "Wet Paint" signs tacked near doorways, and piles of life jackets filling the fore observation lounge with an orange glow. Overhead on the smokestack, a fresh design in gold paint was a flashback to its first decade."

Rainy was totally impressed and told him so.

He continued, full of pride, "The Malaspina left Portland on April 25th to set sail on what our Alaska Marine Highway System called *The Golden Voyage*. From May 1st to the 5th, cultural events and shipboard open houses were planned in Ketchikan, Wrangell, Petersburg, Juneau, Haines and Skagway. Included were two rare day trips to Misty Fjords National Monument and to Tracy Arm Fjord. The romance and adventure of ferry cruising along Alaska's coastal waterways was all one imagined," he said.

"I had no idea….."

"It was a time to power down, to read and play cards, snack and fix your eyes on the beauty outside the windows. The Inside Passage is that and more, especially when the sun spills onto the dazzling high places alongside the unending waterways. From the comfortable seating in the observation lounge, rain may bead the windows or the quiet water may reflect hulking mountains. Either way, you can't stop watching the slow-moving pictures around you. We have the largest contiguous rain forest in the world, the Tongass National Forest. Peace settles in like an old friend, and disembarking leads to adventure." Raising his eyebrows, he took a deep breath and then sipped the coffee beside him.

Rainy didn't take notes but wished he'd get to the meaty issue.

"And then the problems began. Burglaries aboard the Malaspina…on the way to Alaska or after it arrived back in Juneau to begin its ferry life again," Rainy read her notes.

He nodded. "Now, there are eleven vessels that offer streamlined trips between the small towns. I hate to admit it but most of the thefts are concentrated on my boat, the Malaspina, and I'd hoped to find the thieves myself. After talking with Ben in Lark Point, he and I both agreed sending you as a tourist might be the best way to handle it." He heaved a long, frustrating sigh and looked at her with a sense of relief.

Rainy tapped her pencil to her teeth absently. "Where are the other stops and may I see the ship manifest? I understand the ferries travel to more ports besides Juneau, Haines and Skagway."

"Yes, they connect to the South Central and Aleutian Chain lines. It's as easy as switching trains elsewhere, that includes Cordova, Valdez, Homer, Seldovia, Kodiak and the Aleutians in your dream itinerary."

"Let's back up a bit. Can you tell me what changes took place from the time before the ferry was renovated back to its vintage look in Portland and the time it was returned to Juneau?" She checked her notes. "It appears that the thefts began within a few weeks of putting it back into normal service." Rainy looked at the man, wondering if there wasn't something right under his nose he was missing.

He scratched his chin, took another sip from his coffee. "No, I can't think of anything significant.

"Any insignificant changes in day to day activity?"

He laughed. "The only change was a good one. My daughter graduated from college and returned to Juneau. She wants to be part of the ferry system. She majored in Biology, minored in Business Administration. Missy thinks she can take over from daddy when he retires." He chuckled with a soft look in his eyes.

Rainy pondered his answer thoughtfully.

"Once you and your friend get settled in your cabin, Rainy, please be my guests at dinner. I'd like to introduce you to my daughter, Missy. She's a sweetheart and has always been very interested in everything about the ferry system. The restaurant is adjacent to the bar. Say, 6:30?"

Picking up her notepad, she rose and smiled her thanks.

The women walked around the deck, oohed and aahed at the view of the tall snow-clad mountains rising above both sides of the ferry and inhaled the sharp, clear air. They saw every type of tourist on the deck, and compared the exotic view to their own Lark Point panorama.

Cris pulled a hat over her red curls and gripped the railing with her gloved hands and shook a brochure open. "I'm told this is the poor man's cruise ship. If someone is on a baseline budget and quick-footed, one can find deck space for a tent or claim a reclining chair in the fresh air out of the rain. A sleeping bag could be laid out in the solarium where heaters waited. The cafeteria serves salads, fruit, hot sandwiches and gallons of coffee. Fine dining is available, but to save, it's absolutely OK to bring your ice chest and thermos. People can pay for showers, enjoy a book in the lounge and relish the same magnificent views as those folks in the four-berth stateroom with amenities. Ah," she said, "this is quite a gorgeous place and it's nice to know even the middle class can enjoy it. But I'm glad we are going to enjoy the fine-dining aspect of it...." She sighed and raised her freckled face to the sun as it inched its way out in snatches between the gray clouds that followed them up the sound.

Later, as they relaxed in their small two-berth cabin seeing snowy mountains and blue water encapsulated in a post-card view, Cris turned to Rainy and gave her a look. "How much time do we have?" she asked.

Rainy glanced at her watch, locked the door and turned into Cris's embrace. "Enough," she whispered.

Malaspina's deck was littered with men, women and children, each covered in thick jackets, scarves and furry hats. The sun was out and the day might have been perfect but for the wind that rose and fell in chasms across the deck, sloshing huge wakes into the side of the ferry.

Cris grimaced. "My teeth are freezing." Spring in Alaska was certainly different than California, she mused, pulling her hat over her ears and holding it firmly with both hands. She knew there were over 400 people on the ferry along with a lower level of automobiles and trucks, many with trailers. It was an amazing process. She couldn't remember when she'd had such fun.

"Stop smiling and they'll warm up," Rainy snickered as she held the railing with one hand and her stocking cap with the other, blonde corkscrew curls escaping and whipping around her chin. The wind whipped against everyone, tossing conversations and laughter seaward.

Promptly at 6:30, they arrived at the restaurant and followed Locky's wave from the window table across the room. Beside him sat a young woman in jeans, sweater with *Alaska* emblazoned in rhinestones, and the craziest hat they'd ever seen. It had small beads around the edge and a yarn knob on top, a ribbon tied beneath her chin. As Cris and Rainy approached, the woman was fiddling with the tie, frantic to untie it.

Locky stood briefly and pulled out a chair for Rainy. Cris slid into the one across from them and turned to the woman next to her.

The young woman's bright blue eyes welcomed them before reaching a hand with a shy, "Hello."

Cris was charmed.

Rainy chose to hold judgment.

Locky introduced his daughter to the women with obvious pride in his voice. "Please meet my girl, Melissa "Missy" O'Leary. She's learning the ropes and is my best right hand," he beamed.

Missy's face flushed a moment before yanking the last knot from under her chin and removed her hat, releasing a thick cascade of ash-blonde hair. The top and sides were spiked; the back behind the ears grew long past her shoulder blades. Crazy hair at best, but her eyes were soft with a ready smile. She looked at her father expectantly.

"Missy, I wanted you to meet Ms. Nites and Ms. Crissman. They are friends of a man I've known quite some time from California. They haven't been on the ferry system before and are anxious to learn about it from locals. Think you're up to it?" He grinned.

The girl seemed a little shy but nodded in their direction. "Sure. Are you just going to Skagway and then back to Juneau or do you plan on staying in Skagway for awhile?"

Rainy answered languidly. "We want to see everything we can. We understand the ferry will stop in Skagway a few hours so we'd like to see the little town we've heard about...the gold rush, the Yukon and White Pass Yukon Railroad route? Wish we had time to make that trip...We've heard Skagway has less than 1000 inhabitants but doubles during tourist season. Someone told me the town had 30,000 people there during the gold rush. I've heard of the con man, Soapy Smith, who swindled prospectors and all the hoopla that followed."

Missy grinned. "Yes, Skagway has a colorful history and I hope the wind doesn't take you out into the Tayai Inlet. It can be a wild thing at times." She laughed, looked around at the bar filling up around them.

Rainy was surprised to see her track a couple across the room as they left, obviously a man and woman with money. Her diamond earrings sparkled from the lights along the ceiling and the necklace around her neck sending a rainbow of lights toward them.

The women enjoyed their meal and later agreed to meet the next morning for a quick tour of the ferry and watch Haines drift by after a quick stop and then on to Skagway.

As the Malaspina cruised into the bay at Skagway, known as the Gateway to the Klondike, late the next morning, Rainy reached down to caress Cris's arm laying on the cover below her. The bunk bed scenario hadn't thrilled them but they smiled as they both remembered how two could fit on a small bed easily. But they'd both agreed sleeping was another story. Rainy lost the short straw and got the top bunk; they were still laughing about it.

"Skagway today! Rainy, have you any idea how you are going to find the thieves on the ferry? I haven't seen you putting on your private-eye hat since we boarded." She laughed low and inched her way out of bed.

"Not sure. Something seems a bit odd about Missy. She seems nervous. I know Locky told us he wouldn't tell anyone why I was here and I believe he means it. She either knows why we are here or she knows something about the thefts. We have all day in Skagway and then on the ferry back to Juneau. Let's keep our eyes open. You can be my right hand," Rainy laughed as she ran her fingers down the inside of Cris's arm.

"Hey, lady, how can I get dressed when you're doing that?"

"Mmmm… we don't have to get off the minute it docks, you know that, don't you?"

Cris laughed.

The women walked off the ferry at Skagway an hour later than everyone else. Inhaling the cold air, they embraced the peace of the valley, the blue of the sky and mountains surrounding the small town. It was a postcard of perfection. The streets were narrow, there were few cars; little shops decorated the main street. Wind picked up and blew dirt in swirls around them so they tightened their jackets around themselves and proceeded up the main street. Snow-capped mountains rose above and surrounded the tiny town; boardwalks edged the street. They saw shops such as Distinctive Gemstones, Sweet Tooth Café, The Loom, Bites on Broadway Café, Skagway Brewing Company and jewelry shops near the Alaska Shirt Company.

They stopped to stare at the front of an old grey stone building with yellow letters that read Camp Skagway with 1899 above its doorway. Both women wondered what A and B meant, each letter on the top of the outer columns of the roofline as well as the upper edge of the building. Right in the center of the building's roofline the AB met in a circle; a balcony railing in the center of the façade resembled tree limbs strung together in an erratic pattern. It was a town to remember.

Rainy saw Missy O'Leary ahead of them talking furtively with a man about her age who was dressed in Levis and a black jacket with Harley Davidson splashed across its back. Even a block away, she could see he had a tattoo sliding around his neck. It appeared they were having a very serious conversation, almost angry, she thought. Rainy couldn't remember seeing him on the ferry, although with over 400 people on the boat, she wasn't surprised. She tucked it away in her mind for later and pulled Cris toward the brewery. They'd have lunch there and she'd poke around the ferry before the travelers returned.

Cris picked up the menu and they both read the brewery's history as they waited for the girl behind the bar to take their order.

Rainy read, "With roots dating back to the Klondike Gold Rush of 1898, the Skagway Brewing Company first opened its doors to serve thirsty prospectors hoping to strike it rich. Reopened in 2007, we are Skagway's local craft brewery, dedicated to creating fresh unfiltered ales using hydroelectricity and the purest untreated Alaskan water. In our restaurant we're dishing up everything from pasta and specialty burgers to local smoked salmon and halibut fish and chips. Welcoming all ages, we invite you to stop by 7th and Broadway where we work hard, we play hard, and we know how to have a good time."

"Huh. Well, what about the food?"

Rainy saw Missy and the stranger walk by the window, start to enter and then change their mind. Rainy would ask Locky who the man was when they returned to the boat. "Fish and Chips for me," she said, "and the specialty ale your menu mentions," she told the bearded young man who wore a quick smile and a white towel tossed over his shoulder.

He glanced at Cris, who tapped her finger on the smoked salmon and said, "and the ale for me too."

"Rainy, what are you thinking? You look like you're staring into a place where nobody lives........"

She glanced at Cris and pursed her lips slightly. "Not sure, honey, but we need to get back to the ferry. Guess I really have to get to work. But let's enjoy the beer and our food. The boat is not going anywhere anytime soon." Her eyes lit up when the cold beer was placed in front of her and she lifted it in a silent salute.

A few hours later, Rainy had traversed every outer hallway where windows faced the waterway and people meandered toward the ferry for the return trip south to Juneau. She hadn't seen anything that gave her even the merest question of guilt about anyone. She'd turned around and walked the length of the second floor.

A woman came running toward her with a look of panic on her face. "It's gone! I know I left it in the box near the bed and the door was locked but it's gone." She had short, dark hair curling toward her face making her eyes look large and expressive. Her mouth was quivering along with the fat jiggling at her neck.

Rainy recognized her as the woman leaving the bar the previous night with all the diamonds ablaze. Her husband was a few steps behind as the pair jogged down the hallway, arguing. The woman wasn't listening, definitely a woman on a mission.

She stared after them, assuming they were heading toward the Captain's office. Sure enough. As she rounded the corner, a group of others had surrounded them, their voices raised in anger.

"I've been robbed! We had our door locked…what kind of security do you have on this ferry?" The man reached for his wife's arm but she jerked out of his grasp. "Harry, I will not quiet down. We've been robbed and the Captain needs to do something about it!" She was clearly angry. The husband was clearly stumped. Everyone else was anxious to hear what the Captain had to say.

Locky O'Leary's face was a mask of frustration. He caught Rainy's eye and nodded to her, inviting her to bring the couple inside his office. She slipped by the gathering crowd and gently closed the door.

The Captain pulled out a notepad and nodded to Rainy. "Folks, let me get your names and information. This is Lauraine Nites, an investigator who will be working with you. Please give me your names, addresses and tell me what happened. When you left the ferry, what items did you leave in your cabin? We will try very hard to find the answers."

The woman took a deep, angry breath. Rings covered three fingers and a fur muff hung from her waist. The man tried to soothe his wife by rubbing his hands along her shoulder blades. It took nearly fifteen minutes to tell her story, get her information on paper and send them away.

The Captain sagged. "Dammit! I'm glad it happened while you were here but I'm mad as hell it happened at all. So, I guess as they say, here were go again." He slapped his hands on the desk, causing Rainy to jump in surprise.

Suddenly, there was a loud uproar where loud arguing could be heard and the sounds of running feet. "My iPad is gone!" The strident voice was just outside the door and thunderous pounding followed.

The Captain stood up angrily and yanked the door open to find at least twenty people talking all at once. He put his hands up to quiet the crowd a moment before the young woman's tears flew and she repeated angrily, "My iPad was stolen while I was in Skagway. I didn't think I needed to take it with me, for God's sakes. Someone else said they can't find their jewelry bag where she left it. Could that be stolen too? What should I do?!" she wailed.

Captain O'Leary and Rainy heaved weighty sighs as he guided the young woman into the office. Rainy said she would be out and about. He knew she'd be looking for anything out of the ordinary and he was glad to have the woman there; he wasn't sure he could handle the crowd on his own. His staff hovered nearby and he lifted a hand toward three of them, nodding his head toward the gathering storm of people outside his door.

Rainy's heart pounded as she followed the length of hallway before running down the stairwell and into the bar where Cris was waiting for her. "Things are happening!" Her eyes wide, she sat down to skim her scribbled notes.

Cris stared at Rainy, seeing her chest rise and fall quickly; the air around them crackled with adventure. She smiled as Rainy's blonde curls bounced while she whispered her notes aloud.

"There's something here, Cris. I know it. Wait! The burglaries began the end of May." She looked up thoughtfully. "And guess when the Captain's daughter joined the crew on this ferry?"

"What?! You think there's a connection? She's so sweet, I can't believe it. It must be coincidental."

Rainy's eyes narrowed. "I really do not believe in coincidences like this, Cris. You want to be a sleuth? Let's go find the young lady and see what she does to keep busy around this floating barge."

Cris laughed uncomfortably, slid off the stool and tried to keep up with Rainy as she slipped out of the bar and into the main cabin at the front of the ferry. She gripped her jacket tightly and looked to Rainy for instructions.

"You go to the front around the other side and I'll go to the back on this side. When we finish this level, let's do the same on the other two levels. If we can't find her there, let's meet in the dining room. I don't have cell service so we are in the dark ages as far as communication goes." Before Cris could answer, Rainy was gone.

The lounge and open deck area were filled with travelers as they watched the beauty of Alaska fill the windows like a slow-running video. The bleating horn had alerted those still in Skagway that it was time to go and many were already settling themselves in deck chairs. Also, inside the viewing cabin were rows of soft chairs similar to an airplane, only wider seats with more legroom. The tall mountains that hugged the bay and fell into the inlet filled the windows with trees, snow and wildlife. The ferry was dog friendly so it wasn't surprising to see them among the passengers.

Rainy fled along the outer corridor, peeking in windows, looking for Missy as well as listening for conversations that might lead her to a clue or another theft. Her heart thumped under her jacket and she focused her eyes along the long walkway, touching the white steel walls as she turned the corner and headed up to the open viewing area atop the ferry.

Cris had just left the lounge and started along the outer corridor on the other side when she saw Missy. She wasn't alone. She stood with the stranger she and Rainy had seen her with in Skagway. They were arguing and he was pointing at her and poking his finger into her chest. Missy was crying and jerking sideways out of his arm's reach.

"Hey, Missy." Hiding her anger, Cris approached them, as if she'd just planned to say hello, forcing a smile she'd like to slap him with.

The man turned abruptly toward the railing; Missy appeared embarrassed, lifting her hand to her hair, she smiled tentatively. Cris felt animosity flowing from the man and she wondered where Rainy was... they could hardly communicate when Missy obviously needed someone close by. Making a snap decision, Cris asked if she'd like to have some hot chocolate in the bar to warm themselves because the cold wind was slapping them from the open railing.

Missy glanced quickly toward the man and he shook his head at her. "Well, uh...why don't you go ahead and I'll be there in about five minutes? I could use a little something to warm me up," she responded distinctly staring a hole in the back of the man's back.

Cris had no option but to leave them and knew she had to find Rainy. She had to make those five minutes count. Maybe Rainy was right about coincidences. Missy looked to be in trouble. Cris ran up the steps to the top deck and pulled open the door where a staff member watched the travelling passengers from a closed circuit monitor. The man looked up in surprise to see her hold a hand over her chest to catch her breath.

"Hello, how can I help you, miss?" His crisp uniform and inquisitive eyes both demanded attention as he turned to her, holding his fingers stiffly on a keyboard where he'd been tapping away.

"Please find my friend, Rainy Nites. She's helping the Captain with the thefts on the ferry and I'm trying to help her. It's imperative that I know where she is right now. Can your cameras find her?"

The man studied her a moment before turning to the monitor and snapped visuals through several cameras. There, at the doorway to the bar, Rainy was just rounding the corner. She pointed emphatically.

The man lifted the phone by his console, punched in a button and Cris saw the bartender lift his own phone perched on the bar before him. When the man near Cris spoke, the bartender immediately stared into the camera directly at them.

"Please tell the blonde woman with all the curly hair to pick up the phone quickly, Donovan." He handed Cris the phone.

"Hello?" She could see Rainy's confused expression on the monitor as she nodded to the man beside her.

"Hey, Rainy, I found her. Stay there. She's on her way and I have to run back down the stairs. I hope she's alone..."

"What? Why wouldn't she....?"

"Just hold her there, Rainy!" She returned the phone and touched the surprised man's arm, thanking him before turning toward the stairwell.

Rainy glanced around the bar, looked out the window toward the ocean and the majestic mountains beyond. The wind was cold out there and she studied the hale-hearted travelers who sat in the lounge chairs outside. Snuggling into her warm jacket, she removed her gloves and found a table with her back to the window and her eyes on the door.

Missy wandered into the bar a moment later, searching the tables. Rainy lifted her hand and Missy headed toward her. Her flushed face was red, clearly upset.

"Hey, Missy. Please join me? Cris is on her way. Did you enjoy the visit in Skagway?"

Missy seemed surprised. "Well, yes, I walked along Main Street and spent nearly the whole time walking up and down looking for an initial pin like the one my mother bought at a jewelry store there many years ago. She gave it to me, an "M" and I loved it. Wore it all the time.... It was made of pounded gold fifty years ago when daddy bought it for her; I knew it was expensive and mine is missing. I wanted to see if any of the jewelry stores had one like it. Mom's name was Marcia; we were both "Ms".   Rainy watched her babbling and felt an underlying current of tension.

Cris rounded the door at a fast trot and heaved a big sigh when she saw Missy sitting with Rainy already. She glanced around looking for the unfriendly, creepy guy she'd been arguing with; relieved he wasn't inside the bar. She ordered three hot chocolates and took the steaming cups to the table, forcing a calm she didn't feel and hoped Rainy could iron out the issues surrounding the girl.

"Oh, so good...," Missy said after taking a sip. "It burned my tongue but worth it. Thank you." Her shoulders appeared to drop an inch or so.

"You're welcome, Missy. We sure enjoyed Skagway and all the little shops and the brewery. Did you and your friend eat in town too?"

Missy's head snapped up. "My friend?"

Rainy smiled. "Yes, the young man with the tattoo on his neck?" She lifted the hot chocolate to her lips and watched the young woman over its rim. Missy's face was splotchy and she placed the cup on the table, trying to stall for time as her face showed several expressions and her lips tightened.

"Yes, you must mean, Rene. No, we didn't eat in town. He returned to the ship and I stayed to go to all the jewelry stores." She did not say anything further and took another sip of her chocolate.

Rainy glanced at Cris.

"Have you known Rene very long, Missy? He doesn't appear to be one of the staff members....."

Missy laughed. "No, he's not one of the staff. We met in college and when I told him my dad worked for the ferry system and I was heading up here to learn the trade, even though my major was in biology, he latched on to me. He said he'd always wanted to see Alaska. Dad lets him take day trips mostly. Sometimes he gets on like this time...and helps out on the auto deck in exchange for his ride." She suddenly looked worried again and glanced toward the doorway.

"Oh, I see. So your dad knows Rene then. Glad to hear that..."

"Really? Why do you say that?" Her eyes clouded.

"Do you mind my asking if he's your boyfriend, Missy? I couldn't help but notice he was acting pretty nasty to you on the outer deck when I saw you awhile ago," Cris said quietly. "I've been abused by a boyfriend in the past and I didn't like it one bit. And I had trouble walking out of the situation."

Rainy looked up quickly, never having heard that about Cris before and filed it away for another time.

"No, he's not my boyfriend. He likes Alaska and just hangs around….sometimes he just…..," Missy's voice trailed off.

Just at that moment, Captain O'Leary hurried into the bar and spied the women. Quickly joining them, he stared at Rainy expectantly. He reached down and gave his daughter a peck on the check and she reached to pat his cheek lovingly.

"Dad, these nice ladies bought me some hot chocolate. It is really good and it sure warms up the belly. Can I get you one?"

"Sure!" He smiled as she walked off and then turned quickly to the women.

"I think I found the fox that's been in your hen house, Locky." Rainy drummed her fingers on the table.

He was stunned. "Not Missy!?"

"No, but she is afraid who it might be and worries he's up to no good. Cris saw him yelling at her and poking his finger at her chest, arguing loudly in the outer deck. We both saw them in Skagway when we were at the brewery and they seemed to be arguing then too. Something is not right there…."

"Here you go, dad," Missy sat the cup in front of her dad and folded her hands around her own cup. When he gave her a look, her eyebrows rose. "Dad?"

"Missy, I didn't tell you the whole truth when I said I knew Rainy Nites through my friend in California named Ben. That part is true but Ben is the head of the Claims Department at Metro Assurance Company and she is their claims investigator."

Missy turned toward Rainy. "Okay, why the big mystery? I know you've been working with the insurance company trying to figure out who is robbing your ferry people. Why not just tell me up front?" Her fingers mimicked Rainy's as they tapped a fierce staccato near her cup.

Rainy stepped in quickly, "Missy, I asked your dad not to tell anyone, even you. It is the way I always investigate. The less people know what I do, the better. You know I am wondering about the coincidence behind your friend, Rene, and the multiple thefts that have occurred on the Malaspina since the end of May, don't you?"

Missy stared at Rainy, her mouth closed tightly.

"I imagine once we check the ship manifest against the dates of all the thefts since you arrived here from school, we will find the dates coincide with Rene's travelling itinerary?"

The girl's eyes rounded and she brought her hand to her throat. She turned to her father and shook her head. "Oh, no. If that's true, he used me and….oh, I've had questions and every time I ask him about the money he has without a job to earn it, he gets crazy mad. That happened today in town. He told me if I found an M pin, he'd buy it for me. I was shocked. I knew it would be expensive and his ratty clothes and staying in the hostel never showed me he had money. …. Then when he boarded again this afternoon, I found him down on the auto deck in his old pickup truck playing with an iPad. I'd never seen him with one before and when I asked him about it, he got mad." She turned to Cris. "That's when you saw us a little while ago. I was standing at the railing trying to figure out what was going on when he found me there. He told me to stop getting into his business. He was flat-ass furious. I'm glad you showed up." She smiled but tears threatened to spill.

The Captain reached for his daughter's hand. "Where is he now, Missy?"

"He's probably back down in the auto deck with his toy."

He looked at Rainy and patted his daughter's shoulder before quickly walking out of the bar.

When they returned to Juneau, Rainy was ecstatic. Another solved crime. Ben's relief was obvious when she called to tell him security hauled Rene Campos off the Malaspina as soon as it docked in Juneau.

They had one full day before heading home and they filled every minute with sightseeing. They saw the ice field at nearby Mendenhall Glacier, the friendly tour and tasting room at Alaskan Brewing Company and, finally, a 2 ½-hour whale-watching excursion. Ten dolphins came to play as Captain Earl Hubbard maneuvered the boat through the quiet waters of North Pass. The boat was surrounded by intensely beautiful scenery and Cris wondered if she would ever feel the peace and contentment of the past few days enchant her mind ever again.

~

Michael Mallory's nerves were shot.

Cris noticed it immediately.

The cast noticed and not one could understand why he was so nervous, grumpy and secretive, especially Cris who lived with him and thought she knew him so well. She liked his friend, Nico. In the past, they'd shared pizza as a threesome, watched a little television and laughed a lot. Recently, Nicholas seemed changed, the laughter slowed and the conversation became stilted when she entered the room. After a few weeks, she kept to herself when he arrived, talked to Rainy daily and met her for lunch once a week. Their holiday in Alaska was still fresh on her mind and she concentrated on that to wash away her worry about Michael and Nico's personality changes.

One day a few weeks later, she heard them talking low and tiptoed to the door, opening it just an inch. It sounded like they were arguing again but she couldn't understand the words. Shrugging, she closed the door and practiced her Taekwon-Do since it always brought a sense of peace to her mind and body. She'd worry about the guys later.

Michael handed Nico another beer. "You and I both know why we agreed to work for this man. He has my job in his hands because of my felony and you need the money to finish college. I know we agreed mostly because he promised nobody would get hurt. We both hate doing it, I know that too. Now, he's found one more guy to work with us. I don't like him, name's Andreas and he makes me uneasy. You'll meet him later. Keep your cool, Nico. We can't afford to make DAL angry. I have a terrible feeling he might really hurt anyone who does." Michael's voice shook.

Nico felt his beer floating toward the surface and he knew he might be sick. How in the hell he agreed to this in the first place was beyond him to figure out. He'd been friends with Michael a long time and trusted him to do the right thing. Nico hated everything about their new "job" and tried to focus on school…all the reasons why he'd said yes in the first place. Yes, the beer was coming back up.

~

Sam held two phone messages in his hand; one from Charlie and one from the mayor. Elliott sat in front of him, his arms across his chest.

"Sam, they don't like it. We are tromping too closely into their territory." The producer scowled and shook a finger at the notes on his pad. You said too much. Do you want to give the thieves a roadmap to skirt the cops?

Sam's eyes narrowed. "Just because I have the guts to get as close as I can to these punks?" Sam thought his anger was justified and held Elliott's stare.

"But you aren't doing this alone and I don't think you should portray it that way. This is a tough town and Sterling keeps a pretty good stronghold on it. Someone with a lot of clout is on his butt to stop you and you may well better listen. You aren't a one-man show and Brock is getting agitated. That's the guy you want in your corner, Sam."

"Oh, for crying in a mirror. I know I'm skating on thin ice here but if we don't do it, the Democrat will. Freedom of speech aside, this is something that will hold our program on top above the newspaper. I've already had people tell me they enjoy the new format as I look into the camera as if I'm sitting in their living room. I was told it was like a soap opera, something new every day even if it's a tiny breath of light into this damned dark piece of crap who doesn't let up….they just keep stealing."

"Yes, Sam but I have some concerns. I'm wary about your taking this on, taking the mayor on….the police."

"Let's see how far we can go, okay?" Sam tapped his pen on the desk as Elliott left his office, a little distraught but steady.

Phones rang outside his door and his blood pressure spiked just a bit. When Charlie Royce and Mayor Sterling arrived, he'd be ready. He ignored the noise, drank some water and talked his heart palpitations down a notch.

~

Lark Point University campus was thinning out; students packing cars, trudging in and out of their buildings, preparing for the summer hiatus. There were squeals of laughter filling the near-empty spaces where just the week before, students were cramming for their end of term exams.

Tess Berg, however, was not in the crowd. At twenty one, she had a plan and that was to graduate early. She'd already registered for the summer classes she required and although she wished she also had the months ahead to play, she knew she'd made a good choice. She tossed her thick, black mane across her shoulder, whipped it into a pony tail and propped herself against the huge tree trunk she'd claimed as hers three years earlier during her freshman year.

The tree was where she'd first seen Nicholas. He had been studying frantically, tracing his finger down the pages of his calculus book with one hand and tapping his thigh with the other as he kept time to the music flowing out a nearby dorm window.

She smiled at his multi-tasking and had called him a show off. When he'd looked up blankly, their eyes met and they'd been friends ever since. He helped her with calculus; she helped him with English. They shared notes and he paid her to type his homework. She'd offered to do it for free just to look into those eyes of his, but he wouldn't think of it. He wanted to pay his own way. She knew he was from San Leandro, a third-generation Spaniard whose ancestors sailed from Spain to Hawaii and the sugar plantations before settling in California. He was on full scholarship from wrestling and had his eye on energy conservation. He was ambitious, kind, intelligent and had the cutest butt she'd ever seen. She liked his aggressive, clean cut, fast-talking blue-eyed Spanish personality. He studied hard and they spent hours with their heads bent over books.

And he was also going to attend summer classes. Really? Of course she'd made the right decision, she'd be able to spend time with him and graduate the following January. Life was good.

She glanced around the campus and watched the cars streaming in and out of the parking area, young men and women hugging each other, stuffing luggage into trunks, lamps, bedding and books. She scrunched her butt into the crook of the trunk and stashed her backpack behind her as she settled under the leafy fronds of the oak tree. Her watch told her she had two hours to spend in free reading time before Nicholas got out of his Physics class. The anticipation was intensely delicious.

She would enjoy time away from classes but she did not want to pause except for very short breaks. She would earn her Bachelor's Degree in January for her undergraduate degree and then it was on to graduate school to earn her Masters. Maybe a Doctorate one day but one step at a time. She loved the idea of mental health counseling so she could pull some people out of their sick-mental din. She wanted to offer counseling, support and guidance to individuals having trouble coping mentally and emotionally. There were a number of mental problems that she might encounter during her career from people dealing with every-day stress to those with diagnosable mental illnesses and disorders. She wanted to counsel individuals that suffered from depression, Bipolar disorder, anxiety disorder, panic disorder, phobias, addictions or chronic pain. She knew she had to specialize but hoped she would be able to find something in between.

In the meantime, there was the lovely Nicholas and her Kindle Fire. She checked her phone to see if he'd sent her a text but it was blank. Then she tapped her reader's switch and lost herself in Dianna Gabaldon's Outlander Series, inhaled the sweet scents of late spring and settled herself against her tree.

~

Anna buried herself like a hermit in her office surrounded by a computer and research notes amid the safe haven of her writing. Thoughts of Cole Nites were kept at a minimum, barely tingling the back of her busy brain. Her notebooks were crammed with information needed for her book except the one thing still missing; the courtroom sequence and pre-trial notes. She argued with herself daily, pulled out his business card, and then stuffed it back into her desk drawer. It was getting frayed around the edges.

I'll find someone else. Yes, I can call the American Bar Association. She grabbed the phone book, flipped each page and ran a clear, polished nail down each column, hesitating but straining away from the Ns. She slammed the book closed and jumped up from her desk.

Hugging herself and pressing into her stomach to reduce the knot that sat there, she paced back and forth in front of her study window, still amazed at her longing to set eyes on this stranger who touched her so quickly. *Dammit. Double damn.*

Anna heaved a tired sigh and thought of the pristine white, slightly bruised, business card tucked into her drawer. The embossed names, MAPES, LUCAS & NITES, raised slightly in black letters, were rubbed nearly smooth. She retrieved it again and stared at it wondering why she hadn't tossed it out already.

In the middle of an unfinished page, she took her hands off the keyboard, slipped into a sweater and went for a long walk. Sometimes she wanted nothing but the wind. Cobwebs had begun to cling to her thoughts and she needed the smell of flowers.

An hour later, she slipped into her study again, saw his business card staring at her and sat in the overstuffed chair beside her desk. "Watching a court case couldn't hurt really… I'll take my notes, sit in the back and…..I'll take Tess with me!" *Yes, I can do it….*

"Take me where?" Tess asked as she scrambled onto the loveseat in her usual fashion. She sat with her leg dangling over the arm, her other curled beneath her. "Why are you talking to yourself, Mom? Going nuts, are you?" Tess laughed and scrunched down into the cushions as she waited for her mother's answer.

Anna turned quickly at her daughter's voice and reached to hug her closely. "Hello sweetheart. Oh, the court…….."

"…..Are we being sued?"

"That is what an enquiring mind would ask but no, silly. It's that damned research. I found that lawyer named Cole Nites, remember? I told you a few weeks ago after the University Club party," Anna finished lamely, avoiding eye contact with her daughter.

"Mom, what's wrong?"

"Nothing, why do you ask? I just thought you might like to go with me….you know, learn something about our judicial system."

Suddenly more curious because she heard something in Anna's voice, Tess studied her mother's tense face, saw her stiff jaw, and reached for her hand.

"When, Mom?"

Anna poured a glass of wine. Her shoulders relaxed. "Let me call Mr. Nites for a good time to watch the type of case I need for my story."

"Ok.   But remember my best days off are Tuesdays and Wednesdays? What's for dinner? Is Dad coming home to eat with us?"

Anna smiled.   "You give me whip lash with your change of subjects." Laughing, she said, "I don't know and not until later."

Tess creased her forehead and bit a lip as she grabbed a cigarette, lit it swiftly and inhaled, eyeing her mother through thoughtful eyes.

Anna stared at the burning cigarette and wrinkled her nose. "You know I don't like you smoking in the house or period, for that matter...."

"Mom, let's go out to eat then," Tess ventured, exhaling a soft wisp of smoke away from her mother and forming her soft pink lips into a tentative smile. She stubbed out the cigarette and carried the ashtray to the kitchen. She thought idly about quitting as she rubbed her stained fingers.

"Yes, let's do that, Tess."

"Are you ready to go now, Mom?"

"Not yet." She took a sip of wine. She'd let the court appearance and other decisions slide for awhile.

During the next days and weeks, Anna dove into her writing with a quiet vengeance as rain spattered the windows. She wrote furiously, tapping on her keyboard until the pages began to fill the box on her desk and empty ink cartridges piled up. The inevitable court scenes loomed closer each day.

The conversation with Tess was forgotten.   Procrastination continued. Sometimes she would pull out a book to read something entertaining, not too heavy to spoil the need for the contentment of losing herself in a story. Sitting at the computer all day had another side effect she fought against; she'd gained ten pounds since she began writing, her exercise waned, her daily walks were at a standstill. Every time she told herself to start walking again, she'd think of another piece to add to her story, toss her reading book aside and she was back at the computer again.

Now, her exercise program was going to and from the city library. Her walking consisted of walking up and down the steps between floors and to and from her car. Google helped her immensely but there was nothing like pulling those books off the bookshelves and spreading them out before her on a table and tapping out notes. She could diet later.

The library books were filled with precedents outlining court cases and she studied them intently for hours. The library's large marble-walled rooms were calming; the rattling papers comforting. And she began to believe she could finish without Cole's help amid the dark bookcases filled with court cases from floor to ceiling.

~

Cole started to watch Darrin Lucas more closely. He couldn't put his finger on the discontent with his partner; still hadn't found the puzzle pieces to fit together to answer the questions from the old court case that simmered just beneath the surface. He'd continue watching him and maybe talk with his partner, Steven Mapes, but he wasn't sure he wanted to draw him into something that might be nothing.

Steven had his own problems defending corporations instead of individual clients. His expertise was so different from Cole's and Darrin's that he probably had no reason to question the same worries that permeated Cole's mind and he probably didn't care. He was too busy chasing corporate cheats and trying to save the honest ones. No, he'd worry this one out on his own and leave Steven out of his thoughts. The last thing he wanted to become was an office tattle tale when he had no proof of wrongdoing. Yep, probably nothing.

He tapped his fingers on his desk. It was more than nothing, something wasn't adding up. Cole admitted that Darrin's actions had caused ripple effects during previous cases over the years but he hadn't paid attention then. He was now.

Pulling out his legal pad, he began to scribble a list of prior instances so he could line them up, compare and hopefully toss his worries away. As he began to list the old cases on the yellow paper, his hand wrote faster and faster. He was equally surprised and disconcerted as he thought about Darrin and tried to dismiss his apprehension.

The man was a good lawyer and a respected man in Lark Point. He had always kept himself private but everyone has a right to do that. Sometimes it stumped the others in the law firm but they just raised their eyebrows, shrugged or ignored it. Everyone was busy.

For Cole, however, Darrin's actions were sometimes mysterious enough for him to question more than his personality but also his legal character. Too busy to add this complication to his work-day, he decided to shelve his worries and put the pad away. He'd made a list of ten cases that stood out in his mind. Ten cases reflecting questions that arose at the time. Questions that obviously still flit around in Cole's head. Looking at his list before ripping off the page to toss it, he noticed a connection. Ten cases. Ten young men. All charged with theft. Funny, he hadn't realized that correlation before he jotted down the list and now he didn't know what to do with it.

His stomach roiled a bit and he sat back in his chair, glanced out his office window toward the view he enjoyed; the park benches lined the green and trees stood proudly around its perimeter. Today they swayed, leaves blowing across the expanse and rain threatened. Summer was in full swing and fall would soon be on its way. Time was passing too quickly for him.

Darrin Lucas. He exhaled loudly, scribbled the man's name across the top of his yellow pad, and dissected his character in his head. He was a quiet man, stern at times, intimidating and sometimes nasty to his subordinates, but distant always. Cole shook his head for the word he wanted... sly. That was it. For some time, he felt Darrin was a bit sly. But was there more than that? Was he sly about his cases, eager to defend his clients? Was he sly about his life beyond the law firm? Holy Christmas, the man was his senior partner. Of course he had to be sly at times, wasn't Cole as well? Didn't they have to be? Was he justifying the old man's actions or postponing the seriousness of his worries? He wanted Darrin to trust him, so he had to trust Darrin. Didn't he?

He pondered that thought and looked down at his pad. Anna, he'd written. *Damn.*

SIX

Darrin Lucas created a seat of power within his firm that left no doubt who was the controlling partner. Despite his growing up in abject poverty, constant prodding made him the success he clearly showed the public. Steel resolve raised him to a ceiling of corrupt contentment. An illusion. His vitality was equaled only by his ambition and both ran second to his determination. His smile was a warning; it switched on and off like a burglar's flashlight. He never wasted time on people who were of no consequence to him either professionally or otherwise.

He had little regard for other men, even those he knew well, Cole and Steven included. He needed good lawyers and they were good lawyers. He respected their minds but thought little or nothing of their lives outside the courtroom. They were a necessity. They kept the status quo. They protected him. They gave him a measure of respectability. He pretended interest in their business affairs but basically he did his job, went to the bank and lived a life of luxury, albeit far beyond his means. But they didn't know that.

Darrin loved things. He didn't care if it was art, jewelry, people or objects. Just things. He liked touching them, walking into a room seeing the sparkle shine toward him and knowing they belonged to him. He never had enough; his mind cramped demanding more...always more.

He didn't share his life with women; he never wanted to. He was a handsome man but eyes that could turn to steel rarely invited sentimentality or women. He'd trained his partners early on to steer away from his personal life. It was a steadfast rule and neither they nor his staff crossed the line. No one cared and neither did he. He knew what he wanted. He treated his clients fairly, he won cases. He made money. Bottom line. But his law firm was just a front to hide what excited him.

Darrin Lucas was a thief, his legal career a clever façade. He was good in court. Defense attorneys did not like to hear his name when their cases arose; invariably, they lost. Darrin's acute ability to read people saw many guilty parties go free. Then he went after them, bull dozing them into creating an elaborate web of thieves that included an infallible method of bypassing security systems; they were too afraid of him to fight him. They knew if they didn't meet his demands upon request, their butts would be hauled into court again and this time they'd go to prison. He chuckled when he saw their fear and wondered why they weren't smart enough to realize all they had to do was go to the police and turn him in. Yes, they were perfect, brainless and hungry.

Darrin got his art works, jewels, ceramics and collectibles and his men were paid in cash. Everyone was happy to a point; except the victims, of course.

In his early sixties, of average height, he had premature white hair, weathered eyes and an athletic build. He liked to travel, talking vaguely of investments in the Orient. His home, with its exquisite Persian carpets, antique furniture, fine paintings and delicate *objets d'art*, was a feast for his eyes. He was also a cautious man and although secretive, he bragged of old money and his connections to Lark Point founding fathers whenever the need arose. Even as a successful senior partner in the law firm, he knew the old money scenario would avoid too many questions.

Both of his partners agreed that Darrin Lucas was a man to be reckoned with; they applauded his mind, respected his fairness and never attempted to cross the imaginary line he imposed. And despite being partners for over ten years, neither man knew Darrin any better than the day they walked into the partnership. They especially didn't know that their senior partner dropped the façade of respected attorney the minute he left the suite of offices and stepped into his Mercedes.

Sam Berg was becoming his nemesis as the newsman became more and more interested in the burglaries in Lark Point. And Darrin was in the mood for a new slant on his thefts just to see how far Sam would go to look under those rocks he spoke about on the news the night before.

Always on the lookout for the perfect scam, one evening weeks earlier, as he sat in the audience at the local Artists Repertory Theater, his prayers were answered. He'd idly flipped through the program booklet during the play's intermission and saw the headshot and read the name, Michael Mallory and circled it. He fidgeted all through the second half of the play as the actors elicited laughter and applause. He'd found his scam and now the man. Michael Mallory was not a stranger to the criminal defense attorney; he'd lost the boy and now he was found.

The theater audience had trickled into the lobby after the final applause and the curtain fell. In the lobby, an anxious group waited to meet the actors and actresses they'd just watched play the characters in the comedy, *1001*. In the dramatic comedy, the cuckolded King Shahriyar married a new bride every night and beheaded her the next morning. Unrest obviously spread in the Sultanate until his daughter, Scheherazade, takes action.

The main character was Michael Mallory, tall, now dressed in black jeans, white shirt and a loose burgundy tie, his makeup gone, hair perfect. He was the last man to enter the lobby, where expectant energy filled the waiting room. His smile shone bright with the accolades afforded him and the group of actors that surrounded him.

When he looked up to see the older man staring at him, something clicked in recognition and a chill slid down his spine. The lawyer. He broke eye contact, pretending he hadn't recognized the man but the staccato beat of his heart ramped up; the man was making a beeline toward him. Michael was unsure how to react. Not here. Not when he was cleaning up his act, so to speak.

He enjoyed the drama classes he'd taken after his petty theft fiasco. He didn't need a free ride; he was making his own money, working hard, loving the camaraderie of the theater and the feelings of accomplishment. The lawyer reminded him of that frightening time when he wore an orange jumpsuit, wrists clamped with steel behind his back, the judge staring at him as if he was a cockroach on somebody's dirty carpet. The lawyer had arrived as a pro bono defense attorney. But that was almost a decade before. He was surprised the man remembered him but he could see it in his cool eyes as he neared the group. Michael nodded to him. He had no choice.

"Hey, Michael. Nice job. You've come a long way from....."

Michael looked around him quickly, his eyes begging the lawyer to stop the sentence. One word about him being a felon and he'd lose everything he'd worked so hard for. He was the star of the play and Cris would never forgive him for keeping it from her. He fisted his hands.

Darrin Lucas presented a knowing smile. "Can I buy you a drink at Rave's across the street? We can catch up. You can tell me how you've managed to straighten......."

Michael again gave the man a look. ".....Sure, I can meet you there in about a half hour. Need to tell my girlfriend I'll be late."

Darrin nodded to the young man and smiled that horrible smile again before turning on his heel to leave the group of well wishers. He'd made his point and needed to get his trap prepared. Michael had all the prerequisites needed; a so-so salary, a girlfriend who probably liked nice things he couldn't afford, peers of actor friends and the perfect venue base for his big plan.

Rave's was sheltered but filled with a riotous group in front, so Darrin slipped into a back, corner table where he could watch the door. True to his word, Michael had walked in, glanced around and headed toward his table. He remembered the boy's anxious face in the half light and he'd smiled in anticipation. Excitement filled his belly. He'd reached out to shake Michael's hand and they'd sipped cold beers.

He remembered the night well.

"My boy, you are looking good. Nobody would guess that ten years ago you were on the wrong side of the law."

Michael stared at the man. "I don't want my friends or Mr. Champion to know about...what happened then, sir. I've gone beyond that and I'm doing well on my own. That time in my life is over. It scared the shit out of me and nobody knows about it. Thank you again for getting me headed in the right direction." He gulped some of his beer. His deep brown eyes stared at the man across from him.

Darrin smiled before rolling his tongue inside his cheek and feigned contemplation. "Well, I know a way you can repay my kindness and assure my silence, Michael. In exchange for your helping me with my project, I won't send Mr. Champion a copy of your rap sheet." He'd sipped his beer, while never taking his eyes off of Michael.

Michael was stunned and the beer in his stomach roiled. "I'll do anything. Please.......what kind of project, Mr. Lucas?" he whispered as he put down his glass with a shaking hand and gripped the table's edge.

~

Andreas Kassipakis had fallen into Darrin Lucas's lap like a ripe plum waiting for the taking. He was young, angry, mean and hungry. Darrin referred the boy's mother to an attorney who got Andreas freed from the burglary charge. It hadn't been the first time the boy had run amok of the law. Andreas owed him and Darrin liked it that way.

Andreas strutted like a cocky hoodlum when Darren helped him avoid prison. He hated punks and Darrin vowed to change the boy's attitude. One lesson should do it. Andreas liked alcohol. Lots of it. Darrin told him he could never drink on the job and if he did, Darrin would break his arm. Andreas laughed. Andreas broke his word. Darrin kept his. The boy didn't laugh at Darrin's demands during the six weeks wait for the cast to be removed. From then on, Andreas did exactly what he was told.

Nico was another story. He'd accidentally overheard a conversation between him and his brother. He needed money to finish school and support his mother. A college kid who wanted an education. It hadn't been easy. The kid had scruples, he'd fought the idea but he came around. He knew Darrin's project would be the answer to his problems.

His three boys as he thought of Michael, Nico and Andreas, were his team. He gave them instructions, they did what they were told, accepted his cash and waited for the next heist.

Andreas and Nico both respected Michael. Neither Michael nor Nico liked Andreas. As a trio, they all respected, feared and hated Darrin Lucas. They had that in common and it held them together like glue.

Darrin was DAL to the boys. He forbade use of his real name and they agreed; the thought of questioning him never entered their heads.

At first, Darrin had his team rob small shops, just to test them. He promised them immunity because he could. He was a defense attorney after all. They believed him. It was this kind of promise that would push Cole into frustrated confusion during court cases, leaving him simmering with anger.

Darrin's dreams were not small, nor particularly disguised. When the boys questioned where the spoils ended up, DAL, in one of his rarer moments explained that he sold what he didn't want to keep for himself and the rest was stashed in a secret place. The fencing of priceless artworks was a specialty; he'd already stashed untraceable millions. He sold just enough to pay the young men, kept the rest and enjoyed the challenge of organizing each new heist. Watching them follow every detail kept his mind clear and his focus strong.

With great caution, Darrin remained the dutiful attorney. He reveled in his trickery and moved among his cache to touch and adore his things in quiet moments. He placed the Ming vase on his mantel and cunningly applauded his audacity. His life was perfect. His partners never questioned his, sometimes unprincipled, behavior because they weren't aware of it.

Years earlier, his father told him it was impossible to have it all but he had since proved the old man wrong. He would have it all and his belly clenched with excitement thinking about it. Using each victorious theft as his springboard to his long-smoldering desire to have whatever he wanted to touch, to hold, to enjoy created a confidence he'd never had growing up. He'd never feel poor again. Never. It wasn't that he couldn't afford to buy the items, he just wanted them. He was addicted to the taking like a shoplifter was to stealing for the fun of it. He did it because he could.

By the time Michael and Nico realized they were dealing with a maniac, their fear of Darrin overshadowed their lives and clogged logic.

Nearly show time. Glossy hairdos, fancy clothing and flowing wine reflected a richness and delight in the theater's lobby as the attendees whispered and waited. The newest play would soon begin and the minutes ticked toward the magic hour of eight o'clock when the door would close firmly against late arrivals and the curtain would whisper as it opened.

Cris patted powder on her freckled face over the thick foundation and smiled at herself in the mirror after giving her cheeks a pinch to mark the flush. She was playing the part of a woman, just eighteen, and needed to hide her years. At thirty five, she felt old next to some of the newer members of the cast. But for tonight, she'd be eighteen.

The small amethyst and diamond ring sparkled on her finger as she placed her hand on the dressing room table. Michael had surprised her with the gift to celebrate the opening of their new play. She felt guilty taking it but it meant so much to him. And it was beautiful. She enjoyed his gifts so why shouldn't she accept them, she wondered. Rainy had an armful of jewelry and she didn't feel guilty.

She shook her tightly curled red head, repeated the lines she'd practiced with Michael earlier and concentrated on the play. He was playing the part of a gardener always chasing away the kids who liked to play ball in his flowers. He didn't have the lead this time but they'd agreed, regardless of the size of their pieces, they'd study together.

Fluffing her rat's nest of a head, Cris scampered off her chair and slipped into her shoes for Act I before leaving her changing room to scout around for Michael so they could go over it once again. She saw him speaking furtively into the telephone, jerking his head as if to get his point across. When she saw him cover his mouth behind his hand, Cris had an uneasy feeling he was hiding something from her. It wasn't as if she wasn't hiding something from him, but…..

She tiptoed up to him and heard him say, "…….okay you have the name, it's up to you to get in and out fast….."

Cris dropped back, suddenly unsure. She stepped around the corner of the hallway and called his name, clearly stumped.

Michael's panicked face swung around as he finished his conversation, "….yes, that's right. I'll see you later." He hung up and smiled at Cris with a caught-my-hand-in-the-candy-jar look.

"Hey, Cris. Ready to go over it one more time?" His curly blonde hair just touched his collar and his deep brown eyes watched her for any indication she'd overheard the conversation.

"Who was that, Michael?" she asked, pointing to the phone.

"One of my friends…a pool game is set up for later. I know you don't care for some of my friends, so it's no big deal. Let's go over this, okay?" he said headed toward her dressing room, weaving around other cast members also whispering their lines.

Cris was hurt by his lie but reminded herself they'd agreed they each had their own lives. She certainly did.

"Hey, your ring sparkles in these lights like a million diamonds. Someday I'll get you a bigger one," he promised.

"Michael, where are you getting all the money from? Sure I love nice things but honestly, the diamond necklace last week and the studs the week before. This ring today......" Cris looked up at him questioningly.

A muscle in Michael's jaw twitched. His eyes looked angry for a beat before smiling and hugging her to his chest. "I told you, honey, it's my trust fund. My grandparents gave it to me. I have money. Don't worry about it. I just work here at the rep for fun and applause, remember?" He saw the hurt expression and felt contrite.

"Just for fun?"

"Oh, Cris, you know I take my acting seriously, I just meant I don't need the money I earn here. So, I buy you bling. Maybe someday when we get married, everything will come together.

He saw her stiffen.

"Michael, I told you that marriage is not for me."

"Not now but someday.....you mean...."

"No....not ever. Let's study our lines, ok?"

Michael scowled. He hated having the same argument but he felt hopeful he'd change her mind one day. Of course he would.

Cris dove into her character as she always did. Sometimes she wondered where her characters stopped and she began. "Can't you forget this thing, Mr. King? I know it's not for us but really, we must try harder....." Cris struggled to get through her lines knowing Michael's anger simmered.

Lights rose five seconds after the last scene ended. The theater walls shook with the crescendo of applause which expanded Cris's heart to full capacity. Her throat closed with an emotion that always consumed her at the end of each play, both constrictive and tingling.

Warm fingers intertwined with her own as Michael led her towards center stage to reach out to her fellow thespians. His hands trembled in hers, echoing her thirst for the adulation that their work craved. The floor lights were hot and blinding. She felt but could not see hundreds of eyes on her face and reveled in the buzz of conversation amid the thunder of clapping hands. The story had been so rich and complicated, she'd been consumed by her character and thrilled with the communication she'd maintained with the audience. She was alive, throbbing, fulfilled.

Cris glanced at Michael, luxuriated in the warmth emanating from his brown eyes. His smile was for her alone and guilt made her stumble slightly when he pulled her off stage, multiplying her confusion and anger by pulling her into his arms to kiss her deeply.

The applause subsided, footsteps mingled with her own and she was, once again, just Cris-- a woman filled with unanswered questions. The walls, white and austere, seemed to close in on her as she walked toward her dressing room. She was vaguely aware of fond pats on her back, a squeezed shoulder, a kiss on her slim, white neck. Then sanctuary. Lights ringed the square mirror on her dressing table. She slipped in quickly, closed the door and felt the hard wood slam against her back. She felt choking sobs rush upwards from deep in her belly. Squeezing her green eyes closed tightly to crush the onslaught of salty, wet tears, her right hand shakily covered her face. Her greasy, theatrical makeup smeared across her face but somehow she eased the roaring in her ears.

"Michael, what are you hiding?" Her mind went into overdrive as she replayed the phone conversation she overheard earlier. The scent of body perfume filled her nostrils; the atomizer had leaked, stifling the small room with its pungent sweet smell. Cris wrinkled her nose and rinsed it in the sink.

The Artist's Repertory Program billed Cris with a glowing list of accolades.

> María Crissman made her theater debut with "Other People's Money, written by Jerry Sterner. It was originated by the Hartford Stage Company in a New York production. She has worked in regional theaters across the country including Alaska Repertory Theater, Virginia Stage Company, The Barter Theater, Arizona Theater Company, Snowmass/Aspen Repertory, Empty Space Theater and Tacoma Actors Guild. Her credits included Truvy in *Steel Magnolias*, Brooke/Vickie in *Noises Off*, Helena in *A Midsummer Nights Dream*, Catherine in *The Foreigner* and Gloria in *Gloria Duplex*. "Cris" made her home in Lark Point and taught Taekwon-Do.

Cris stared at Michael's name in the program on her dressing table, wondering what on earth he was up to. He was talented and such a good guy. She traced the words with her finger.

> Michael Mallory returns to the rep where he was last season as Charles Condomine in *Blithe Spirit*, and as Will Masters in *Bus Stop*. Rep

audiences will also remember Michael for his roles in *A Moon for the Misbegotten, Home, Artichoke, The Foreigner* and *Gossip*. He plays Lawrence Garfinkle in *Other's People's Money* and most recently appeared as Del in the Salt Lake Acting Company's production of Stephen Metcalf's *White Man Dancing*. His extensive regional credits include work with the Virginia Stage Company, Empty Space Theater, Intiman Theater and Tacoma Actor's Guild. Some of Michael's favorite roles have been as Brick in *Cat on a Hot Tin Roof*, Tom in *Creeps*, Konstantin in *The Seagull*, Jerry in *Betrayal* and Bohan in *You Never Can Tell.*

Her green eyes blurred. She wouldn't question him. He could just keep his secrets. She had her own. She would not get in the middle of it, she vowed and slammed down her brush.

Darrin Lucas paced his office. The wrinkle in his day started the night before when he listened to Sam Berg, the one-man vigilante, on the news. He grumbled, "All the newsman needs is a cowboy hat, pointed boots and a six shooter on his hip. Why don't the cops stop him from the foolery he was stirring up, standing in front of that camera like a private eye? Darrin slammed his hand on the desk. He must find a chink in his armor. Sam Berg, you will be out of a job when I get through with you."

His mind ticked through names at the Lark Point Police Department, trying to pinpoint the best one to call. Somebody must muzzle him. He wondered, loftily, how the police could run an investigation with the media spilling their beans. He'd stop Sam Berg from screwing with him. He snatched up his brief case. Heading toward the elevator, he stopped at Cole's office.

"Cole," Darrin looked into his partner's office. "I didn't like what I saw on Channel 14 last night. That Sam Berg has to be stopped from interfering with a police investigation. Those burglaries can't be solved with the media putting in their noses. Help me find something on the guy." He gave a nasty grin and rushed down the hallway to the elevator to meet a client, leaving Cole staring after him.

SEVEN

The Lark Point Democrat newspaper featured the burglaries in a breaking news headline and Sam Berg read the article with growing frustration.

Homes in the northeast Lark Point and Irvington neighborhoods were hit by eight similar burglaries within a four-week period. Police warned residents to lock their doors and windows at night. The burglar or burglars hadn't confronted the residents of the homes during the string of early evening break-ins. Every robbery has occurred between 8:30 and 10:30 p.m. It can be assumed this is an organized burglary ring preying on the rich based on the type of artwork, jewels and family heirlooms taken.

The Police Chief, Sebastian Grant, thought he should cooperate with the television station to use any means possible to curb the crimes, but it was against his better judgment. As the gangs became a major factor in Sam's insatiable quest to break the-news first, the crimes continued to grow in magnitude. The police were stumped while fear spread throughout the neighborhoods.

Sam had an inside source at the police station who trickled information; just enough to keep his show the most-watched program. Elliott loved it. Sam loved it. He saw his dream expand beyond his wildest expectations. Elated, feeling his much-sought-after career on the horizon, he earnestly fought to keep his town clean. He hated injustice. He was real. He observed oddities in the thefts as things turned outrageously from bad to worse. The LPPD conducted a sweep through "old town" and ran a number of boys into jail to no avail. The thieves became more brazen and still ran free.

As the days turned into weeks, Sam's popularity grew. The thefts continued. The citizens of Lark Point started thinking that Sam was the only person trying to fix the problem. The police kept a wary eye on him, as they followed every lead to piece together clues to the thefts that wouldn't stop.

As more thefts occurred in the city and investigations doubled at the station; Sam worked longer hours; his already-meager social hours dwindled. The steam generated by the constant maze of the investigation balanced between writing the news and interviewing witnesses. He was stunned over the number of phone calls he received.

The stress fed his creativity. He knew a large segment of society was attracted to strife, anxiety and anger. He also knew they looked to the media for answers and he ached to give it to them. He'd seen hard living, endless streets and bitter disappointments and he knew his new position would give him what he needed. He wanted to win.

Thriving on the intensity of his job, he lost track of his personal life. Typically, Sam's love for journalism was paralleled only by his love for his family but he continued writing, mouthing words silently, editing and moving to the end of each story. Normally the producer and editor worked together, selecting portions of video and then the voiceover with Sam's comments completing the fully edited piece. It usually took over an hour for a ten minute segment to be finalized on a good day, sometimes longer.

Bigger and better stories chugged around in his head, leading him deeper and deeper into the television abyss. His few indulgences were cigarettes, which he puffed madly and Tess, whom he doted on as often as possible. Anna was still an unanswered question while loving her beyond reason. Driving himself insatiably from one story to the next seemed to keep his doubts about their marriage corralled. In fact, at times, he felt Anna was lost in the crowd but avoided mental examination.

He loved his job. He had to get the news first hand. And he had less time to dwell on his marital relationship; instead, he concentrated on himself and the station around him. That denial warped his sense of time and place. It wasn't long after his night of glory and his societal entrance at the University Club that work began to dominate his life. Despite his addiction to news and the station, Sam tried to fit in Tess between the cracks but during a particularly hectic schedule, he was harried and depressed when a messenger popped his head in the door. "Phone call, Mr. B."

"Take a message," he yelled.

Everyone in the station paused. Several eyes met, some shoulders shrugged, unasked questions vibrated through the offices.

A moment later, the messenger returned timidly. "It was your daughter, Tess, Mr. B.......said she'll call back about 11:00."

Sam slowly stood and closed the door to his office. He wondered what in the hell was wrong with him? He sat down at his desk and spread his hands on his desktop watching the clock. Shuffling papers beneath the green desk lamp, he pretended he wasn't counting the slow minutes to his daughter's promised call.

When the phone rang, he lunged for it but it wasn't Tess and he quickly ended the call. His forehead creased. Anna rarely called and Tess's calls were becoming less frequent. Sam lifted the receiver, dangled it in his left hand and rested his forehead on it a moment before hanging it up again.

A light tap on his closed door snapped Sam out of his melancholy mind games.

"It's your daughter, Sam, line one."

"Hey, dad, can you have lunch? I texted you earlier but you must have been busy. I'm between classes and have three hours to kill. You were first on my list," she teased over the telephone that Sam had perched between his shoulder and chin.

"Great timing, sweetie...meet me at the Red Peacock in half an hour?" Sam's grin split his face and his eyes blurred when he hung up. His leather chair squeaked when he leaned his elbows on his desk and smoothed his graying hair back from his face with each hand.

He called Anna. No answer. "Dammit." He'd forgotten she went to the beach. Again. She'd been there off and on for weeks. He hung up. His eyes were thoughtful and his mind was awash with frustration. When he checked his phone, there were no messages from her.

Loosening his knuckles still tightly wound around the receiver, he stood up, pushed his hand into his rear pocket and removed his wallet. Flipping to the plastic pages, he stared at Anna, seeing the laughing brown eyes looking back at him innocently, loving him. She'd been a twenty-three year old college senior and he'd adored her. Years had changed them both. He admitted she hadn't looked at him like that for longer than he could remember. A bleak sadness overwhelmed him as he grabbed his well-worn jacket and headed out to meet Tess. He pushed the theft investigation to the back of his mind. This afternoon, Tess was more important and he'd be damned if he'd let thieves take time from her.

He stormed out of the newsroom as he pulled on his dark jacket. "I'm going out."

"Out!? The script isn't finished yet."

"If anybody calls or comes looking for me, tell them to stay put or leave a message. I'll be back when I can."

"Where can I tell Elliott you're.........?" The young woman was talking to air and wisps of dust.

That afternoon, his office door burst open, revealing Elliott's smiling face.

"Sam, get your notebook. We're meeting the sheriff in half an hour. Elliott jangled his keys inside his pocket and nodded his head toward the door. "I'll drive."

"What's up, El?"

"Those damned burglaries have multiplied and seem to be zoned in the middle-class area of Woodland Peaks and Forest Hills. There have been twelve in the last two months. The sheriff and Metro Assurance asked me if your show could be their soapbox." Elliott smiled at Sam's stunned face.

"Hell, yes!"

Elliott was glad to see a glimpse of the old Sam. Smiling with his notebook pumping the air, the men walked down the corridor toward the bank of elevators, words tumbling over one another.

"Tell me....." Sam started.

".......The thefts are always at night after 8:30 and before 11:00. No one is ever at home....we don't know how they know the homes are empty. Nobody's been robbed in the daytime or when anyone's home.

"Any leads?"

"The sheriff is embarrassed. The mayor is pissed. The insurance carrier is losing tons of money and they want you!"

Sam's excitement mounted. It reminded him when he and Anna both wrote for the Tribune years ago. His steps flagged momentarily thinking about the thrill of the job and working it with Anna.

Fifteen minutes later, they were ushered to a hearing room at police headquarters. They grinned at each other.

"You go on in, Sam. I'll find us coffee." He left Sam at the door to the hearing room and rushed down the hallway. He'd get it himself instead of asking the sheriff's staff. He wasn't helpless and knew Sam needed to make a solo entrance.

The hearing room wasn't large; an oblong table filled it nicely, long windows boasted a view of tall trees, their leaves beginning to turn orange, many on the ground below.

The men waiting for Sam didn't notice the view and probably didn't care. They circled around one another the first moments after Sam entered the room like a wolf with their prey. The men felt grumpy, having to depend on a television investigator, but they focused on their mission. Hope stared them in the face and they stood in unison to shake Sam's outstretched hand, offered names and sat. Expectancy filled the room as each waited for the other to begin and then they all started at once.

"Sam, I......."

"We want......"

"What can I.......?"

All the men laughed and tension lessened. Elliott caught the lingering smiles and pushed the door closed with a foot before unloading the tray with five cups of steaming, fresh coffee. Everyone's brows shot up; fresh coffee was a rare find in their business. They sipped as conversations began in earnest while Sam and Elliott wrote furiously.

"They're fast, clean and gone before the homeowners return home. Thieves are selective, good stuff.....oil paintings, engravings, sculptured statues, jewelry. They rarely steal anything breakable....makes me wonder where they unload it. Maybe it's important, maybe not. These guys can't fence the stuff without some of our people hearing about it. I also do not think they are just your garden-variety thug. They seem organized; they're so smart...they bypass the security alarms, for Christ's sake!" The sheriff took another gulp of coffee and pursed his lips.

Sam looked at his iPad and held his stylus ready to continue making notes. "How long ago did you figure there might be a connection between these burglaries?"

"Three weeks," the sheriff mumbled, "and it pisses me off they're still making a haul without a stinking lead!" he finished out of breath. Reaching for his coffee, he slurped and turned to the man beside him.

The mayor made a steeple with his fingers, elbows on the table; his coffee forgotten. "When they robbed me, I figured it was an isolated incident and nothing has been found at pawn shops or on Craigslist over the internet. We've checked eBay, watched the papers. Nothing has surfaced. My wife is on me every day for answers. I've been pestering the sheriff here and now we are all kicking the cat to find where, how, who?" The mayor's face was red, his fingers splayed before pulling the coffee to his lips again. He turned toward the insurance man to see if he had anything to add.

"So far," Ben Russell said, "insurance claims have topped over six hundred thousand dollars. My people are yelling bloody murder and I don't have any answers," he blustered, eyeing the sheriff.

"That's not fair, Ben," we're joining forces, aren't we?"

"Well, I have both my insurance investigators on the case waiting for a break. We need one before these idiots bankrupt us." Every time there's a new claim, they study everything about the event, make their list of missing items, speak with the victims and the paper trail is longer than a puppy playing with a roll of toilet paper. I need answers. They are getting frustrated and everyone in this town is getting tired of our claims department putting them off. They don't give a damn how busy we are or why we are having problems taking care of anyone else's claims. They want us to help them and that's the bottom line. That's why I agreed to sit in on this and by the way, thanks for finally realizing we needed help.

"And that's why we are here, Ben."

"What's on your mind where Sam Berg's concerned, then?" Ben continued his rant.

Sam cleared his throat.

Ben gulped his nearly-cold coffee.

Sam's eyes met Elliott's with raised eyebrows as the men listened to the others argue. They quietly waited for the sheriff and mayor to outline their thoughts about how the station could help their investigation.

"You're vocal, Sam. You have a visual place in the community's homes…Every night at six o'clock you visit most of the living rooms in our town. Your face has become their trusted friend. The way we figure, if the thieves know the police, insurance company and the media---namely you--- have decided to run them down in a collaborative effort, maybe they'd make a mistake…give us some clues. Maybe we could scare the hell out of them or what would be even better, when they made a mistake, it might lead us to them." The sheriff finished and shook his head.

Five sets of eyes studied the table.

Then all the men smiled.

"It's a go, then." Elliott said and shook his head.

"Let the games begin," Sam responded strongly. Instead of offering his listeners bits and pieces, he'd be at the core of the investigation and my god, wouldn't the Lark Point Democrat have its nose out of joint, he thought. Good, he liked that.

Elliott read the excitement on Sam's face and though distressed over the burglaries, he was delighted with the opportunity to help the city and also the man who'd become a good friend by giving him something to chew on. They got down to business, each commenting, writing, sometimes agreeing on the best route to take. How much information to release, how much to hold as classified. More arguments, more agreements. More coffee.

The men brainstormed well past ten o'clock. The windows were dark, empty cups strewn amid Chinese food containers that had been pushed to the end of the table. Chairs scraped across the floor. Standing, the men stretched and shook hands. Their thoughts straddled one another as they left with promises of something in the air versus the frustrating problems that entered the room several hours earlier.

Sam already had the beginning of his next script in his head, "In a move to protect consumers and reduce confusion among Lark Point residents, the city fathers have chosen to supplement our police force's need for volunteers. A study made by the sheriff's office has concluded…….."

Anna drew a resigned breath as she left the cottage and the raging ocean behind; thunder clapped above. Raindrops threatened. It was time to leave her haven, *Mirafleures*, and return to Lark Point. She'd been gone two weeks this time. Her manuscript was near completion but every time she pulled it up on her computer, she spent hours editing it all over again. *Will I ever finish?* She stashed a bag of dirty laundry into her Audi with her extra pair of shoes, her book draft in a box and seashells she'd collected along the beach. Her beach.

She'd lived at the little cottage off and on for years with her Grandmére. Anna could still hear her grandmother's cane tapping across the floor if she listened hard enough. She did that sometimes, just for the memories because she missed her so much. Between the cottage and La Verdiere in the south of France, she could feel her presence, feel the old woman's embrace and that was probably why she found both places her refuge

Ashby was a small town on the ocean not far from Lark Point. A tight little community with a few artsy shops, a little bookstore, a coffee shop that promised fresh, spud donuts. It didn't offer specialty coffees like Starbucks; just fresh, black and an abundance of cream. There was another, larger cottage next door to Anna's that was owned by a non-profit writer's colony. She'd been asked to speak on several occasions and had become good friends with the mentors of the group. She loved the little town and most of the inhabitants knew each other by their first names. It was far enough away from Lark Point to be too long for a day trip but close enough for a life in both places.

Anna didn't want to leave *Mirafleures* yet. Lately, she never seemed ready. Torn with indecision and restlessness, she knew it was time to leave her haven; Sam's earlier phone message was pissy.

Autumn leaves blew erratically, spurning the metal grey clouds hovering above trees littering surrounding yards. She had a blurry view of the street; the pavement was wet, covered with gold and reddish leaves that devoured the road in thick clusters. Rain spattered the glass, drizzling in rivulets that inched down the pane and smeared the view. Her thoughts were in accord with the fall scene as they swished above her, blowing in every direction. But it was time to go home. She tested the word as she pulled onto Highway 1 because she really didn't know where home was anymore.

EIGHT

Tess threw her arms around Nicholas when he walked in the door. She'd stubbed out her cigarette the moment she saw his lights turn into the driveway.

"Hey! What a welcome," he said as he kissed her deeply on the lips and pulled her close against him. "I love it," he whispered as he fit her body into his.

"So do I, Nicholas." She hugged him quickly and drew him into the living room. She pointed to the chair and he promptly sat.

"Okay, Tess, I'm ready."

Tess grinned, stood up in front of the fireplace and began reciting her speech for Speech Class. "......and the reasoning behind my theory is that regulated drug therapy within the confines of a mental health facility would mean......" she continued for ten minutes.

When she finished, Nicholas burst into applause. "You are great, Tess. You should get an A, nothing less." He jumped up and swung her in circles.

Her laughter dissolved in kisses as they ended up curled together on the creamy leather couch. Moonshine slipping through the windows added more than a little romance to the interlude. Tess reached up to pull Nicholas close, savoring the thrill of his hands on her ribcage as they moved slowly upward.

Nicholas loved her but he was afraid; his life was a mess and he pulled away.

Hurt, Tess looked into his face. "Nicholas?"

"Honey, I think I love you," he whispered as he touched the edge of her mouth with a tanned finger making small swirls near her lips.

"That's bad?" she asked in confusion.

"God, no, it isn't bad. I love how we feel. It's just that I can't make a commitment to you until we're out of college and I want to have a job that can really support us," he finished lamely.

"Nicholas, stop thinking. Just hold me close. We can worry about the future later. Tell me again about the love thing… That part, we can deal with now," Tess said with dazzling determination as she slipped her fingers beneath his sweatshirt and felt him tremble.

"I love you, Tess Berg."

"And, wonder of wonders, I love you Nicholas Alonzo. Now, we're even. Let's go find something to eat."

"Where are your parents?"

"Mom's at the beach house writing on her book and dad's at the television station. He's been given a new show and he's so excited he just wants to stay there and work on it to iron out any bumps in the agenda."

"Nice. What kind of show?"

"Mmmmmm. Well, it's called *Sam Berg, Man with a Story*. He's been doing it awhile. I mean that's how it begins and ends. But now he's working with the police and it's morphed into an investigative show, you know…trying to stop crime, getting to the core and ripping it out by letting the city know how to combat it, that sort of stuff."

"Crime? What kinds….murder and that type of thing?" He was suddenly very interested, dark eyes curiously thirsty for specifics.

"Oh, you know, anything that's driving the police bonkers. Dad will look into it, try to find the bad guys and his show will rip their lives up by….just investigations. Boy, you seem interested all of a sudden. Are you going to apply for a job at the station?" She teased as she applied a mock fist at his clean-shaven jaw.

Nicholas smiled. His eyes twinkled while she made them sandwiches; they ate and shared a bottle of beer. Then, she lit a cigarette and blew the smoke upward.

"Do you count how many of those stink sticks you smoke a day?"

"No," she answered simply and stared at him.

"Okay," he responded, knowing when to shut up.

After another moment, she stamped out the cigarette in the glass ashtray beside her plate. Her eyes grew large and liquid as she gave Nicholas a steady, unwavering look.

He smiled; he wanted to hold her close and never let her go.

The next night, Nico and Michael met at Rave's just in time for the six o'clock news. The men turned to the television. The rumor had it that the television station was now working with the police. Nico's insides were sick, knowing it was Tess's father who might lead them to jail time. The irony was not lost on him.

"The city of Lark Point has been invaded steadily by a gang of thieves who strike under the darkness of night and always when the homeowners have left for the evening. It seems they have a sixth sense when to hit, who to hit, what to steal…and they have to this point always slid away unscathed. Until now….."

Sam stared into the camera.

"Now, we are watching you. There are people around the city waiting for you to make a mistake. You will be under surveillance, so remember the next time you go out to slither into someone's home; we will be close behind you, like the neighborhood watch groups, only stronger. Your false illusions of grandeur will no longer hide you. They will not keep you safe. They will not allow you to steal much longer. There are now protectors around Lark Point where you least expect them."

Abruptly, Sam turned from the camera and approached a bespeckled man coming out of the doorway on the corner of First Street and Alder. He wore a plaid jacket with a turtle neck to hold his body heat in and the windy coolness of the evening out.

"What do you think should be done to the thieves who are demoralizing our neighborhoods, sir?"

The man squinted into the camera as if it was a fly under a microscope. He was thoughtful a moment before answering harshly, staring a Sam and his microphone.

"Hang 'em. They invade our privacy, steal our things and so far they're getting away with it. They should be stopped, so I say hang 'em. You say you are working with the police. I say it's about time we see where our taxes are going instead of nowhere."

Sam raised his eyebrows slightly, thanked the man and stood in front of the camera while the autumn breeze tossed his dark hair around his face, showing crow's feet around his eyes, fervor in his stance.

"This is the overall consensus among the people of Lark Point tonight. There are angry rumblings and many have voiced this man's thoughts because we haven't found these perpetrators yet. Everyone wants them caught. Everyone wants them to pay for their crimes. But we must find them first and we are going to do it. This must be stopped and it will be stopped. We are rattling a few cages and will bring an end to this madness as we work alongside your police department, the mayor's office and Metro Assurance Company. Sam Berg, Man with a Story. Good night"

Nico and Michael sat like stones.

Across town, Anna and Tess applauded, their hands tingling and burning. They looked at each other and laughed outright, "Boy. He's made it big time, huh, Mom?"

Anna nodded. *Yes, big time*, she thought uneasily. "He talks as if he's speaking directly to these thugs. They should be wary, right? I guess he is but it's a little frightening actually. They know dad is after them. It's not just the police but a specific man with a name and a face in front of them every night." Anna was unable to erase her uneasy feelings.

"I know, Mom, but it's wonderful. I'm so proud of dad. He will get to the bottom of this, just watch. It'll be great," Tess said with sparkling eyes.

Anna glanced at her watch. "Honey, isn't Nicholas coming soon to take you out to a movie?"

"Oh, right. I better get changed. I feel sweaty and dirty from my Taekwon-Do class. Cris is so good and I can't believe she finds time to teach when she also acts at the Repertory Theater. Maybe we can go see her in a play sometime? Tonight, I need to shower and want to wear something special. I must look my gorgeous self for him. Isn't he great, Mom? I'm crazy about him. He's the finest man I've ever been with and he makes me feel wonderful all over...." Tess finished as a look of wonder spread across her features.

Anna's eyebrows raised a notch. "All over?"

Tess laughed and jumped up from the loveseat they shared. "Yes, Mom, all over," she said as she leered toward her mother and sped out of the room and up the stairs to her bedroom leaving a trail of delicious laughter behind her.

Anna sighed loudly and stared at her rose-colored fingernails, scrutinizing them. Life could be so strange. Her beautiful daughter was in love, sharing herself intimately already.....she knew it...and Tess was thrilled with it all. Sam had his own television program, feeling contented after working so hard for it, thriving amid the chaos. She knew the thrill was consuming him. *And Anna. Where was Anna?* She sighed again. Holy Christmas, she was getting dramatic. *It's either PMS or I'm getting old.* She switched on a lamp, got up and punched off the television.

It was dark and quiet. The men waited in the shadows until the tired maid left the kitchen, stepped into her car and drove away.

Nico and Andreas glanced about, nodded to each other and began their night's work after disarming the alarm with the cutters Darrin had supplied. Michael had never given them false information yet and as promised, the owners were out, no doubt applauding Michael's acting at the very moment their assets were being lifted from inside their home.

They had paintings, jewelry and a little bronze statue bagged within ten minutes, timing was down to a thumbnail of perfection. Nico yanked the last piece off the table, stuffed it into the bag and pushed Andreas toward the doorway. "God, I hate doing this."

Andreas studied Nico's face in the moonlight from the open French doors. "Really? I love it. It makes my blood spin. This job was made for me," he said with a laugh as he reached back to latch the door.

Nico looked at Andreas while his heart slammed in his chest. He would never get used to it. Never. And he couldn't understand how this kid from the streets could think it was an adventure. He'd obviously never spent time in prison. Nor had Nico for that matter and he wanted to keep it that way.

Tossing the large bags into the truck, they slid down the driveway without lights and slowly inched their way up the street. After two blocks, Nico switched the lights on and turned toward the Amtrak station. If there were large pieces of artwork or paintings, they were instructed to place them inside a steel door near the drop site. He had a key to the building as well as the building where they met DAL on Saturdays near the theater.

Darrin Lucas liked the train station because the neighborhood was half industrial, half slum amid truck yards, machine shops and warehouses. Derelict cars and weeds sat in dusty stretches of vacant lots and unused oil drums were hidden from the street beneath an old overpass. It was perfect, a veritable junk yard and cemetery for old boxcars. And it was right next door to a building he owned under an assumed name. He didn't leave anything to chance.

Hidden behind the farthest train tracks were custom-made, yellow oil drums that were not oil drums at all. As always, the young men gently placed the bags inside the barrels with false lids. They hid the larger items inside the brick building and then they were swiftly on their way. Now they'd wait until Saturday morning to get their cash from at the old brick building in town.

Nico dropped a swaggering Andreas off outside the Dragon's Nest. As he swung into traffic again, he sighed. How he detested Andreas. Nico thought of his college tuition and knew regardless of the shit he had to go through, he couldn't quit yet. Half a scholarship had been great until his dad died. He couldn't take money from his mom. He'd finish college and then walk. DAL couldn't make him stay, he knew too much about the man.

Anna thought Tess had the clear, translucent skin of a child. Before the sun went down, the last rays picked out the flecks of silver in her blue eyes, set deep in a delicate heart-shaped face. Her slightly parted lips had given her the look of expectancy and it seemed to anticipate the smile she was saving for Nicholas Alonzo.

After the old Chevy drove away taking her daughter with it, the silent room made Anna sag. With a tightness in her throat, she moved to the window. Incredibly weary, she traced a raindrop with her finger as it slid down the pane. And then she smiled when she heard the old song, *From a Distance,* filter into the room. Anna hummed along with Bette Midler while she banked her papers together, pleased with what she'd accomplished at the beach. She stood up straight, bowed toward her desk and danced around her chair. "Yes!" she said aloud, and then sat down to her computer once again.

Chuck Champion, the owner of the Repertory Theater welcomed Cole Nites into his office and they clasped hands warmly. They'd been friends a long time. Cole's law firm and especially Darrin Lucas was their largest benefactor. Chuck always made time for his friend and they hadn't seen one another for awhile. He was pleased knowing Cole and Rainy were season ticket-holders who attended most of the plays the theater offered. Tonight was opening night for a new play and he was glad Cole could attend.

"Rainy has the Rep's end-of-season party planned and wants me to confirm that it's a go. Her calendar is good for September 13th or 20th. Our house. The law firm is covering it."

Chuck's finger ran down the calendar and the 13th was good. Smiling over at Cole, he said, "That is so generous of you, Cole. We all enjoy the celebration at the end of a good run of plays. Thanks so much. Where's Rainy?" he asked, interested.

"She's out schmoozing with a glass of your wine. I'll find her when the curtain goes up. She may even be backstage visiting Cris. You know they're very good friends.

Chuck laughed. When I found her in Tacoma playing the lead in *Other People's Money*, I knew she'd be perfect for our theater. When I offered her the lead here in *Gossip* four years ago, I was thrilled when she agreed. Cris is definitely a good friend to have. I tell her she's my protector. She's a Black Belt in Taekwon-Do, you know."

"Oh yes. I knew that. Rainy became friends with her just after that first play and they've been buddies ever since. She's definitely a good choice to have one's back." He looked at his watch. "Well, almost show time. I can see you are getting antsy. Let's have lunch one of these days. Just call me, huh?" He got up and they walked out into the lobby together."

It was after eight when Sam drove his Jeep out of the underground garage at Channel 14 headquarters. As usual, he drove his own vehicle even though the station offered him the use of a station car; one was always available as part of the job but he'd traded his truck in for a Jeep as quickly as his old tweeds were exchanged for Dockers and golf shirts. A few minutes later as he turned onto Fowler Street from Smithson heading east, his mind was still on the broadcast he'd just concluded. He smiled and tapped the wheel as he headed home.

He thought of the story and then his image on the monitor, knowing the show had been hasty but his reporting good. Elliott said it was one more solid performance. Elliott always gave his ego a boost and Sam ate it up. It usually lifted his spirits but instead, thoughts of Anna turned his face somber.

With sobering honesty, Sam admitted he'd been ignoring the problems between him and Anna and caught his breath wishing it weren't so. He didn't know why, but he knew their lives were speeding in separate directions. And he didn't know how to stop it, or if he could, or if Anna wanted to. So, he was afraid to broach the subject at all. He grimly asked himself why he was so weak at home yet so strong at the station?

Although raised in a middle-class background in Oregon, he'd received his early journalism training in Ohio. He felt as if he was two men. Which one did Anna love? Which one did she miss? Did she want neither? Questions bombarded him as he wound his way homeward.

Dammit. I have to be me. He slugged the steering wheel. He'd followed the plan he'd set for himself; investigate and tell the story after gathering the facts. If he was contradicted, he'd confirm or disprove the facts. Why, then, did he feel inadequate at home but in control at the station? He pulled into the garage as if he was his own worst enemy.

Dim lights shone from the kitchen. No movement could be seen elsewhere. He knew Anna was undoubtedly at the computer. She and that damned computer seemed attached at the hip. Sam turned off the ignition and sat in the car, closed his eyes and leaned his head back on the seat.

Anna now. Anna then. He'd wanted her since he'd met her in college. He'd stared at the photo in his wallet, gone over the old memories often. She had a lively mind and on occasion, a sharp tongue. She didn't accept nonsense from anyone. It had always endeared her to him. Now, it was a deterrent. Who had changed the most? Her? Him? Sam heaved a sigh, grabbed his keys and opened the door. They had to talk. He stepped into his home with quiet determination and headed toward the kitchen in desperate need of a scotch. Yes, he'd have a drink first, hoping for a warm welcome, but expecting none.

The sound of ice brought Anna's attention away from her writing with a mild prick of frustration at the interruption. Sam was home. She tapped save on her screen, switched off the lamp and walked to meet him with a forced smile.

"How's everything in the writing world?" He was pleasantly surprised to see her smiling face.

"Good, I finished three chapters today. It's running smoothly and I feel good about it." Her voice held warmth he hadn't heard in awhile.

She watched the contours of Sam's face as he lifted his glass to his lips. "Rough day?" she asked quietly.

"Yes. You watched the news?"

"Yes, Tess and I watched it together. It was good, Sam. But then, you know that. It was a little unsettling though, the way you seemed to be talking to those hoodlums. They know your name, your face...and everything. Nobody's been hurt yet but...well, they can hide. You can't."

His face showed surprise at her analysis and tried to think of an intelligent comeback. He couldn't.

"Well, don't you think it's a bit unnerving, Sam?"

"No. I don't."

"Come on, Sam! You are so busy gathering the news you forget the human beings who make it. THEY ARE REAL."

"I know that, Anna. Christ, you act like I'm playing make believe. It is serious and I'll get to the bottom of it."

"But you aren't doing it ALONE and you make the listeners think that you are. You are not Superman, my dear husband. You are a newscaster." Anna was sorry the minute the words came out of her mouth but could not retrieve them.

"No, I'm not Superman," Sam whispered. He lifted his glass in a silent toast, gulped his scotch and poured another. Then he left her and proceeded into the living room.

Anna caught her breath, unsure what Sam really needed from her.

That night, still troubled by what had passed between them, Anna lay awake and realized Sam's breathing was uneven, knowing he also couldn't sleep. Both restless, both with minds alive with frustration, neither attempted to discuss the problem but they each knew the day would come.

~

"He must be stopped!" Darrin's voice thundered ruthlessly.

"What do you suggest, DAL, unplugging his TV?"

Darrin scowled at Michael, his fingers itching to knock him down but instead, stared at him until Michael dropped his eyes.

"Oh, okay, shit. What are we supposed to do? Should we just stop hitting places for awhile?" Michael looked at the old man hopefully.

"We stop when I say we stop. And I'm not ready to stop. I want to hit places under that idiot's nose before we put the skids to our project. In the meantime, here's your next job." Darrin pulled a piece of yellow paper out of his pocket and held it out toward Michael.

Michael held his temper and took the paper between his fingers.

Darrin waited for his reaction and wasn't disappointed, gauging it perfectly.

"What the hell?! Hit the god-damned guy's house? You really want to make fireworks jump, don't you?" Michael's voice shook.

Darrin smiled. "Hmmm....Yes, fireworks will do nicely. Order some. As soon as the boys rob the place, send some up. It will be my little message to him personally. It will give him some crunch for his evening news.

"DAL, we can't. My God, it could be a real trap for Nico and Andreas." Michael was shaking with fury and his eyes flashed.

Darrin's steely glare stopped further conversation as Michael's boldness peaked with adversity. He chose his words carefully. "Tomorrow night. I want the house hit at 6:15 whether anybody's home or not. I want it during his program. At the precise hour of 6:15 when he's ready to go off the air, but not quite..., I want a note delivered ON THE AIR. I don't care how you do it but make it happen while he's still on the air. 6:15. No later. Call Nico."

Michael's insides were drugged with frustration. "Dammit! What should the note say?" Already dreading the rest of his day and sick about hurting his friend, Tess, he knew he had no choice but to follow instructions. Was his job at the theater worth it? Was Cris? His mind was rattled.

It should read, "I'm one step ahead of you. Your home this time, smart ass. Now! Come find me." He watched Michael's face and knew the young man wanted to slug him.

"Ok, 6:15 tomorrow. Anything else?" Michael's eyes snapped.

"Yes, I want a timing device to go off at 7:00. That should just about be perfect for his arrival home.

"My God, not a bomb?!" Michael shouted.

"Keep your stupid voice down. Of course, not a bomb. A burst of firecrackers, that's all. You think I'm a killer? I just want the man to leave me and you boys the hell alone!"

Darrin strode for the door. "Don't screw this up, Michael!"

Michael watched the older man leave. When he slammed the door, the apartment shook behind him. The man had never come to his place before and Michael didn't like it one bit. His body felt heavy, his brain sodden. He dreaded calling Nico without having a drink first.

Cris ran for the stairwell when she heard a growling voice from inside her apartment. She'd just struggled out of the elevator with a bag of groceries in one arm and her sports bag twisting across her thigh, lifted her key toward the door and heard the man yell, "Don't screw this up, Michael."

Now, peeking through the stairwell door, she tracked the man with her eyes. He looked about five ten or taller, about two hundred pounds and wore a long, dark overcoat. As he stomped away from her apartment door to slap the elevator button with the palm of his hand, the hall lights glinted off the large ring on his finger and blazed in Cris's head.

She waited about two minutes before letting herself into the apartment. Michael stood at the window, staring down at the street with a glass of wine in his hand. He turned quickly when Cris entered, spilling the red wine across his sweater and the creamy carpet. He stared at the stain.

"Who was he?" she asked urgently as she dropped her bag, ripped off her coat and sat the grocery bag on the kitchen table.

Michael lifted his eyes from the carpet stain and into Cris's frightened face. "Who?" Michael looked at her blankly.

"Who? Dammit, you know who I'm talking about. The man nearly ran me down and his voice alone scared me into the stairwell. Who is he? Tell me!"

"No. We agreed to keep our business private. Anyway, the less you know about that creep the better. Don't bother about him. He's nobody." Michael gulped the remainder of his wine, set the glass down carefully and touched Cris's cheek.

She stared up at him, a little afraid.

"I have to make a phone call while you start dinner, ok?   It's private. Please understand, Cris."

She huffily headed for the fridge while Michael slipped into the bedroom and picked up the phone at the exact moment Cris cradled the phone to her ear.

The next morning, Darrin punched his office building's elevator button and waited impatiently to be whisked upward. His fingers twitched around the handle of his briefcase and his eyes moved rapidly to encompass the people near him. Peasants, he thought. Then, casually dismissing them, his mind rehashed his discussion with Michael. He liked the boy and he didn't want to like anybody. Michael had asked Darrin a barrage of questions.   Did he have enough? No, not yet.

Michael had responded instantly, "You know, Sam Berg's going to be right on our asses pretty damned quick. Did you think about that?"

Darrin had refused to answer except to say the race was on and he wasn't stopping for anyone. It's the principle of the thing.

Michael asked, "The principle?" with a bemused expression.

Darrin said, "When someone has the upper hand like I do and a guy who makes his living off of other people's lives tries to stop me... well, I won't allow it."

He hadn't liked Michael's response to that statement either.

"Great thinking, DAL. He just happens to be working with the police and one of these days he's going to find the right clue that will lead him back to me. My God, the last ten weeks, we've hit twenty two homes and the victims have all been at the theater watching me. I can't believe the police haven't figured it out yet. What are they doing, playing tiddlywinks?"

"Or playing with themselves....who the hell knows, I just know I'm not done yet," he'd shot back.

"Will you ever have enough, Darrin?" Michael asked him tiredly.

"I told you not to use my name."

Darrin could barely wait for the firecrackers. He smiled maliciously before stepping out of the elevator, scowling at the fog outside the windows. That's what he got for having an office in the sky and it seemed to creep toward him as he walked down the hallway to his office.

"Good morning, Mr. Lucas," the receptionist said eagerly.

He continued on, nodding.

"Good morning, Mr. Lucas, your messages are on your desk," a tall blond remarked in passing, hurrying to get out of his way.

Darrin glanced at her in annoyance. Weren't they always on his desk? He watched her sit down at her desk outside his doorway; saw her dress slide up her thigh. When she yanked it back down to her knees, he smiled. She was nervous but tried to appear busy.

He chuckled and raised an eyebrow. "Ask Cole to come in to see me when he has a moment, will you, Allison?"

Dark eyes turned to him. "Yes, Mr. Lucas."

He smiled stonily before lifting his briefcase and hung his heavy coat behind the door.

Cole thumped lightly on Darrin's office door a few moments later with a question on his face. "Morning, Darrin," he said crisply.

Darrin looked up as Cole strolled in his door looking fresh and in control. "Order us some coffee, will you, Cole? I have something I want to go over with you," Darrin asked, spacing the words evenly.

Without hesitation, Cole asked Allison to bring two black coffees with a friendly smile.

"Sit, Cole."

Cole raised his brows and sat in one of the easy chairs before Darrin's desk, crossed a leg across his knee and looked at his partner expectantly. "What's on your mind, Darrin?"

Allison quietly entered, bringing coffee in a chrome pot, two cups and napkins. Darrin noted her nervousness with pleasure.

Cole waited.

"Cole, remember a few months ago when we tried to get that kid off for robbing three jewelry stores in a row and found out later that he actually did it with the help of four accomplices?

Cole remembered vividly which case Darrin mentioned. The frustration of that day never quite left his head. Uneasiness filled him, remembering how Darrin seemed to use his own witness as a patsy and enjoyed watching the man squirm. It was the day he listened to Rainy talking on the phone with her lover. "Yes, I remember, Darrin, why?" He watched Darrin with half-closed eyes.

"Yes, I was sure you would. I know how angry you were with me and I also know you kept it bottled up inside. You made the remark that I was hiding something. Well, Cole, I was. That kid was my nephew."

"What?!" Cole sputtered.

"Yes, my nephew. We got him off by sending his friends to prison. He's been arrested again....only this time, he's innocent. Completely innocent. Sam Berg's trying to railroad him into jail. He's trying to prove he's somehow mixed up in that gang of thieves he's trying to yank out of our city for the good of Lark Point," he said with a sneer.

Cold stared at Darrin.

"How do you know he's innocent? Maybe he is one of them."

"No. He. Is. Not!" Darrin said vehemently.

"Seriously? Okay, what do you want from me?" Cole countered.

"Get him off."

"What? Why me, Darrin?"

"Because you can do it. You're good and you know it. I can't take the case because I'm his uncle, you know that."

"Ask Terry."

"I am asking you, Cole. Only you. I don't want my name mixed up in it at all and Terry is still wet behind the ears." Darrin handed Cole a manila folder.

Cole stared at the folder and then at Darrin.

Darrin placed it carefully on the table beside their coffee cups and sipped his coffee, staring at Cole across the rim.

"This means a lot to you, doesn't it Darrin?"

"Certainly, he's my nephew."

"There's more to it. What is it?"

Darrin's look sharpened. He never liked it when people questioned his motives. He finished his coffee and got up to look out his office window. "That's it. He's expecting you within the hour. His case will be heard this afternoon at two."

Cole's eyes sparked. He grabbed the folder, drank the last of his coffee and stood up to leave.

"Oh, Cole, one more thing…. I'm having a little get together tonight at six o'clock sharp. Bring that lovely wife of yours. I have a wonderful new work of art that I want to show off."

At Cole's surprise, Darrin chuckled, enjoying the expressions racing across Cole's face. "Well, I can't be standoffish forever, can I?"

"I'll call Rainy to see if she has other plans and let you know."

"Oh, I've also asked Steven and Moira and a few other friends. Just a small dinner party….try to make it, won't you?" Darrin made it sound more like an order rather than an invitation.

Cole repeated, "I'll see, thanks for the invite." He left the room suspicious but curious. Quickly tossing the folder on his desk, he called Rainy. Resenting the reminder of that infamous day a few months earlier, he grimaced when he heard her voice. Still disgusted, he set the time and place. Then he left to see the nephew to plan a defense.

Anna arrived home from the beach with her mind aflutter. She'd decided to go to France alone. She would pack a bag and then tell Sam he was welcome to go with her, but she knew he would not leave his precious television station for a month. All she needed was a swim suit, a week's worth of clothing and her laptop. She'd make her reservation after her commitment in San Francisco. Suddenly the thought of a few days on the Bay brightened her day. She pulled out her luggage and passport and then surprised herself by humming along with the radio. She hadn't done that for too long and it felt good.

Michael caught Nicholas as he was leaving the LSU campus. He watched him cross the grass, catch Tess in his arms, hold her face between his hands and kiss her gently. He smiled, enjoying the luxury of watching young love. His mood changed though, remembering his reason for being there and honked his horn; two short blasts, one long.

Nicholas looked up, still holding Tess. His face clouded. He said something to her and loped across to the car. Michael could read the unhappiness on Nico's face. He knew how he felt.

"What?" Nicholas asked, panting slightly."

"Get in the car a minute," Michael said seriously.

Nicholas looked back at Tess, waved and held up one finger before slipping in beside Michael. "What now?"

"You won't like this any better than I did," he began. DAL has been going ballistic ever since Sam Berg's been out for blood," Michael finished hastily.

Nicholas stiffened at the mention of Sam's name. "What?" he asked, steeling himself for something rotten. "Another hit already? It's only been two damn days and there's no play on Wednesday night. I hate it when we have to go through this damn game so often. Tess is asking questions."

Michael hung his head and exhaled deeply, hating himself for what he had to tell Nico. "Yeh, another hit, Wednesday or not. Tonight at exactly 6:15 p.m. There's more but I have that part taken care of." He looked at Nicholas, watched him wave at Tess again and saw her wave back, looking young, carefree and beautiful. "She's sure something, Nico. You really......."

".....what's the address, Michael? What's the matter with you?"

Michael wrote quickly on the back of a Burger King receipt and handed it to him. Sweat was pooling under his armpits and his blonde hair was damp. It wasn't even warm outside.

Nicholas glanced at it, squinted and looked up at Michael. "This is Tess's address, Michael." He stared. "You're kidding, right?"

Michael shook his head regretfully.

"Well, I won't do it! What the hell's the matter with the man? My God, that's my girl's house. No way, man! No flippin' way am I going to do this!" His fist crumpled the receipt and he smashed it into his thigh.

Michael reached over and grabbed Nicholas by the arm. "Look, bud. I don't make the rules and neither do you. We just follow them. Nobody will get hurt. Nobody ever does. DAL promised us, right? So, big deal, we steal a few things. They have insurance. Just make sure Tess and Anna Berg are not at home, that's all I can say."

Nicholas jerked his arm out of Michael's grasp. He saw Tess walking over toward the car. Grabbing the handle and looking at Michael once more, he said, "Christ, how the hell did I get into this mess? Huh? I'll get Andreas and we'll do it but by God, I'm going to quit this. I've had it up to here! He yelled at Michael while making a slicing motion across his throat. He jumped from the small car and walked toward Tess, forcing a smile on his face.

Tess waved to Michael and grabbed Nicholas' arm pulling at the sweatshirt, pretending to rip it off. He started chasing her across the lawn as Michael slowly drove away, his mind already on the rest of DAL's requirements. Fireworks. That man was overboard nuts.

"Hey, skinny, come back here," Nicholas yelled as Tess ran in front of him.

"Hey, mister, don't call me skinny...." She laughed up into his face, clinging to his neck. "Am I really too skinny for you? You didn't say that last night....." she said softly. "In fact, you said I was rounded nicely....now is that your idea of skinny or were you lying? You never lie to me, do you, Nicholas?" she asked innocently.

Nicholas stopped and looked at her as he tried to remove the brick that seemed lodged in his chest. "No, little girl, I do not lie to you. I love you," he said before grabbing her and pulling her into his lap. He held her so tightly she began to squirm.

"Nicholas? What's wrong? You didn't miss me that much between classes did you?" She kissed him and lurched away while grabbing her books. "I have to hit the library on the way home, do you want to drop me off?"

After brushing off his jeans, he stood and brushed his hair off his collar, shoulders straining the sweatshirt. He took a deep breath and pulled Tess along to his car and pushed her inside without saying another word. He would call DAL when he dropped off Tess; he'd refuse to do it.

"You okay? Did Michael say something to upset you?"

Nicholas jumped slightly. "No, let's go."

Tess lit a cigarette and drew on it deeply, exhaling out the window. The leaves swirled around the car as they drove. Each enjoyed the view for different reasons.

"The leaves are gorgeous, don't you think, Nick?" She snapped a photo with her iPhone.

"Free, that's what they are. Free to move as they like," he added in a lower, huskier voice.

"That's a strange thing to say, but yes, you're right. They are free, like us." She laughed, snuffed out her cigarette in the ashtray and slid close to him, placing her hand on his thigh.

Nicholas pulled her close, willing the day to be over. "Tess, what are you doing later? About 5:30 or 6 o'clock, I mean."

"Mom is picking me up at the library about five and we are going shopping. We're going to the Mid City Mall and eating out. Ever since dad got his daily show, we often eat out. He's rarely home. We should be home after seven, why....what do you have in mind?" She looked up into his well-defined face, smiled and moved her hand up and down his leg. "You feel good, you know?" she whispered.

"So do you....Are you sure you have to go to the library?"

Tess pulled away, squeezed his leg and grabbed her book bag. "Sorry, my love, but I must."

He pulled over and she jumped out. "Come by about eight?" she asked with a broad wink.

Nicholas laughed and shook his head, nodding yes.

Tess closed the door and disappeared into the large marble building. Nicholas sat still. He fought rising panic and frustration and wanted to kick DAL to hell and back again. Then, he drove to the pub to pick up Andreas. He was early, so decided to drink a beer. He thought it was exactly what he needed to calm down but he doubted it would.

Andreas saw Nico walk in and sit at the counter like he was an old man. Both elbows hit the bar and his hands brushed through his thick black hair. Andreas watched him a little longer before joining him.

"Hey, Nico. Party time, huh, man?" Andreas munched on a handful of peanuts and sat next to Nick with a plop.

Nicholas looked at the kid, trying to hide his dislike. "Yeh, Andy, we got a hit," Nicholas said quietly after looking around to make sure nobody was within earshot.

Andreas moved closer, eyes dancing, excitement bubbling inside him. The high he got from stealing and getting away with it made him jump and he was ready to roll. "Where? When?"

"Waverly Drive, tonight at 6:15 sharp."

"Huh. Sounds like the time means something, huh?"

"Yes, it does. DAL has something up his sleeve and I don't know what it is. Let's just get in and out fast," Nicholas said in a whisper as the crowd grew. He looked at his watch. "We have an hour. Let's have a beer and then leave."

Andreas pulled away quickly. "Hey, no beer for me until AFTER. I ain't dumb," he said before slinking away from Nicholas and the smell of beer. The memory of that broken arm was never far away.

Nicholas watched beer foam jump when the bartender slapped the glass down in front of him. He lifted the cold glass to his mouth and gulped it down all at once before placing it on the bar and asking for another.

Andreas itched for a beer. Why meet at a bar before a job when Nico knew he couldn't drink? It pissed him off to watch Nico enjoy one and he almost caved. When Nico swung around looking for him, Andreas heaved a sigh, following him out of the bar, relief mingling with disappointment. He shrugged it off, got into Nicholas's old Chevy and rubbed his hands across his knees, tapping to his own tune.

They crawled toward Waverly Drive.

"I don't like hitting a house in broad daylight. DAL's losing it, I think," Nicholas said under his breath, anger slicing through him like shotgun blasts.

Andreas just grinned and stared at the houses as they moved along the tree-studded neighborhood. Large houses loomed in front of them, painted siding, perfectly-manicured lawns with brightly-colored mums lining the sidewalk in all the autumn colors. The houses stared back at them. Andreas' eyes narrowed in anticipation. His fingers squeezed the brown plastic bags ready to fill with stolen items for DAL. He thought of everything they stole as DAL's things. He never thought about keeping anything, just the fun of stuffing the bags.

Suddenly, the car pulled into a long narrow driveway. Nicholas parked at the back out of sight near a small door painted bright yellow. Side windows framing the door beckoned them.

Andreas waited for Nicholas to open the door before jumping out of the car, following Nick's lead, as always. They crept along the outer wall toward the door as Nicholas pulled out the long, narrow piece of wire they used as a *key*.

Suddenly, the bushes beside them shook and the men jumped backward ready for the intruder. Nico's face paled.

"Nico, it's only a stupid rabbit. You almost knocked me down," he whispered loudly. He kicked his foot toward the bushes.

"No, leave it. Let's go," Nicholas said hurriedly. "It's 6:10, time to go in." They were groping along kitchen cabinets within seconds.

Nicholas dreaded the minutes ahead. He saw Tess's smiling face alongside Anna's on the wall beside them. The lump in his throat was surpassed only by the feeling of nausea.

"Come on, Nico!" Andreas stuffed small figurines into kitchen towels from the counter along with the jade lady from the shelf above the dining cabinet. They didn't usually steal anything breakable but DAL said all rules were off on this one. He had one sack full and was just finishing the second when Nicholas heard a noise.

Both men came to a sudden halt. Their eyes met before inching back the way they'd come in. Movement outside caught their eye as a small boy ran to pick up a white soccer ball beside the wheel of Nicholas' Chevy. The boy studied the car curiously, and then looked toward the house. When his friend called him, he shrugged before kicking his ball back down the driveway.

Nicholas thought his chest was exploding.

Andreas laughed.

At 6:16 p.m., they drove out of the driveway hunched down away from the boys in the street. They sat up a block away and looked in the rearview mirror to see the boys still playing with their ball, nothing amiss. Extracting a huge sigh of relief, Nicholas drove toward the Amtrak station.

Andreas whistled beside him, fingering the bag's contents with delight. He reached over, switched on the radio and beat his thigh in time with the music, barely aware of the fury sitting next to him.

Nicholas stared ahead.

~

Darrin Lucas's large imposing home, formerly called the Sistern House, was fronted in beige stone with a large columned portico at the entrance. Leaded glass doors were framed by burnished wood and stood below a small balcony and wrought iron railing reminiscent of New Orleans. Eight front windows in the two story house had dark gray shutters and a sculpted garden marked the edge of the columns beside the circular driveway. It sat on a crest of land in the hills above Lark Point where he'd lived more than thirty years.

Darrin hadn't been this excited in a long time. He almost wished his stupid father could share the evening with him. Almost. He'd proven the man wrong over and over again; he'd become a lawyer and could buy and sell anything he wanted, even people. But that knowledge only proved that his father hadn't known squat. He had more money than he could spend but it wasn't about money. It was the excitement of the hunt, the thefts, getting away with it and holding all the pieces of art, looking at the paintings, touching. That was more valuable than items money could buy. No, it was the sweet anticipation of opening those oil drums out in the open, gathering the cache and laughing aloud because he could do it. Ah, the beauty of it all. He glanced at his watch again and poured himself a glass of scotch and chuckled as he lifted it to his mouth.

Cole and Rainy approached the house with trepidation, as did Steven and Moira. The partners gave one another a look.

"This is really strange, Cole," Steven whispered.

Moira nodded to Rainy and they all agreed.

"What's up? He's never invited us to dinner except on business occasions. I didn't know what to think when he called me and invited us over," Steven said under his breath.

"Yes, and it seemed like he was almost playing with us. That's dumb. Maybe he's trying to finally form a relationship with us?"

Steven laughed at Cole. "Seriously?"

The women joined him and Cole shrugged.

The large brass knocker sounded harsh and loud. Rainy tapped a bright red fingernail against Cole's arm as she leaned into him. Her blonde curly hair looked like a halo next to his thick, dark mane. She glanced up at him and held onto his arm like a possession.

Cole glanced at her disdainfully while pulling his arm free, surprised when he saw her confusion.

A maid invited them into the house, stretching her arm toward the entrance hall. An antique foyer table stood against the wall littered with too many beautiful things to take in at once. The entrance wall and small shelves beside the doorway were covered with art. Rainy stood mesmerized only a moment before it dawned on her what she was looking at, a museum of sorts. The value of the contents inside the house was clearly beyond belief.

Cole and Steven were offered drinks from a tray just inside the main room after their coats were taken. Darrin stood by the fireplace, his arm slung across its width. He didn't move, just nodded to the newcomers which added to the mystery of their invitation.

The room was large. Two picture windows were adorned by mauve linen and brocade drapes with a thin film of cream beyond. Brass flowerets were fitted along the side holding the drapes back to allow the outside in. Large billowing green plants covered tables squarely in front of each window giving the illusion of an inside garden.

Cole was mildly surprised at the tasteful room after encountering the gaudiness of the foyer. His thoughts were generously shared with others around him. He caught Steven's eye and nodded toward a large black pedestal table topped with grey marble. Directly in the center stood an oriental figurine about twenty four inches in height. The body was solid jade, the eyes diamonds, the cape draped with minute rubies. The gems all reflecting in the candelabra from the ceiling made it sparkle. It was set directly below the light for a perfectly dizzying effect.

Darrin watched his partner's reactions, disengaged himself from conversation and walked slowly to join them.

"Like her?" Darrin asked in his deep timbered voice.

Cole stared at the figure, quite unable to take his eyes off her. "Yes. My God, Darrin, she must have cost a fortune. Did you get her when you went to Hong Kong last year?"

Darrin's mouth twitched. "A gift," he said smugly.

Cole turned to stare at Darrin, meeting Steven's eyes beyond his shoulder. Steven's eyes widened and he shrugged his shoulders.

Darrin reached a hand up to each man's shoulder and drew them toward the fireplace within the group of men stationed there. Conversation flowed as Cole watched Rainy flutter among the other women, amazed she knew no strangers. That's why she was so good at her job he thought vaguely. He watched her juggle Champagne and stare at Darrin's art objects. His eyes squinted. She was such a puzzle. He knew she still had a lover but he was damned if he could figure out who he was. He ripped his mind away from her and tried to pin down the uneasiness he felt permeating through the room.

Darrin's eyes kept darting toward the clock on the mantle. Cole remarked on it to Steven who stood beside him. "I can't figure this out…..." he whispered and looked at others in the room to see if they noticed his furtiveness also. The people around both men chatted, drank and moved around slowly to sip and look at the art seemingly unaware of anything out of the ordinary.

"Dammit, why can't we just accept he might want to be friends with us? Maybe he's just trying too hard or….." Steven jabbed Cole into silence and nodded toward their senior partner.

Darrin touched his flat-screen TV. "Let's hear how Sam Berg is doing with his *Man with a Story* gimmick. He tapped the remote and Sam's face filled the screen. Darrin looked like a cat that just ate a canary.

Cole and Steven looked at one another again quizzically.

"Good Evening, Lark Point. This is *Sam Berg, Man with a Story*, coming to you tonight at 6 o'clock from Channel 14. When I left you last night, I told you we would have some more answers for you tonight. The police have decided to watch old town a bit closer, grab kids out after curfew and haul them into City Hall. It seems we have had several interesting cases lately where troublemakers have been put in jail only to hit the streets again within hours."

Sam stared into the camera and shook his head.

"A local young man who has been brought in for questioning several times was seen in the burglary locations at the time of the thefts. Ironically, this young man has relatives in the judicial system. He was released from jail on technicalities. Don't get me wrong, I'm not saying this young gentleman is one of our culprits but it's a rotten life for our police force when they are out there on your streets fighting for your rights and they can't even hold them over night."

He shook his head again.

"Tonight, plans for a new venture will definitely slow down our ring of thieves called Lark Point Activists. It is a committee of citizens to man their own streets. LPA will take calls right now at 378-2314. Call now and register for your neighborhood. The police chief will set aside an officer to be on call for the captain as we continue to fight for justice."

Sam Berg seemed to join everyone inside Darrin Lucas' living room. Darrin's eyes narrowed before glanced at the clock again. Nobody noticed but Cole, who continued to watch him curiously. Everyone watched the segment until Sam was closing the program and a flustered young woman burst before the camera and quickly fled. Sam looked down a moment then up at the camera with a few seconds to go. Struck with indecision, he chose to open the note.

Everyone in Darrin's living room stared at the television screen. Darrin walked over to retrieve his scotch, glancing at his guests with a triumphant gleam in his eyes and his mouth twitched in anticipation.

Suddenly, Sam's face tightened, clearly stunned at the words scrawled on the paper in his hands. He uncharacteristically signed off immediately.

A momentary hush filled the room.

Cole turned quickly toward Darrin who stood looking out the window silently sipping his drink. Cole shrugged, wondering if the note had anything to do with Anna Berg and his mind flew off in another direction. Anna was a refreshing thought. He remembered her leaving the University Club, blue dress blazing beneath lights and candles. He grew warm wondering what she was doing and why she hadn't called for a look-see at a court case for her book. Maybe he'd just call her and then just as quickly brushed the notion aside. No, no way.

Steven sidled up to Cole. "What do you make of that maneuver to bring Sam Berg's news show into the room with us?"

"I was just wondering that myself, old man. I couldn't begin to unravel Darrin. It is odd though, that every time Berg's name comes up in conversation, he goes a little off center, don't you think?" Cole sipped his drink, grabbed some cashews and offered the small dish to Steven.

Later, Cole idly wondered if the maid cooked the delicious meal. The BBQ pulled pork and baked beans with molasses alongside creamy coleslaw surprised him. He enjoyed his dinner, nodded at his partner and reached for his water glass where a neat slice of lemon clung to ice cubes.

The ambiance soon slid toward moodiness. The partners ate silently, each wondering why, what else? Uneasiness clamored in their heads but neither could put their finger on it. After a small glass of Port back in the living room after dinner, they watched Darrin Lucas caress his art pieces as he walked by the tables. They studied his strange actions and wondered some more. Then, it was as if Darrin dismissed his classroom. Everyone faded toward his front door as they clung to the uncertainties held within the house.

NINE

Sam's heart constricted. The small white piece of paper lay scrunched in his hand. Sweat gathered beneath his shirt and dripped down his neck and slid into his hair, which felt matted. He held the smile by rote until the red recorder light blinked off.

Elliott lurched toward Sam as he tore past him for the elevator yelling behind him, "Call Charlie Royce, those bastards robbed my house while I was on the air. I don't know if Anna and Tess were home!" The elevator doors swallowed his last word.

Orders tumbled out of Elliott's mouth and the phones began to ring. The note had proven to be a bigger draw than the news story before Sam even left the building. He wondered what the world was coming to and wiped his forehead with his white handkerchief. Everyone wanted to know what was in that god-damned note.

Sam jumped in his Jeep in the underground lot and impatiently waited for the door to roll up and let him out. His thoughts of Tess and Anna gave vent to anger that was hard to contain. Neither answered their cell phones. Tires squealed as he hugged the corners and raced for his house five miles away. His hands shook trying to fit the key into the lock after sliding into his driveway on two wheels.

"Tess?! Anna?! No answer. Apprehension warred with relief. He tore down the long hallway into the living room, grabbed the door frame and swung his large body into the dining room. He stopped still, staring at the shelves above the table. His eyes blazed. The shelving was bare. All of Anna's Hummels were gone, her favorites saved over the years. There had been sixteen sitting there when he left this morning. His chest rose and fell as he continued through their house, seeing figurines, oils and a tapestry no longer where they should be. The house was missing half the mementos from their life and the women he loved. It felt emptier than ever before and so did Sam.

Anna had been right. The show! The bastards feel threatened. Suddenly, he smiled. Yes, the show. It was working. He grabbed his suit coat, threw it on again. Police sirens loomed closer and he hurried to the door, hitting the auto dial on his phone to call Anna again.

Two little boys had been playing ball in the street and nearly collided with one another running to the curb when they heard sirens from several police cars as they converged along Waverly and into Sam's driveway. Tousled heads, dirty jeans and eyes full of excitement, the tallest boy grabbed the other, pulling him down beside him. They sat on the curb to watch the events at Sam's house. Freckles and dirt covered their faces while they held the soccer ball between them.

Lieutenant Charlie Royce was the first man out of the car and met Sam in the driveway. Sirens stopped blaring.

"My house was robbed, Charlie. Thank God nobody was inside," he said angrily.

"Sorry, Sam. Dammit." The policeman whistled between his teeth and gazed toward the brick house. Curtains filled the windows, green plants could be seen just inside. Flowerbeds were trimmed beside the house evenly as if it was a gardening-magazine photo. He looked at Sam.

"Most of the things missing are small items, figurines, some oil paintings and all of my wife's Hummels. They even took the tapestry off the dining room wall beside the damned door," Sam exploded. He glanced toward the curb and saw the neighbor boys sitting with eyes as big as quarters staring at him, listening to every word.

"Corey, did you or Jimmy see anybody come to my house a little while ago and take some things out of it without anyone home?" Sam yelled across the grassy area.

Corey yanked Jimmy up beside him, happy to be in on the conversation and itching to stand closer to the policeman. "Didn't see nobody take nothing, Sam."

"No cars were here?"

Corey thought a moment, dropping his chin. Momentarily, his face lit up and he said, "Only Tessie's boyfriend was here awhile ago but I didn't see him, just his old car." He stared at the gun in Charlie Royce's holster that hung level with his small face.

"No, Corey, I mean strange cars…you know, like a truck. Did you see anybody you didn't know around my house?" Sam let out a long audible breath.

"No." Corey stared at the policeman.

Jimmy stared at the gun.

"Who is Tess's boyfriend, Sam?" Charlie asked, interested.

"Oh, Nicholas Alonzo, a nice college kid Tess has over all the time. Don't worry about him; guess the kids didn't see anyone….."

Just then, the air around them filled with loud bursts of noise as the firecrackers ignited, popping like a woman's staccato heels along a marble tiled floor. Balls of smoke spurted in every direction causing the men and two children to reel in shock as a putrid smell erupted around them.

Charlie twisted one of the boys behind him. At the same time, Sam grabbed Corey and pushed his face into his belly. The other policemen ran in all directions unsure where the noise originated. Eyes wide with surprise, they ran around to their lieutenant with smoking bits of cardboard in their hands from the flowerbeds under the front windows.

The noise stopped as quickly as it began. Sam and Charlie pushed the boys behind them as people began to crowd the sidewalk, pouring out of nearby houses, or looking out their windows and driving slowly by his house. Charlie bent to pick up a fishing line that was stretched across the driveway and lifted it while Sam watched curiously.

"Well, this is from a timing device," he said, impressed with the ingenuity involved by someone trying to impress Sam.

"Timing device?" Sam looked quickly around the yard, following Charlie and another policeman as they knelt down in his flower bed to remove bits and pieces of firecrackers.

"See here?" Charles showed him. "….and here…..and here…..?" He pointed toward the dirt, the fence and garage beyond. His dark blue jacket was spotted with grey, used burnt fragments. Sam and the boys followed him around the house.

Sam grunted as he twirled the fishing line in his hand. It was attached to several groups of firecrackers, perhaps five hundred in all. They continued to the end, seeing the fishing line lead toward the fence, behind the garage. Gravel spun underfoot as they inched around the garage, the boys tagging along, feeling important and bursting with excitement. The boys bumped into the men when they stopped abruptly and they heard Charlie say, "There!"

Red bricks made a path between the garage and fence, grass neatly trimmed beside it. On the bricks was a two inch square piece of very rough sandpaper, held solid between three heavy rocks. Sam's forehead wrinkled as he examined the area seeing a wooden match that had scraped across the sandpaper setting off a long fuse. The fuse ignited the first set of firecrackers, each setting fire to the next batch until they marched around the flower borders to the front of his house. Just in time for him to arrive from the station, Sam mused.

Charlie held the boys back. "No, let's stay back for now. I'm going to have a look around to see if we can find any clues. Maybe these guys left something stupid that might lead us to them."

The men returned to the driveway, hauling Corey and Jimmy along with them.

An hour later, Sam was back at the station, still wondering where Anna and Tess could be and his frustration level was over the top. The thought of someone setting up that match and other paraphernalia while he was undoubtedly in his house looking around, made his skin crawl with renewed anger.

He was determined to find those responsible and decided to call in his markers for any information. Someone out there knew something that might lead him to them.

His mind careened through the facts he'd dredged up and aired to his audience. Excitement soon placed his anger. "That's it! Damn, but the message is clear. I'm getting close and they don't like it..... ." He dialed his insurance agent, related the incident and waved Elliott into his office, hoping for any news from the crew or callers. A pattern was beginning to emerge as the police and investigators compared the nightly robberies with each victim's whereabouts at the time each theft occurred. Studies dictated the picture; the team was pumped. They chipped away at each lead offering Sam the basis for each evening show with the ultimate goal of publicly denouncing and luring the thieves into jail.

"Come on, Sam. Give," Elliott said, his ears straining to hear every word. The man had been yelling orders since Sam had run out of the station and he was exhausted.

"......then I was standing in my driveway with the neighbor boys and the police and then the firecrackers went off...zap...zap, it sounded like gunshots. Everyone raced for cover. We each had a boy buried in our bodies because we didn't know what the hell was happening."

"And what about Anna and Tess?"

Sam frowned. "Thank God they weren't home. I need to tell them but they aren't answering their cell phones. I left messages but if they get home without listening to them, I hate to think what their reactions will be." Sam put his head in his hands.

"Look at this, Sam," Elliott handed a folded newspaper toward him and stabbed one item with his finger for Sam to read. "It's in the Lark Point Democrat. This might have pointed your house in their direction even without your Story program.

Sam read the article quickly.

IN DEPTH

Initial publicity consisted of radio and T.V. public service announcements, brochures and speaking engagements. Ongoing publicity has been fundamentally the same until Channel 14's Sam Berg grabbed the tail of the community's rage and displayed an avid interest and intense need to find answers. See tomorrow's story for further details.

Sam grunted and handed the paper back to Elliott. He reached for a Marlboro and twisted the unlit cigarette in his fingers. "Where's the woman who brought me the note?"

"She works in the back. I don't know her name."

"Well," Sam said, like a teacher to a student, "she might be able to lead us to whoever gave the note to her to give it to me."

"Oh, of course," Elliott said grimly. "Of course. Let me call Martha and find out who she is. Just a minute." Elliott reached across Sam's desk and lifted the receiver. He had the answer within seconds.

"Trudy Knox, they're sending her in."

"Good!" Sam thoughtfully examined the paper on his desk.

A slight knock against the window brought both men's attention back to the present. A tall woman hesitated before entering. "Hi, I'm Trudy Knox. Martha asked me to come to your office."

Elliott moved to allow her access to the other chair in the room.

She nodded toward the men.

"Who gave you the note you gave to me while I was on the air earlier?" he said, not wasting time with small talk.

The woman's shoulder's lifted, her almost-purple eyes stared back at him. Her smile was warm, her features even. Long lashes framed her eyes as Sam leaned forward waiting for an answer.

"Well?" Sam whispered urgently.

"I don't know who gave it to me. Someone propped it up in my keyboard with a yellow sticky attached to it that I brought with me." She handed it to Sam, her navy sweater dipping slightly.

Sam blinked at the display of pale skin before reaching for the sticky note. Glancing at the tiny printing, he read it aloud, "Give this envelope to Sam Berg at EXACTLY 6:15 or Karen will be very late for school tomorrow."

Sam looked at Trudy again. Her eyes glistened and her breathing was shallow. "Please relax, Trudy. I'm not going to beat you," he said sympathetically. "Who is Karen?"

"My little girl. She's six and just started first grade." Her shoulders heaved forward and her breath caught.

"Ahhh…" He sat back in his chair.

"So, you see….?" She said softly with lavender eyes begging for understanding.

"Yes, I do. Elliott, would you please go call Charlie Royce and tell him about this? He said he wanted to question Trudy and is probably already on his way." Sam handed the sticky note to Elliott, who shrugged and slipped out of Sam's office.

"Do I frighten you?" He watched her bottom lip tremble.

"No, it's just that I've only been working here two weeks and already I'm in trouble. I just want to do my job and live a normal life and here I am in the middle of something….." She said it so fast Sam had to tip his head to make sure he got it all.

"How old are you?" Sam asked her softly.

Trudy looked surprised. "Can you ask me that?" A smile hovered on her lips. "Don't you know you don't ask a woman her age, Sam?"

"Sorry, it's just that when you first walked in, you didn't look much older than my daughter and yet you have a quality about you that appears older, and….."

She smiled. "I'm forty two. I had Karen when I was thirty six. My husband died of cancer two years ago and we girls are just getting our act together again. That's why I don't want to lose my job. I love working here and want to learn as much as I can about the kind of reporting you do," Trudy said in another rush of words.

Sam chuckled. "Well, I'm not going to fire you. Besides, I don't hire or fire anyone. I work here just like you do."

It was Trudy's turn to laugh. "Right. *Sam Berg, Man with a Story,* just like me…." Her laughter had a gentle tinkling sound. Her reddish hair touched her shoulders and her clear eyes crinkled when she laughed.

He liked her. "So, you want to learn my kind of job? Well, can you come in about 5:15 tomorrow evening and I'll show you how it works before I go on? Maybe you can help me. Everyone starts somewhere. I learned from Shelby Stone. Do you know of him?"

"Of course. He's been on the news for years. Where is he now?"

"Los Angeles. They offered him a deal he couldn't refuse. But me? I'm happy in Lark Point," Sam finished proudly.

Elliott's voice cut into their conversation. "Charlie Royce is on line two for you, Sam."

Trudy eased herself out of the chair as Sam picked up the receiver. His eyes followed her out, admiring the woman in tan slacks and navy sweater as she turned the corner.

Tess and Anna finished dinner a little after seven and lifted their shopping bags to join the crowd. As they neared the car in the mall parking lot, Tess checked her phone. She didn't want to miss Nicholas' call since he was coming over later. She tapped her dad's voicemail message and put it on speaker phone as Anna pulled out onto the road.

"Hey, baby, I need to find you and Mom. I've left messages on both phones. I hope you listen to this message before you get home because you'll have a nasty surprise otherwise. To put it bluntly, we've been robbed. I'm ok but there's a lot of missing things in the house. The police were with me and little Corey and Jimmy were outside. Nobody got hurt. I'm mad as hell. They stole your mom's Hummels. All of them. And the tapestry…please call me to let me know you are both all right. I'm at the station. The creeps coerced a woman into giving me a note telling me he was robbing me during my program so it was live. Shit. Nasty stuff. Call me. I love you."

Anna pulled over quickly and stared at Tess's wide, frightened eyes. She reached for her hand and grabbed her own phone to punch in Sam's number. He answered on the first ring.

"Sam! We just got your message. I'm mad as hell too. You know they hit our house because of your investigation, don't you? And Tess and I could have been home! It was just a fluke we were at dinner and shopping. I know, I know…but I'm livid. My Hummels for God sakes. I know they are just things but….. At least we're safe. Tess and I are driving home right now. Yes, of course, we'll see you when you get there. Yes." She stabbed the cancel button and tossed the phone in her purse.

"I told your dad he was asking for trouble when he started that damned program, staring in the camera like he was egging on those guys but he just wouldn't listen. He thinks he can handle things. He's not Superman. I told him that too….."

Tess stared at her mother. "But mother, he must be getting close because they are trying to stop him from coming after them, right? Isn't that a good thing?"

Anna squeezed the steering wheel. "Yes, it is a good thing to catch them but it's not a good thing if they decide to come after us too…like they did today….in order to stop dad. I'm angry at him for not taking that into consideration. Instead, he's like a little boy, anxious to be the important kid on the block. And I am worried!"

"Okay," Tess said, fading to a hushed stillness.

Anna took a deep breath. "Now, when we were walking to the car, you were telling me about your Taekwon-Do classes. Tell me again what Cris said about your stance and when your Yellow Belt test takes place. I want to attend of course. Maybe I should join the class. I could use some self-defense moves…"

Tess chuckled. "I had a good class today. There were five others and Cris takes such great care to help each of us. I really like her. She's so caring and interested.   After the class, I told her about dad's program....I know....I know.... Anyway, I told her how he's trying to catch the thieves and she had a very odd response."

Anna looked across at her daughter. "How so?"

"Well, she asked me all about what the police know about the victims, how they think it's being done, if they have any clues about who might be part of it.....and, well, she gave me the impression she might have a clue but she's afraid to share it. Maybe it's just my imagination, but I don't think so. The other thing is she's invited me to attend the end-of-the-season Artists Repertory Theater party next Saturday, September 13th. She said dad will get an invitation so all four of us can go. My gut feeling was yes, so I sort of RSVPd for all of us. You don't mind do you?"

"It does sound like fun. Four? I'll write it on my calendar. Where is the party? And Tess, your gut feeling is usually the best truth meter you can depend on," Anna said cryptically.

"Yes, I know you are right about gut feelings.... Not sure where the party will be held. The fourth is Nicholas, of course. Cris said it was at a friend's house. I'll find out."

The Three Lion Bakery had already prepared and delivered the food for the party that would begin in a few hours. Rainy ticked off her fingers to count the people she could expect. Twelve cast members, Chuck and Laura, Darrin Lucas, me and Cole, Sam and Anna Berg, Tess Berg and her friend Nicholas...twenty one. She'd ordered enough food for twenty five. She loved to cook but cooking for twenty five? Not so much. Cole was in charge of the bar. She hadn't wanted to invite Darrin but since he was the largest donor to the theater, she grudgingly admitted it would be uncouth not to do so. If he just had a little more charm it would make it a lot easier.

She hadn't seen Cris in three days and couldn't stop smiling. She set the table with glass bowls filled with nuts and smoothed fig spread over the Brie to bake. She would bake chocolate chip cookies just before the party so the chocolate pieced were melty and warm. She looked down at her waistline and grimaced. Yes, she liked to eat but Cris liked her just the way she was, so by damned she'd bake the cookies and eat them too.

Cole had skimmed the guest list; after reading Chuck's, Darrin's and the cast's names, he didn't read any further. He'd been disinterested in most things lately and hated feeling so lethargic. Rainy had her life and he had his; they'd lived that way for years now; although she'd endured sex early in their marriage, now neither was interested and it made life easier on both of them. He knew he could've asked Rainy about the affair and she might have answered frankly, but did he really want to know the answer? No. Yet, paradoxically, the questions that lingered just generated new ones. So, it was just another party to tend bar, smile and greet.

Rainy's off-white slacks were ironed to perfection, her red blouse billowed around her hips and her diamond studs sparkled. She was ready.

Cole had the wine lined up alongside the hard liquor and was chewing on cashew nuts when the doorbell rang at seven. "I'll get it," he yelled and pulled open the door.

Anna, Sam, Tess and Nicholas stood among the laughing cast members clustered together on the porch. Darrin was walking up the drive as Chuck and his wife arrived. Cole stared a beat before inviting the crew inside.

Anna was dumbstruck. *Cole's house*? She thought the cast party was being held at the owner's house. She turned to Tess with a question on her face. Her daughter grinned, completely unaware that her mother wished she'd stayed home.

Sam ushered his family in and pulled Nicholas along with the chattering cast members to shake Cole's hand. "Thanks for inviting us, Cole. We didn't realize it was being held at your house. It's nice to see you again." He looked around and was impressed by the décor, furniture and the inviting scent of cookies.

Darrin nodded to Cole, accepted a glass of scotch and surveyed the group, his eyes lingering on Sam Berg. He couldn't decide if he wanted to slap the newsman stupid or boast about stealing from him. Having Nico and Michael in the room added to the bittersweet euphoria he tried to tamp down.

Cole watched Anna mingle and thought how beautiful her daughter was. Nicholas seemed a nice young man. Unable to keep his eyes off

Anna, Cole moved behind his bar on tenterhooks, itching to give her a glass of wine so he could look into those eyes again.

Anna was afraid her heartbeat was trumping the classical music coming out of the speaker system. She tried to calm it by placing a hand over her chest but she was sure it could be heard over the laughter in the room. She wanted wine but her legs wouldn't take her to the bar. Anna looked toward the bottles and the man behind them and scoffed at her nervousness. Big sigh. She gave in.

"What can I get for you, Anna?" he asked with deceptive calm. He didn't take his eyes off hers for a beat before reaching for a wine glass and placing it in front of her. "You look good.... Red or white?"

"Red, please. It's nice to see you again," she murmured. Her warm brown eyes met his and held.

A fleeting pang bit him; if only she was his wife, Tess their daughter and ... He shook away the crazy illusion and poured Cabernet Sauvignon into the crystal stemmed glass, complimenting himself on his steady hand. Smiling, he lowered his eyes to the napkin, sure his emotions were transparent. *Where were you when I was single?*

Anna reached for the glass, thanked him and turned toward the group. Nobody seemed to notice she was floating across the floor or that she would have enjoyed sitting at the bar talking to Cole for hours rather than mingling. Nobody noticed her heart was beating so fast it felt like a trip hammer. But she did.

"Welcome everyone," Rainy said as she raised her glass. "I hope everyone has a glass in their hand? Let's make a toast to the cast of the Artist Repertory Theater....To Chuck who makes it all happen and to Darrin who believes enough in the Rep to make enormous donations. Thank you for coming. You all know my bartender....." Everyone laughed. "and Sam Berg and his lovely wife, Anna, their daughter, Tess and her friend, Nicholas. And of course here's Laura who always gets Chuck to the Rep on time." Laughter followed her toast and everyone sipped their drinks. "Dinner will be served at 7:30 in the dining room so please find a stranger to talk to." Rainy smiled and winked at Cris.

Cole looked at the group, wondering if Rainy's lover was in the room. He watched her flit from one person to the next and tried to recognize a special touch, a special smile. One cast member seemed to draw her attention and he watched them but didn't feel air crackle around them. His eyes slid to others before landing on Anna and watching her study the books in the corner shelf. He chuckled quietly when he watched her cock her head to read their spines.

Nicholas held Tess's hand while avoiding Darrin like a bee sting. After guiding him toward Sam, she was pleased they were enjoying an easy conversation. When she looked for her mother, she noticed a strange luminosity about her as she carried a glass of red wine away from the bar. She turned to Nicholas again and saw in his face a determination and strength she was coming to love. What she also noticed was tension and wondered why.

Cris followed Rainy into the kitchen. "Mmmmmm, those cookies are to die for. Can I have one before dinner?" She lingered just inside the doorway so she could see anyone coming around the corner and mouthed, "I love you."

Rainy lifted a warm cookie to Cris's mouth and touched it to her lips, urging her to open her mouth and taste the chocolate melt on her tongue. Her eyes warmed and she swayed toward her.

Cris opened her mouth, tasted the cookie and sent a delicious message to Rainy with her eyes. She chewed it slowly and glanced into the hallway again, wishing they were alone.

Both women were surprised to hear upraised voices, the tone of an argument coming from the living room. The unmistakable voice of Darrin Lucas could be heard above the music. Rainy hurried from the room.

"I think you should leave it to the police, Mr. Berg. You are a newscaster, sir, not a cop. A television investigator is no match for the kind of thieves this community is up against." Darrin huffed loudly.

"...But it is working. I know they're uneasy. Why else would they rob my house? Why shouldn't I help the police? People watch our show because we are doing something about it."

Cole was flummoxed. Curious, he moved from behind the bar and stood beside Sam. He looked at both men. "Darrin?"

Darrin shrugged and strode to the bar, poured himself another scotch and gulped half of it down. Chug chug. "I am just a little tired of Sam trying to be someone he isn't, Cole. This man has lived in our community just a couple of years. He thinks he's smarter than our sheriff and the entire police force. I needed to tell him what I thought, nothing more." He drank the remaining liquid and poured a third glass.

Cole and Sam stared at the man.

Nicholas moved to the corner of the room, wishing again that Tess had not invited him. The last thing he needed was to be in the same room with slime. If he'd known DAL was attending, he would have found an excuse. He walked over to Anna who seemed a safe haven.

Cris watched Michael sit down on the couch as if his legs couldn't hold him up. She studied him and looked at Darrin. Darrin was looking across the room at Michael with a scowl on his face and the two men mutely lifted their glasses at the same time. She inched down beside Michael and he put his arm around her.

Rainy's eyes fairly smoked but she was too clever to lose her temper. Instead, she worked her way toward that side of the room. Several cast members circled the men. Lily and James looked at the fireplace mantel and tried to name the painting propped against the wall. Some others were teasing Cris about the number of curtain calls she got in *Gossip*.

"You can't resent me for that," she bantered, enjoying the camaraderie and the adulation they gave to her while trying to change the subject of news investigations and burglaries.

The cast surrounded her and they squeezed together for a selfie photo. Within minutes it was on Facebook.

Michael whispered, "I'm uncomfortable here. Let's leave early and stop at the deli to eat."

Cris's eyes flared. "What? This party's for us, we can't run out on everyone. What on earth is wrong with you? She looked at Darrin again. She'd heard his name bantered about because he was a big donor for the theater but she'd never seen him at the theater. There was something oddly familiar about him.

"Okay, Cris, but I want to leave as soon as we can." He purposefully ignored Darrin's gaze.

"I think Sam Berg's doing a good job, Michael. He's got the community thinking. I don't know why Mr. Lucas is making everyone so uncomfortable. Sam is a nice man. Tess is proud of him and the work he does. The news program is top notch, I think." She looked up to see Darrin Lucas standing next to her, flushed and angry.

"I would say, young lady, that you should stick to acting and playing house….not thinking." Cris was astounded, clearly startled.

Rainy was stunned and went directly to Cris like a protective mother bear.

Cris sat speechless. She felt Rainy's hand stroke over her frizzy hair, trying to calm her before it dropped to Cris's shoulder.

Michael looked at Rainy as if she'd sprouted horns.

Cris tried to dismiss the criticism airily and gulped her wine.

"Darrin, you're out of line," Cole said urgently. "What in the hell is going on with you tonight?"

Darrin turned to his partner. Without a word, he walked to the bar, placed his glass down and bowed to Rainy. "Yes, I think I am out of line and I apologize. I believe I will skip dinner and hope you have a nice evening." He nodded to Chuck and the group of cast members. "Good job and good night." With that, he turned on his heel and walked out the door.

Everyone stared after him, relieved but mostly curious. Cole was filled with an interested amazement. His eyes moved to Rainy where she sat on the arm of Cris's chair and vaguely wondered why when there was an open chair next to her. *Strange woman*, he thought. He nodded his head pointing to the dining room and she took the hint.

"Dinner will be served within five minutes everyone. Please be sure to refresh your drinks and follow me." She shepherded them into the large, open dining room. The music was piped in and added a calmness the group needed.

Bottles of wine were passed around the table. Anna filled her glass again. As she lifted it, she noticed Rainy watching Michael with animosity and it stalled its trip to her lips. Anna frowned and glanced toward laughter at the end of the table. Sam and Cole. She knew it was unfair to compare them, but she did. Sam was a good man living his life through others. Cole, by contrast, breathed vigor, firm independence and mystery while exuding strength and grace to others.

Back in the living room, conversations ebbed.

Nicholas urged Tess out the door.

"Shall we also leave, Anna?" Sam asked his wife.

Still deep in thought, Anna jumped in surprise.

"Thank you for dinner, Rainy. Those were great chocolate chip cookies." Sam grinned as she handed him two more wrapped in a napkin.

From behind Anna, Cole said, "I've enjoyed talking with you, Anna. I'd like to help you with your book. I promised, remember?"

Before she could answer, Sam was at her elbow shaking Cole's hand. "Good to see everyone and thanks for the wine too." Sam looked at Anna and she followed her husband, waving a hand to everyone. A feeling of déjà vu came over her when she glanced back, straight into Cole's silvery-grey, unwavering eyes.

The clock chimed eleven when Anna finished her ablutions. Sam was propped up reading the newspaper when she climbed in beside him.

"You talk in your sleep," he said. "Did you know that?"

Anna laughed. "It's a good thing I have nothing to hide then, isn't it?" After a short hesitation, she said, "I think we've been playing this game too long, don't you think?"

"He glanced at her and put his paper down. "What game, Anna?" He searched her pale face.

"Us, Sam." She started to say something further but he cut her off.

"We're tired. We're blurring at the edges. Wish we could just take a long rest somewhere but not now. I can't now, Anna."

Anna waited and stared at the bedcover.

"What's wrong, Anna?" He watched her carefully and saw her trace her fingers along the satin coverlet corners, saw her swallow hard, saw her mouth tremble.

"Everything's wrong. It's supposed to be right, but it's not. And I don't know how to fix it."

Sam held out his hand. "Anna, I love you...." His words trailed and his hand dropped as he watched a tear escape Anna's sad brown eyes.

"I can't...." she lifted moist eyes to his.

"We're tired, honey. What can I say?" He turned off the lamp.

She didn't move. "I suppose you can just say good night so I can go to sleep," Anna muttered.

As Sam interviewed the mayor for the third time, a nugget of information slipped that the mayor thought wasn't important. Sam certainly did. During the past few years, the mayor and his wife's seasonal seats never changed and they befriended people around them. When the mayor mentioned one of those friends had also been robbed, Sam perked up and he noted the man's name. Excitement pumped through him. Coincidence? Probably not. He called the man immediately and they agreed to meet near the college campus. A link, perhaps? Should he call Charlie or should he wait until after his interview? After, he decided.

Tony Cilantro was a big guy, probably close to two hundred and fifty pounds. Seeing him squeezed into the booth in the little café made Sam smile. Promising himself to stop eating fast food, he slid into the bench across from him and shook the man's hand.

The man smiled, they ordered coffee and Sam pumped him full of questions Tony readily answered, clearly upset.

"My wife is frightened, I'm mad as hell and the insurance company says they are so far behind in the claims department, they can't promise when an adjuster will call us.

"When Mayor Sterling told me you were also a victim, I thought it was pretty coincidental. Do you know if anyone else in the theater group has been robbed?" Sam asked urgently, sure he was on the right track.

"Yes, now that you mention it. Alyssa heard a woman, who sits in front of her, discussing it a couple of weeks ago with her companion. I don't know if Alyssa knows her name but she lives alone and her voice was very shaky, obviously still upset. She heard the woman say she was relieved she'd been at the theater when they stole a painting her late husband painted and her heart was broken to lose it."

Sam's excitement mounted. He peppered the man with more questions and Tony's answers were more than he'd hoped for. They finished their coffee and stood to shake hands. Sam asked if he could use his name as a source if needed.

"Sure, and we'll watch your program later."

A disheveled Charlie Royce picked up the phone.

"Hey, Sam, slow down....what?" Sam started over and the policeman listened. His eyebrows rose and his dark eyes rounded in surprise, frustrated the mayor hadn't mention it earlier.

"He hadn't thought it was important, Charlie. He just mentioned it as an aside in aggravation. Everyone is scared, angry. I think there's a connection. When he mentioned the lady sitting in front of them, it clicked. I want to discuss it in my program tonight." Sam was elated, but hesitant to cross the bounds of the verbal contract made with the police.

Charlie listened.

"Tony said we could use him as a source and the mayor would love the free media attention," he finished expectantly.

Charlie Royce didn't miss the excitement in his friend's voice.

Sam could almost hear Charlie's mind circling the wagons. "There's another play tonight so we can't wait, right?" Sam wanted to start on the script right away.

"Do it, Sam. Call the theater's owner and......"

"I already called Chuck Champion. I told him I'd like to see the database for his season-ticket holders. He refused. Maybe he'll give it to you? And I trust you'll share it with me?"

"We'll see Sam. It's an open investigation but there are some pieces of information you aren't privy too. Let me work on it. Do your piece tonight and I'll get back to you." Charlie's voice sounded final and Sam recognized it for what it was.

When Sam rushed into the station, Trudy walked through the lobby, both pleased that their paths crossed. They'd become friends and she was a quick learner. If she wanted to be an investigator as she told him, he had a plan and the anticipation lifted his spirits.

"Trudy, how'd you like to help me on a project that could help get your investigative juices flowing?" He smiled at the way her hair swung around her shoulder when she tipped her head, listening with interest.

"Of course, Sam. What can I do?" She took a frank look at him. "Can you break away and come to my office? I'm going to see Elliott. I have breaking news and my teacup runneth over." He winked at her.

She laughed and rushed toward her cubicle with a promise to meet after she met her deadline. She'd already learned a lot from him. She tried to ignore the warning bells because spending time with Sam was the most special part of her day besides picking up Karen. Tamping down emotions, she slipped into her chair, surprised to be attracted to a man again. Jake had been her life and losing him had shaken her so badly that she wondered if she'd ever be whole again. And it had to happen with a married man. Damn. Thank God she had her little girl.

Sam stormed through Elliott's open door, panting as if he'd run a mile.

Elliott head shot up. "Sit, Sam. Catch your breath. What's up?"

"BIG break, El, from a conversation I had with the mayor. He didn't think it was important but you will. It's about season ticket holders at the Artists Repertory Theater…same seats year after year, so they make friends with ticketholders around them. Today, he said some of those people have also been robbed!"

Elliott's eyes held a gleam of interest and his white eyebrows shot upward. Pursing his lips, he nodded to Sam for more.

Sam took a breath. "Sterling's wife heard another patron talk about being burgled. She lives alone and was frightened. She lost a very sentimental painting, among other items, and said how glad she was to be at the theater during the robbery." That's three patrons robbed while at the theater. See a pattern here?" Sam's eyes danced.

Elliott slapped the table. "Did you call Charlie? Did you contact the Rep for a list of their other patrons?"

Sam grinned. "Yes to all. Chuck Champion wouldn't give me the list. Charlie is calling him. I want Trudy to help me put this together. She's a quick study and anxious to help. Do you think Tom Watson would mind if I grabbed her for this?"

Elliott didn't miss Sam's interest in Trudy but attributed it to helping the young woman find her way into the investigative world of television instead of copywriting. "I'd say grabbing her might raise eyebrows," Elliott answered indulgently, "but an assistant eager to learn would be a plus and this could be big. Damn good job, Sam!"

Sam jumped up and disappeared.

Elliott stared at the empty doorway thoughtfully before grabbing the phone to call the mayor.

TEN

Cris was anxious to watch Sam Berg's news show. She fought her uneasiness and reproached herself for thinking Michael might be involved in the thefts. Working at the theater plus teaching martial arts classes, didn't leave much time for television or the news. However, she would make time today after learning there might be a connection to the theater. She prayed she was jumping to the wrong conclusion. She knew coincidences existed but too many strung together weren't coincidences at all. She mentally listed her facts to compare with what she'd learned from Tess.

Connecting the victims to the Artist Repertory's audience made her heart blink. Add that fact to the conversation she overheard between Michael and someone…a few weeks earlier kindled and burned in her mind. . In fact, as she thought back over the past months, he was often on the phone just before curtain call. Damn. Then there was that old guy he argued with and the call about fireworks he made afterward. She'd kept her own counsel after listening to his conversation and then Tess's house was robbed and fireworks were involved. Had she been so blind?

She called Rainy. Knowing she was also investigating the thefts, Cris wanted to do a little investigating herself. She left a message asking to see her either before the news or afterward. She was shaking.

Within minutes, Rainy called to meet at the deli near the Rep within the hour. She was working hard to close the claims cases for her Metro Assurance and if there was anything Cris could tell her about the Rep's connection, she didn't want to delay.

Rainy was already seated when Cris arrived. Two tall glasses of tea with fresh mint leaves and lemon floated among the ice cubes when Cris sat down. They grinned at one another for too many reasons to count and lifted their glasses.

"Ok, what has your panties in a knot, Cris?"

Cris laughed. "They are definitely in a knot. Tess Berg was in my Taekwon-Do class this morning and we started talking about her dad's news show on Channel 14. I've never watched it. I remember how he bristled at the party when Mr. Lucas snapped at him. Tess told me her dad is collaborating with the mayor, the police and your boss through the television station."

"Yes, I watch him and he's good. His *Man with a Story* angle is a bit eerie because he looks into the camera and talks directly to the thieves." She shook her shoulders as if cold, saying, "Glad he's not after me. He made the bums nervous enough to rob him too so he must be getting close.

"Now they've connected victims to our season-ticket holders....."

"What?" Rainy's forehead wrinkled. "Do you think these thugs have the patron list? Hmmmmm, I'll call Chuck to see who has access to a list like that…Sorry Cris. Go on."

Cris weighed her words carefully. "I imagine there's more than one guy or girl? It must be a gang like everyone suggests in the paper. Who would have the ability to be at the theater and also rob these people? I mean it's always during show time, I understand. Well, maybe one person there and several others do the jobs?"

Rainy looked at Cris and responded slowly. "I suppose if the person works at the theater, he or she would have to make a mistake. Throw money around or something. The person on the inside at the theater must get paid a pretty penny to set something like that up, right?"

Cris bit her lip. "Yesssss, he would."

"Are you suspicious of someone, Cris?" Rainy's eyes narrowed. Rainy knew Cris well enough to recognize when she was holding something back and pushed her for an answer. "Well, Cris?" Rainy leaned forward to make her point.

"I'm not sure," she spoke in a suffocated whisper.

"But you think you know something?"

"I *said* I'm not sure."

"Well, Cole and I will be at the play tonight. He wants to talk with you. He suspects someone too. He wouldn't tell me and you won't tell me, so we'll just be one happy mute threesome," she finished mockingly.

Cris took a breath, sipped the lemony tea and let her mind calm. She'd watch the program tonight at the theater and make her own judgment call. She was not going to throw Michael under the bus unless she was sure and even then, could she?

"Now, let's talk about something delicious," Rainy said as she looked around to see how close they were sitting to other tables. "I've been missing you and right now what I really would like to do is hold you and kiss you until you moan."

Cris felt stirrings begin at her toes and work their way up. "Yes, that is much more delicious than talking about burglaries. Will we ever have that freedom?" she asked Rainy, trying to read a future in the blue eyes. She felt Rainy's leg press against hers under the table and the warmth just kept moving into all the right places.

"In a perfect world......" Rainy whispered.

"When you decide what's more important...me or your fancy life? You know you are not being fair to Cole or to me." Cris sighed.

Rainy's eyes dropped. "We've talked about this before, Cris. I'm not sure if we can handle snide remarks or our losing friends and...."

"In *today's* world? There are too many women marching for gay pride for me to believe that's what you are worried about." Before Rainy could answer, Cris looked at her watch and grabbed her black leather bag. I need to get going. I'm playing a bitch in tonight's play and I already seem to have my bitch hat on." She crossed her eyes and looked fierce; getting the laugh from Rainy she'd hoped for to lighten the mood.

"See you tonight then....." Rainy's voice was a velvet murmur.

Cole was restless while he waited for Chuck. He'd arrived earlier than usual and snagged a glass of wine before the cart opened for business. *Good to have friends in high places.* If Rainy was right, Cris might know something. The thought of someone having access to that database made him cringe. HIPAA rules regarding privacy would be breached and poor Chuck would have a hell of a time proving he hadn't sold it or left the storage file unlocked, which was mandatory.

Sipping his Merlot and munching on almonds, he waited in the lobby deep in thought. He'd seen Sam's program earlier that evening and his probing questions made sense. If the list had victim's names on it, there's a problem for Chuck....especially if the list held all of the victim's names. If there was someone on the inside, which obviously there must be, that person had mighty strong willpower not to toss his dirty money around. Wouldn't someone have noticed? Wasn't there someone who wasn't acting normal? First the list....

Chuck came around the corner and walked directly over to Cole. "I got your message, Cole. Come into my office…" Chuck didn't waste any time on pleasantries. His face was so serious that Cole wondered if there was something else he should be worrying about it.

"Ok, your message asked me if there was anyone who has access to the patron's list. Two people. Me and the bookkeeper. She's been with me ten years. I would vouch for her honesty as if she was my own mother. I don't sell lists, nor do I even think of such a thing. And the file cabinet is always locked." Chuck ran his hands through his hair.

"Whoa, I'm certainly not accusing you of anything, Chuck. We are your legal counsel and our job is to protect you. I had a conversation with Rainy today that got me thinking. She said someone in the troupe may know something about the insider here at the theater. He or she can't be carrying out these thefts alone and probably doesn't even step inside the victim's house, but I think he or she gets the ball rolling and it may start with that list." Cole took a breath.

"Sam Berg called me today and so did the sheriff's office. They want a copy of the list to compare with victim's names. So you are on the right track, I think. Must I hand it over to either of them? Am I protected from the HIPAA privacy law's standpoint?"

"I'd say yes to the police but no to Sam. I know he's breaking his ass trying to solve these burglaries but I doubt the community would like their names and addresses in the public media and to be honest, I wouldn't. Rainy is also investigating this for Metro Assurance, but no to her too. But, hell, let me see it." Cole grinned at Chuck and saw him push the paper toward him.

"Don't take it out of my office, Cole. Get a list of the victims and we can compare both lists here in my office."

"Sounds like a pregnant idea. Put a call into the sheriff. Scan and send it to him or Fax it over. I'll sit here during the play to compare the names. Agreed?"

Chuck reached for his phone.

"I'll go find Rainy and argue with her. She'll want to be in on it but I'll plead HIPAA and we'll lock the door. She wants to see the play anyway and is worried about Cris."

"Cris? Why?"

"Oh, that slipped. It was Cris who Rainy thinks might know something. She asked me not to mention names... I didn't, right?"

Chuck shook his head and rolled his eyes as he picked up his phone. While he called the police, Cole left to find his wife.

Late that night, Cris heard the phone ring and struggled awake, wondering who could be calling so late. Late-night phone calls spelled emergency. She jumped up, ran for the living room and grabbed the phone before the caller hung up. It could be serious, after all.

"Hello?" She said urgently into the phone.

No answer.

"Oh come on, a crank call? This isn't funny," she hissed.

"Stop with the questions, lady, or you won't see tomorrow."

"What?! Who the hell is this?" she demanded in a shrill voice.

"Pay attention! Stop giving sage advice about the burglaries. I will be watching and listening!" the voice hurled the last few words with such menace that Cris fell wordlessly into a chair. She couldn't move even after she heard the click.

"Cris, who's calling so late?" Michael yelled from the doorway rubbing sleep out of his eyes. When he saw her face, he rushed over and pulled her hands into his, urging her to talk to him.

"I don't know who it was. It was a man and he was warning me to stop asking questions about the burglaries." Cris whispered.

Michael sat still and let the anger seep out of his pores as he gripped her hands. "Who are you asking questions about, Cris?"

"What? I don't know what he means. What do *you* mean? I'm not asking anyone questions about the burglaries. After the other night when Mr. Lucas was so filthy nasty to me, I haven't said anything...." Her eyes cleared. "He was really snotty that night...why would he care about what I say, anyway?" Her brow furrowed and she bit her lip. She didn't notice Michael's discomfort or that he avoided her eyes.

"Let's go back to bed. That was awful. Maybe I should call the police? Or maybe not, he said he'd know if I didn't pay attention. My

God, this is reminding me of a very scary movie and I'm in it." She slipped her hands out of his and retraced her steps. She turned back to Michael who hadn't moved off the couch. "You coming, Michael?"

The next morning, Cris called Rainy about the late-night call.

"My darling, how bizarre. Yes, you should tell the police, for sure," she soothed. "Do you want me to call them?" Rainy's voice told Cris how worried she was and she was almost sorry she'd called.

"No, I'll decide what to do. The only people I've asked questions about or said anything to are you and Cole. I don't have any solid answers or clues; I just have questions without answers. I'm truly spooked, Rainy, but I am sure that was his intent. I know I can defend myself from most people but I'm no good if someone comes at me from nowhere like this. The other night at your party was bad enough with Mr. Lucas. I was very shocked just like you were. He is one weird man."

"I agree with you there, Cris. I'm sorry this happened, honey; please call the police about it?" She cajoled. "

~

The Golden Gate Bridge and twisting streets had welcomed Anna with open arms. When she'd breathed in the Bay's air, tiny chips of stress fell to the ground and she'd had an epiphany. She didn't feel lonely like she did living with Sam. How could that be? Walking through a city of strangers, she felt peace but walking through her life with Sam, she felt lost, lonely. She'd made her decision, but one step at a time. An audience waited and her notes were clearly outlined for her afternoon lecture.

Two hours later, the applause was deafening as Anna closed her notebook and stood back from the wooden dais. Suzanne Larkin, a large woman with graying hair, walked to the podium still clapping and smiling broadly. Reaching toward the microphone, she adjusted it to her taller height and nodded toward Anna before turning to the crowd.

"Thank you, Anna. It was a delight to have you here the past two days. From the feedback, I'd say we can't wait to get home to begin writing! Please think about coming back for the April seminar in Phoenix if you are between writing projects?"

Another round of applause greeted Susan's invitation and Anna answered sporadic questions, while watching the clock at the end of the large room. She was wilted. Finally, chairs scraped against the wooden floor; a human tide of writers eagerly prepared for lunch and goodbyes.

It was nearly an hour before Anna finally walked through the lobby of San Francisco's Fairmont Hotel. Leafing through the hotel's information brochure while she held the Tourist Booklet of San Francisco under her arm, she was ready. She attached a small flat purse around her waist, shrugged down her white sweater jacket and danced down the wide steps toward the crowd. Walking under wispy clouds, she watched them waltz along the skyline and enjoyed the late September air. She loved San Francisco and couldn't believe her good fortune when the Bay Writer's Colony asked her to teach a class at their annual writer's conference.

Despite the fact that she was elbow deep in her first novel, she was thrilled to leave the problems that plagued her at home. She had guiltily assessed the situation and admitted she wanted a divorce after agonizing months of indecision. The trip to San Francisco had shaken it all loose for Anna. No more smoke and mirrors. Was it Sam? His job? Was it Tess's graduation looming in a few months and her turning to Nicholas? She refused to bury herself in her work to avoid the truth one more day.

Mind chatter followed her down the streets of San Francisco, up and down the hills the city was known for and her brain chugged on. It might have been easier if she'd allowed herself the luxury of making close friends when they'd first moved to Lark Point. She should have a friend to confide in; she certainly couldn't share these thoughts with Tess.

A new inner peace triggered a smile and her cinnamon-brown eyes glowed. Yes, she'd run away. With the decision to divorce Sam made came a freedom of spirit she'd only dreamed of but had been too weak to pursue for fear of hurting those around her. But, it was time. She swung both arms out like an airplane, twirled around like a ten year old and headed for the Powell Street cable car. She heard the trolley clanging its bell before she got to the corner. She wrinkled her nose in disappointment when it lumbered down the street and passed her. It was filled to overflowing as the Powell and Mason car continued toward Lombard. She could see the man at the helm using his brake and telling stories as he yelled at honking cars to entertain his passengers. Anna smiled again.

She looked down at her tennis shoes, looked toward Fisherman's Wharf, gauged the distance and decided to walk. It didn't look too far. She turned back the way she'd come, walking west, then north along Hyde

Street. She passed narrow streets and saw houses built so closely together that they touched each wall, no spacing in between. Black wrought-iron grilles covered most windows, some doors, entrances to small bricked patios and around small balconies at upper windows. She inhaled the smells, reveled in the sights and felt a measure of contentment.

Her arms swung in tandem with her footsteps and the bay came into view. *Yes, it is like a window on the world.* She had the rest of the day and was determined to enjoy it. The all-day presentations had kept her busy the past two days. Now it was just her and the City. Shops emitted delectable smells all around her as she continued to wind her way up and down the streets. Feeling slightly winded, she admitted the distance to the wharf was deceptive as she walked down Hyde Street.

A small, corner grocery caught her eye and wakened her appetite. With a warm spinach calzone and bottle of water, she stepped onto the sidewalk and sat at a small table to eat before continuing toward the water.

Afterward, she saw Fisherman's Wharf adjacent to the bay. Tourist boats slipped in and out of the marina as the Golden Gate Bridge loomed beyond. Anna sat down on a round wooden stump by the dock to rest. People milled around her and seagulls dipped for fish and food on the ground. People-watching was one of her favorite pastimes. She studied large men, small children, trendy teens and harried mothers, mentally adding them to her character dossier list.

A second wind conquered her withered state, so she followed a long walkway that stretched into the Bay for sightseers. The seagulls screamed and left bird droppings everywhere but it didn't stop her. As she wandered across the bridge, she saw men fishing from the sides of the bridge, others flirted with girls, kissing, laughing. Pulling her camera out, she placed it on top of the rock wall and walked over to a Chinese fisherman. "May I take a picture with you?" she asked impishly.

He smiled a shy, toothy grin, nodded to his fishing pole and quickly pulled up the line. Anna hurriedly set the 10-second timer on the camera and approached him once again. She posed beside him, but to her dismay, he quickly placed a smelly, wriggling fish in her hand just as the camera clicked, visibly catching her by surprise.

The fisherman laughed and grabbed the fish from her hands. "You wanted a memorable one, right?"

Anna was surprised at his English and angry that she'd been profiling. With dubious thanks, she rubbed her sticky hands down the sides of her jeans and walked toward the end of the pier with her camera for a closer view of Alcatraz.

The man's laughter followed her. She glanced back at him and laughed too. "That should be a memorable one all right," she murmured.

Two hours later, lugging a bag of treasures inside her new leather backpack, she stood at the corner of Ghirardelli Square. Forcing her throbbing feet up the stairs to a small restaurant, she lifted her feet to a railing and ordered a glass of Pinot Noir. A pianist wound his music around her and she lifted her glass in a silent toast, mirroring his smile. An audible sigh escaped her. As she sipped the wine, she hungered for the sounds of a cable car, knowing the return walk would be impossible.

When her glass was empty, she strode away with her bags and contemplated a taxi in the early dusk. As she rounded the corner by the candy factory, she spied a small shop that lured her inside with colorful books propped up inside a glass case. Drifting into the warmly lit shop, she heard music playing that took her back to high school. *I feel like a child, always ready to be surprised and delighted.*

"The day just keeps getting better and better," she mumbled to herself as she marveled at the many rows of books around her. Old ones, new ones and collectibles lined the walls. *Rock Around the Clock* suddenly tumbled through the sound system and she danced in time with the beat as she bent down to a low shelf tripping her fingers over the titles.

"Well, it definitely is Anna Berg….and dancing too?" said a voice behind her.

Anna stood quickly. Dark hair slid across her face and her foot bumped into the leather backpack on the floor. Startled, she turned slowly toward memorable grey eyes with tiny flecks around the irises.

"Cole Nites." She stared.

"Yours truly," he said, enjoying her surprise.

Anna looked around him and then down at herself. She still smelled like a fish and felt utterly helpless.

"What are you doing here?" was out of her mouth before she could think properly.

"Why, Mrs. Berg, I followed you straight from Lark Point and let me tell you, you have given me a run for my money," Cole said quite seriously.

Anna stared at him blankly.

Cole laughed. "Actually, I watched you lift your glass toward the pianist and then saw you duck into this shop. I couldn't believe it was really you so I followed you to make sure I wasn't fantasizing," Cole said, his eyes half closed, smiling. Warmth consumed his body as he looked down at her.

Anna continued to stare, weak kneed. She reached down and grabbed at her bag, trying to get by him without the fish smell permeating their surroundings, books forgotten.

Cole followed her to the door, passing a heavy-set woman who stared at them through thick glasses.

"Are you alone, Cole?" she asked, suddenly intent on his answer.

"Yes." He looked at her, his grey eyes searching deeply into her brown ones as his voice dropped to a husky tone.

"Oh…." Her voice faded to a hushed stillness.

He lifted his right arm, pulled back the wrist of his dark grey sweater and looked at his gold watch. Glancing at her impishly and determined to spend the evening with her, he made a quick decision.

"Have you eaten?"

"Yes. I mean, well…a few hours ago I ate a calzone on the run…" her voice dwindled. She looked around her, the wind ruffling her hair as goose bumps rose along her arms. "Cole, why are you here? I mean, really?"

"Seriously, I have several clients in San Francisco and I usually fly down three or four times a year. I can't believe we chose the same weekend. Why are *you* here?" They stood on a wide cement sidewalk with people moving around them steadily. Cigarette butts littered the cement and great cracks, some hairline, reminded Anna of spider webs spreading in every direction.

She looked at Cole. "I gave a two-day presentation to writers on how to keep their notebooks filled with sights, smells and other things to enable them to better their writing habits. Since it is a slow process, learning how to write and then another process feeling confident enough to do it, I try to make a dent in writer's heads by telling them how I began to give them a jumpstart. It's over now and I leave tomorrow afternoon."

"So do I. The 3:20 flight with Southwest?"

"No, I'm on the 1:20 Alaska flight," she answered as she started to walk slowly toward the cable car station, knowing it was just around the corner. She was at a loss as to what to do next.

Cole settled her indecision quickly as he grabbed her elbow and steered her in the opposite direction. Her dark hair blew across her face as the wind decided to play and he pulled several curls away from her mouth.

Her breath hitched.

"Let me do three things for you, Anna," he said, pulling her toward a navy Mustang. "First, I'll take your bag and throw them in the car like this," he said, spacing the words evenly, tossing it in the trunk. "Then, I'll take you to my favorite restaurant and feed you," he continued while pushing her into the passenger seat. He walked swiftly around to the driver's door, got in, hooked up the seat belt and turned to her. "Then, I'll drop you off. Where are you staying?"

Anna felt the car close in on her. His eyes were just as beautiful as she remembered and his smile just as arresting. A weight pressed in on her as emotions filled her throat. She struggled and finally answered,

"The Fairmont."

Cole's eyes shifted momentarily.

"Okay, we're off. I know I'm not being fair, Anna. I'd allow you to go back to your hotel to change but I'm afraid you'll disappear on me..... again," he said quietly.

She lifted her head and said softly, "Please let me change, Cole. I'm sure you can smell the fish on my jeans. A fisherman thought he was being cute...I promise I won't disappear. Besides," she said with a laugh, "I'm suddenly starving. Where are you taking me?"

"You'll see. Do you have comfortable walking shoes?"

The car was filled with electricity as he headed toward the hotel. He was stunned. *A book store in Ghirardelli Square?* He shook his head. *Really? A book store.*

Thirty minutes later, Anna's stomach fluttered with misgivings. She felt her hands go up smoothing her hair again with fluttering fingers. She fluffed pillows, smoothed the bedspread, pushed her bag under the bed, rummaged for lipstick and finally ended up near the telephone. Without hesitation, she dialed home. Tess's cheery voice answered on the recording. Waiting impatiently for the beep, she said, "Hi. I'm off to dinner. My plane arrives tomorrow at 2:30. Alaska Air. See you then."

Cole tugged at the crease in his grey flannel trousers, straightened his red sweater and tucked in the white collared shirt beneath it. Pulling on his dark jacket, he grabbed his Fairmont keycard and dropped it into his pocket. He looked around the room, killing time, hoping he wasn't making a mistake. He refused to miss an opportunity to spend time with her. He wouldn't! *It's only dinner, for God's sake.* Time crawled toward seven o'clock and he was finally out the door, down one flight of stairs and knocking on Anna's door.

She opened it immediately, her face welcoming. She had changed out of her jeans and sweatshirt and into a soft yellow sweater and black slacks. He noted the black low-heeled shoes approvingly. Black and gold beaded earrings danced from her earlobes as she stepped into the hall.

"Mmmmmm...you smell good even though the fish stench was growing on me."

Anna smacked his arm. "A gentleman would *not* have mentioned that," she said with laughter spilling out of her near the elevator.

"Whoever said I was a gentleman?" He grinned and guided her toward the open doors, wondering if she had any idea how sensuous her voice was? He reached for her hand as they left the hotel but she gently pulled free. Walking along Clay Street and through Chinatown, they saw hundreds of burning lanterns while stock keepers pulled wares into their shops. Children ran through alleys and across streets and laughter embraced them.

The odors of cabbage, bread, fish and garbage filled the air, as they proceeded toward Columbus. The smell of garlic assailed them as they walked through Washington Square at the Italian section before turning up Pacific. Anna thrilled at the view of the Golden Gate Bridge.

Cole was quiet as they walked past a small alley up the hill towards Broadway. They laughed when they saw *Vesuvius* on Columbus, a bar that displayed North Beach artist's works, known to offer sanctuary and wine to writers and occasional curious tourists who ached to get away from their every-day lives. They agreed every city needed one.

Brandy Ho's sat between Grant and Columbus between Chinese apartment buildings and various cafes. Cole eased Anna into a brightly-painted doorway at 18th and Hartford; Chinese emblems covered the walls. The dim establishment was filled with diners. Tantalizing aromas made Anna's stomach yawn; her mouth watered. A gilt-edged sign above a red dragon spelled Brandy Ho's On a far wall, gigantic letters proclaimed, Absolutely NO MSG.

Anna glanced at Cole and smiled.

The restaurant was nothing like she expected. No glitter. No bells and whistles, just shelves full of glassware, soy sauce, plum sauce, then farther up the stairs, beer and wine. She was intrigued with the ceramic masks adorning the wall. Black and white plates sat on black and white table tops. Cole watched Anna take it all in. A friendly girl, about fifteen, led them to a table in a corner. She called Cole by name. He gave her a dollar and pulled out a wooden chair with a round, tufted black vinyl seat.

After they were seated, Anna was very much aware of Cole's disturbing good looks and the spark between them. Now uneasy, she knew it was not right, her being there. She was violating her own sense of honor, not just flouting convention. She'd fought his mysterious attraction since the night they'd met but it was just dinner.

"Do you keep track of the young girls in here or do they keep track of you?" she asked with a trace of laughter in her voice.

Cole chuckled and waved to the bargirl. He ordered two Bud Lights but received Michelob bottles. They laughed as a metal pot of hot tea joined the beers in front of them.

Anna glanced at the white paper napkins, upside down tea cups, chop sticks, and the checkerboard tiled floor with worn grouting. Lifting her eyes upward, she touched the pink Brandy Ho's logo with her finger.

Cole marveled at her curious expressions.

She brought her eyes back to Cole and chuckled. "Thanks, Cole."

"I make a point of eating here when I'm in town. I love the place."

"What do you suggest?" She studied the menu, reading the names of dishes while noticing the plate of hot oil on the table.

"Onion Cake with Peanut Sauce and Steamed Dumplings? After that, Chicken Salad, strips of fresh chicken with slices of cucumber and translucent rice noodles prepared from an old sauce recipe," he read."

"Sounds good to me," she said, matching his devastating grin.

The waiter nodded happily, pen poised.

"Make that two, Harry."

She stared after the man when he left them. "Harry?"

"I can't pronounce his real name," he said with a laugh, "so it's always been Harry to me."

After a bottle of beer, they relaxed, ate and listened intently to each other. They shared quiet moments, heard clattering dishes and friendly chatter while enduring the sweet pain of sitting close.

"This is hot." She licked her burning lips and blinked quickly.

"You can order the degree of spice you like. I ordered mild plus."

"Mild plus?" she blurted, eyes watering.

"Mmmmmm good," he said, watching her disbelief.

Later in the dimness, they spent half the night telling each other about themselves, their politics, their families, their tastes in music, food, books and movies; their interest in skiing, walking. Both hated jogging.

Anna was filled with yearning and the effect of the beer upended her thoughts. She felt steam and wanted to caress his foot with her toes. Instead, she steadfastly swallowed the rice, vegetables and peanuts before washing down small bits of chicken with her beer. *I like his face and the tenderness around his mouth when he smiles.* Although attracted, she knew she would do nothing about it. Unthinkable. Cole wasn't the type of man to bear guilt any more than she was. Stalemate. But for tonight, she'd enjoy magic.

Cole suppressed a desire to cover her fingers with his as she picked up her beer. *God, she's warmth cutting through snow.* He placed a hand over hers. "It's funny," he said in a soft, serious tone, "but I feel like I've known you all my life, Anna, and that's not a pickup line. I mean it."

His words caught her off guard; a part of her felt bewildered, ready to run. Yet another part felt comfort in his eyes, a feeling she could tell this man anything and perhaps everything. She cleared her throat and tried to suppress the roller-coaster emotion raging within her.

Their eyes met and locked.

Shivering as they left the restaurant just after midnight, Cole drew her thick sweater around her shoulders. His hands felt warm against her skin as they brushed the nape of her neck. Anna refused to analyze the sensation, the implications too disturbing. But it was impossible to deny he aroused sensations in her that Sam hadn't in years.

If their lives depended on it, she could not have recalled afterward what they ate or in fact, if they had eaten at all. The aromas of chicken and onions and the view of the open kitchen were lost to her.

Back inside the Fairmont, Anna was struck with the fact that Cole was still beside her. "You don't have to walk me in, Cole." she asked, suddenly wary.

"I've already been here two days," he answered, watching the emotions flit across her open face. He lifted a keycard. "406."

"Oh." She headed toward the elevator. When the doors opened, he followed her inside with a smile tugging at the corners of his mouth. The elevator descended in silence.

"Thank you for a fairytale evening, Cole. I loved every minute," she whispered. The beer seeped into her senses; she knew if the moment was right, if things were different, she would have reached out, touched him and silently invited him to kiss her.

"It doesn't have to be a fairytale; I want to see you again...can we share breakfast?" His thumb grazed her lips.

She sobered instantly and swallowed hard. Fighting not to curl her cheek into his palm, she said, "We can't, Cole. We're married and...we can't." She stepped off on the third floor, thanked him again, and let the elevator close behind her. She found her door and went inside.

Three minutes later, Cole knocked on her door.

It was thrust open.

Cole walked inside and closed the door. It clicked neatly, letting silence fill the room. Anna stared at him, circling him with her eyes. Her heart beat fast; sure he could hear it as she fretted inwardly.

Cole reached out his arm and pulled her to him slowly.

She felt tears clouding her eyes. "Cole, you don't want to do what you're thinking......"

"I don't believe I can stop myself."

"You should try."

"You're not moving away." His eyes met hers. "And you probably should." He gave her a wry smile.

"I am trying."

Then Cole kissed her, so gently she thought of butterfly wings. She reached up and kissed him again, letting her arms circle his neck as she breathed in his maleness. He groaned and pulled her tightly against him. "Anna, stay with me tonight."

Anna achingly stepped out of his arms and touched his face.

He didn't move. He couldn't. He looked at her questioningly, his hair falling just over his forehead. Her hand was warm on his cheek and he didn't want her to take it away.

"Cole, I'll just touch this moment," she said softly as she looked at him searchingly, "now please go."

"I want to see you," he murmured, moving his lips to her fingers.

Anna had always been good at resisting the persuasions of physical attractions. It had never been important to her before. But with Cole, each time she was near him, she felt herself slip a little farther, a little deeper. She ignored it as much as she could, but swayed toward him. "I'm not ready for this," she heard herself say.

"Neither am I." Still, he drew her closer, held her tighter. Cole reached up and covered her hand with his and moved his lips to her palm, staring into her soft eyes. He pressed his mouth gently into its smooth softness and brushed it with a silent kiss that seared her skin and caressed her soul before he let himself out.

She stared at the closed door. Then she locked it behind him and trembled. She wanted him. With massive effort, she shoved the treacherous feelings back down into the depths of her subconscious and turned her attention to a shower, bed and home.

ELEVEN

The landing gears made a thumping sound. She visualized, had hoped Tess was with Sam but knew she could not be so fortunate. No, she had to do this alone.

Get up. Get your bag. Walk down the aisle. Smile. Nod. Thank the stewardess. Smile at the pilot. Walk out of the plane. Anna felt like she was in kindergarten, her legs lead weights as she placed each foot in front of the other. She tried to keep Cole's face and sweet kiss from clouding her mind. It wasn't fair to Sam and he was waiting.

Anna's knees shook perceptibly when she saw him waving. She was glad Cole hadn't been on her plane. She could not have born it. She was shaken by the fact that she immediately compared Sam's smile to Cole's. Her decision had already been made. Before the kiss, she reminded herself. Tess was nowhere to be seen. She was, indeed, on her own.

"Hello, dear," Sam said as he reached down to kiss her. She gave him her cheek, chattered about the convention and pretended she didn't notice the hurt look on his face. They strode to the car in silence.

"Do you want to talk about it, Anna"? Sam said quietly as he pulled out of the airport lot.

"I'm tired, Sam. Let's talk at home, okay?"

The trip was silent and static. Anna gripped her purse and watched Sam's hands tighten on the wheel. The twenty minute drive seemed to take hours. She felt him glance at her periodically; her stomach muscles clenched.

"Sam, I want to go to *La Verdiere*. I'll make my reservation soon. Alone. Tess is so wrapped up in school and Nicholas; I doubt she'll miss me too much. I know I don't usually go until the middle of November, but I want to go sooner this year. I know your schedule has been tight lately too and I need to do some serious thinking." she said, as a brief shiver rippled through her.

Sam's gut twisted from belly button to backbone as he pulled into their garage without answering. He pursed his lips and grabbed her bags, before following her inside their home.

"Why go alone?" Sam's voice was an octave higher than normal.

"Sam. Sam. We're a mess. Don't deny it. I have finally faced reality. This constant denial is killing us," Anna said, begging him to understand and agree with her.

He followed her into their bedroom where she removed her jacket and kicked off her shoes. He began loosening his tie while his brain worked furiously, trying to form words that might allay his worst fears. He could not lose her. He would not!

Anna turned around and looked at Sam before sitting down on their bed for long minutes, feeling lost and confused. Her trip to San Francisco had made her feel happy and carefree long before Cole found her in that bookstore. Then her emotions spiked. Those heady emotions were now missing. She wanted them back. She'd once been happy with Sam and he'd been happy with her. Where had that love gone? Had it disappeared completely? Had she changed? Had he? Was Tess now their only link? She swallowed hard and squared her shoulders.

Sam watched her as another uneasy feeling gripped his gut.

"My darling Sam," she began. "I want a divorce so we can put an end to this sad charade. You know we've lived separate lives for months. Please understand I love you and hold our memories bittersweet but I am not *in love* with you anymore. The love we shared for so long is lost somewhere in the midst of your job, my writing, and the time that fell in between. We have both changed so much. Lately, you must admit, neither of us fit the mold we made for ourselves so long ago. The only thing we have in common now is Tess." She let out a long sigh and looked at Sam steadily as tears seeped past her brown eyes and ran down her cheeks in silent appeal. She caught a sob with her hand at the look of utter desperation and raw pain on Sam's face.

He was on his knees instantly in front of her. Both his hands grasped her rib cage and he buried his head in her lap. An anguished, "No!" escaped his lips as he held her captive and their tears flowed and mingled as one.

"I'm sorry, Sam," she crooned as she rocked back and forth, holding his head between her hands, stroking her fingers through his hair.

"No, darling," he cried again. "I'll try harder. I'll stay home more. I'll have Elliott hire an assistant. Tell me what I can do to mend our marriage." His broken words filled the room.

Anna slid gently from underneath Sam, rose and walked over to the window where she stood looking at a view she'd seen hundreds of times before. Eventually she turned and said, "How well do we really know one another, Sam? Truly know, I mean. There are secret parts to both of us. Parts we don't always know ourselves."

Sam looked at her without moving. Then, he gradually raised himself, took a deep breath and said he would be back in a minute. He agreed they needed to talk this through.

Anna stood still beside the window, more than relieved she had finally been able to voice her feelings. She felt the burden lift, glad a dialogue had begun and released her breath. *Now to tell Tess.*

Sam walked into the room with the sound of ice clinking in his glass. "Scotch, that's what I need first."

Anna looked over at the man she had been married to for nearly twenty five years. They stared at each other. Sadness filled her so thoroughly for the hurt he was enduring that she could barely move.

He lifted the drink to his lips, clearly at a loss for words.

She noticed that he held the bottle of Scotch in his other hand and he filled the glass twice more before he began to talk to her.

Anna said, "Maybe, if we........"

"....Anna, you wan' a divorce...I don't. I'll change..." he slurred. He poured himself another drink, sloshing it against the rim of his glass.

"I'm not implying you did anything wrong, Sam," She walked back toward the bed and sat down. "What I meant was......."

Sam lifted a brow questioningly.

"Sam," she whispered as she lifted her head to look at him once again. "This has been a long time coming. We haven't connected emotionally or physically for longer than I can count on two hands," she said quietly. "Dealing with our reality is far better than continual well-intentioned fabrications."

Sam jerked away quickly, spilling some Scotch on his pants. He looked down at the floor and then up at her, his brows drawing into a frown. "Is that what this is all about? Have I complained that you never want me in bed? Sex, is that it? Have you found someone who turns you on when I don't? Is that it?" He rasped out each word louder than the one before, his drunkenness shaping his words until he was almost yelling. Sam stared hard at Anna and he saw her face flush. Her stricken expression spoke volumes as far as Sam was concerned.

Suddenly Sam was incensed. Pacing faster and faster in front of Anna, he raved about his acceptance of her aloofness, his fear that she'd stopped loving him. "You're all I want Anna, don't you know that? It isn't just a matter of screwing. God, making love to you was once the greatest thing… lately you haven't enjoyed it. I know that. Is it just me, then? Not the fact that you have lost interest? You've lost interest in *me*? Not sex? God, I have been so blind in my love for you. Jesus Christ on a cross, help me understand this, Anna," he cried.

Anna's face was ravaged as tears ran into her mouth and her sobs shook her body. "No Sam, stop beating yourself up. Sam.....?" she cried, her eyes turning dark with regret.

He suddenly halted in front of her.

"You must understand, Sam. I feel trapped and we just don't fit one another anymore. You must see it!"

"Why?" Sam mumbled. "Why would you suddenly feel trapped and feel like we don't fit anymore?"

"Don't you think I've asked myself that a hundred times lately, Sam? I DON'T KNOW!" she snapped. "I just don't know….."

"Maybe you have a man hidden away....?" His voice drifted.

"Oh, Sam, pleeeeease….," she answered quietly, vehemently. Anna spoke slowly to give even greater emphasis to her words, "Sam it's as if our marriage has been held together by prayer and spit." Brown eyes stared into blue and time stood still.

He placed his glass on the side table thoughtfully. "You have to give me another chance, Anna, before you haul your ass off to France again. We c'n make our lives good again," he stated with deceptive calm.

Before Anna could guess his intent, Sam pushed her down onto their bed and began kissing her face, eyes and neck while whispering his love. "Can he do this? Does he touch you here...and here...?" Sam ran his hands over her body roughly and continued his onslaught until Anna began to push at him, grabbing at his hands, moving her lips away from his, pushing harder and harder as she tried to move out from underneath his large body. "Sam, please stop this!" she cried. "You're not yourself. You don't know what you are saying. I am not having an affair. Stop, Sam!"

Her words incensed him and he tore at her black slacks and yellow cotton sweater. She was stunned when it ripped off her shoulder and he kept on relentlessly. She rocked her head back and forth to avoid his Scotch-slobbering kisses and tried to block out his words. Words she had never heard him utter before were staggering her mind. Words filled with a coarseness and graphic vocabulary that made her feel sick. This wasn't the Sam she'd known and loved, but a revolting stranger.

Within seconds, he had climbed on top of her and his large body was ramming inside Anna again and again as salty tears streamed down her cheeks. She finally lay still and tried to pretend she was dreaming. This was happening to someone else. It was a movie scene. It wasn't real. It wasn't Sam and Anna. Anna could feel his fingers digging into her soft skin, as he seemed to devour her neck and shoulder with slobber and kisses, pawing her. His climax shook them both and he sobbed at the end.

Suddenly it was over.

Sam rolled off of her.

Anna squeezed her eyes shut, refusing to look at him. She heard him breathing hard beside her and knew he was staring at her, willing her to look at him.

"Oh my God, Anna, I'm sorry, sorry, sorry...." Sam cried brokenly. "Please forgive me. My God, what's happened to us?" His crying unnerved her but his words couldn't erase his actions.

Anna turned away from her husband, pushed her face into the white pillow case, feeling bruised and stiff, broken. Fury choked her.

"Talk to me, Anna," Sam begged urgently, soothingly, the rape instantly sobering him. He was like a small child needing forgiveness as he voiced his justification and sorrow simultaneously.

Anna lay still as a stone. Quiet pain engulfed her like a heavy fog over the ocean. No recriminations. No shouts. Nothing.

Finally, Sam left the bed, stood above her forlornly, reached out and gently covered her with the bedspread. He showered, dressed and looked at her from the doorway one last time. Feeling dead inside, he sat on the stairs a moment and buried his face in his hands. And then he wept as hope scurried and died.

Anna still had not moved when she heard him drive away. Her thoughts were dictated by all the words they shared. Her mind traced back over the past hour and skittered away from reality. She accepted some of the blame. She refused to accept more. She did not hate Sam. She just wanted to be away from the chaos despite his conciliatory words.

She pulled herself up off the bed and walked across the plush carpet in her bare feet. Her mind was blank except for her aching need for a shower, talking to Tess, and driving to Ashby, her port in the storm. She would leave the house before Sam returned. Tess would have to understand; but she would not tell Tess the worst; that would be forever between her and Sam she hoped. Only her and Sam.

Under the streaming hot waters of the shower, she bent her head backward, letting it pelt her face and eyelids. There were too many emotions swirling around her head for Anna to even feel vaguely in control of herself. Purple bruises were already forming on her thighs, belly and neck. She made an effort, straightening up and trying to untangle how she felt. And then came the ache. It caught her like a stitch in the side after a breathless run uphill. It hurt so sharply that for an instant she could not breathe for the pain.

Anna's letter waited inside an envelope for her daughter.

Airline reservations were made.

She would leave for France in four days. Her packed bags were in the trunk of her car. She kept her mind from thinking of anything except driving the two hours to Ashby and holing up in her cottage by the ocean. She would soon see *La Verdiere* and then she would be okay. France would soothe her hurt heart and soul. The beloved village would untangle her thoughts. She could find her life again and put her feet on the ground.

Please Tess understand, she thought fervently as she walked through her house, touching the candle holder Sam had brought her from New York, feeling the tablecloth that covered the antique table she'd kept from her Grandmére's home and running her fingers lovingly over the cabinet that once held her Hummels. Just a month, she promised. Then, she'd come back and work on the next step, but for now, France calls.

Anna replayed their conversation before the drinking, before the rape and she shivered.   It was strange that such simple declarative sentences were all it seemed either of them could summon to express the feelings that boiled inside each of them.   They'd lost what they'd had. Where had it gone, the love? Frozen. Never to thaw out again.

~

Cole tapped his fingers in time with the instrumental flowing from his car's XM radio. Glancing down idly to read the name of the tune, he chuckled. *Song for Anna* by Chet Atkins. How appropriate. A few moments later, he arrived home from the airport to an empty house and starving. He was glad Rainy wasn't home. He didn't want to face the woman after the searing kiss he'd shared with Anna. His chest hurt from the emotion and he knew he'd turned a corner in his life. Glancing around the kitchen, he admitted nothing in the room made him feel at home. Too much like a showplace in a magazine to suit him. It didn't feel cozy…had it ever? He peeled the ham from the package, added jalapeño cheese, mayonnaise, a sliced pickle and a hunk of lettuce. Grabbing a cold beer on his way into his study, he noticed the phone machine blinking so he sat everything down to punch the button. Maybe it was Rainy.

The voice sounded distorted, "….Hey, sweetie, I loved being with you last night. You made me feel like my insides were on fire. I wonder sometimes if I can handle the dead time in between our being together. Poetic justice…wouldn't you agree? Call me soon? I know Cole's gone and I'm alone. I love you." Cole heard a smooching sound.

Cole's eyes narrowed. The caller was obviously trying to change his voice since the timber was sporadic. It pissed him off. Grabbing his sandwich and his beer, he cautiously did not erase the message. He didn't want Rainy to know he'd heard it until he confronted her. *Poetic justice, my foot.* He paused and stared at the phone. *And, I'll be damned if that didn't sound almost like a woman's voice at the end.*

He took a deep breath and focused instead on the lovely Anna, the conversations, the laughter, the fullness of her…Was he really any better than Rainy, lusting after another man's wife? He gulped the beer and bit into his sandwich savagely

~

Her Audi traveled the serpentine road that late afternoon, its headlights leading her from the pain she left behind to her beach haven and the unknown. Anna pushed in a selection of music from her CD player and the sounds of Jacques Brel's *C'est la Vie* filled the car. The music welled up inside her as she rolled down the window so the scents might overwhelm her.

She drove quickly. She was glad she'd packed last week for France. Had she an inkling before her trip to San Francisco that she'd be running away? She looked at the clock. Six thirty. Sam's program was over. She idly wondered if he'd skipped it after the ra....... She stumbled over the word. Skip his program? Of course not. Yes, she was bitter. She wouldn't pretend otherwise.

Now sitting in her cottage, the *cafe crème* she'd made sat cold beside her chair. Her stomach rumbled but she ignored it. Beyond caring and still feeling numb, she willed Tess to call and could only assume she hadn't read her letter yet. She hoped her silence wasn't because of anger, but refused to dwell on Tess's feelings. It was time she focused on her own.

Her cell phone lit up in her lap and Tess's face filled the screen.

"Mom?" Tess's voice sounded fragile, shaking.

"Hi honey. I'm sorry I just ran out like that," Anna apologized hesitantly, "but I couldn't take the pressure anymore and dad and I…...."

"…Mom, why'd you leave so late? Dad's acting real weird and won't talk to me. Did you two have a big fight?"

"Yes," Anna snapped.

"But….." Her voice was shaky.

"Darling, listen, I'm flying to *La Verdiere* in four days. Please take care of things. I will call you again before I leave and keep in touch when I get there. Please understand I need to go. Support me, huh?"

"Are you and daddy okay…....?"

"Tess, I left your father. We've separated. I'm sorry but that's all I can tell you right now. He and I…........."

"What?! Come home, Mom. Don't go. You can work it out," Tess cried. "Dad needs you. He's drinking a lot and won't talk to me except to ask me every ten minutes if you called yet."

"No, Tess. You do not understand. I know this is hard on all of us and I wish I could've talked to you before I left, but.....but I am going.

Trust my decision, honey. I need you to understand. I love you. Please.......this is where your counselor training kicks in....." Anna said, pleading, her voice cracking.

Silence on the other end of the phone confirmed her suspicions. Her daughter was weeping.

A small choked voice could barely be heard, "Mom, dad is all alone. You're not being fair...just running away. What are you running from?" Tess's voice stopped wavering as sudden anger changed her tone. "There's something going on here. What is it?" she demanded.

"Tess, please...don't."

"Dammit, mother, you have no right to just........"

Anna snapped. "I don't have a right?! This is something between your dad and me, Tess. It's very serious. I'm hanging up now." She silently tapped the end button, turned off her phone and cried; tears from deep within, tears she couldn't stop, as she listened to the crashing surf outside her windows.

Later burrowed into her bed, she watched the night light slip through the blinds thinking she'd spent all the tears she had left but she was wrong. More tears welled to sting her eyes. Her chest spasmed painfully and she muffled a soul-deep sob in her pillow. She cried for Sam. She cried for their broken marriage. She lay there not knowing where she ended and where the world began. She wept out fear, disappointment, loneliness, and sorrow. Beyond the window, the hiss of sporadic traffic down the patent leather streets finally lulled her to sleep.

Ashby was a typical little coastal town, not very interested in the outside world. Although she was friendly, Anna's pain was of no consequence to them; the attitude was that stranger's deeds meant little. She was still an outsider. Despite seeing the residents while walking the beach or eating at the Bay House, her life was too private for them to question, so she was left alone for four days, mending and waiting for her plane to depart.

She confronted the bitterness that might have destroyed her and worked with it. She wrote sporadically, sometimes all night, walked miles on the beaches, read a lot and only occasionally wondered what she was going to do the rest of her life.

One day as the clouds rolled in and the white-capped foam scampered toward her, she pushed her toes into the sand slowly at first. Before long, she walked at a dizzying speed to stay one step ahead of her thoughts. By the time she reached the lighthouse, she was jogging and out of breath. The breeze had blown away all the clouds and the ocean spread out before her like a jeweled blanket. It reminded her of Monet's *"La Terrace de Sainte Adresse."*

Tess called twice, crying, surprising Anna as she'd always been a strong young woman. She was spending more time with Nicholas and kept busy with Taekwon-Do classes. She and Cris were becoming good friends and Anna was relieved.

But, mostly Anna drifted, too numb to let Tess's unhappiness break into her thoughts. *Where is my life? Where is the thrill of another day?* Sadness permeated her being and fed her hopelessness. It was all very well to tell herself to snap out of it. She hoped the answers that eluded her in Ashby would be found once she stepped on French soil.

Sam did not telephone.

After living in denial so long, Sam's actions had opened a dam in Anna. The rape etched her decision in stone where before it had been possibly drawn only in the sand.

Tess had driven to *Mirafleures* the day before but their visit was stilted and unsatisfactory. "Come on, Mom. Dad is so sad. Whatever you fought about must be resolved. Please tell me why you're separating."

Anna and Tess had sat on the patio overlooking the Pacific Ocean as seagulls swooped, dipped and fought for scraps of fish that littered the sand. The ocean had crashed while the breeze tossed their hair. They drank iced Limón. Tess had stared at Anna, challenging.

"It's too big Tess and final. I'm not going to live with your father again. It was just too big......" her words trailed off slowly.

"Don't be impractical, Mom," Tess said, chilled suddenly. "You and Daddy will go on forever. Please." Tess felt her world tipping and she had a sudden fear of being alone.

Anna reached out to clasp her daughter's hand, but Tess pulled away and stood quickly.

"Darling, try to understand my feelings."

"No, Mom. I can't believe you're leaving Dad over an argument," Tess cried, wiping her cheek and staring down at Anna's surprised face.

"What could he have done to you that hurts that badly? You seem so very angry and different somehow, Mom."

Anna's resolve snapped and she gripped the arms of her wicker chair, the knuckles turning white. "You do NOT want to know what the argument was about, my darling," she blurted, scarcely aware of her own voice. The words slipped out, just above a whisper and then all the fight went out of her. "I just want peace and quiet now....." Her physical bruises were purple and still hurt. Her emotional bruises she had no wish to share with her daughter.

Tess stared at her mother before turning toward the ocean, taking herself far away. She stood transfixed and felt like she'd opened the door to the wrong room. Certainly as though she had been made to dance to someone else's tune. She had asked and had received no answer. Several seconds of tense silence passed.

"There's something you're not telling me. I see that look on your face."

Anna's eyes pooled. "I can't say."

"Mom, you're sensitive, caring and honest. Why are you putting up this brick wall? It pisses me off that all of a sudden you're not open with me when you've always been before. What?" Tess implored her mother, "I'm a big girl now, a woman...."

Anna reached for her.

"Seriously, Mom?" Tess whispered. "Dad's like a caged lion at home......because he's there and you're here! That's why you should go back and talk......"

Memories that had been half buried surged forth with the clarity of yesterday. ".....Nobody's perfect, Tess, not your father and not me." Anna looked at her daughter steadily and chose her words carefully. "You're going to encounter disappointment throughout your life. Everyone does...and it would be good to know how to cope with it."

"Sounds like a great plan. I want to begin now, okay? ...Why are you going to *La Verdiere* early and why did you leave me this strange letter when you knew I'd be home an hour after you left?"

Anna hadn't answered.

Tess had sniffed before quickly turning into the house through the French doors. Anna's hand had dropped into her lap and convulsed into a fist as the sounds of spitting gravel echoed in her head when Tess had pulled away from the cottage.

Anna now sighed at the memory and stood, stretched her arms above her head and took her lemonade out onto the patio. The pale sunshine bathed her face as she sipped the cool liquid, although she was shivering within minutes. She felt like an old lady at a nursing home, wheeled into a garden for fresh air and she was furious at the analogy.

The day before her plane would fly her away from California, she took one last walk along the beach, past the restaurant where she waved at Sarah through the window. She began the trek northward, the sandy beach littered with sea grass, broken shells and spirals of yellow bubbles. It was a long, uphill walk that she took at a fast pace. She'd started out strolling again and her mind's crowded thoughts raced through her head. As she stuck each bare foot into the sand toward Haystack Rock, she felt bits of flying sand stick in her hair and eyes. It was getting colder now that fall was midway toward Christmas and she hugged her jacket tightly.

When she arrived at the rock, she found an outcropping where she could watch others walk the beach, follow children and toss sticks in the air for their dogs. When she saw the rainbow-colored kite, her thoughts immediately returned to Tess and the fun they'd shared so often on the same expanse of beach. Her heart tugged.

Using a walking stick, she dragged herself back to the cottage, all the while thinking how her life had spun out of control. She'd taken too long to see what was happening. Now she was beginning to realize that the only way to stop it….to bring her life back into balance, was to be bold. She hoped Tess wouldn't get caught in the crossfire but the girl would have to struggle through it. Anna would learn to be herself without anyone's permission.

Anna rested for awhile, staring at the ocean from her cottage. An orange-pink hue engulfed the horizon, reflecting off the water in shimmering light and dark patches. Warmth stirred inside her, something she had been out of touch with for years. She smiled optimistically, recognizing the courage in her decision. She felt an ounce of hope that she might find music in her soul again under the layers of buried unease.

She wasn't like Cole and Sam, she thought. Boldness wasn't in her nature but she would sure as hell put it there. "Stand up for yourself," Grandmére said a hundred times. "Do what you must for your own heart.

All else will follow, *petite-fille*." She'd said it when Tess was born, evidently seeing something in Anna's life that pulled the words forth. Anna had laughed at her then. She wasn't laughing now.

~

Sam's drinking escalated.

Tess didn't know how to support her father; not even Nicholas seemed to lift her spirits. She was angry at Anna for leaving. She was angry at Sam for letting her go. When she heard him come in the house at ten o'clock a week after she'd tearfully left her mother in Ashby, her nerves were too jangled to make sense.

She followed the sounds of ice clinking. "Dad?"

Sam turned toward her quickly, his glass midway to his lips. "Hi Tess." Sipping the scotch, he walked slowly into the living room.

"Dad, please go get Mom." Her eyes begged him to pay attention.

"I can't, Tess." He couldn't look Tess in the eye.

"You mean you won't. I know I'm acting like a little kid, but if there's anything I can do to push you, I will." She stared at him angrily.

He lifted his head to look at her. "No," he said quietly. "Not because I won't. Because I can't. I treated her very badly."

"But she'd listen to you, Dad!" Her voice broke.

His face blanched. Taking a deep swallow of the drink in his hand, he pulled his thoughts together. "Would *you* listen to someone you loved and trusted who threw you on a bed, held you down against your will, whispered filth and raped you? When you begged that person to stop and he wouldn't...and he just kept pounding into you? Would you listen, Tess?" He covered his face with his hands.

"Oh. My. God." Speechless, she stared as rage slashed through her. Her legs weren't much steadier than her stomach and there was a headache brought on, she supposed by the shock, kicking behind her eyes.

He began talking slowly, squeezing his eyes closed while sipping his scotch. He told Tess all the reasons why it happened, the drinking, the anger, the hurt. He blamed his job, his lack of attention, their months of unhappiness, remoteness. A dam had been unleashed as he replayed the scene over in his head, wondering what he could have done differently to avoid the drunken rape. Could he live with his undeniable guilt?

Tess sat so still he forgot she was there until she jumped up with a sob. She didn't know where to turn. Like a caged animal, she twisted around in circles. Then Sam was behind her and she froze, panting. Her white face had tears streaking down her cheeks.

"Go away, Dad."

"Tess......."

"Leave me alone!" she snapped.

"Let me explain what I was feeling."

"Why?!" she thundered. "What was Mom feeling?" She whimpered, "And I left her angry to commiserate with *you*. Now she's in France. She refused to tell me what happened. I begged her but she didn't even try to explain. She just let me hammer away at her. She was hurting so much and she still protected you. Oh, God," she sobbed and covered her face with her hands.

Sam reached for her, came nearer and put his arm around her shoulder, held her. She sniffled into his neck and Sam felt her arms go around his waist; small hands rubbed his back as their tears ran together.

Neither believed for a moment the issue had died with the conversation.

TWELVE

She arrived in Paris on a cool morning as the sun rose above the city. Anna passed quickly through Customs where she took a shuttle train from the Charles de Gaulle Airport to the Gare de Lyon on Boulevard Diderot and before riding the fast train to *Aix en Provence*.

"*Je suis Arianna Berg*," she said, glittering with eagerness. "*J'ai reserve le automobile*." The girl understood. I am Arianna Berg. I reserved a car. She was soon in the driver's seat of her tiny, blue Fiat, turning toward her most favorite place in the world, *La Verdiere*.

She meandered northeastward through the countryside; the car window was down a crack, just enough for the whiff of Acacia to tumble through and tickle her nose. She felt an immediate peacefulness settle across her features. Memories of past visits to *La Verdiere* in springtime cascaded across her mind like a cacophony of spring flowers. Now, in October, she could almost hear the breeze sighing through the grasses as she drove leisurely toward the quaint village. The miles ticked away as she headed for the only place on earth she believed in childhood dreams.

She laughed when a young man honked brashly and shot around her like a bullet. He passed her with a wave and a smile and disappeared from sight before she blinked twice. Anna passed through flat plains interspersed with hills and mountains. Quaint villages dotted hillsides as she meandered toward *La Verdiere*, the village of her youth, the flicker of blue sky above the terracotta roofs.

She missed the yellow mustard flowers, *moutarde fleurs* and red poppies, *coquelicots* that bloomed in springtime but a few wild flowers still edged the roadside. She felt a brief euphoria from the scents, the nip in the air and her palpable excitement.

The small village of *La Verdiere* loomed ahead. The castle atop the hill silhouetted against the blue skyline. Anna squinted as the afternoon sun lowered behind the small stone houses where flowering vines laced around doorways and the sign of *La Verdiere.*

Slowing, she made an abrupt right turn into the village and pulled over into the first cobbled street wide enough to park. Perched in three tiers on a charming hilltop, the village was a series of compact, rose-colored buildings. Protected in its spiraled setting against the fierce *mistral,* the village was tightly spaced; its narrow, rock and pebble streets looked more like alleyways than main avenues.

She dropped her anxious fingers into her lap as the keys jangled in the silence. Her eyes strayed to trailing vines climbing up the side of the nearest stone building. Pots of vibrant fall flowers sitting a foot apart along the nearest porch hummed with color beside a small arched door set inside a foot-thick cranny. The air was fragrant with lavender and olive trees. Garden scents mingled on the afternoon air with cooking aromas.

Anna *fondit en larmes*, burst into tears. "I'm home...but not home," she whispered. She swiped her cheeks and put the car in gear. The village looked beautiful in the late afternoon sunshine; cherry-colored roof tiles and a warm honey glaze rose over the beige stucco walls. Her roof was barely visible through the thick foliage as Anna drove slowly up the curving gravel driveway past the swimming pool to be welcomed by the large stone terrace like a long-lost friend.

"*Et, voilà!*" Anna crunched to a stop and jumped out. She gaped at it. Tall yellow flowers pushed out of a tangle of bushes lining the driveway that sprouted every few feet from the car to the house. She was surprised they were still blooming in October.

The stone house sat on the outskirts of the village where one could stretch the eye for miles toward the Mediterranean. Arched bricks fanned each doorway, window wells a foot deep framed by shutters could be closed from inside. At the end of the sitting room, double French doors fit with antique hardware led out to the garden; light window coverings hung from dowels over the five-foot tall windows. A place to dream about.

Anna dropped her bags and ran her hands across the freshly cleaned armoires, the piano and leather-bound books in the tall bookcase. She whispered hello to her grandparents and tears welled up again.

Food? Sure enough, inside the cold fridge held a baked chicken, slices of ham and chilled Chardonnay. Pots of jam, butter and bottles of water shared the shelf along with custard topped with berries. On the sideboard, a large jar of mushrooms swimming in olive oil, two long baguettes, fresh pears, late-harvested strawberries and a small wheel each of Gouda and Edam cheeses waited. Aurore, friend, housekeeper and confidant, had put her loving touch on everything. The note was propped against the window sill next to a lavender-filled vase which read, *Bienvenue à la maison, ma cherie* – Welcome home, darling.

Outside, the mid-day sun of Provence warmed Anna's cheeks. Birds chirped in the magnificent canopy of two olive trees that hung over the patio. Anna's eyes turned warm as peace invaded her mind and limbs, calming her whirling thoughts. Her tired body sagged, belying the tenseness within.

She glanced toward the courtyard and visualized Grandmére laying out plates, grandfather pouring red wine in little glasses. She could almost hear the voices and laughed, wondering where the napkins were stored? *Ceci est votre serviette. Il est pour la semaine.* Here is your napkin. It is for the week. Each fit into fabric envelopes where they resided between meals. She pushed open the arched gate flat against the outer stone wall. Anna smiled at the old bell that hung above the round table, the antique buffet with the candelabra sitting in the center, the candles unlit. The dining room was cozy; the table covered with a flowery-sprigged oil cloth.

Thoughts of her daughter stilled her wandering mind. Tess would understand……eventually. The last word came unbidden. She sank onto the chaise beneath the arched window and inhaled deeply, slowing at last. Anna had been caught in a world filled with people. She'd rushed through daily routines, living for Sam and Tess. Rushing. Rushing. Rushing.

Her mind skittered toward Sam. *Fury spit through her. I hate him. No, I don't.* She sighed. *......but I will never live with him again.*

Cole. *No.* His face crushed into her thoughts. *Is this what it's all about then? A married man?* "Holy shit," she spat out. Jumping up, she felt tears against her eyelids for the hundredth time. The man was messing with her head. "I just want to be me!" she said aloud as she flung herself toward the house. *I don't want to be lost anymore. Cole..... Dammit.*

The next day, turning into the colorful French kitchen filled with copper pots and warm antiques, Anna quickly packed a lunch of sliced ham and cheeses along with the fresh baguette bread lying beside her backpack. Yes, the backpack. She remembered buying it in San Francisco just before....Cole again. She grabbed a bottle of Rosé, as light as lace. *Maybe I'll just drink it out of the bottle.* Laughing at the vision, she wrapped up a glass along with her phone, iPad and light jacket.

An hour later, she drove into Aix en Provence, found a little park beside a fountain and uncorked her wine. Carefully, she laid out stuffed olives, dark and purple in their briny juices, a long baguette and a hunk of grapes. Next to this, she sat with her glass of wine. Gathering her thoughts, she began to write. Unwinding as birds sang, she ran the tip of her finger along the rim of her wineglass and pondered again the intricate emotional web she left behind. A lump worked its way up into her throat. "I know this place can restore my balance and soothe my soul." She sipped again. "….Yes, of course it will."

She shivered. Gathering the remains of her lunch, she walked down cobbled streets and found a flea market where she lost herself for another hour before ambling back to the car. She scanned the newspaper she'd found, read about Digital Equipment Corp downsizing their sales force. Then, Dow Jones & Co., publisher of the Wall St. Journal, said earnings fell. Anna's head swirled. She tossed it into the car, leaned her head back and closed her eyes. *The world's still moving and so will I.*

A fountain sat in the corner of a large courtyard near her car. She saw a homeless man murmuring quietly to himself. On the other side of the fountain pigeons flocked in frantic motion. Someone had tossed a croissant and they were shredding it to pieces. Several teenage girls in black leotards stood nearby puffing madly on cigarettes, staring at their phones. A man leaned against a wall playing music on a harmonica. The vision calmed Anna and a tentative smile lifted her spirits as she drove by.

For the next week, she underwent deep soul-searching such as she had never known, going back over the entire course of her life with Sam, who'd always been gentle. The more she pondered, the more she realized it was his self absorption with being a news star. It wasn't for her or Tess. It was only for Sam. It had been unfair to expect her to stroke his ego continually when it was the very thing that started their lives crumbling.

At that same moment back in California, Sam sat hunched in his easy chair with a Jim Beam while he smoked cigarette after cigarette. Desperately casting about for some magic beam to turn back the clock, he stubbed out the last cigarette. He sat there all night while stubble darkened his jaw and the sun rose behind him.

Sam had always been obsessed with the fear of failure. His father, a journalist now dead over twenty years, had never stopped pumping his diatribes into his son's brain, an almost insane belief in the need to achieve, to succeed. Above all else. "No matter how much success you have," his dad often said, "life can pull the rug out from under you if you aren't diligent. Don't relax for a moment once you get there, son. Don't rest on past laurels; keep striving for the next story because one mistake in this business and you lose."

Sam had grown up with the conviction that any success he achieved was merely a precarious toehold in life. He must not relax his determination to continue onward, upward.

He wasn't sleeping well even before the *event* as he called it. When he ate, he existed on antacids. At home, he was resented and misunderstood. He slurred loudly, "Well, dad, I listened to you. Now I'm alone in a house with a wife across the ocean that I raped and a daughter who thinks she's unimportant but hey! I have a successful job." He held up the glass of whiskey with a look of infinite sadness. "Salud, Dad."

~

Meanwhile, another man was thinking about Anna Berg. If he heard Tess's voicemail message say, "Anna's gone for awhile," one more time, he'd scream. *Gone where??* For some weeks, he'd indulged himself with the notion that she might call him. Lunch? Coffee? But eventually he admitted she wanted no more to do with him. And he felt an inexplicable sadness in losing a gem he'd never had in the first place.

One morning, two weeks after Anna disappeared, Cole sat at his desk moodily sipping coffee, nodding at Darrin as he walked by his doorway. He fought a gnawing sense of regret. By lunchtime, his reports left unread, he gave up. Whatever was done was done. He would go on. Standard operating procedure; keep his head in the sand? Jump off the bandwagon? He sat quietly and let the phone messages stack up on his desk. He was a lawyer. Good God he was pining after a married woman and he wasn't free to do so. How old was he anyway? Sixteen.

~

Anna's days were slow and lazy. She felt like a flower blooming in the sun under the French sky, *Épanouir*. She had done nothing more complicated than take long walks along the red-dirt road beside the house and think. In the evenings she had listened to music, read books and watched French television. She had gone beyond the wish to throw dishes, stomp around the house, smash everything in sight, hurl food or toss clothes. She was, however, becoming a stir crazy.

By the end of the third week, Anna boarded a fast train to Paris. The lilting French conversations pulled her into a safe harbor. When the train slowed, she grabbed her shoulder bag and laughed at the absolute rashness of going to Paris for a couple of days.

Once entrenched in the Hotel Studia in the Quartier Latin District at 51 Boulevard Saint-Germain, she propped herself up in a soft wing chair. As she scribbled down her thoughts, night shadows filtered into the bedroom. During such uninterrupted moments, her hand raced to keep up with her mind, frantically keeping pace as words filled the pages. She felt the fusing of her story turning into an integrated book and time stood still.

The view from her hotel window the next morning showed her a sky leaden with a threat of rain, so she pulled a rain jacket out of her bag. It was early October and the sun was still bright but the air was cool. She deposited her key with the blonde woman at the front desk, gave her a cheery "*Au revoir!*" and trotted down the hotel steps.

Turning west on Boulevard Saint-Germain, she walked to Rue Saint-Jacques. She passed a boulangerie, a charcuterie, La Poste (post office) and dodged pedestrians. Intent on walking to Notre Dame, she inhaled dizzying scents, soon spying the Seine. She grinned as she crossed the river. Boats moved slowly between the left and right bank. Ah, the wonder of Paris. Seeing the tall cathedral spires took her breath away as she neared Notre Dame. Bird droppings covered the sidewalk and adjacent statues as she stared at the gargoyles far above the awesome cathedral. When she walked through tall wooden doors, candles glowed and sunlight angled through small, paned windows. People were a hundred deep, some sitting on wooden chairs, the remainder standing at the back. Feeling the rush of reverence, Anna's breath hitched as magnificent choir voices filled the cavernous room. She met the kind eyes of a large woman in front of her, who made room for Anna to move closer.

Anna was caught in the silent crush as others moved forward. She realized she was standing in the Holy Communion line. *I'm not Catholic. Should I?* Then, she was next. The priest smiled, held the wafer aloft and said, "The body of Christ." Mimicking others, Anna whispered, "Amen" and extended cupped hands. The priest placed the small opaque wafer in her hand and she moved on. A small glass of wine was lifted. She sipped as choir voices rose above Anna's pounding heart.

She shuffled past stone columns, side chapels filled with tables, statues and holy pictures. Flickering candles beckoned. Her searching eyes found the donation box, so she scrambled for a coin. Her elbow brushed a young woman as she lit a candle from a burning flame. Anna knelt and closed her eyes. She hadn't been to church in ages and wasn't sure she remembered how to pray. But that day in Notre Dame, her vision blurred.

She was so tired of tears. Once outside in the sunlight again, she walked across the park beyond the huge stone rider on his mount. Standing at the stone wall above the river, she stared down into the Seine, unaware of the milling crowds and inhaled deeply.

Paris, the city of lovers. Her fingers caressed the stone wall as she looked across the street to see a Kodak shop on one side and to her abrupt right, a Metro station and farther still, a boulangerie, bakery. Next to the bakery was a wine shop, *Le Vin*, beside a deli. She wanted to step into all of them, but first she'd find a cafe, a chocolate croissant and *café au lait*.

Paris was not clotted with tourists but there were enough of them to turn the city into a romantic enchantment. She mused, when one goes to Paris, anything can happen and memories are created for any number of reasons...all because it happened in Paris. The city was a balm to her heart, a place to heal from Sam's attack and from Tess's reactions.

An internet café caught her eye and before she could change her mind, she dropped in the coins and logged onto Gmail. She grimaced at the foreign keyboard but smiled. There were twenty emails from Tess. She apologized for her anger and hoped Anna was unwinding, she loved her but wished she was home. Anna tapped a paragraph, sent hugs and signed off. Things would be right again.

"Now I'm going to Paris!" She whispered aloud with a touch of defiance and started walking. Something she'd read once said the longer one walked, the smaller one would become. *Good, after eating chocolate croissants and drinking steaming café au laits I'll need to walk a lot.*

She located the St. Michelle Metro to visit *Montmartre* but headed for *Sainte-Chapelle* first, the church of stained glass windows. It was a royal, medieval Gothic chapel, located near the *Palais de la Cité* on the *Île de la Cité* in the heart of Paris. Strengthened with resolve and tense with haste, she felt like a drawn bow as she found her favorite spot in Paris.

Suddenly, she hugged herself and spun around. She would sweep the cobwebs from her mind and push away whispering voices and galloping thoughts of Sam, Tess and Cole, the most intriguing man she'd ever met. She struck a pose for only a moment before listening to the grand City call her.

She walked most of the day. As Helen Keller said, "Life is either a daring adventure or nothing." When she reached the *Champs-Élysées*, she stopped to gaze up that long wide boulevard to stare at the *Arc de Triomphe* in the distance. She could barely see the tricolor flag caught suddenly in a bullet of wind, causing her to smile suddenly.

She found a sprawling café that first night in Paris and treated herself to an inside dinner, knowing it was more expensive than ordering and walking away with it. She started with a thin soup, a puree of vegetables, carrots, potatoes, zucchini and onions followed by pieces of crusty bread. When they removed her plate, they brought a casserole of zucchini with cream sauce and fromage, the soft cheese melted and browned to perfection. Then, a plate was placed in front of her with scalloped potatoes, a cold rice salad with tomatoes and cucumbers. A lamb chop nestled nearby. More steaming hot bread. She picked up a piece of bread and dipped it into the casserole sauce. A cheese plate of Camembert cheese stared at her. She was stunned when he returned with fresh grapefruit and baked apple pieces. And wine.

Afterward, the waiter, with a serious nod of his head, brought a sample tray of dessert. Anna chose Calvados, an apple brandy from the French region of Lower Normandy, took a sip and decided it was by far the finest liquid that had ever passed her lips. He brought her chocolate truffles; she popped one in her mouth. At once, the chocolate began melting and her tongue involuntarily curled greedily around it. She didn't give a toot that it cost her a week's groceries back home, but she was so full, she could barely waddle away.

Her feet throbbed. Despite being full of croissants and Panini's, Anna promised herself one more day. She was finally starting to hear the music. And she'd missed the music. She slipped into a sidewalk café near the Sorbonne and sipped chilled *citron pressé*, a refreshing non-alcoholic citrus beverage using only lemon juice, water, and sugar, a French twist on the classic lemonade drink. Leaning back, she watched people stream past. A man near the door slipped a *Gauloise*, from a Mediterranean-blue packet, between his lips. After lighting it, he lingered over the first deep inhalation. She took a long swallow of her drink, enjoying its tartness and studied the man's peaceful enjoyment.

Anne Murray's voice intruded gently from the music system......a song Anna knew well about crying a tear, about her sweetheart wiping it dry… she was confused and he'd cleared her mind….." Anna whispered the words along to the end. She knew them all. Her throat was too choked to swallow any more of her drink. She sat her glass down on the small bistro table, glad to be in a corner. "I needed you and you were there….." Her eyes blurred.

After all her soul searching, she knew she was singing about Cole Nites, not Sam Berg. She sniffled and heard Anne Murray finish the song about him giving her strength to stand alone again…. to face the world on her own again and needing her….over and over again.

Music now stirred up too many emotions. She'd been looking for the music in her life and it was now overcrowding her thoughts. She'd listened to Jacques Brel stirred by his intensity. She couldn't keep her shoulders still as she chair-danced to Yves Montand. Then, Charles

Aznavour's voice crept into her soul and his music raced through her head. In spite of being drunk on music, Anna knew it was time to go back to Lark Point. Despite Paris being a mesmerizing jaunt down quaint and enticing alleyways filled with patisseries, charcuteries and chocolate shops and tiny boutiques that only sold enameled porcelain brooches, she was homesick. Rocky curbs and cobblestones made her smile but her home was in California.

~

During the weeks of Anna's absence, Sam spoke with Tess at length. He'd finally accepted Anna would not return home as his wife. Nicholas was always under foot and seemed to soothe her and for that he was thankful but he also knew until Anna returned, his daughter could not be consoled.

His news show was ramping up and he was relieved to stay busy. The hours were long but he had nobody to worry about him being late. Nobody to fix his meals, do his laundry or listen to him at the end of the day. He accepted he had a burning desire to be the best damn journalist he could be. It wasn't just his dad pushing him. It wasn't that he'd majored in journalism. It wasn't that his ego overwhelmed logic. He loved what he did. He loved finding answers to questions, solving cases, beating the odds and whipping the Democrat into second place, moving readers to television news.

But was it worth his marriage? No. Now it was too late and he would concentrate on his daughter. She was a young woman on her own in so many ways. But he couldn't stop remembering the sweet times when she'd rushed toward him at the end of the day with small up-stretched arms. It had made his day worthwhile all those years. Yes, he loved his job, but he loved Tess more and he'd be damned if he'd lose her too.

Tess counted the days until her mother's return. Skype was impossible. No internet service in *La Verdiere*. She wondered if her mother would forgive her angry outbursts. Would her mother forgive her father? She doubted it. Rape was rape in any language regardless of whether you are married to your partner. It was too sad to fathom.

With a pinched expression, she sat cross legged, writing an essay on the laptop balanced precariously on her knees. Words swam before her eyes. Even with Nicholas, she was subdued. When her mother left, she'd feared life would never be the same. She wanted her mother home. At least she'd finally answered her emails. She angrily stubbed her cigarette out as the doorbell jerked her from melancholia.

"Hey!" As she pulled Cris into the house, her features cleared. They'd become close friends during the past months, drawn together by Taekwon-Do. Tess was glad Nicholas suggested she learn self defense and Cris's friendship was a bonus. They liked each other immediately and Tess was now working toward her Blue Belt. .

"Cris, so glad to see you…I'm really in the dumps!"

Cris breezed into the living room radiating her usual warmth, clutching a Trader Joe's bag. Her frizzy hair bounced as she plopped down on a cushion beside Tess on the floor.

"Wine. Michael's off somewhere so here I am. Glad you're home," Cris deadpanned before squealing, "I got it!"

"You got the part in *Passport Passport*!?" Tess screamed.

"Yes, yes, yes!" Cris responded. She genuinely liked Tess. She didn't have to stay on constant guard like she did when she was with Rainy or Michael. She pulled the bottle of two buck Chuck out of her backpack as Tess ran for a corkscrew and glasses. Cris watched her young friend skim across the room, admiring Tess's unflagging vitality.

Tess opened. Cris poured and they tapped the rims. The clink filled the empty spaces of the house and they both giggled.

"Here's to *Passport Passport* and to us." Cris toasted.

"Yes, to that and to us," Tess mimicked.

They sipped the wine and tapped rims again. It didn't take them long to finish the bottle. Her essay forgotten, Tess leaned her head back and closed her eyes.

"Heard from your mom since that last email?"

Tess blinked rapidly. "No."

Cris patted her hand, a flicker of sympathy crossing her face

"She'll be home soon, sweetie."

Tess smiled unsteadily. She couldn't explain to Cris why her Mom left; her answers would be garbled. Relationships were hard, she knew that. She loved Nicholas. Would they end up like her parents? A marriage was supposed to be solid…last forever!

The wine brought introspection. Tess turned to Cris, "What does Michael say about your trips with Rainy? I know it's fun for you, but ......"

Cris turned thoughtful. "He doesn't like it. But we do as we please. We aren't married, you know? We argue about it sometimes. I've learned to wait until the last minute to tell him if Rainy asks me to go with her on an insurance investigation. I must have gypsy blood. If someone says go, I pack bags and Michael can't stop me..."

"Well, you've been together so long..." Tess said. "You're an established couple, no matter what you say about marriage.

"Not really, Tess. We share expenses. It's just been a few months that, well...our relationship changed. With police swarming the theater since your dad connected the patron list to the thefts, life has been a nightmare. Everyone is jumpy. You'd think the cops could nail down this mess since it's been nearly a month. Michael is jittery and I think......."

Tess interrupted her. "Cris, did you know Nicholas and Michael meet a guy on Saturday mornings at that old building by the theater? I've seen them when I grabbed breakfast at the deli before classes......."

Cris sat up, suddenly alert. "Who was the other guy?"

"Mmmmm," Tess answered, blowing smoke away from Cris, " I asked Nicholas. He seemed......well, sort of strange. Surprised or a little argumentative actually...." Tess creased her forehead. "Come to think of it, he never did answer me."

THIRTEEN

Anna's breath hitched, glad her feet were on American soil once again in more ways than one. The first thing she did after arriving back at *Mirafleures* was to walk across the sand to the Bay House and find her friend, Sarah. Her feet sank in the loose sand nearer the grasses but she didn't care. She'd slip off her shoes at the back glass door and grab them on her way out again. France had been exactly what she needed to decide she would make choices for herself, nobody else. She had to go all the way to France to hear her grandmére's voice remind her to "be alive while you're alive." She finally knew what she meant and no longer walked the path of confusion.

Sarah joined Anna briefly at her small, linen-covered table where the ocean's view blended into a beautiful sunset. She patted Anna's shoulder. "Here's your shrimp salad and a nice chilled glass of your favorite Chardonnay, darling. It is so wonderful to have you back again. May I sit a moment? I want to hear about *LaVerdiere* and find out why you looked like you lost your best friend a month ago and tonight, you look vibrant and ready to take on the world. Was it a wild fling?"

Anna laughed.

Sarah sat across from her with her own glass of wine and they talked together for over an hour. Taking a measured sip of wine, she looked at Anna above its rim, a sorrowful look on her face. "You should have a life, a real life. So, Sam is not the one. I am sorry, *mon petite.*"

Anna swallowed the lump in her throat. "I came to the same conclusion. I will not return to him. It is definitely over." Glancing out the large glass windows, she stared at the breaking waves and watched darting seagulls hunt for dinner. The sun was a large ball of fire on the horizon. The day was waning just like her marriage had already.

"You will meet a man someday, little one, even if it is far from your mind today," Sarah said as her husband came to stand beside them.

"I hate to break up this little *tete a tete*, ladies. Sorry, Anna… but these guys want food, Sarah," he said with a twinkle in his eye. He raised his right hand as if to invite her to dance.

"Okay...okay...he'll work me to death one of these days, Anna," Sarah said, beaming at her husband and waving a finger as she walked toward a group of men standing at the bar.

Anna shook her head as if she was dreaming as she watched Sarah walk away. One of the men at the bar resembled Cole. She chuckled at her wild imagination before ticking off the first thing on her mental list.

First, Tess. She was relieved Sam had talked to her during her absence. She'd been very apologetic when Anna called her earlier. Although hurt by their divorce, Tess wasn't stupid. She'd noticed some of the problems for longer than she cared to admit. She knew about the rape.

Second, Sam was another story. He was moving out of their house in two days. She would stay in Ashby before returning to all the changes.

Third, her book. One piece still missing…that elusive court scene. She toyed with her salad, sipped more wine and glanced toward the bar again. It was getting noisier. Turning her head to stare outside at the surf, she saw her reflection in the window. *How I love the beach.* She felt as if the breakers vibrated through her soul. Like coming home. Like a fresh smelling flower after a spring rain. Like seeing a rosebud open for the first time. *Thank you, grandmére, for leaving me Mirafleures. I feel you.*

More noise from the bar attracted Anna's attention, knotting the muscles in her neck. The man standing at the end of the bar certainly did look like Cole. Anna shook herself. Holy Christmas. She was seeing him everywhere; the way a man stood, smiled, laughed, even the way he tipped his head. She stared. *My God, that guy really does remind me of Cole.*

He was number four on the list. Slightly confused, she sighed deeply, lifted her glass again and stared out the window. She saw a muted reflection of candles with wavering lights flickering back at her. The ocean view blended with reflections within, including Cole's face? She turned around slowly and met his wide grin.

An answering smile trembled over her lips. "Cole," she said breathlessly.

"Anna, you *aren't* a mirage then? I thought you dropped off the face of the earth. I called your home several times and your daughter finally told me you were in France. You left so quickly after San Francisco... Are you going to tell me it was planned that way?" Cole asked earnestly.

"No." she answered. A smile of enchantment touched her lips.

"No, what?" He was still standing, still a reflection in the window.

"No, it wasn't planned and no, I'm not going to tell you why. Won't you sit down? I won't even ask what you are doing here in Ashby, a small ocean town away from the city. Just please sit down and let me look at you." Anna said softly.

"I'd love to," he murmured.

Cole raised his arm for Sarah, requesting more wine.

"Yes, another Chardonnay will be fine," Anna said, without taking her eyes off Cole.

Sarah watched them quizzically and gave her husband a look. Something was going on with their Anna and they should watch her.

"A toast," he whispered. "...to good friends".

Anna's eyebrows arched an iota before nodding and tracing a tentative tongue to catch the condensation around the glass's edge. "Yes, to friends," she repeated, watching his fingers grip the crystal wine stem.

"Let's just pretend we're old friends getting to know one another again?" he whispered, willing her to respond with his eyes.

He was not truly handsome, Anna thought, but she liked his looks; his face was alive with curiosity and intelligence and humor and he looked at everything with such intensity. Right now he was looking at her as if he wanted.... not just in a casual way with carelessly spoken social phrases. "Cole, the last time we were together we talked for hours so I suppose we really are old friends.... In San Francisco I was floundering, but these weeks in France truly helped me see life as it should be. We didn't really delve into our personal lives then...can we talk about it now?" Sitting back in her chair, she tilted her head to one side expectantly.

"Well, I am as private a person as you are. Mmmm...." he began, pursing his lips slightly in thought after sipping some of the chilled wine. "I grew up with an older brother who was killed in a car accident when I was twenty-two and he was twenty-eight. I was very close to Judd and it nearly killed me............I was in college at the time and so glad school kept me too busy to get lost in the pain. He was a good guy and we were very close......"

"I'm so sorry," Anna said as his voice died away. Her insides tripped as she watched the way his lips moved and his eyes turned cloudy for just an instant. He looked up abruptly, lost for a moment.

"Go on, Cole," she urged gently with open curiosity.

Cole nodded. "Then, I fell in love with a girl while I was in college and we planned to marry after graduation."

Her eyes perked up. "Rainy?"

Cole laughed outright, finding the idea extremely amusing.

"No, her name was Shari. Sharon Lawrence. She made me laugh and I felt valued and indestructible." He sat still. Then he gulped the remainder of his Chardonnay. He looked at Anna, seeing her absorption.

"Leukemia," he said bleakly. He turned his head toward her and a short swathe of hair fell casually onto his forehead.

Anna was mesmerized.

"She died two weeks before graduation. I nearly did too, all over again. Losing both of them nearly pushed me off the edge."

Anna reached over and covered his hand, gently caressing the skin between his thumb and finger.

He smiled at her empathy and placed his free hand over hers, enjoying the smoothness and warmth. "It was ten years later that I met and married Lauraine Heinz. I was thirty two." Cole sighed. "She was my mentor's daughter. She was smart and funny, but distant. Her father kept pushing her at me until I finally said yes. I hadn't planned to marry...ever, and she seemed to feel the same way. But we were married anyway. That was eighteen years ago. It seemed the thing to do. I was sick of being alone. Her father was an attorney in my first law firm in San Francisco before I joined Darrin and Steven in Lark Point." He paused. "Our marriage was warm but it had no depth. I was raised to believe divorce wasn't an option. And, of course, there were some good times. But was I ever happy or content? No, I wasn't. I was too busy building up my law firm to think about discontent, so I just spent more and more time at work. In that way, I was able to avoid dealing with it."

Anna peered into his eyes while pulling her hand away.

Cole looked at her steadily. "As for Rainy, she seemed to have everything she wanted. The money was rolling in. I built her the house she dreamed about. She went into interior design and then fund-raising and volunteer projects led to her business. And then, of course, there is the claims' investigating that takes her around the country. She keeps herself busy, as do I."

Anna sipped her wine, her eyes breathing warmth into the conversation. She could see he had more to tell. She watched the serious nod of his head, his heavy brows plaited together in concentration.

"Several months ago, I learned she was having an affair. I'm sure she still is….someone she met became more important than our marriage and I realized I didn't care one way or the other. The affair should have come as no surprise, as the marriage has been passionless for years. We are both workaholics. We pass one another in the hallway, occupying the same space, yet living separate lives. So, I let things ride. I guess I shouldn't be telling you all this," he said but there seemed to be no apology in his voice. "But nothing is as it seems." He took a generous draft of wine. "My own marriage," he said bitterly, "is a symbol of what I mean."

There was a moment of loaded silence.

He seemed to expect her to say something but she was at a loss for words. "At the beginning, we liked each other. We were from similar backgrounds. But there was something odd in the room; since I had nothing for comparison except Shari during college, I shrugged off my uneasiness and married her without love. She organizes benefits for every agency under the sun; I attend, mingle, and say all the right things. I create an atmosphere for business contacts. I make friends...She travels around the country solving mysteries and helps Metro Assurance settle claims. We're friends of a sort and I tried to ignore her other life." he finished lamely. "Here we are nearly a year later."

"And you're…....."

"……..still with her? Yes. It seemed to be enough until…….."

"Until……?" Anna prompted.

He glanced at her upturned face. "Until I met someone to shake the status quo and turn my belly inside out."

Anna sighed deeply and then pinched the bridge of her nose.

"I don't want things to ride anymore," he whispered meaningfully as he picked up his wine glass, sipped the liquid and watched her.

"I'm very sorry," Anna said carefully, unmoving. "You deserve more, Cole," she answered with a sense of conviction that was part of her character.

"That has begun to cross my mind lately." Cole studied the tablecloth and took a deep breath. To lighten the mood, he changed the subject. "So.... back to you. When did you first realize you wanted to be a writer, Anna?" Cole's eyes softened as he watched her.

Anna laughed, suddenly unsure how to answer but glad the conversation shifted. "You know, Cole, as I think back, I know exactly when it was. It was my 12th birthday. The house was full of family and neighbors. Mom had given me a new cream-colored leather binder for school. My name was stamped in gold. It zipped closed." She was quiet a moment and glanced out the window, staring at the miles of sand and surf nearly shrouded in darkness.

He waited, interested.

"The binder was filled with lined paper, lots of it. I followed the lines with my finger and itched to fill in the blank pages. The room was noisy with people and I started writing what I heard, who I saw and how I felt. Words flowed frantically from my mind and a writer was born. Actually, I've not stopped writing since. It's like I want to write everything down, every day. Sometimes late at night when no one is around and there's nothing in the silence but my thoughts, that's the best," she finished and caught her breathe. "Wow, where did that come from?" she picked up her wine glass, lifted it and silently toasted the man across from her.

Cole's eyes smiled and then his lips while they both shared a laugh laced with inspired contentment.

"Wonderful," he said softly, his eyes not leaving her face.

"Cole, the mind is very powerful, but it can be manipulated with music, images, memories, sounds, smells and words. I chose words. I love to write, bringing characters alive and moving toward a common goal. And, you..... Cole, why the law?"

"Law. I learned a long time ago that it takes more than one lawyer to make a difference. The call for justice and all; but I enjoy everything attached to it and try to capture whatever takes my fancy."

"And what is it that takes your fancy?" she asked.

He sat still and looked at her. "You do," he said quietly.

Anna caught her breath; saw the setting sun dancing on the ocean's surface. Violin music drifted through the dimly lit room. *I want him. I want to tell him what I'm thinking, what's inside of me. Because I think he will understand. I want to make love to him....oh God.* "No," she said firmly, almost faint with longing as she straightened in her chair.

"Anna, do you truly love Sam?" he asked bluntly.

Anna was startled and felt her face warm. She hesitated a moment, unwilling to discuss the divorce with Cole. "Yes, he is Tess's father."

"That's not what I asked, Anna."

She didn't answer immediately. "We have always clung to the positives and glossed over the negatives. Couples should be more honest, I guess. More realistic. No marriage is perfect. So where's the cut-off point? At what point is there more bad than good? At what point do you say enough? I clearly reached it before Sam………." She stopped suddenly and looked up at Cole. "I will always love him because…of Tess."

"Are you IN love, I mean?" Cole prodded.

"That's none of your business, Cole!" Suddenly the wine hit her and she felt ill-prepared for the situation. She quickly pushed back her chair. "Listen, Cole Nites, you know damned well I'm attracted as hell to you and you're pushing my buttons to the limit. I spend my days busy writing, talking to people… but as soon as I slow down, the first thing I think about is you. I've been analyzing these feelings so damned long since I met you, that I don't know which end I'm on half the time. My trip to France was wonderful. My time away from Sam was wonderful. There, I thought about you every day also! Please go back to Lark Point and leave me alone!" she whispered urgently. She wiped her eyes with the back of her hand, grabbed her purse and nearly ran for the back door, out onto the sand, away from Cole and her wild thoughts. The sun had set and the last light had disappeared at the edge of the sky.

Cole was stunned. *Thank you*, he breathed silently, knowing in that moment how much he loved her. *But, my God*, he thought, *to love this woman…. After I've lived all these years in limbo… never imagining such a woman existed. Could it be possible?*

Anna ran the length of the beach toward *Mirafleures*, mumbling into the wind, "Damn man...can't leave well enough alone...think I'm made of stone? They're all alike... their needs are first, first...first. Damn Damn Double damn..." Her words melted into the surf as sand flew behind her.

She threw herself into the back door, locked it behind her, ripped off her jacket and threw it across the room. She forgot her shoes on the restaurant patio so she couldn't throw them too. As she tossed her belt, an insistent tapping invaded senses. The front door. She abruptly stopped her tirade. Anna jerked the door open and looked at Cole's face, etched with concern and gentleness.

She threw herself into his arms as his lips found hers in a kiss that shook their souls. She arched toward him and ran her fingers through his thick hair as she heard the door click behind him. His hungry lips reached for her neck and slid slowly downward as she pushed toward him.

Anna groaned and pulled his face into her breasts, begging for the closeness his caresses promised. She knew there were no shadows across her heart anymore.

"Anna...."

She pulled away and stared into his clear gray eyes, seeing the warmth of his smile echoing in his voice as he whispered, "Anna, I cannot stay away from you. Don't send me away this time."

Anna went limp against the wall. She touched his head, moving her fingertips through his hair and her breath caught. "Oh, dammit, Cole," she murmured.

Cole's lips moved down the front of her body as she hugged him closer and heard him moan slightly, deep in his throat. The room began to spin with the sweet emotions rippling through them. *This feels too beautiful to be happening.*

I'm lost, Cole's head was roaring, his desire leading. He slowly lifted his head and looked deeply into Anna's searching expression.

"I want you, Anna. My God, I won't deny it," he said slowly, each word vibrating through the quiet room.

Anna shook with emotion. The scent of his aftershave assaulted her nostrils and she briefly wondered if he shaved around that soft beard? She inhaled deeply, enjoying the smell of him and the feel of him. Placing her right hand in his left, she slowly pulled him toward the hot tub across the room while he pulled off his shirt.

She switched it on and bubbles frothed instantly. Stepping out of her slacks, she stared up at him until he pulled her toward him. Anna gave a start at the shock of his skin on hers. Her breasts were flattened against the dark hair on his chest; his large hands moved over her back, her buttocks, her waist, her thighs, as if shaping clay and then her long sigh broke the silence.

Anna again reached for his hand and led him to the gurgling hot tub, nodding for him to step in ahead of her as he walked out of his tan corduroy trousers. Leading him to a small wooden bench, she pushed him down before sitting beside him. She reached to unlace his shoes, not uttering a single word.

Cole's eyes lighted, surprised. Unwilling to break the soft spell that lay woven around them, Cole didn't move. He smelled the wood, the perfume in her hair and was still.

Then, she bent to kiss his chest, as the lights glimmered and reflected against the glass blocks that surrounded the hot tub and invited an intimacy she craved. "You are beautiful," she said, suddenly grinning, lightening the moment.

His hands came up from his sides. He placed a palm on each of Anna's flushed cheeks and pulled her face within inches of his own. "Men are handsome," he said chuckling, "You're the beautiful one." His lips touched the sensitive area beside her mouth and his finger tenderly traced the line of her cheekbone and her jaw.

She craved the feelings his touch invoked as she let the intensity invade her senses. *Don't stop*, she thought.

"Don't stop?" he asked, smiling.

Anna's face was filled with surprise as a soft and loving curve touched her lips. "You're reading my mind, Cole."

"No, sweetheart, you said it aloud and I loved hearing it."

Within seconds, Cole stepped down into the gurgling, swirling pool that pulled at his naked skin. He felt warmth seep into his body and a contentment he had only dreamed about. *Anna... I knew it could be this way with Anna.*

She stood on the edge, poised, uncertain momentarily and excited. "This is so sinfully delicious," she whispered; as she placed her right foot onto the upper step.

Cole's hand clasped her ankle, encouraging her to join him now that she was naked and he could not take his eyes off her. He continued watching her, aching to grab her and pull her toward him instantly.

Instead, he moved toward her slowly, stood up and moved his mouth to kiss the honey softness throbbing before him.

Anna stood still, transfixed. Eyes flying open, she watched Cole caress her in a way she had never known before. His arms encircled her buttocks and moved so gently up and down her thighs, she thought she was dreaming. The sensations wrought from Cole's mouth mesmerized her body, paralyzing her until she wanted so much more as he loved her profoundly and deeply with his kisses.

The next moment, Cole gently pulled her into the foaming depths. Her tan skin bounced near his chest as the curling hairs met her small breasts. He held out his arms and she flowed into them, needing surcease from loneliness, lost dreams and disappointments. Anna let herself feel a euphoria she had only read about as he pressed her with relentless enjoyment. His smile was nearly as intimate as his kisses.

"My turn?" Her words fell into the bubbling cascade around them.

Cole felt her tremble and pulled her down beside him and she felt soft music. A gentle peace invaded the softly-lit room where before had dwelt so many uncertainties.

"I love you, Anna."

"I know you do," she whispered into his neck while kissing him gently. She savored every moment as warm water invaded every part of their bodies, their hands insistent on the other.

When he pulled her down to straddle him on the hot tub's ledge with the water rumbling around them, she felt like she'd really come home. The kisses did not stop and the gentle movement and fire took them each by surprise as they climaxed just moments apart. Then, they were still, savoring an afterglow neither could remember sharing before.

Gradually their hearts stopped pounding.

Brown eyes met grey as they gazed at the other in wonderment. They dried one another with thick towels as intimate smiles moved across their faces like a slow summer cloud before working their way over toward the bed. Then, they crawled beneath the covers and held one another all through the night. And magic settled over them like fairy dust.

The next morning, Anna awoke to find Cole gone. She sat up quickly to glance at the bedside clock. Six o'clock. The sensation of panic was short-lived when he came in wearing jeans and carrying a newspaper under his arm. He balanced two steaming cups of coffee in each hand.

"I found this when I jogged up to get my car and my luggage. When you de-clothed me, I had nothing fresh to wear this morning," he teased as he handed her the coffee and caressed her hand as she took it from him. Sitting on the edge of the bed, he opened the newspaper and sipped the steaming coffee as a pervading calm invaded him again.

She watched him, loving him. All she really had to do was look in his eyes to see the longing there. No man had ever looked at her quite like that, not even Sam.

It wasn't long before Cole winked at her, swatted her through the covers and tossed the paper. One of his hands slowly moved up to her cheek and he stroked it with the back of his knuckle. "Let's go for a walk on the beach."

"All right, give me five minutes," she said as she jumped up, totally naked and felt his eyes follow her across the room. The comfort with her nakedness in front of Cole astounded her. She had never felt it before and added it to her list of feelings since he'd walked into her life.

Cole waited on the patio, downing a second cup of coffee, while staring at the shoreline. When she joined him, she was wearing the bright sweatshirt he remembered from San Francisco. They walked toward the ocean hand in hand, enjoying the silence and warmth from one another.

Anna stopped suddenly, leaned forward and kissed him. "You are the nicest man I have ever known, Cole. If the world had a pause button, I'd use it to prolong the bliss."

"Well, you make me nice and you helped me face the world again," he answered, gently pushing the curls from her face.

"No," she laughed. "You did that for me."

They each smiled and continued walking, arm in arm.

"How's the book coming?"

"Very well... still need that court scene...."

They both laughed as they remembered the night at the University Club when they first met. The court scene had plagued her then and it was still left undone.

He looked down at her. "You said it had to be a murder in self defense...I have been working on a case for several months and the court date is set for next month. How long before publishing do you need it?"

She thought a moment. "I have two other pieces to write. It's amazing how lost I become while writing this book, how exciting it is to create a story out of thin air. My agent calls me every week hoping it's ready but I want it to be just right and I refuse to be rushed. When the book is finally published, she will arrange book signing events starting in New York City. Tess and I hope to make a holiday of it. So, my guess would be New York in nice weather, say April or May... so a month waiting for the court scene would definitely work."

"Good...it will give us more time together too."

Wind whipped Anna's hair, the surf beat in time with their thoughts. She looked at the horizon and the openness around them. Where does one begin to make the changes that support new feelings? How does one survive hurting others to make those changes? Would they really have a time in the future together? The roiling surf and flying sand drifted through her frenzied thoughts.

Cole watched her, filled with chaotic thoughts of his own.

"What's going to happen to us?" she asked quietly, amidst the seagulls screaming and the surf whipping alongside them.

"You mean, are my intentions honorable? You know they are, once we push through the weeks ahead," he said, a serious note entering his voice. He pulled her close and wrapped her arms around his neck.

"Let's touch this moment, then," she said as they began walking back toward *Mirafleures*, leaving deep, matching footprints in the sand behind them. "I am beyond tired of twisting in the wind."

Cole and Anna spent the long afternoon in the quiet cottage.

Afterward, Cole put a bottle of Chardonnay in an ice bucket that he'd borrowed earlier from an inquisitive Sarah. He loaded the Bose player with three piano CDs from his car and the mellow music filtered through the room like soft petals falling from a basket.

Cole watched Anna lower the blinds against the afternoon sun and inquisitive beach walkers. Afterward, they lay on the bed, talking, laughing, touching, kissing, then talking less and kissing more. Cole undressed Anna silently and marveled at her sleekness and sauciness, uncaring of the stretch marks from her pregnancy on her abdomen and breasts. Every curve and angle excited him, filling him with a great tenderness. "You are gorgeous," he whispered, "and you've pulled all my tangles out. I didn't think it could ever happen."

Warmth spread through her body. She was aflame, hungry for him. His hands explored her gently, not forcing, never hurrying. Their touching went on and on until Anna found true desire, overwhelming all else, aching to feel the hardness of him inside her, aching to be joined to him, to be part of him.

Their touching, once his clothes covered her pile of garments on the floor beside them, pleasured them both. Her soft cries and breathless murmurs of excitement delighted him.

When they came within seconds of one another, he buried his face in her throat and called her name again and again.

"You're the loveliest thing I've ever seen in my life."

"Am I?" she murmured softly.

"Oh, yes." They snuggled, their legs entwined, holding each other for a long time. He fell asleep but she did not. Anna rolled to face him and they lay eye to eye for breathless, hushed moments while he slept. Later, she worked her way free to sit at the small, round table facing the ocean and opened the blinds a few inches. She gazed across the sand and the canopy of trees lining the shore. Cole. She loved him. But he was married and he thought she was also. She would tell him today.

"Stop over thinking," he whispered from across the room.

"I'm not. Not really."

"I want to stay here with you a few days, Arianna. I don't want to lose this," Cole whispered as he came up against her and massaged the nape of her neck, gently rubbing, caressing.

Anna smiled at his use of her full name. No one ever had except grandmére. The name conjured the warm, lined face of a gentle white-haired lady. The old woman was smiling. Anna shrugged away her longing for the woman she loved so well and repeated one of her many philosophies. "My grandmére believed we all have a place that is right for us, with people who are right for us and when we find it, it is foolish to waste time searching for something else. So....no, Cole, as lovely as that sounds....today I go back to face reality and my daughter."

He looked at her a moment, wanted to have just one more day and started to begin his plea when she stopped him, putting a finger to his lips.

"Cole. I left Sam when I went to France because I had already decided to divorce him," she stated simply.

Cole's face was startled.

Anna took a deep cleansing breath.

"Amen," he said as he moved his hand from her neck and replaced it with his lips.

She relaxed against him and felt like she'd come home.

"Anna.... I don't do one-night stands. I want to get my house in order, it will take a bit of time but when I do, I am absolutely without a doubt, all yours. Can you live with that?"

"Mmmmm," she whispered, straining toward his gentleness. She reached up, stroked his face thinking he felt like warm velvet.

He smiled against her neck. "What was that?" he whispered.

"That was a Yes. I. Can. Right now, I just want to touch you," Anna pulled his face down to hers.

Cole bent his body to entwine with hers and time stopped. His mouth fit hers perfectly, his kiss insistent, determined, passionate, everything that was Cole. His hand cupped the back of her head, drawing her into the heat of his mouth.

FOURTEEN

In the week since she'd returned from France, she'd met with the attorney, cried with Sam and argued with Tess. And she kept sweet memories of Cole close, to smooth out all the wrinkles in her head. She told Sam she didn't hate him after what happened. She also told him she loved him like a brother and it was not what he chose to hear. Since he'd moved into a townhouse near the lake within walking distance to the television station, they had only spoken twice.

She walked in front of the curio cabinet on her way to the study and paused to contemplate her missing Hummels and the history the thieves took with them. She told herself they were material items that could be replaced. She knew they could and would be, if possible. But when she looked into the empty cabinet at that moment, she focused, instead, on the fact she and Tess were safe. She knew the theft wasn't really Sam's fault but simmered because his investigative reporting brought them into her house. And they still hadn't caught the thieves.

Twisting in the Wind still lay unfinished. She promised herself, without interruptions, she would send it off to her agent after Cole's trial. She felt a welcome surge of excitement. Anna sat down at her desk, pulled her keyboard forward and began tapping the keys. She realized she could make some steamy edits to the love scenes...and the smile just wouldn't go away.

Cris got to the theater early. Her Taekwon-Do bag slapped her hip and her cosmetic bag nearly slipped from her arms. She was struck dumb to see Michael and Nicholas turn the corner by the theater and walk into the brick building next door. There was a man yelling at them. He went around the back and the guys went in the front.

She put her gear down quickly. After darting a look in all directions, she sped after them, inching her way into the front door. The brick building had been vacant awhile and there'd been talk of expanding into the area for a little café to be part of the theater's wine and dessert area. She knew Chuck was talking to backers. Maybe this guy was one of the men with money? The man obviously had a key.

Random thoughts swished around her brain as she quietly closed the door and noticed the ceramic tile floor. Her heels would give her away and she wanted to sneak after them. Hurriedly toeing off her shoes, she tiptoed forward, following the loud, arguing voices.

Cris squatted down to place her knees on a piece of carpet wedged between some boxes. The door was ajar, so she watched them through the crack in the door. Their words were garbled. What were they yelling about? Michael was jabbing his finger in the air and Nicholas was dodging it. It became curiouser and curiouser.

An older man faced Nicholas, his back to Cris. His voice hissed as if he was trying to whisper and yell at the same time. She leaned forward, cocking her head to listen.

Nicholas was staring at the man, refusing to budge. Warning bells should have been clanging in his head but his mind sped elsewhere. He took his eyes off the man only a second and it was a second too long. Darrin's fist lashed out at him and knocked him to the floor.

"Nico, my friend," Darrin said softly, "You and Andreas, go get that girl or she will be dead instead of only kidnapped. I'm going to stop her father from his damned meddling and she's a valuable piece of the puzzle. I will brook no argument!" His foot slammed into Nico.

Nicholas groped upward, lifting himself onto his elbows and stared at the older man angrily. "You don't own me, DAL!" he yelled.

Cris knew he was scared and still the pieces in her head didn't fit.

When Darrin kicked him in the ribs again, she flinched in shock. Nicholas was smashed into the wall so hard that it jarred the door near where she crouched. Twisting away, she crept into a closet, closing the door almost shut. She cursed inwardly. Why couldn't she have hidden closer? Although still barely able to see the men, she lost most of their words, only the yelling.

"Nico, go get the girl," Darrin repeated menacingly, "Go. Get. Tess Berg. Now." Cris saw the man's fist shaking in the air.

Nicholas inched up, grasping the wall until he stood, slightly doubled over, holding his ribs. He stared at Michael whose features were pained but obviously too afraid to cross Darrin. Nicholas hurled himself straight at the old man, but Darrin smashed his fist toward his face once again, flinging him down on the floor again.

Cris heard nothing but the wild beating of her heart as she hunched over, holding her belly, willing for it to end.

"So, my little friend, you like to play?" Darrin's voice hardened.

"DAL, you'll kill him," Michael rasped. Darrin turned to stare at him with a look that didn't invite further comments so he shut up.

Nicholas turned toward Michael, missing Darrin's foot as it lashed into his shoulder. He cried. "No more, DAL, please, no more….."

"No more?" DAL said with a sinister smile.

"No, DAL. I quit," he mustered some strength and started crawling toward the door. "I don't want to hurt anyone. You said nobody would get hurt. Just get lots of loot, you said. It's not Tess's fault her old man is trying to nail you. Go after Sam Berg, not my Tess!" Nicholas's voice was broken as he kept pulling himself to the doorway.

Glittering blue eyes followed Nicholas as he nearly crawled out the door. Darrin motioned Michael near. "Get the girl. Leave Nico to me," the older man said quietly.

Michael sighed angrily, but moved toward the door.

Darrin glanced around the empty room slowly. He retrieved his jacket, removed a piece of lint off its sleeve and followed Michael, walking toward the closet where Cris crouched behind the door. Her hands covered her face, trying to stifle any noise that might alert them of her presence.

Nicholas moved as quickly as possible, his skull aching, pain stabbing him with each step. He made it outside the brick building and across the street into the deli two doors away, the smell of sauerkraut and sausages invading his nostrils.

"Nicholas….hey you a'right?" the old man yelled from behind the sandwich counter while running to help the crumpled figure in the doorway. He leaned down, noticing how frantic the boy appeared, trying to get up.

"Phone, Jimmy. I need…..my phone…..Hide me quick." Blood dripped from his head onto Jimmy's hands. He moaned with every breath.

The old man dragged the half-conscious boy behind the counter and pulled him into his back room. They both heard the front bell jingle. Nicholas stared at Jimmy and held his finger to his swollen lips.

Jimmy raised his grey eyebrows and nodded quickly.

"Hey! Who's minding the damned store?" Darrin bellowed as he looked behind the counter and into every corner of the deli. His eyes were glassy and he was heaving as if he'd run a mile.

"Sorry, mister. I had to take a toilet break. What can I get for you?" Jimmy asked as he nonchalantly wiped down the glazed countertop, looking at Darrin expectantly.

"Did you see a kid run by or come in here a moment ago?"

"Hey, if anyone'd come in here, I'd've heard the bell just like I did just now. This is a small place, nothing gets by me," he said matter of factly, pointing to the door behind Darrin and the bell above.

Darrin's eyes narrowed. He lifted his hand slightly, gazing around the sordid little place, hearing the whining of the radio. He nodded, looked around once again and walked toward the door.

"No sandwich today, sir?" Jimmy asked, twisting the screw.

"No," Darrin growled.

Jimmy remained standing, facing the door with a smile pasted on his face until he saw a silver Mercedes slowly drive past his front window.

Nicholas edged his cell phone out and dialed, pain shooting from all directions. He listened to the phone ring for the third time and nearly gave up when Anna's harried voice said, "Hello?" and waited.

"Anna! I need Tess quickly." Nicholas bleated.

"Nicholas? She's not home, can I……..?"

"…..Listen carefully, Anna. They're looking for Tess! I couldn't stop them. They're the bad guys and they want to stop Sam's investigation through Tess. You have to get to her quick!" Nicholas cried. His cheeks were wet when he dropped the phone and Jimmy placed it back into his pocket.

"The bad guys, Nicholas?" Jimmy asked, straining for an answer. Blood seeped onto the floor and he grabbed a towel off the counter.

Nicholas moaned again and struggled to keep a toehold in its climb toward unconsciousness. And then he fainted.

~

Horrified, Anna stood a moment before slamming down the phone. She grabbed the nearest jacket, Tess's old blue denim, and a blue stocking cap along with her cell phone. She raced out the door toward the corner grocery hoping to catch Tess inside. She began to run. "Oh God, not Tess....." she screamed. "Damn you, Sam, I told you to take them seriously...." Tears blurred her vision. Her jacket flapped around her as she ran. She barely noticed the screech of tires and then the sound of lurching brakes told her it was already too late to run.

In an instant, rough hands grabbed her and shoved her face down on the dirty floor of what appeared to be a van. Frozen with terror and disbelief, she lay still. A man's cowboy boot wedged its point against her backbone. She was more frightened than she'd ever been and her skin grew cold from sweat. Her heartbeat clanged into the dirty carpet as she fought for breath and tried to scream. Struggling, her eyes went wild as the boot held her down behind the driver's seat on the gritty floor.

The van was moving again within seconds.

"Hey, that was easy, man," Andreas snickered, moving his foot against Anna's back like he was rocking a bag of potatoes.

"Shut up!" Michael said through gritted teeth.

Anna's head jerked. *Michael?* She couldn't move; her insides hurt and she felt as if her hip was being ground into rocks while her heart socked against her ribs.

The man, sitting on the seat above her, snickered again. "Well, we got her didn't we? Just like DAL said. This should shut up Berg for sure," Andreas continued. The excitement had his other foot tapping, the boot perilously close to Anna's head. He tapped his thighs to a quick beat Anna couldn't hear.

"I said shut up!" Michael turned to glare toward the back seat, rolling along the streets over the speed limit and breathing heavily. If he'd just said no all those months ago when Darrin Lucas had cornered him, he wouldn't be driving a van holding a young woman against her will to pay the price for her dad's interference. Nor would he be putting up with the jerk behind him. His muscles were so tight he could barely drive.

Andreas stared down at the woman on the floor. "Don't move, kid," he said when he saw her inching toward the front seat away from his boots. He angrily pushed his foot against Anna's butt again, poking at her when he saw a cell phone inching out of her jacket. He scooped it up. All they needed was for her to call someone for help. No, not on his watch. He rolled down the window and tossed the phone, grinning as it crashed to smithereens in the road.

"Leave Tess alone!" Michael shouted at Andreas and stared at him through the rear view mirror. "Just leave her alone, Andy," he said in a less belligerent tone when he saw how agitated the guy was getting.

Anna froze, her mind working wildly. *They think I'm Tess. Of course! They saw Tess's jacket. But Michael will know.* Her fear doubled but she silently blessed their asinine error. Keeping her face hidden, she didn't know if Cowboy Boots had seen Tess before or not.

"For God's sakes, Michael, I'm not hurting her," Andreas whined. The tapping on his thighs got faster, his boots joined the concert. "I need a cigarette but I'm out. Give me one when we get there?" Getting more frustrated by the minute, she felt Michael accelerating into the turns. Andreas held on to his seat belt and watched the girl being tossed against his hard-tipped boot. He jabbed her again.

She whimpered and tears formed in her eyes. Squeezing them closed, cursing Sam again for the hell he'd opened for them the past months, her mind screamed. *Sam! You did this*, she shrieked to herself as anger and fear melded into one and stiffened her bruised body. Each bump jarred her hip bones and jaw as her body slammed repeatedly against the hard floor.

Michael looked in the rear view mirror again and saw Andreas' eyes glazed and shining. He couldn't leave the guy with Tess. The idiot must be on drugs. Plan B, his mind swiftly calculated. There's no way he'd let Andy touch Tess. He'd hate himself even more than he did already and Nicholas would kill him too. Michael strained away from those thoughts while trying to create new ones. He pulled jerkily into an unpaved driveway, pulled into the back of an unkempt house and jammed down the emergency break before jumping out.

Andreas' hands shot down toward Anna. The side door jerked open and he started to yank the girl toward Michael.

"I'll get her, Andy." Michael reached for her carefully. "Please just do exactly as I say and you won't get hurt," he said apologetically.

Andreas scowled, really needing that cigarette.

He helped Anna up and his eyes shot wide. "You're not....."

"Not what?" Andreas asked, suddenly uneasy. He looked at the back of the girl's head and Michael's face, interested but wary.

Anna whimpered and her eyes pleaded with Michael.

Michael's heart beat a staccato flip against his rib cage.

"Not what....?" Andreas repeated as he stared between them.

".....Not as tall as I thought," Michael said in a low voice.

Andreas grunted and followed them out of the van and up the walkway such as it was. He had slightly hooded eyelids and a wide, fleshy lower lip that instilled a growing menace around him.

Anna caught her breath, her eyes wide and her body aching. The porch was old, rickety and filthy dirty. The hinge on the door looked like it'd been ripped off, possibly damaged with a hammer. Paint peeled off the outer wall and there were mouse droppings all over the porch and window sill beside the door. She gagged as Michael pulled her inside, nearly tripping as they stepped across the damaged threshold. He tossed Andreas a package of cigarettes and watched him catch it one handed.

"Don't talk, Anna," he whispered in her ear urgently. "Not a word, please!" Michael glanced at Andreas through the window. Calming himself, he placed a palm on his rapidly beating heart and took a deep breath. He hated being thrust into the fire but now he had no choice.

Anna nodded, afraid again. She sat in a hard chair, hands and feet tied. A cloth was cinched around her mouth. She saw Cowboy Boots smoking just outside the door. Smelling the smoke, she was glad to be distanced from him. He really did frighten her.

With one eye on Andy out the dirty window, Michael turned to Anna. "I don't want to hurt you, Anna, and I didn't want to hurt Tess either. Nico got the hell beat out of him for trying to stop this from happening. Shit! None of this would've happened if Sam hadn't tried to play God on his TV program. Man with a Story...Shit."

Anna stared at him, unblinking. Could this be the same man Cris has been living with and the actor she'd applauded for at the theater? She'd always trusted her instincts before but now wild doubts assailed her and she felt sick.

"I have to leave but I'll take Andreas with me. I don't trust him at all. Don't try anything stupid or we'll have to grab Tess. I don't want murder on my hands too. I just want out Anna. I never wanted in! The old man blackmailed me into stealing for him. I'm in so deep now....you must have already figured out it's me and Andreas and Nico too......." Michael turned thoughtful. "I like you and Tess, Anna. And I like Sam too. Nobody was ever supposed to get hurt," he said wearily.

"Nico?" Anna queried.

"Yes, Nico...Nicholas." Michael glanced out at Andreas again so he missed the stunned look on Anna's face.

"So, that's why....." she started.

"Why what?" he grilled her.

"Why......Nico is Nicholas?"

"Listen, Anna, I have to leave. The old man's waiting. He's pulling some stunt that's tied to us grabbing Tess. Cris doesn't know anything about this. She thinks I get all my money from a trust fund. That's how I've been able to buy her jewelry and things. It makes her happy. I keep trying to just make her happy....but there's always something more, something missing...maybe it isn't the damned money at all. Maybe it's me...Oh hell, I'm going on......." His eyes misted and he wiped them angrily.

Anna continued to stare at him, intent on hardening her heart.

"Hey! Let's get this show on the road," Andreas yelled. "Get moving!" He tossed the cigarette butt and started moving toward the door. "The boss said to be back before the six o'clock news to watch Berg when he gets the note."

Michael stood indecisively a moment before running toward Anna. Crouching down, he cut the twine at her wrists. He stared into her angry eyes. "Wait ten minutes before leaving, Anna. Please! Ten minutes!"

Anna smiled tentatively trying to blink back the tears and leaned toward him. Her elation made her weak. She was afraid he'd change his mind or that Cowboy Boots would catch him. She held her wrists behind her after the twine was lifted away.

Michael sniffed hurriedly, blinked again and ran outside. "Let's go!" he told Andreas as he walked across the gravel toward the driver's side of the van.

"I stay, man!"

"No, Andy, you and I'll both go watch that guy read about his little girl all tied up," Michael said with a harsh, raw voice. He stared at Andreas, daring him to argue and tapped the roof of the van.

Andreas' face was a dictionary of indecision.

Michael pushed him toward the van and started counting minutes in his head.

"Hey, man, okay…okay," he whined, anxious to make Michael happy despite fearing DAL's anger. He jumped into the van and they spun quickly out of the driveway tossing gravel in all directions.

Anna exhaled loudly after ripping the stinking gag out of her mouth. Time crept slowly. How could she count ten agonizing minutes without the clock on her phone? Silence creaked around the house as she ran to peer outside after freeing her ankles. She slipped out the door and started running, thankful she'd put on tennis shoes. For the first few minutes, she just flat out ran and the streets melted away from the old house. She paused. Where the hell was she anyway?

Her chest hurt. She had to think. *Cowboy Boots tossed my phone and I need to call …..I must get to Cole. He'll know what to do.* Words fell over themselves in her head as she fought for breath. Her hair was ratty and sweat ran down her face. She'd lost the hat. She began to run again, her legs pumped faster and faster, her coat tails slicing through the wind.

A café loomed ahead. Flying inside, she begged breathlessly, "Can I use your phone?"

The woman at the counter stared at Anna's disheveled state.

Anna was panting, her frightened eyes begging for help. The words, *fear is ineffectual*, slipped though her mind. Her tear-streaked face smiled as the woman handed Anna her cell phone. Smiling her thanks, she dialed Cole's office with shaking fingers; she was glad there was nobody in the café to witness the crazy scene.

"Lucas, Mapes and Nites. How may I help you?" a woman's soft voice answered.

"Cole Nites please. It's an emergency," she cried. Anna grasped the phone, willing him to be there.

"May I ask who's calling please?"

"Anna Berg!"

"One moment please." Recorded music filled the line for only a moment as she thought, hurry, hurry…She whimpered into the phone.

"Cole Nites."

"Cole! It's Anna! I need help *now*!"

"Anna, what's happened?" Cole stood up, instantly alert, fear lacing his voice.

Words strangling one another, she tried to relate what happened over the past hour. She was hoarse, crying and frantic. The woman standing next to her had eyes so large Anna feared they'd drop onto the counter next to her.

"Stop, sweetheart. I'm coming. Where are you?" He was already grabbing his coat and keys while straining the phone cord from its base.

"4th and Fresno at the *Silván's Paella Café*."

"Go up Fresno to *Henry's* on 5th. Wait inside, but watch for me." Disjointed thoughts flickered through his mind and some of the puzzle started fitting together. His heart hammered so fast, he had trouble getting the key into his ignition. When his BMU flew around the corner, he was clenching his teeth so hard his jaws ached.

Ten minutes later, Anna ran out to Cole's car the second he drew up to the curb. The people in *Henry's Pub* stared after her. She'd looked a little worse for wear but hadn't said anything as she stood just inside the doorway. She slid across the seat and tunneled into his arms, disregarding the transmission shift knob and anything else that got in her way. Her face was smeared and dirty both from tears and the van's floor. Cole held her tightly before pulling back to look into her dear face.

"Sam's supposed to have a note delivered like the last one while he's on the air at six. They grabbed me by mistake but thought they had Tess. It was Michael Mallory! He recognized me after we got to the house, but didn't tell the other guy they'd grabbed me instead of Tess. He untied me at the last minute and took the other guy away with him. Andy somebody….didn't want to go…..he scared the crap out of me. Michael said he never wanted to do any of it, he wants out of the whole thing but the old man…that's what he called him….God, Cole, we have to find Tess and tell Sam and… He'll get the damned note while he's on the air and think Tess has been kidnapped and…" Her hands shook and tears were on the brink of her eyelids ready to slosh over face again.

"Shhhhhhhhhhhh….we'll get right to it. Hang on." Cole ripped away from the curb. Anna leaned her head back, closed her eyes and gripped both hands between her knees.

Sam was surprised to see Anna and Cole rushing into his office; she was dirty and scraped, her face ravaged. He jumped up, vaguely wondering why Cole was with her but too upset to get past the frantic clutch in his belly.

"It's your insatiable need to be in the limelight with your damn program. That's what it is!" Anna's wrath knew no bounds as she poked his chest with her index finger and started crying.

Cole pushed her into a chair before turning to Sam. He shook his head, wondering where to begin. There were so many questions he couldn't answer that it was difficult forming words for the man when Anna could have been killed. He wanted to grab Sam around the neck and start choking. Cole hoped his face didn't show his emotions because he was having trouble controlling himself.

Sam looked from Cole to Anna and back to Cole again.

"What the hell is going on?"

"Sam, your show has started a snowball effect that is putting your family in danger. You must have realized that when you were robbed. This time, it was much more serious. These thugs kidnapped Anna and that was hard enough to accept…"

"What?!"

"…..But their focus was Tess. Anna just happened to have Tess's jacket on when they grabbed her. Luckily, one of the kidnappers knew Anna and it appears he was coerced into finding Tess in order to stop your investigation. He helped her in the end but we're still in trouble."

Sam looked horrified.

Cole stared at him with a thunderous expression.

Anna shook so badly, she had to hold the chair with both hands.

Ten minutes later, Sam stood before the camera, neat and ready; the red light flashing the countdown before him. His face exhibited a calmness he was far from feeling. After learning what happened, he knew he must act as if his life depended on it until Tess was found. The kidnapping was a shock but when he learned his daughter was missing, his mind clouded. Could he pull it off? The red light stopped blinking. He cleared his throat and became Sam Berg, Man with a Story and waited. This time, he was ready for the man's note and he fought back. He could show no fear this time.

"Today is a turning point in the Lark Point burglaries," he began after introductions and smiling as if he hadn't a care in the world. "There's a man out there who thinks we are stupid and I want to tell him that my promise to cuff crime is still in the fast lane. Between the Lark Point Police Department and this program, we will find you, so be aware! Where's your head, man? You are going to make a mistake. And when you do, we will run you to ground." He focused on controlling his voice and stared directly into the camera. He took a deep breath and dared the man as if he could walk through his door with a six gun blazing. He ended the show, a little distraught and the station was quiet.

Elliott flew into Sam's office afterward, angry and red in the face. He slammed the door behind him. "You take too many liberties, Sam! There's a script prepared that I expect you to follow. This isn't the first time you've changed bases on me during your live broadcast and I don't like it! We are a team. You are not a one-man vigilante!"

Sam's facial muscles twitched nervously. He had difficulty keeping his hands steady as he reached toward his water bottle.

The producer continued, "Believe me, Sam, we all know how hard it's been on you with Anna being kidnapped, Tess's boyfriend being beat to shit and then him disappearing. All we know is what Michael Mallory told a kid with cowboy boots. We know you've been under a lot of stress with Anna and the divorce coming at you......."

Sam flinched.

".......But dammit, Sam, you're letting your feelings get in the way of good reporting. You're better than that. You can do it and you know it. It's not the brusqueness I have a problem with. Having cut my teeth in the old, male-dominated newsroom, allow me to clue you in. I read somewhere that we're chain-smoking, ink-stained, fact-obsessed derriere-kickers, to put it politely. And it's true. There's always someone who'd like to chew us up and spit us out. These are tricky times. We already know there's somebody out there trying to take you down personally and today proved it. Why in the *hell* are you trying to aggravate the issue? Charlie Royce and the mayor are on their way over here right now. They called me the minute you got off the air and told me to keep you here." Elliott took a deep breath. Their exact words were, "Hold his butt there!"

"So, what are we supposed to do?" Sam growled. "Sit with our thumbs stuck where the sun won't shine? We have to stop them before they hurt other people, not just my little girl and my wife. This has gone beyond professional journalism, I know that. This is my family and I'm sorry it upsets the mayor and Charlie. I'm gunning for this guy and I won't back down. What else can we do?" He stared at Elliott grimly.

"What else can we do? We get the bastard the right way before anyone else does, of course, and then we go get shit faced."

Sam hunched back in his chair gritting his teeth as he watched Charlie and the mayor storm into his office. This time, Elliott closed the door quietly, pulled up two more chairs and they all stared at one another.

"What in the hell did you think you were doing? Get your head out of your ass. We have serious work to do and you are interfering big time." Charlie jabbed his finger into the desk top and stared at his friend.

"Sam, we know you have every reason to take this personally and we are all looking for your daughter. Anna Berg just left the station after signing a report about what happened and I'm glad to say we finally have at least two names to link to these damned burglaries. But we all know we need the big fish, not little pollywogs. Dammit, get your head on straight. Do it right. We made a deal, remember?" The mayor ran a finger around the neck of his shirt and took a breath.

Elliott piped up with, "Hey, Charlie, are you looking for Michael Mallory and his sidekick or do we let that ride while Tess is still missing? You know they may have her by now and jumping all over Sam isn't putting those two in jail. Let's focus here, ok?"

Charlie jumped in with both feet. "Sam, you were out of line. If this was my station, I'd sack you." He stared at Elliott to get his point across.

Elliott grinned. "You think I should fire the best damn newsman in the industry because he's made the Lake Point cops mad? You mean I should fire him because he's the man who connected the dots? Are you telling me I should knock the piss out of him as a thank you?

Sam's eyes closed and he placed both hands on his desk. "Ok, so you guys can put me on the naughty step if you want to, but we have some serious work to do. First off, let's get our asses in gear and find my daughter. If it takes me bluntly voicing the fact that I have a personal axe to grind over it, so be it. But I will not back down. I will not play Mr. Nice and you guys better damn well have some answers and keep my girl safe.

All three men sighed deeply.

Sam stared the men down.

They shifted in their seats.

Elliott stood, opened the door and they filed out.

Sam hitched his thumbs in his waistband and said, "Ok, boss. Let's get drunk. I have no clue where to look for Tessie and everyone has my number. Shitfaced, here we come."

Elliott followed him out as he lifted a thick hand to Sam's shoulder and waved to everyone in the studio so they could start breathing again.

FIFTEEN

Michael was shaking visibly when he dropped Andreas off at his apartment. He flicked a wave and drove the van back to the brick building where he placed the keys under the mat as instructed. And then he hurried across the alley to enter the theater. The other cast members weren't due for a couple of hours and he was relieved. He wanted time to catch his breath and regroup. He wouldn't be Darrin's pawn anymore. He was sick of Andreas and scared spit-less he'd be caught and didn't know where to turn. He'd earned the kudos the theater promised and refused to sacrifice that or Cris over his fear of others finding out he'd made an ass of himself as a young man. It was time to fess up and toss DAL if he had to.

He would bare it all to Cris. She'd have an idea.....the police? Leave town? No, he'd fight for his chance to continue his acting career. The lawyer wouldn't stop him. Yes, Cris would know what to do. He retraced his steps, pulled out his cell phone to tap her number when he heard voices coming from her dressing room. He smiled. Great, she was already here.

The dressing room door stood ajar as he approached. Michael started to push open the door when he staggered backward. Hearing the whispered words, he eased closer to eavesdrop. Disbelief marred his features as he inched behind a panoramic screen just outside the door.

Rainy listened intently to Cris, bending her head a fraction to soothe and lament. The thief was right under her nose and she missed it; she didn't like Michael before; now she added burglary to the list.

".....and then the old man started beating Nicholas and then.....I couldn't hear it all, Rainy. Michael looked frightened but didn't help

Nicholas. I couldn't understand it. And then Michael.........." Cris gulped and took a breath.

"And then Michael what...?" Rainy urged her to continue, breathless to hear the story. She held Cris in her arms and laid her chin on the top of her red head.

".....and then Michael just stood there. I could tell he was angry but he just didn't know what to do. What could he do? The guy was kicking, hitting and so cruel. Michael probably thought he'd be next...it was about kidnapping someone. The old man thought it would stop someone from investigating those burglaries. Those guys must all be in it. Michael has to be part of it. I heard him talking on the phone weeks ago and now that I think back, he must have been telling others who was in the audience here at the theater, who to rob and....he always had money...the rings, necklaces and..." Cris sobbed as Rainy pulled her close.

"Oh, darling," Rainy whispered. "Look at me...we'll figure it out. Who was the old man beating Nicholas?

"I couldn't see his face. He looked familiar but I was too busy trying to be quiet and scared to death so I must have had my eyes closed when he walked by me."

"Damn. Well, I need to tell Ben Russell and go to the police. I hope Tess is all right! Do you want to come with me?"

"No....... poor Michael. I need to talk with him first."

"*Poor* Michael? I say he's a rat," Rainy sighed with exasperation. She pulled Cris closer rubbed her back, kissing her cheek, her neck and finally their lips touched and held.

"Oh, Rainy, what would I do without you?" Cris moaned, "I love you so....." She looked into Rainy's eyes and smiled, tears almost forgotten and touched her lips again, roaming over her face and eyes. Their lovemaking was gathering steam when they heard a noise that pulled them apart quickly. Then silence.

"Let's go away again. Ben wants to send me to Hawaii when this burglary issue is resolved and now that it is, let's do it. One of his largest clients seems to be missing items in a warehouse on Maui. I can reserve our tickets. Let me know the schedule for the rest of the season and we'll set our calendars...and then some Piña Coladas and alohas!"

Cris grinned at Rainy. "Yes, aloha...but I need to talk with Michael first. He must be scared."

"Scared, my ass…but okay." Rainy tossed her hair over her shoulders, the golden curls slapping her face in a show of defiance. "Good luck with that. I'd like to slap him but you know him better than I do," she whispered, blowing a kiss. She stepped gleefully into the dark hallway and rushed through the back door. She could hardly wait to tell Ben. She'd tell Cole too. Her stomach knotted with giddiness tying all the loose ends together. The thought of removing Michael from Cris's life for good gave her such a feeling of elation, that she wasn't sure what to do first…… call the police first? Sam Berg?

She left Cole a message on his cell after pulling into the parking lot of Metro Assurance. She was anxious to get Michael arrested and out of Cris's life. "I got him…" she said aloud, a smile stretching across her flushed face. "Hawaii, here we come…I'll help her forget she ever knew him….make her forget her guilty conscience at turning him in…," she breathed.

Michael wasn't sure he could move from behind the screen. The words in his brain were moving in slow motion. Cris and Rainy? Cris and Rainy! He fisted his trembling hands and bit down on his lip until he drew blood. He'd loved her! He'd offered her the moon and back and she was a..…one of *them*….he couldn't even say the word. His eyes burned, his chest exploding, heavy, tired. Pulling himself up from his crouch, he felt the gun in his pocket. It felt cold, hard, deadly. Darrin's gift to scare Tess with. Things didn't quite work out as he'd planned at all.

He couldn't get Cris's voice out of his head …., "Oh, Rainy, what would I do without you?" He'd heard the kiss, the moans. The outer door clicked shut. Why hadn't he stopped Rainy, Michael asked himself fiercely as he gripped the gun with trembling fingers.

Cris pulled her legs under herself, contemplating the horrific day, the beating, Michael, calling Rainy afterward, the frightening revelations, her fears. She sat down at her dressing table, held her head in her hands and pushed the cosmetics off its top to smash against the wall. "Damn and double damn!" she cried. "Why did it have to be Michael?!"

Michael Mallory walked towards the dressing room door Rainy had just vacated, the room she'd just made love to Cris in. His face was red, mean. Pushing the door open, he saw Cris at her makeup table, her hands on each cheek, staring into the mirror as the myriad of lights reflected from her large green eyes.

There was a flicker in the glass of the dressing table mirror. She looked up and saw Michael's reflection staring at her. Acting kicked in, she swung around and hoped he would tell her what she'd already witnessed and explain himself. "Hey, you're early too," her voice died away at the look on Michael's face.

"Yes I am, *darling*," Michael sneered.

"Michael?" Cris's knuckles suddenly turned gray as both hands gripped the table, her nails nearly blue.

"Come on, *darling*, I know you're hungry….but not for food," he laughed harshly and walked toward her like a stalking panther.

Cris stared at him, standing up to face him. He towered over her outweighing her by fifty pounds. She always thought she could defend herself from any man. Now she wasn't so sure. Her anguished brain screamed and she wasn't ready to relinquish her grasp, still pretending. "What do you mean, Michael? You sound as if……."she started.

He was now inches from her face. "You bitch!" He slapped her so hard her neck snapped, throwing her backwards. It would've hurt more if she hadn't prepared for the blow, shocked but prepared. She slammed into the small white table, the mirror swayed, the remaining bottles smashed to the floor. The scent of perfume filled the room.

She stood up again, her stunned face staring at him. With a trembling hand, she reached up to touch the red welt already swelling on her jaw, her eyes gleaming with tears. "Michael, stop!" she yelled back.

"You slut," he said, low and menacing. "It's not enough you figured out …… I hate myself for being part of it, but did you have to tell your *friend*, Rainy? You loved all those diamonds…all the shit I've bought for you. You just kept taking, leading me on, letting me think you loved me and all the time it was *her*!" He came toward her again.

Cris backed away one step at a time. She heard his voice whisper obscenities, filth. She couldn't believe what she was hearing.

He snaked out his hand, pulling her roughly against him and ground himself into her. Grabbing her hair, his fingers wove through the frizzled mane and he forced her mouth to his, kissing her until she was light headed, rubbing her lips tightly across her teeth.

Cris was too frightened to move, stunned at the onslaught. She began to tremble and could not stop.

"Does that bitch kiss you like this?" he whispered, a silken thread of warning in his voice. Tears slipped down his cheeks and his voice cracked. "Does she!!?"

Cris stared at him as understanding dawned. He'd been outside her door when Rainy was with her; her worst nightmare. She closed her left hand into a fist bringing it to her throbbing lips. Her green eyes were wide with fright and she wished the floor would open and swallow her within its cellar. His tears disarmed her. She could not think.

Michael's face was crazed. His right hand dove into his jacket pocket while his left hand held the back of her neck like a vice. "Why, Cris? Why?"

It was then she saw the gun. Her eyes nearly burst from their sockets, tears lodged in her throat. "No," she barely squeaked in a frantic whisper. It was then she felt Michael relax his hold, sensing her wild fear. Sanity slammed into her in that split second and she brought her right foot down on his instep. Hard.

He howled and raised his arm to grab her but she was faster. She slammed her elbow up into his solar plexus. His eyes bulged. She didn't stop. She threw a jumping front kick, crashing into his chest and knocking him toward the floor.

He raised the gun, shaking it in her direction and shot wildly when she kicked his wrist with an inside crescent kick with the inner edge of her foot. The gun flew towards the wall where the wild bullet was lodged. She heard it thud against the wall but did not take her eyes off of him.

Michael grabbed her ankle in defense, trying to knock her off balance but she tightly laced her hands together and brought them down onto the back of his neck. His body jerked and fell against her dressing table, the corner of the mirror piercing his temple.

Silence followed the smell of cordite from the gunpowder. Her thoughts were in slow motion. Where was the smoke? Didn't guns always have smoke? Didn't a shot smell like ammonia? She sat down, dumfounded and stared at Michael's inert body. Her breath came in short gasps until the sound of footsteps broke through her subconscious. She felt arms around her shoulders, a damp towel on her face.

"For the love of all that's holy, Cris, what in hell happened in here?" Chuck demanded.

Cris stared at him, glanced at Michael again, and promptly fainted.

Lily, Cris's understudy ran into the room, surveyed the scene and started crying. Chuck gave her a look and glanced at the phone. She lifted the receiver slowly and dialed 911, while never taking her frightened eyes off Michael's bleeding head and unmoving body.

Chuck dialed Cole's number and left a voicemail message. He was pretty sure Cris might need a good defense lawyer.

Tess traced her pale finger in circles on the flat, white sheet while her right hand gripped his lax fingers. She ached to see his eyes flutter, the lashes lift and his dark brown eyes focus on her own. The circles became larger and larger, becoming swirls outlining the nurse's remote call button beside the pillow where his black, tousled head lay so still. The dimly lit lights from the hallway sent a stream of yellow toward them. Nicholas still didn't move.

The doctors and nurses had finished stitching his lip, his cheek, the swollen left shoulder and his left hip. The rips in his flesh were deep as if an animal had attacked him. Bandages covered yellow-orange stains all over his skin. One eye, his right, was swollen shut. He couldn't have opened it if he'd wanted to, Tess thought. She lifted her left hand off the bed and smoothed it across his fevered forehead.

"Is he coming around yet, young lady?" The nurse wore light blue Betty Boop scrubs and had been quietly checking on him since they'd brought him to the room from ER. The smell of medicine followed her.

Tess appreciated her quiet, caring voice. She looked up at the woman and shook her head as the nurse marked notes in Nicholas' file. She took his pulse, noted that too and left them quietly.

Gently disengaging her fingers, she stood up. Stretching her hands and arms high above her head caused her to grimace. Her body ached. She glanced at her watch and wrinkled her nose. She'd been there three hours. It was nine o'clock dark. She fished in her pocket for her cell phone and walked into the hall to call home.

A policeman, lounging next to the nurse's station, moved quickly to intersect her path. "Good evening, miss. Is your friend awake yet?"

"You mean Nicholas?" She looked at him with a question in her eyes not understanding why he'd want to know about Nicholas. Then it dawned on her he probably wanted to know who put him in this terrible predicament.

"Yes, Nicholas Alonzo."

"No, he isn't awake. He's been stabilized, but he's a mess; three broken ribs and a fractured jaw. His assailant must have punched him in the face and then his attacker must have kicked him viciously in the side. Have you found the creep who beat the shit out of him?" Tess's voice was shrill. The niceties had left the building.

The policeman stood next to her, his blue shirt starched stiffly, pondering the young woman a moment. "Can we talk?" he asked kindly.

Tess hesitated, seeming to sag toward him. "Yes, of course, but I need to let my mother know I'm okay. Can you wait a minute?"

He started to say something, instead nodded and motioned her toward a lonely green and blue plaid couch inside a small waiting room. There was one man sitting in a chair near the lamp playing solitaire on his iPad, so intent on the game he barely noticed their entrance.

Tess called Anna's cell phone but it went directly to voicemail so she hung up and called the home line.

"Tess?!" Anna barked into the phone.

"Mom. I'm sorry I didn't call you sooner......"

".....Honey, where are you? We've been worried sick. So much has happened. My God, Michael Mallory kidnapped me because he thought I was you...... when I ran out to find you after Nicholas called......."

"Kidnapped? Nicholas called you?" Tess whispered. "What time was it? What did he say?" Tess's mind was zipping in circles and didn't want the policeman to listen, so she moved toward the man with the iPad, as she furtively watched the hallway.

"Nicholas told me someone was going to grab you." Anna's voice was shaking with relief. She closed her eyes and swung them upward as she gave a huge sigh.

"Mom! The time! What time was it?!" Tess demanded.

"Why, Tess? Are you okay?" Anna's short-lived relief changed to fear as Tess's voice and the fear she heard transferred across the phone.

"Yes. I'm okay....what time?" Tess repeated.

"It was about four o'clock just after you ran up to the store this afternoon. I was on my way to find you after he called....."

"Mom, did Nicholas say how he knew this was going to happen? Wait, did you say Michael Mallory? What the hell? Mom, I'm scared... and Nicholas is hurt very badly......"

Anna's head jerked up. "Where are you, Tess?" She pressed her trembling hand to her chest.

Sam waited tensely in the doorway. When she nodded to him, he wasted no time and grabbed the phone from her hand. "Tess! Where are you?" He gently pushed Anna into the side chair and started pacing across the living room, agitated and scrubbing his face with his hand.

"Dad, I'm okay. It's Nicholas who is hurt! Some old guy from the deli by the theater named Jimmy called me about five thirty. He dialed the last number Nicholas dialed when he spoke with Mom earlier. I ran here to St. Elizabeth's Hospital and I've been here ever since. He's bandaged from head to toe and hasn't woken up yet." Her voice broke.

The policeman stared at her. Turning her back and covering her mouth, she noticed the iPad man perking up, suddenly very interested in her conversation so she moved farther away and urgently asked, "Dad, Michael Mallory took mom......? Why??? Is she really okay?"

"Yes, she is...especially now that you've called. Michael let her go. The other guy probably would have hurt her if Michael hadn't helped her. It's all tied into this damned burglary thing. Maybe Nick knows something. My God, he must! He told Mom they were going to grab you in the first place. I'll be right there..."

"No, I'm staying here and there's a cop waiting for Nick to wake up. I'm going to talk to him now. God, daddy, they almost killed him." Tess's shoulders shook and she sprayed tears when she wiped at her face. She looked up and the blue starched shirt was inches from her face. The man held out a steaming cup of black coffee toward her.

"Bye, dad, I'll call again later." She hung up and sniffed loudly, gripping the cardboard cup in both hands and nodding her thanks. She was cold, shivering slightly, and the coffee was exactly what she'd needed, aware suddenly that she'd forgotten her sweater.

"Do you know who hurt your friend?" he asked quietly.

Tess's mind reeled away from Michael and didn't answer. She shrugged and lifted her coffee to trembling lips.

He noticed her hesitation, felt she knew something. "You want us to catch whoever hurt him, don't you?" he said kindly.

"Of course, I do" she snapped. She was so torn she wasn't sure what to say until she spoke with Nicholas. The thought that he might not wake up at all left her shaking so badly she had to sit down or spill the coffee all over herself.

"Then we need help. All old Jimmy knows is Nicholas stumbled into his deli and tried to call you. He knew Nicholas and hid him in the back room when some big guy in a Mercedes came looking for him. Your friend was in a bad way. When Nicholas called you, he got your mother instead, warned her to find you and then he passed out. Someone, two men actually, tossed your mother into an old van….it is a long story I'm sure she'll tell you. In the meantime, we want to get our hands on them. If he was trying to help you, they must've tried to stop Nicholas and here we are." The policeman eyed her, urging her to trust him.

Tess stared at the man, seeing his slicked-back brown hair, bushy brows and sincere eyes. Taking a deep breath, she vowed to talk with Nicholas first; too fearful of getting him into trouble. She couldn't imagine what mess he'd gotten himself into. The beating was enough for now and she needed answers. "I don't know anything about it except Nicholas is hurt badly and he hasn't been awake since I got here. I've been here three hours and want to get back to him." She jumped up and slipped down the hallway and into the darkened room again.

The policeman followed her and spoke from the hallway, "I'll be waiting out here, Ms. Berg."

She looked at the man outlined in the doorway without answering and didn't relax until his shadow disappeared from the light streaming in from the hallway.

"Nicholas, please wake up!" Tess gently squeezed his arm and pushed her face into the pastel coverlet covering his broken body. She jerked her head up when she heard him moan softly and move his head back and forth on the pillow mumbling, "No, DAL. Please…. not Tess….. I won't do it," he whispered brokenly.

She stood up immediately and placed both hands on each side of his face to hold his head still. "Nick! It's me, Tess."

He raised one eyelid, the other too puffy and swollen to budge. A tear slid down his cheek. "Tess, thank God. Come closer."

The nurse walked in beside the policeman when they saw Nick's arm wrapped around Tess, but they couldn't hear the conversation.

"Nicholas, glad to see you're awake," the man's voice said as he approached the bed. My name is Clyde Mark and I want to ask you some questions starting with who hurt you."

"I didn't do anything," Nick whispered out of swollen lips.

"Nobody said you did, son. Help me get the guy who did this to you. I can't help you until I have a name." The policeman stared at him and Tess shrunk back, wondering what Nick would tell the man.

"Don't know who he was," he said in a muffled voice and looked at Tess before staring back at the policeman.

"You don't know? Come on, one name and I'll leave you two alone. I know this young woman's safety and her parent's depend on you talking," the man continued grimly. His brows scowled as his words cut into the silence.

The nurse hustled him out of the way and wrapped a blood pressure cuff around Nick's arm. "Really, this guy's had enough for one evening. Can you come back in the morning, officer? He'll have a night's sleep and a little healing behind him...maybe he will have some answers for you when he isn't so groggy," she said as she pumped up the cuff.

Nicholas stared at her with a strange look in his dark eyes.

"But.... I must...." The detective's eyes narrowed.

"Please...out!"

Detective Mark left but not before looking back at Nicholas steadily and shaking his head. "See you in the morning, then..."

The nurse removed the cuff, told them her name was Cecelia and promised to keep the police out until morning. She felt his forehead and smiled at Tess. Then she gently closed the door behind her.

"Why did you lie to him, Nicholas?"

"The man would kill you if I told the police his name, that's why."

"But, if we tell the police, they can arrest him...put him in jail," she responded naively. "Did the man you are protecting send Michael to kidnap me? I know you called mom and when she tried to find me, men grabbed her and threw her into a van, thinking she was me," she cried and wiped her nose with her hand.

Nicholas stared at her mutely before nodding tiredly.

"Was it Michael who beat you up?" she hissed, shaking her hands toward his broken body, anger seeping through her tears.

"God, no, it wasn't Michael. He knows what D…what the guy would do to him, me…any of us. The guy has a wicked temper and his heart is made of stone. I never realized it…had no idea…when I agreed to…….shit…what a mess. But I never wanted to hurt anybody. He promised nobody would ever get hurt. Just until I paid for school….."

Her eyes snapped. "What's Michael and this guy got to do with your school tuition? Dammit, Nicholas," she whispered as her anger increased. She dried her face again.

"Tess, leave it. Come close. Sit. We'll talk later. I'm just so tired……" His eyes closed and he drifted to sleep again.

"Oh. My. God. What are we going to do?" She nestled close to the bedside and held his hand tightly. The faint murmuring at the nurses' station outside the door was the only indication they weren't all alone.

He was glad Tess was there when he woke again. Minutes, hours, days could have elapsed for all he knew. Since time had no relevance in a hospital, Nick's disorientation was augmented further. The moment he opened his eye again, she leaned over.

"Hi."

Her long hair fell forward; his fingers caressed the strands and he gave her a lopsided smile. It was nerve racking, not being able to see her clearly. Only one of his eyes would open. He realized that his head was swathed in bandages and his entire body ached like a toothache.

"Where is she?" The smell of the hospital was a nostril-flaring mix of disinfectant and medicine amid sweat and worse.

The detective had just neared the elevator when a man he immediately recognized as the television newsman came storming out with a woman he guessed was his wife. She looked harried and frightened. Her eyes swung left and right along the hallway before settling on the tired policeman.

Nurses at the station near them warned the group to quiet down but Sam ignored them. Anna looked at them with an apology in her eye as she left the men and quietly asked the nearest nurse where Nicholas Alonzo's room was located. The nurse eyed her warily.

"Are you a relative to the young man?" she asked tersely.

"No, I'm his girlfriend's mother and need to find her. I'm sure she's with him…" Anna's face was not just harried but a little haggard. Cecelia led her to Tess while the men continued their loud-whispered conversation.

Sam watched the nurse lead Anna down the hallway out of the corner of his eye. He abruptly left the detective's side after a brief nod and left him standing in front of the elevator. The policeman tracked him with his eyes, shrugged and punched the elevator button.

Tess shook herself out of her reverie when Sam's huge body was framed in the doorway. "Dad, I asked you not to come down…I am okay, I told you."

"You're okay. You mother's okay. I'm okay. Nick's okay. Hey! Little girl…something's going on and I want to find out what it is. Things are *not* okay," Sam answered with an uneven voice.

"I was scared, Sam, but I think it was the fear that made me strong. Inside, I was mush but I am okay. How are you, Nicholas?"

"Yes, Anna. I'm glad, but I need answers now….." said Sam, ignoring the depth of her emotion. He knew Anna would survive.

Tess stared at her father and saw Anna's eyes snap dangerously. "Your damned investigation again, dad? What about us? Mom could have been killed. I could have been killed but she was my surrogate this time. I know something's going on too but you can't get anything out of Nicholas tonight….and not until he's ready to tell you, *if* he tells you!"

Sam stared at them, seething. "And just what the hell does that mean?" He looked at Nicholas meaningfully and then back at Tess.

"It means, Dad, that he's scared. Please leave us alone. Mom?"

Nicholas moaned again and thrashed and moaned a little more.

Anna rushed to Tess's side and threw her arms around her daughter, kissing her pale cheek.

Sam studied them before decided he'd look for the cop. Maybe he had some answers.

"You okay, sweetie? I mean really? I had to make sure. I've been a screaming maniac all evening not knowing where you were and reliving the nightmare. I just wanted to hold onto you a minute. Forgive me?" Anna murmured, half laughing, half crying.

Tess's sense of humor took over and she laughed with a little hysteria mixed in. "Forgive you? What, for taking my place and nearly getting killed? Sure, you're forgiven..." Her sad eyes met her mothers and they both looked at Nicholas, who slept beside them. Her anger resumed and fear returned as Anna told her story.

"......then I found a phone and called Cole..."

"Cole? Why not call Dad?" Tess was alert to the change in her mother's voice and stared at her.

"Guess I thought I needed an attorney," Anna answered quickly to cover her unease.

"Well, Mom, I know a little," she whispered as she glanced at the doorway, "but this is Nicholas' life. I won't let Dad intimidate him for a damned story. I mean it," she finished fiercely.

Anna touched Tess's shoulder, noting the polish beginning to chip around the edges and felt panic bubble into her throat. *Dammit, I'm worried about my chipped nails?* I love you, darling."

"I love you too, Mom.....so much," whispered Tess as she allowed herself to be encased in her mother's warm arms.

Sam stood in the hallway outside the doorway undecided; clearly upset the detective had gotten away.

~

Across town, Cole walked into the house, puzzled at the look on Rainy's face. "What's going on?" You look like you just lost the lottery."

Rainy winced. "You obviously weren't listening to the news on the way home. Didn't you get my voicemail message about my visit with Cris this afternoon? It's Michael who is the thief from the theater!"

"What? I was listening to music and haven't checked messages." Instantly alert, he felt the first stirrings of unease. "What happened?!" He reached over to turn up the television above the kitchen counter. The breaking news ribbon that had Rainy's attention as he walked in was no longer sliding across the bottom of the screen.

"Cole," Rainy said in an emotionally ragged voice. "Channel 2 news reported that someone was killed at the Repertory Theater. I met with Cris at the theater a short while ago. She told me it was Michael and then I left her alone to go meet Ben at Metro to tell him we had our thief.

Cris was alone when I left." Her chest rose and fell in a quick, soundless gasp.

"You think it was Cris?" he asked hoarsely.

She couldn't answer, her face mottled with fear.

~

When the policeman had read Cris her Miranda Rights earlier, she clawed her way up through gray mist. The words blurred in her head as she tried to make sense of the past couple of hours.

"You have the right to remain silent. Do you understand?"

She whispered, 'Yes."

"Anything you say may be used against you in court. Do you understand?"

"Yes."

"You have the right to the presence of an attorney during any questioning. Do you understand that?"

"Yes, I think so."

"If you cannot afford an attorney, one will be appointed for you free of charge before any questioning if you want. Do you understand?"

She shook her head.

"Please say yes or no, Ms. Crissman."

She looked up at the man who stared at her with eyes slightly narrowed. She pressed her hand into her chest to slow down her heartbeat. "Yes, sir." Her voice shook and tears slid down her face. Everything happened fast and Michael was dead. Her thoughts slammed shut again.

"Do you wish to waive these rights?" The officer waited.

"I...think so." She looked up at them, clearly unsure of an answer. They smiled.

She'd stared into a camera for a mug shot, her purple jaw standing out like a swollen eggplant. They'd taken her diamond studs, her amethyst ring and her watch. She'd signed an inventory form before being led into another room.

Cris stared at the swirls of black ink covering her fingertips. Her face was blank as she sat in the straight-backed chair and listened to the questions slung at her from two different directions. Their voices sounded as if they were in a tunnel and she was baffled. Her eyes blurred the men's images as they paced back and forth. She thought she would vomit.

With a loud bang, Cole crashed through the door nearly tearing it from its hinges sending ripples of reaction throughout the room. Cris turned her head at the noise, barely registering the scene. The chair was hard, the table was cold and she wanted to lie down.

Cole came to her swiftly, knelt down beside her and gripped her cold hands as he glared at the officers standing beside the table. One cocked an eyebrow, the other's expression clouded in anger.

He stood up stiffly. "She's already been booked! What happened to interrogating a client with their attorney present?" he growled with barely restrained fury. "Leave us please....she's not going to run away. Look at her!"

Both men shrugged, put their hands up in mock surrender and quickly closed the door with a snap.

Cole looked at Cris as she slowly lifted her face to his. Her left jaw was purple, swollen; her eyes puffed and red from crying. "Are you alright? To talk, I mean," Cole asked gently. "Tell me what happened."

Cris shook her head, touching her chin to her chest and her eyes filled with tears. She closed them tightly and thought back, all the way to Michael. And she shuddered as the rambling dialogue with voices in her head fought to surface. Sobs shook her body and she placed both hands on the table, fingers splayed before her. Mascara rolled down her freckled face and her red hair sprung coiled around her face like Orphan Annie. She looked up, smothered another sob and said clearly, "It was self-defense, Cole. He heard me tell Rainy he was part of that gang of thieves and he tried to kill me. I had to....had to.....but it was an accident, I swear. I just wanted to stop him, not kill him. He had that gun and he shot at me...Oh," she wailed, "....not Michael."

"And you were there alone with him?"

Her green eyes stared into silver in mute appeal. "Nobody was there but us. I told Rainy I knew he was part of the burglary ring...and he heard me tell her. I tried to stop him from hurting me but I ended up hurting him....No, killing him, Cole." She wept aloud rocking back and forth.

"Cris. Shhhhhh. It's all right, honey." He held her closely, protectively, like a child. Brushing at her fire-red hair, he wiped her tears with his hands. He had to know everything. "Is that all, Cris? It is so hard to believe he'd want to kill you just for ratting him out. I know he adored you." Something didn't fit. He knew the District Attorney would love to make a name for herself with something just like this.

Cole saw Cris's face close up like a cornered animal.

He waited.

Her face flickered minutely, some kind of emotional reaction, gone too swiftly for Cole to interpret it. "Yes, that's all, Cole," she said quietly. Staring at her fingertips, she gripped her hands together on the table as if in silent prayer.

Cole frowned. "Maybe we should start at the beginning. I need to record our conversation, do I have your permission?" he murmured, opening his legal pad, ready to write and placing his cell phone between them.

She nodded yes and he leaned closer, straining to hear her words as she began to tell him what happened from the minute Michael walked through her dressing room door until Chuck entered the room after he heard the gunshot. Her red coiled hair gleamed in the lighting overhead. Cole wrote furiously, wanting to catch every word even though he was recording the conversation.

"......the artwork and jewelry. He stole from all those people who watched us perform... He cased the patrons in our audience and called Nico. They disarmed alarms if they had one and robbed their homes while Michael and I entertained them, setting up his alibi at the theater. They called the old guy Dal. I can't remember for sure but I thought one of them called him something else once but it was muffled in that closet...I'm sorry, Cole. I just can't remember."

"Yes, Cris, got it. Let's get back to the confrontation in the dressing room. Tell me everything that happened and everything he said from the moment he came into your dressing room. The words, how he said it, when, what you said, where you both stood in the room, the time he came in. When did he show you the gun? Everything. I have to know it all to defend you, dear. Go slowly, don't rush. I know how hard this must be for you. But telling me now while it's fresh in your mind is best before you forget something.

She hung her head and took a deep breath.

"And then, I'll try to get you released on bail as quickly as I can. Your arraignment should be within forty eight hours where you'll be formally charged by the prosecutor in a written statement. You will be listed as a defendant and asked how you plead. You will, of course, plead not guilty. Do you understand, Cris?"

"But, how?"

He came to Cris and put his hands on her shoulders. "Cris, you didn't kill him on purpose. Just remember that."

She bit her lip and nodded. "But Cole, I'm just so scared."

"Then have faith in what I do."

She nodded numbly. "I already do, Cole."

He patted her cheek and left to call in the sergeant.

Later that evening, Cole stared into the dark corners of his office. Beneath the quiet of the building, questions stirred and became insistent in the silence. He called Chuck Champion at the theater and thanked him for the call even though he hadn't heard it until after talking with Rainy.

"I'll never forget walking into that dressing room, Cole. She was like a robot and I was so worried, I couldn't think straight. Michael was slumped on the floor and blood seeped from a head wound. I wasn't sure what to do first. Thank God, Lily was there early. None of the other cast members had arrived yet. I'm sure just the two of us were there in the entire building with Cris when we heard the gunshot. I just can't figure it, you know? That guy loved her. Even if she did find out he was in on the burglaries, he loved her too much to kill her over that. I'd bet my life on it." Chuck sighed deeply.

"That's the same feeling I have, Chuck. Something just seems screwed up on this one. Until I talk to Nicholas and figure out who the punk is who was with Michael when they grabbed Anna...."

"God, I heard about that too. From the worry over burglaries to kidnapping, murder...what else can possibly happen? I'm actually not sure I want to know. They say it comes in threes?"

Cole pursed his lips. "Well, let's concentrate on getting Cris out of this and try to keep the burglaries separate from this fix she's in."

"Right. Well, the play will go on tonight but never thought I'd have two stand-ins at once. The entire cast is so upset; I hope they can pull it off. Gotta go. Let me know if you need me for anything, huh?"

Cole hung up and stared at his legal pad, closed his eyes and hoped Anna was sinking into a nice hot bath after what happened to her earlier. And I wish I could be right there with her, he thought…smiling at the vision before he pulled the pad toward him again.

He turned on the recording and listened to Cris's voice intently, clicked and listened again. She paused a few too many times and it made him uncomfortable. After going over their conversation a third time, he noted details and only then when he thought he had all he needed to pull off murder by self-defense, his mind whirled looking for something else. He missed something. He could feel it. He knew she was innocent of premeditation; it was a clear case of self-defense. Michael shot a gun at her. That was real. His having a gun in the first place, the whys of it just didn't make sense. He had to construct his opening and closing arguments so strongly that the jury would find her not guilty of first degree murder. He would make them see it. He expelled a breath and shook his head. Or it may not even go to trial. Cole could hope.

Generally, if someone attacks you and you are in imminent danger of death or great bodily injury, you may kill your attacker. If your fear of such danger was reasonable, the killing is completely justified. Either way, he had his work cut out for him. Hopefully, she'd be arraigned tomorrow. And the bail? He would recommend it immediately.

Cole reached for the bottle in the cabinet behind his desk. *Courvoisier* was amongst the four leading cognac houses in the world. Legend had it that the emperor Napoleon himself chose *Courvoisier* as his preferred cognac; therefore *Courvoisier* was often referred to as "The Cognac of Napoleon. Cole was sure it probably was since it was priced like gold. He took a long draw on the cognac, closed his eyes as the fluid hit his throat and smiled when he felt the surging warmth in his veins.

SIXTEEN

Cris tried to stop crying but the tears just kept coming. The woman on the other cot wouldn't stop staring; she hadn't said a word to Cris since she was led into the cell the night before. Shivering, she remembered the long white hallway, the clanging sound the steel door made when its bars slid across the cement floor. She grimaced thinking back to the loud *thunk* as it locked into place after she shuffled through. Her orange jumpsuit was stiff and foreign. They'd taken her jewelry, her clothes, and shoes. But nothing prepared her for the horror that followed; she was forced to bend over for the female guard to search all her private places. She shivered again while her cellmate continued to stare at her.

There was a small window in the cell but so high it didn't let in much light. The steel-framed bed had a very thin mattress and the pillow felt like a towel she'd bunched under her head once at the beach. She was hungry and cold. Closing her eyes tightly, she hugged herself, too afraid to let her mind wander further. When she blinked open a few minutes later, her cellmate was standing beside her bed. Cris's heart rate sped up and she pulled the grey blanket up to her chin.

"Hey, girl. I won't hurt you. Some of them out there might because you're mighty cute but stick close to me. I'll watch over you but you gotta do everything I say, got it?"

Cris was instantly awake. When the door swung open and the female guard called her out, she nearly tripped getting through the doorway. She looked back at the woman who stared shrewdly after her.

"Your lawyer is here. Go into door number five. You can talk through the glass. I'll be waiting right here for you," the big, irritable woman told her.

Cole was indeed in the little cubicle. She slid into the white plastic chair, put her hands on the table top and smiled at him. Holding back her tears, she felt her throat close up; she was so happy to see him, she thought she would faint.

He motioned to the phone on the wall. She lifted it up to her ear and watched him do the same.

"Hey, Cris." He smiled gently with eyes so full of apology, she nearly cried again. She was sure sick of crying.

"Hey, Cole."

"Rainy sends her best." He noticed her cheeks flush.

"Thanks. What's happening?" She was getting agitated again and worked at calming herself, using her Taekwon-Do meditation but it didn't help much. She hadn't planned on needing it in a place like this, a tiny closet with a piece of glass and a telephone between her and the outside world.

"The arraignment is at nine, Cris. A criminal arraignment is a short hearing before a judge. It will formally begin the courtroom proceedings where you will be charged with one or more crimes by prosecutors in a written statement, which will label you a defendant. As a defendant, you will be offered a chance to request court-appointed counsel, but I will stand up as your counsel. At that time, you will offer a response to the prosecutor's written statement, which will, of course, be a not-guilty plea.

"Oh, God," she uttered with the shake of her head and a sick look on her face. She ran all ten fingers through her hair, crumpling the curls only to feel them bounce back out of control.

"I know it's a lot to keep in your head, Cris. I want to explain it all to you anyway. The judge will establish a tentative schedule for future courtroom proceedings, including preliminary hearing, pretrial motions and potentially the trial date itself. The judge will also establish the bail amount, which may be revoked, raised, lowered or decided as a release on one's own recognizance.

"Bail? Who could I possibly ask to do that for me?" she cried.

"Just listen for now...During your arraignment, no juries are present. There will be a judge, the prosecutor, you and me in the courtroom along with other defendants, their counsel, and other members of the public. During the arraignment, you will receive a written notice of charges filed against you by the prosecutor, you will make an initial plea regarding these charges, which is not guilty and the judge will review your bail status, which can be changed pending defendant requests and prosecutor requests. A date is scheduled for hearing pretrial motions or upcoming hearings not related to pretrial motions. Are you still with me?" Cole asked as gently as he could.

"Not really," she whispered with a voice as reasonable as she could manage. Vomit threatened again. "I can't stay in that cell, Cole. Please make it happen. I *really* want to go home."

"I know you do. I will do the absolute best I can. You know that. There's no reason for them to think you're a flight risk or a detriment to the community. Chuck Champion and Rainy will both be there."

Her face lit up and she smiled for the first time since she'd walked into the cubicle. Cole saw it as a plus but wasn't quite sure what brought on the change. Regardless, he was glad to see it. He looked at his watch. "The guard will take you to the courtroom in a police van from here. Sorry, Cris, I wish I could take you but rules are rules." He smiled goodbye and replaced the receiver.

When he got up to leave, Cris's nervousness returned. The guard opened the door and she was led through the maze of locked doors clicking behind her, echoing hallways and worst of all, her feet and hands were manacled for the trip.

~

Sam's script was prepared; news of Michael's death on top. It was surreal, knowing the victim and the woman who allegedly killed him. He was relieved Cris got out on bail, thanks to Chuck Champion at the Artists Repertory Theater. Despite not having deep pockets; he'd managed to come up with the money and posted her bond. He smiled as he thought about how special friends were to a person. As a newsman, he had to keep bias out of the report but it galled him. Of course, she didn't mean to kill the young man. The red light blinked. And then Nicholas getting pounded.... My God, and the burglars still out there thieving and loose. He responded to Trudy's smile just behind the camera with a grin. She was learning fast and he enjoyed....... Red light. He was on.

Rainy smoothed the coverlet and put fresh flowers in the vase beside the bed. She checked her watch and rushed to put fresh towels in the guest bathroom before going downstairs to make sandwiches. Wine was chilling, chocolate chip cookies cooling and the butterflies finally stopped flapping inside her belly.

The past twenty four hours had been the cruelest of her life. Nervousness and fear for Cris while discussing Michael's death, jail and the arraignment with Cole left her exhausted. Seeing Cris in that orange jumpsuit with her hands and feet manacled made her faint. When the judge ruled bail was acceptable, she flew home to get the room ready. Cris would be there in her house for at least a week. That is, if she could talk her into it. She smiled, set the table for three and waited. Cole, as usual, was in top form. She wanted to hug him. Almost…maybe a kiss on the cheek. She felt faint when she heard his key in the front door lock.

"I smell cookies," she heard Cris say. Laughter followed her into the kitchen. She looked good, relieved and maybe a little bit frightened still, but Rainy rushed to hug her while Cole took her overnight bag upstairs. She watched him go up the steps and then swung Cris into a bone-crushing embrace.

"Oh honey. I am so glad to see you I could cry." Rainy looked into Cris's face and saw the tears start to spill. "Come on; let's see if food will cheer you up. And cookies," she said with a husky whisper as she remembered sharing one at the end of season party.

Rainy brought sandwiches, wine and chips toward them.

"I have to eat and run, Rainy," Cole said as he lifted his wine in a toast to Cris. Everyone sighed loudly, sipped and began to eat. Cole thought of his desk full of files, his notes to study and a trial to prepare for. Rainy thought about Cole leaving and having Cris to herself. Cris thought about being out of jail, away from her cellmate and dreading the funeral on Saturday morning.

Before Cole had taken a bite, the phone rang. "I'll get it, you two eat." He reached for the phone and wished he hadn't.

"Cris, it's for you," he said apologetically. He held his hand over the receiver and said, "It's Sam Berg. Whatever he wants, tell him no."

Cris's eyes grew wide as he handed her the phone. Rainy and Cole grimly stared at one another. She listened to Sam for quite some moments, then looked at Cole and firmly said, "No, Sam. I will not be on your show. I'm going to Michael's funeral Saturday. I am preparing for court and then I'm not sure what will follow." She listened a minute more. Her face flushed and she shook her head negatively.

Cole reached for the phone, took it gently from her and heard the last words that Sam said… "But, Cris, Michael was in on this and we can't get this resolved without your help. You may know something you don't realize you know…."

"No, Sam. This is Cole speaking as both her friend and attorney. I know you want to catch that old guy she saw and the young punk who grabbed Anna. I do too. But you'll have to do it on your own, buddy." He hung up.

Both women stared at him for a beat before lifting their wine.

"Guess it's just you two ladies alone for now," Cole said and proceeded to finish his lunch.

He missed the intimate smiles between the two women.

Back at the office, Cole spread out Cris's file and started piling up bits and pieces of information so he could delegate the help he'd need to pull in all the answers. His gut instinct told him there was something missing. He could not believe Michael would try to kill his sweetheart because she told Rainy he was a thief. He stabbed his pencil on the tablet and the broken lead pitched off his desk. Maybe Sam is right…there might be something she knows she's not aware of. *Is that it?* No, it was something else. His mind went round and round as he made doodles on the yellow legal pad.

When he looked down, ready to make some phone calls, Anna's name stared at him. Not only her name but AAAAAAAAAAA. Like a school kid. He promised to get his house in order, make changes. But with this uproar, he knew he had to concentrate on Cris and getting her out of the court system first. He knew she never would have purposely killed Michael with or without Taekwon-Do. She wanted to help people, not hurt them. He was stumped. Lifting his right hand to rub his thumb over his bearded jaw, he started making notes after removing his "A" page.

1. Cris saw an old guy leave the apartment after arguing with Michael
2. Michael called him Dal and another name Cris can't remember

3. Michael called someone from the theater before curtain calls and that someone undoubtedly robbed the patrons during the plays
4. Nicholas was with Michael in the brick building when the old guy beat him up. (a) Where is Nicholas now? (b) Where did he go afterward? Cris said he was beat up pretty bad. (c) The brick building near the theater – Who owns it? Who has access to it?
5. Who was the punk who grabbed Anna with Michael Mallory?

His pencil lead broke again. The thought of Anna in those thug's hands made him so angry, he couldn't see the pad in front of him. When she'd called him, he was so distraught he couldn't get to her fast enough. He wanted to protect her, love her. He grabbed another pencil. *I have to concentrate, dammit.*

6. He had to find Nicholas, talk to him. He could call Anna to get his last name......

Early the following morning, yellow oil drums, near the railroad yard beside Lark Point Steel Corporation, shone in the sun. A large sign, its ten-inch letters newly painted, boldly advertised the premises. Maple and oak trees lined the back of the property, far away from the commuters sitting in the historic station.

"No, DAL," he repeated stubbornly. "No."

"Well, now like I said, it's just you and me. Where is Nico? What do you think will happen if we don't find him?" Darrin hissed at him.

"Ah....think....well....nothin'....I guess the robberies stop. I haven't done nothin' since that bitch killed Michael. I just waited for you to call me. You asked me to meet you here and well.... here I am." Andreas was sullen, unsure.

Darrin grunted, disgusted with the smell of diesel everywhere.

"Sam Berg is still digging. After grabbing his daughter and then having her miraculously escape from you idiots made me very unhappy," Darrin said quietly, distastefully kicking dirt off his shoe. He glared at Andreas.

"I won't tell him nothing, DAL, you know you can count on me. The trial will nail that redhead and it will be over. Michael bought her all that bling and she goes and kills him!" Andreas spit into the dirt and then methodically ground it deep into the soil with his heel. He fumbled for a cigarette and held a lighter to the tip, his hand shaking slightly.

"How's your drinking, Andreas?"

Andreas was so surprised at the change of subject, he dropped his lighter. Suddenly wary, he slowly bent down to pick it up and thought frantically, wondering what DAL was getting at.

"Do you still brag about your adventures to your buddies down at the tavern, Andy?" Darrin's thumb rubbed against his other four fingers, round and round as he talked. Moving slowly toward the end of his car, he chuckled seeing the fear in the kid's eyes.

"I'm okay. I said okay! I don't talk. Why? You wanna pay me so I can leave town...is that it? I wouldn't need much." A ray of hope lined his insipid features.

The response hardened Darrin's features and his lips thinned. "Where would you go, Andreas?" Darrin asked with a silken voice.

Andreas turned away, pointing east. "To Montana to get a job on a horse ranch. My big brother lives there and he said he could get me on."

The sound of the gun being cocked was the last sound Andreas ever heard as a neat hole was blasted into the back of his head. His body was slammed face down into the dirt and the shadow of the yellow oil drums fell across his shocked features. Staring eyes were focused into dry, brown dirt and a train's shrill whistle sang his epitaph.

Darrin Lucas stood a moment staring down at the young man, choking on the smell of burnt gunpowder. "That's two," he said. Then he reached into his jacket pocket and pulled out a large white, freshly ironed handkerchief. Fatigue settled in the pockets under his eyes as he knelt down and carefully wiped the splatter of red blood off his silver fender and the side of his door. He pressed the red cloth into the boy's pocket and slowly drove out across the tracks glancing only once in his rear view mirror. Then he chuckled quietly. "But where's number three hiding?"

~

Nicholas was mending. He'd answered the detective's questions although the man wasn't happy. Too afraid for Tess and her family, he refused to tell him about DAL or Andreas. The shock of learning about Michael's death left him weak. A swift shadow of anger crossed his face. He'd been in the hospital two days and he wanted out. Winter term wasn't going to happen. Planning a visit to Ashland and his mother was a better idea. She loved the new town where she'd moved just last year and he hoped for a job to earn money by working in the big hotel near the Shakespearean Festival venue. But DAL knew where he lived. Leaving Tess would be hard but in a few months, he deduced, he could earn enough to make it count but he couldn't go to Ashland. He would tell Tess in the morning. She wouldn't like it but he had to go somewhere and soon.

Before midnight, Andreas' body had been removed from the railway yard, the outline of his corpse, yellow crime-scene tape and dark stains on the ground the only indication a man's life had been snuffed out. A railroad worker nearly ran over him when he left his seven o'clock shift. He'd braked in disbelief as the dust stirred around him, nearly smashing his old red truck into some oil drums. The story had been pieced together without much to go on and delivered to the reporters at the police barricades after the press asked their questions. Several photographs of the surrounding areas and a few hundred feet of video tape had images that would be edited down to a hundred seconds on tomorrow's television newscast. Clouds hid the fragment moon. The area was nearly empty; the only light came from the headlights of the passing train.

The death of Andreas Kassipakis held only an obscure corner of the Lark Point Democrat the following morning. A railroad worker found him. The man thought he could save the boy before he realized the boy was cold and a bullet hole was lodged in the back of his head. Yellow crime tape surrounded the area, the tire tracks were measured, investigated and the open case was stumping the police. When Anna read the small article, she scanned the remainder of the page before moving into her study. It kept her mind busy to sit in front of her computer. Write, write, write.

She hadn't seen Sam since he left the hospital the night before. She'd only seen him briefly before that to discuss the house, the divorce, the final killing of twenty five years of marriage. Her anger wasn't directed at Sam anymore. Now it was Tess. She was sitting on a kitchen stool when Tess came into the kitchen yawning, her eyes darting towards Anna. Behind her a shiny array of burnished copper pots and pans hung over the island.

Tess turned on the small television above the counter and stood, barefoot, pouring hot coffee into an earthenware mug. "Morning, mom."

Anna looked up.

"Can we talk please?" Tess asked firmly.

Sitting down on a rattan chair, she faced her daughter with the television behind her. She pointed to the other chair.

Tess poured quickly, her heart slamming in her chest. "I was so wrong, Mom." Tears blinded her eyes and choked her voice. Wet glistened on her pale, heart-shaped face as she tossed her hair over her shoulder. I should never have said those things to you last night after we got home. I know you were worried. I was so scared about Nicholas and mad at Dad. When I saw those divorce papers on the dining room table when we walked in, I lost it." Her face burned.

Anna didn't move. "You, wrong?" she asked, swallowing hard.

"Dad was wrong. I was wrong to accuse you of anything. I didn't really mean it. I hurt inside and I guess I.....I don't know but I love you and I hate this anger between us. Please love me again?" she whispered as her mouth twitched and a hot tear escaped over her cheek.

Smothering a sob, coffee forgotten, Anna raised her arms toward her daughter and pulled her down onto her lap. "I never stopped loving you, Tess. But you need to step back from this. In fact, if you don't get up, my legs will drop off," she said with relieved laughter in her voice.

Tess's lips still trembled with a need to smile. A tentative sense of humor was restored and she laughed, standing up and reaching for the coffee pot. "More coffee, mom?"

Anna nodded, holding a cup in both hands toward her daughter.

The TV commercial ended and both women glanced at the monitor curiously when they heard the news flash. "The body found last night at the railroad yard with a single bullet in the back of his head has been identified as Andreas Kassipakis, son of Julian and Marianna Kassipakis from Kalispell, Montana. There are no leads to his killing but the police feel it may be linked to......." A photo of Andreas filled the upper right hand corner of the screen.

Anna walked closer and her face drained of color, the rim of the coffee cup perched at her lips. "Oh. My. God."

"What, mom? Tess followed Anna's shocked gaze but the screen had changed to another local story about schools.

"It was that kid!" she answered, her mind racing.

"What kid, mom?" Tess pulled her mother around to face her.

Anna's brown eyes panicked. Running her hand through her dark curly hair, she ran back to the table and tore into the newspaper, whipping through the pages until she found the article. She read it again quickly and laid it down in front of them. She pointed and gripped Tess's hand. "Who should we call first, Cole or Nicholas? Both! Call Nicholas, Tess…now!" Anna's eyes were glazed with fear. "And hurry!"

Tess dialed Nicholas' cell phone, her eyes never leaving Anna's white face. It rang three times before she heard a sleepy, "Yeh?"

"Nicholas. It's Tess….."

Anna jerked the phone out of her hand and patted Tess's cheek quickly. "Nick! It's Anna. Listen to me. Wake up!" she yelled.

Tess was stunned.

"What, Anna?" he said, instantly alert.

"Get dressed fast. I will be there in ten minutes. Get out of there and meet me at the emergency entrance. Ask someone the way, just get there. Move, man, now!" She hung up, grabbed Tess, running to her Audi explaining to Tess what she wanted her to do.

"Take this money and credit card. Take your car to the old Jiffy Lube that's closed out on Scholls Ferry Road. I'll bring Nick to you. That kid that was killed? He was the one who kidnapped me and I think the old guy Cris saw beat up Nicholas is probably his killer."

Tess was stunned.

"Nicholas could be next and probably will be unless we get him as far from Lark Point as possible. Go to Sarah at the Bay House. I'll call her after I drop off Nicholas. Then you drive back immediately from Ashby, less questions that way." Her heart fluttered and she stared at her daughter, whose face filled with questions. "You can do this, Tess! Do not tell anyone what we're doing. *Nobody* and that includes your father." She jabbed at the gas pedal and the little Audi spun wheels toward the hospital.

~

Cole Nites got off the elevator at St. Elizabeth Hospital and approached a nurse in the hallway a few feet in front of him. He lifted his briefcase in a more comfortable position and approached her while the questions he had ready for Nicholas Alonzo went round in his head. After learning from Anna the night before where Nicholas could be found, he'd gone to work again.

The nurse pointed toward the end of the hall and he headed that way, glancing into rooms, slipping by the cleaning cart as the hospital smells hit him like a bad-smelling rose. He hadn't been in a hospital for a long time, not since Shari, his college sweetheart, died. He wouldn't be walking down the hallway now if it wasn't imperative that he speak with the young man. He needed answers to give strength to Cris's testimony. He knew Michael had been in deep and it was Cris's word against the prosecutor's when the trial started. To think Michael and Nicholas had both been inside his home not long ago…….. casing his house?

A nurse stared after him, file in hand.

Cole's eyes narrowed and he pushed his way in. The bed was empty. He swung his head around. The toilet? The door was closed. Standing a minute with indecision, he placed his briefcase on the floor, sat on the chair by the bed and pulled out his legal pad. He'd wait. His graying head was bent over his notes as he scribbled in the margin. After a few minutes, he lifted his head to listen for any noise coming from the toilet. He chewed the inside of his cheek a moment before getting up to put his ear to the door. "Nicholas?"

No answer. He tapped on the door. Still no answer. Putting his head into the hallway, he caught a nurse's attention and quickly explained his dilemma.

She lifted her eyebrows and followed him into the room. Noting the covers were strewn half on the floor, she wondered if the patient had to run for the toilet fast. Lifting her hand to knock, she opened the door when there was no answer. The toilet room was empty. Conflicting thoughts raced across her face. "He was here just moments ago. Maybe they took him to x-ray? Let me check his file notes," she told Cole. "I'll be back." In extra large lavender scrubs and matching clogs, the big woman headed for the nursing station, gray hair bouncing as she walked.

Cole sat down, pulled his pad into his lap again and resumed his wait. He needed to talk to this guy and he wasn't leaving until he did. He thought about the conversation Cris had rehashed for him again and again. Her story was a little erratic but basically the same. Michael heard her talking to Rainy, he came into her dressing room after Rainy left and came at Cris with a gun filled with anger and bullets. But to actually shoot at her when he so obviously loved her just didn't add up. He slapped the yellow pad on his thigh. *"Dammit, what am I missing?"*

Lavender Scrubs returned with a frown on her face and a clipboard. "He wasn't set to go anywhere. His vitals were taken an hour ago and his doctor is in the hospital and expected to visit Mr. Alonzo any time now. I have no idea where he could be. You are welcome to wait but I need to find out if anyone saw him leave his room. He may be walking the halls but his ribs are still so painful, he had trouble moving. He is still a broken young man so I don't know what I can tell you," she finished apologetically.

Cole stuffed the pad in his briefcase and followed her. He looked up and down the hallway and began walking toward the elevator as he watched the heavy nurse whisper to other nurses, pointing toward Nicholas' room. He saw the women shake their heads. Nobody seemed to know where he was. If he was that broken up, he couldn't have gotten far and why would he leave before the doctor saw him anyway? Cole turned on his heel and retraced his steps, opened the little closet by the bed and found the answer. Empty hangers and a balled up hospital gown, nothing more. He let out a bark of disappointment and left.

Cole's questions multiplied as he drove back to his office. His BMW took the corners neatly while Joe Sample's piano music played gently from a CD. Why would the kid leave? Why not wait for the doctor? Where would he go? Where does he live? He's a college student, maybe he lives in a dorm at LSU? But, where was home? His head beat to the rhythm Joe spewed out of his speakers. Hmmmmm. He's Tess's boyfriend. She'd know something. He suddenly smiled. He could use it as an excuse to hear Anna's voice again.

Anna pulled up to her front door and aligned her Audi next to her sweet-smelling winter Daphne, its scent easing the stress from her neck when she opened the door. She was breathing fast. She was glad she'd made the decision to follow her gut-feeling instead of the way she'd lived her life in the past. She wouldn't make choices based on what others thought. She wouldn't keep quiet when something upset her. She'd voice her opinions; stay vocal, fight for what she believed in. And she believed in Nicholas. He'd made some bad decisions, yes, but he was essentially a good guy or Tess wouldn't be in love with him. Anna had liked him instantly. She only knew part of his story, but she decided being a protective mother lion fit her just fine. She was proud of her actions the last hour and nothing would change that. Her cell phone was ringing by the time she entered her kitchen. She tapped it open and smiled. Cole.

"Hey, Cole." Her heart rate increased with the memory of his arms around her.

"Hello there. Am I calling at a good time?" His voice was low and purposefully seductive.

Anna laughed. "You could never call at a bad time. How are you? I heard that Cris is staying with you and Rainy. What a tragedy. I'm sure she is very depressed, so glad Rainy is there with her. How will that work as her attorney?"

Cole chuckled, "She'll be here for a few days. It is a strange one and I have questions.... Anna, is Tess there? I went to the hospital a bit ago to ask Nicholas Alonzo some questions to help me with Cris's case but he's flown the coop. The nurses couldn't find him. "

Anna took a deep breath.

He continued, "You and I both know he's involved somehow with Michael. Cris saw an old guy beat the crap out of the young man. I want to know who it was. The nurse told me the police had questioned him. Why wouldn't Nicholas give him answers? If he had, Sam would have had it for the entire community to mull over on last night's program."

The breath seemed to solidify in her throat. "Oh." She spoke carefully. "Tess isn't here right now, Cole. I'm surprised he was gone when you got there. He may be on his way to the police station as we speak?" Her voice was shakier than she would have liked.

Cole rubbed his short beard, noting the timber of her voice. When he spoke again, his voice was tender, almost a murmur. "Are you doing all right, Anna? You sound a bit off. I know this trial is going to put off some life choices for me but I will make them...please don't think I have changed any of my thoughts since I saw you last. Dirty face and all, I love you."

She gloried briefly in his words and could barely lift her voice above a whisper as anxiety spurted through her. She hated keeping Nicholas' whereabouts from him but her determination kept her focused. "Cole, you do what you have to do. I will be here. I wish I could see you, but I understand and you must concentrate on Cris." She moistened her dry lips.

He smothered a groan. "Yes, Cris. I will do some checking to find Nicholas but if Tess knows where he is, please ask her to give me a call?"

A delightful shiver went through her. "Yes, certainly," she whispered as her troubled spirits quieted.

After he hung up, he pulled out his notepad and drifted through the questions he'd prepared for Nicholas. He had to find the young man and focus.

Darrin Lucas stood in his doorway. His stern face and thin lips told Cole he was upset about something. Craggy face beneath the prematurely white hair added to the disgruntled features as he came into the office. "Do you have a minute?"

"Sure, Darrin. I'm struggling a bit. I was able to get María Crissman out on bail. It's a clear case of self defense but now I'm missing one of the witnesses. The news this morning gave some indication that the boy found dead at the Amtrak station may have something to do with Michael Mallory and that theft ring but nothing concrete.

Darrin's eyebrows rose and his jaw jutted out. He crossed a leg across his knee and pinched the crease in his suit pants. When he looked up at Cole, his expression was clouded. "Missing witness, huh? Maybe the police know where he is. Who are you looking for?" he asked Cole innocently, cool blue eyes shining like cobalt.

"A college kid named Nicholas Alonzo." Cole consulted his legal pad. "He was attacked and hospitalized but skipped out of Dodge."

Darrin scowled. "So the police haven't talked with him? They don't seem able to solve much of anything in this town! You'd think they would have….."

"Oh, they talked to him the night he was beat to a pulp, I understand, but the kid said he didn't know who his attacker was. Cris watched him getting beaten but she doesn't know who the old guy was either. The police are pounding the pavement to find him. It has to be part of this damned scheme because Michael was in the room with them and didn't stop the fight. Maybe he couldn't. If that bastard was beating someone in front of me, I'd think twice before stepping in too…but there are just so many unanswered questions."

Darrin perked up. "Your client saw an old man beat on your witness? Interesting. Could she recognize him? What happened afterward? Do we really know why she killed her boyfriend? Sounds like you have your hands full, Cole." He stood up quickly and left the room.

Cole was baffled by his behavior but had no time to think about it.

Darrin Lucas was livid. How could those boys cause such a ruckus and ruin his project? He steamed back to his office, pulled out his cell phone and dialed Nico's number. No answer. No surprise. Shifting to the large window in his office, he ignored the beeping phone on his desk and concentrated on the woman. She was out of prison thanks to Cole and she would be easy to find. He grabbed his coat and left the building.

~

"What do you do when you can't get access to the main players in an investigation like this, Sam?"

He looked at Trudy and lifted his coffee cup, thinking how to answer her question. "Well, when someone you want to interview refuses to cooperate; you go in the back door."

"The back door?" She gazed at the table a moment before lifting her eyes and smiled. "Ok, Mr. Berg, explain."

"I want to talk with Nicholas. He doesn't want to talk with me. I want to talk with Cris. She doesn't want to talk with me. Think about it, Trudy. They are hiding something and my conclusion is fear. So, who are they afraid of? We go after that person. Cris saw someone beat up Nicholas badly but neither will say who did it. This person must have some clout either around town or in their group of acquaintances. We narrow down the list. Nicholas is a college student dating my daughter. Cris is an actress working at a theater that we now know was a burglar's nest. They must be related. Michael was in the room with Nicholas when he was beaten half to death. Michael is dead. Nicholas is missing. Cris is frightened and fighting for her life in the courts. Why isn't she telling all? Why isn't Nicholas? Where is Nicholas? And where is the kid who was with Michael when they kidnapped Anna? The back door means we are on the right track but going in the wrong door."

Trudy smiled. "Sam, you amaze me." She jotted down some notes, glanced out the window and turned back with questions in her eyes.

He admitted he wanted to get to know her outside the station. Was he ready? Maybe. Was she? Maybe. "Talking about the back door, would you be interested in going to dinner with me on one condition?" He grinned at her expression.

"Depends on whose back door you want to walk into and the condition." Her face was an open book and he liked that.

"We make it a threesome. I would like to meet Karen. I'm pretty good with little girls. Despite having only one, I think I did a pretty good job raising her….although, of course, I can't take all the accolades there. Her mother is a great mom. But I like children and would be pleased to be around a little one again."

Trudy's face shadowed at the mention of Anna, wondering about the broken relationship. Did Sam still harbor feelings for his ex-wife?

"Hey, if you don't like the idea, no pressures. Just dinner and…."

"No, it's not that, Sam. I know Karen might like a man at our table again. I'm cautious because you are still technically married……"

A weight filled Sam's chest before answering. "I am on my own, Trudy. Anna has another life now. I am lucky enough to still be part of my daughter's life. If you ask if I'm still in love with Anna, I can't tell you because my head and heart are in flux right now. I can tell you that I like you and spending time with both of you would make me very happy."

Outside the window, a mass of dead leaves scuttled across the flagstone patio as a cool breeze softened the sun's glare. "7:00 o'clock Friday night then? Karen is in bed by 8:30. Would I be forward asking if you'd stay for a movie afterward?

Sam grinned. "Yet bet. Friday, 7 o'clock it is."

"Great. Bring wine and grapes." Sparkling eyes answered him.

"Grapes?"

"Yes, Karen loves grapes. The wine's for me."

He laughed, enjoying the warmth slipping through his gut.

SEVENTEEN

Charlie Royce handed a cup of coffee to Detective Clyde Mark. "So, no answers, huh? What else have you got?"

The detective pulled out his book and ran down the list. "The old guy at the deli said a guy with white hair came in looking for the boy. He was a big guy with cold blue eyes and a nasty manner. If he was the abuser, he'd have to be nasty." His eyes followed down his list and his pencil stopped. "He also said the guy drove away in a silver Mercedes." How many of those are rolling around Lark Point?"

Charlie smiled and pointed to the door.

Clyde headed for the end of the hall looking for Candace Shelton. She was a sleuth with the motor vehicle department and a whiz on the computer. He thought it might close the case. He hummed, finished his putrid black coffee and tossed the empty cup in the waste bin outside her door.

Charlie studied the white board's bits and pieces of scribbled notes and names strewn from top to bottom. Three guys that they knew of...Michael Mallory for sure based on María Crissman's story. A punk who helped him kidnap Anna Berg also based on her story, an accomplice named Andy based on Anna's statement. He tapped his pen on the metal table. If the activity surrounding those oil drums was any indication, the kid they found dead last night could very well be that punk. Andy could definitely be a nickname for Andreas. He made a note to show the photo to Anna Berg. With that identification, he'd have his third thief. But the white-haired man had him stumped. He hoped Candace could give Clyde the answers to the Mercedes. He tossed two Tums into his mouth and called Sam Berg. Maybe he had some ideas Charlie missed? Sam had opened a hornet's nest with that program, pulled the bad guys right out of the air when the police investigation had stalled. Charlie found it vaguely disturbing but at least the mayor had gotten off his back. He found it quite interesting that just one small comment by the mayor opened Pandora's Box. He made a date to meet Sam for a beer at seven, maybe a hamburger at that deli…and they could talk to old Jimmy again.

Rainy was worried. Cris wasn't eating much and her tears hadn't abated. She'd finally agreed to relax in a bubble bath; Rainy tested the water, splashed in lavender scent and fluffed the towel.

"Cris, the bath is ready, come on, honey." Peeking into the guestroom, she held a robe for Cris to shrug into while searching her face. "It will make you feel better. You can just sink into that warm, frothy bath and let your stress float away. Cole will get you out of this mess and then we can fly to Hawaii just like we planned," she managed in a hoarse whisper.

Cris followed her to the bathroom, dropped her robe and stood naked a beat, her eyes swung to Rainy's and her mouth curved in tenderness. She placed a foot into the tub, noting the perfect temperature and sat on the edge before sliding in. Foamy bubbles hid her breasts as she laid her head back on the foam pillow attached to the tub with rubber suction cups. "Ah….Rain, you're right. It feels sooo good…." She clasped Rainy's hand, reaching for her solid strength.

Rainy smoothed Cris's red curls with a hand and sensed awakening flames in Cris's eyes, so Rainy joined her.

"What? Six silver Mercedes in Lark Point? Never would have guessed that." Clyde took the printout from Candace, winked his thanks and headed back to the case room. It was already six and the building was clearing out except for a few diehards.

"We have six hits, Charlie. Ted and I'll check them out tomorrow." The detective shook the sheet of paper at Charlie and bid him goodbye.

Charlie still stood in front of the whiteboard, rubbing his chin. The whiteboard stared back at him. Three young guys and one old guy. The railroad yard and brick building. The theater and brick building. His jaw snapped. The brick buildings. Who owned the brick buildings? Was there a connection? He'd check land records first thing in the morning. After grabbing his jacket, turning off his laptop and brushing his fingers through thick honey-colored hair, he was ready for that beer with Sam. Another angle. A grin spread across his lips and his shoulders relaxed.

Cris didn't want to go into her apartment. She didn't want to face the silence, Michael's clothes or his scent. But she knew she couldn't put it off any longer. She'd stayed with Rainy and Cole long enough. Was she ready to face the funeral tomorrow? The trauma of going home?

She stood in the doorway. There was thick dust, empty beer bottles in the sink, stinking garbage and a sense of timelessness as she sat down at the table and stared around her. Quite some moments later, she drifted into the bedroom before looking through her closet, seeing clothes she never thought she'd be wearing to Michael's funeral. A funeral that would not be happening if she'd been more careful, more …. She stopped and sat on the side of her bed, unsure what to do next. It was harder than she'd imagined.

Her cell phone rang and Rainy's number popped up on the screen. "Are you all right? Do you want me to come over?" Rainy hadn't wanted her to leave and they'd argued.

"No, I mean yes. I'm all right. No, please don't come over." When the line went dead, she held the receiver in her hand a moment before hanging up. She needed coffee. Soon, the aroma of the fresh brew filled the empty apartment and she was on her second cup before she opened her closet door again.

For November, there was a chill to the morning that even the sun couldn't penetrate. She studied the tired image that confronted her in the mirror. Slender arms wrapped protectively around a body she barely recognized as her own, red hair framing a face etched with lines of exhaustion that even careful makeup hadn't been able to erase. She wondered how she was going to get through tomorrow. Or today.

The sounds of morning drifted up the stairs and down her hallway while she looked through the layers of clothes hanging in front of her. She owned nothing black, never had. Navy blue? Her hands, shaking slightly, plucked the dress from the hanger. Something caught, and instead of stopping to disentangle the unseen snarl, Cris simply yanked at it. The rasping sound of a seam giving way raked across her nerves and she knew she was going to cry again. She angrily swallowed them back.

Suddenly hungry, she decided food might help and pulled some appetizers from the freezer into the microwave. However, within minutes, she was having difficulty concentrating on what was happening and ran for the toilet. After a moment, she turned her head and vomited up all the spinach puffs.

Later, she went to her dresser where her eyes fell on Michael's picture inside a frame filled with memories. She'd bought it for that particular photo she'd taken the year before in San Francisco. The Golden Gate Bridge scampered across the top and surrounded his smiling face that now seemed to mock her. Now the tears did come. Cris backed away from the picture, sank to her bed, and buried her face in her hands.

That was how Rainy found her. She paused at the door, watching her and her heart ached but felt unable to comfort. She crossed the room to sit beside her and with gentle hands, touched Cris's face and kissed her. "Honey, is there anything I can.....?

".......do?" Cris said between tears. "I think we already did it."

Darrin Lucas was incensed. Two down and one to go didn't sit well with him when the last one had disappeared and a woman was running around with too much information in her head. He should have finished Nico when he wouldn't grab the girl, he fumed. Instead he'd just hit him a few times. Wondering where the kid got to afterward made him angry all over again. How far could he have gotten? He thought back to the old man in the deli, but shook his head. No, the guy looked too honest. To think he'd been at the damned hospital..... If he'd known, he could have paid him a short visit....

Then there's the girl. He'd been stunned to learn she'd witnessed him pummel the boy. She hadn't recognized him; good thing he had his back to the door...at least that's what she's saying. She might recognize him though. He tapped his fingers on his chair arm. And where the hell was Nico now? He stood up and stared out the window. He'd worked too hard to let one or two loose ends spoil things. He had to find him before Cole did. He placed his hands belligerently on his hips. Watching the plane in the sky above his building turned his thoughts to the case he should have been working on. His white head turned to the desk with a fleeting image of curly red hair and green eyes. The girl. Maybe he should concentrate on the girl. How could he be assured of a guilty verdict? It would sure get her out of town. He chuckled.

On Waverly Drive, Anna tried to concentrate on her manuscript. The editing had begun without the missing court scene.... If she screwed it up, the reader would question the validity of the entire story. Her readers were intelligent; she owed them accuracy. She Googled criminal court trials and was astounded with the wealth of information she found. However, no clear court scenes. She thought, ruefully, how she'd wanted to listen during a self-defense trial and now Cole would be defending Cris. The irony of her original request and the reality gave her chills.

On one hand, she thought of finishing her book after the trial but cringed because it would be so emotional. On the other hand, she didn't want to wait the length of time it could take to go to trial. Glancing at her watch every few minutes didn't help either. Tess should be back soon. She hated to call her while she was driving, unsure if she'd ever paired her iPhone with the Bluetooth in the Mazda...but if she didn't arrive soon, she would throw caution to the wind and call her anyway.

Anna held the new iPhone she'd purchased that afternoon to replace the one Andy smashed to bits and slapped the keyboard. Pacing the room, she decided a glass of Rosé would smooth her thoughts as she wrapped her arms around her body. Squeezing her eyes shut wearily, she pulled the cork out of the bottle and reached for a wine glass. Would her life ever be normal?

It was six o'clock. She punched the television remote to see Sam's smiling face looking back at her, his voice animated. Yes, he was cocky now that the investigation that opened up his Man with a Story program was born. She was worried about Nicholas and what the death of the boy at the railway station could mean to him. She sipped her wine, swirled the glass thoughtfully and wondered about the kingpin who was blackmailing these young people into stealing for him.

Her eyes rounded. *Maybe I'll use the story for my next novel.* She emitted a murmuring sound that sounded like bitter amusement. Did she regret all the changes she'd encountered in the last few months? No. The freedom was intoxicating; she probably didn't even need the wine. She tapped the stem with her fingernail. Her dark, curly head lay back on the chair, her wine settled in her lap and words for the last chapter scrambled through her brain. She had to make a decision there....Her cell phone rang and she smiled as Tess's photo lit the screen.

"Tess!"

"Mom, I'm just leaving. It took awhile to convince Nicholas you knew what was best. He called his mother in Ashland and he explained what happened up to a point. She thinks he's working for the winter. He wanted me to stay with him but we agreed you were right. If I go missing too, everyone would know I was part of his disappearing act. I'll be home about eight." She sighed loudly.

"Thanks, honey. I was starting to stare the hands off my watch and will be glad to have you back here. We have to think about what to do next. Cole called asking where you were because he hoped you could lead him to Nicholas for questioning. He is sure Nicholas can shed light on Michael's actions for Cris's trial or at least help with her defense. I hated lying to him," she finished, a heaviness centered in her chest.

"Well, he sure can't know where Nick is...I'm on my way," she hurriedly ended the call with *I love you* and hung up.

Anna tipped back her glass and finished the last drop. She hoped she was doing the right thing. Trying not to question herself, she shrugged out of the chair. "Tonight's a two-glass evening," she said aloud and tipped the bottle.

Cole hit a brick wall looking for Nicholas Alonzo. He knew the young man could be the impetus to getting the district attorney to drop the charges against Cris. He banked the notes in front of him and studied the summary he'd created. His stomach rumbled but he ignored it. Too busy to eat, he realized he'd skipped lunch and after checking his watch, he realized it was dark outside, nearly nine. He went over what he had one more time. He knew he was tired when the words began to blur.

Darrin and Steven both left hours earlier. Darrin was clearly agitated but Steven was smiling because he and Moira were going to visit their new grandson. A grandson. Cole smiled. He and Rainy hadn't wanted children. Thank God. She wasn't mother material and he was unsure if he could have met the commitment either. His thoughts turned to his marriage. Before meeting Anna and got smacked in the gut, it was a subject he'd consistently steered away from.

He'd met Rainy so long ago. He remembered her father's worry because she wouldn't date. When he insinuated Cole should take her to dinner to make an old man happy, he did so. Cole couldn't even remember the date. She was a woman with a lot of attributes but she never seemed passionate about anything other than art, events, sleuthing and cooking. It hadn't bothered him. He wondered if he ever cared and wondered also why they'd ever married but of course he knew why. It made the old man happy, Cole gained a hostess for his clients and his heart wasn't on the line. They all won. Now, not so much. Despite being anxious to address his quasi-marriage with Rainy, he shook his head to focus on the legal pad. He had to help Cris first by finding Nicholas.

The district attorney really wanted to sink her teeth into this one. Cole wondered if it was the notoriety or serving justice as Lyn Corelli proclaimed.

Everyone liked Cris, a woman who enjoyed teaching self defense through Taekwon-Do. She was proud she'd never had to use it. Now it was going to bite her in the ass. He doubted she had a mean bone in her body, although she was a bit cloudy in her roles between acting and who she really was. Cole found Chuck's remark interesting. With each new role, Cris seemed to become that character. Could she be really just acting innocent? Could he be reading her wrong? All of the cast members agreed she was a good person and that she'd cared about Michael. Michael. He tapped his pencil against his close-cropped graying hair. What would make this guy turn on a woman with these attributes? A woman he lived with and loved? If she was hiding something, as he surmised, he could not figure out what it could be. What reason would she have to lie? She was clearly devastated about his death and her part in it. He glanced at the pad again. The DA thought she had enough evidence for second degree murder. Did she? No, it was ludicrous.

He scribbled out the words, voluntary manslaughter. A murder can be reduced to voluntary manslaughter if the defendant acted in the heat of passion. Killing in the heat of passion requires 1) the defendant was provoked, 2) the provocation caused the defendant to act rashly and under the influence of intense emotion, obscuring his or her judgment and reasoning, and 3) the provocation would have caused the average person to act rashly.

In other words, to qualify for heat of passion/voluntary manslaughter, the jury must find the defendant was so provoked by what the victim did, and reasonably so, that he or she killed out of intense emotion rather than deliberate judgment. But the gun, the spent bullet, the fall and the crack to Michael's skull? He tossed the pencil and pushed papers into the files, stashed them in his drawer and left the office. On the way to the car, he knew he needed to call a Pre-Trial Hearing. He'd call for a meeting with Corelli. He knew she didn't have peanuts and he was determined to prove it. Damn, but he wished he could find to Alonzo.

Darrin Lucas was powerful and unstoppable; he gripped his whiskey glass and scrunched down into the grey wingback chair in front of his fireplace. Dark windows near the lamp reflected a mask of anger. His jaw clenched. Drinking the liquid, he enjoyed the burn in his throat as he gazed around the open room, lighting on each sculpture, each piece of artwork on his walls and the brass greyhound that fronted the fireplace corner. He turned his head toward the lady filled with gems and his face changed from the usual ugliness to contentment. Nobody could really touch him. Wherever Nicholas was, he was too frightened to come forward. The stupid actress who took Michael away from here would have to play it out. He wondered idly if Cole could pull it off but in the next instant he didn't doubt he would.

The house was quiet, always so quiet. He didn't even want animals to mar the smell of his home or the noise they made. Man's best friend? "Not for me," he said aloud. He glanced around the room again, took another sip of the fiery liquid and knew where his best friends lay. They were stashed in the secret room of his basement. He wasn't sure what he'd do with the Hummels, not his style. The tapestry was nice. Maybe he'd hang that in the back bedroom when his sister visited. She'd like that. Hell, maybe he'd give it to her. Yes, things would be all right. He tossed back the last of the whiskey.

Suddenly, he felt tired. Darrin Lucas' last thoughts before he slid into bed were that he should stay close to Cole during this case with the woman. It was never too smart to let things slide. He never could have reached his success in the community if he had.

~

Sam opened the door to his new townhouse and flipped on the lights. Too quiet, too empty, too lonely. He didn't call Anna anymore. She told him it was bordering on harassment. Not quite believing their marriage was over; he'd last asked if she'd have lunch with him. Her response was testy.

Trudy Knox, on the other hand agreed to have lunch with him a couple weeks earlier. Sam enjoyed her company so much, he'd invited himself to her house for dinner with her little girl and he'd enjoyed every minute. He liked her but would it go anywhere? Did he want it to?

He slid off his tie, kicked off his shoes and pulled a can of soup from the cupboard. Rummaging through his newly-stocked pantry, he found a pan, some crackers and some peanut butter. Can't have crackers without peanut butter, he told himself. The soup was full of potatoes and vegetables with a few minute pieces of stew meat. He looked into the pan…very minute pieces. He hoped Trudy would invite him over again. He wasn't a cook and wasn't sure he wanted to be.

Elliott was on his butt because he hadn't interviewed Nicholas. He couldn't get past Tess. That girl was like a bird protecting a nest. He never let a little girl stand in his way before when there was a story and a witness to interview, but he'd never run across one like Tess before. He laughed. Just like her old Dad, he thought. Elliott said to wait until he's out of the hospital and try again. When he'd called the hospital and found he was no longer there, Sam had called the fraternity house. He wasn't there. Tess would know but he dared not call her or Anna.

He poured the soup into a bowl, smeared peanut butter on several crackers and popped open a cold MGD. He mulled over the facts he had for his program the next evening. He had to find something before his audience looked elsewhere. That's what Elliott feared. Sam had reminded him they couldn't stay number one all the time.

Elliot's face had turned red as he had asked, "Why?!"

Slurping the soup and washing it down with beer his mind kept clicking. He couldn't interview Cris because Cole was in his way. He couldn't talk to Nicholas because Tess was in his way. Michael was dead.

Andreas Kassipakis may have been part of the gang and he was dead. The victims could rest easy, he hoped, now that the gang was probably dissolved. That left the old guy with the white hair. An old guy with white hair….. He got up and called Charlie while he stuffed another peanut-butter filled cracker into his mouth. He needed a news headline and by God, he'd get one.

Nicholas drank the steaming black coffee, trying not to think about his clenched gut and headache. His ribs screamed every time he bent over, stretched his arm to get something out of the cupboard or took a shower. The pain woke him every time he twisted in bed. His mind wouldn't shut up. His mother wouldn't stop calling and there was Tess. She wanted answers and her questions were wearing him down.

It was a shock to learn Andreas and Michael were both dead. Dead! My God. Who would have thought when this began that this could happen? Would he lose Tess over it all? Would she ever trust him again? The magic with her happened on a cloudy day a year ago September. He had to hold onto it and knew he'd lose it if he wasn't accountable for his own actions.

The sounds of the ocean outside the cottage were muted through the windows. Walking outside to the back deck, he knew he shouldn't be hiding. He should be helping somehow. DAL had to be stopped but when he thought of him, the beating impinged on his mind and he froze. He'd never been really afraid of anyone before. But that was before he got mixed up with DAL. And that man scared the crap out of him.

Glancing at his watch, he knew Tess was due to call. He smiled. Life had to get straight. He could not imagine life without her. But he had to stand up like a man. Nicholas pulled out his phone and scrolled down the contact list again. He'd added Cole Nites to his phone that morning. He was sure the man would help him and he wanted to call him. But he'd talk with Tess first. Anna trusted him and he had to trust her too.

EIGHTEEN

Lyn Corelli doodled on a notepad as she listened to Cole Nites list all the reasons why she should drop charges against María Crissman. She glanced over at his face. She noted his short hair was threaded with silver, the neatly-trimmed beard had a small area of grey about the size of a dime and his eyes were deep silver. Eyes that looked at her so earnestly. She thought he was the most handsome man she'd seen in awhile, felt stirrings of interest and doodled some more.

"Let me get this straight, Cole. You think since people like this red-headed woman that I should rethink my charges for second degree murder. You think because she's your wife's friend and yes, I know she's living at your house which I think is strange to say the least…. that she's a pillar of the community because she teaches Taekwon-Do and is a accomplished actress, I should drop the charges. Stop and think about it from my side of the desk. Taekwon-Do is a non-contact martial art but she beat the shit out of Michael Mallory. He hit his head and died in her dressing room. She's a good actress and she is screaming self defense. She's playing her part well, I think." The DA's dark eyes below naturally-arched eyebrows were dynamic and not just a little mesmerizing.

They stared at each other.

"I think," Cole said evenly, "that you do not have enough evidence to prove second degree murder. I think setting a Pre-Trial Hearing with the judge would be a healthy step in the right direction. I will put Ms. Crissman on the stand, you can list discovery, I can rebut and we'll see if the judge will drop the case or set trial."

A flash of humor crossed her face. "Let's have a pizza and beer across the street. My treat, counselor." She stood up and walked provocatively toward the door, her hips swaying in obvious invitation.

Cole hunched over, his arms resting on his thighs and rolled his eyes. "Not this time, Lyn. I have a case to put together. I will be contacting the judge for a Pre-Trial Hearing. You can bet on it."

She pinched the bridge of her nose and walked stiffly to the door, let him pass through it and then slammed it after him.

Nicholas shook the sand off his feet and then shoved his toes into the sand. Staring at the ocean from the deck, he saw a boy and his dog scramble over the rocks. When the boy fell and the dog yipped and jumped around wildly, Nicholas jumped off the porch and raced to the boy. A small foot was wedged between two rocks and the boy's elbow was bleeding. The noise was deafening as wind rushed around them, breakers crashed. He looked at the boy, put a finger to his lips and lifted the rock aside to pull the boy loose. The small terrier sniffed at Nicholas' toes and whined as he sat on his haunches. A woman's voice yelled over the wind an instant before both parents arrived beside them.

"Thank you!" The woman reached toward the boy as the man lifted him up in his arms. They soothed their son, thanked him again and walked away with the dog happily barking and running laps around them.

Nicholas' ribs screamed like the seagulls above him when they walked away. He'd been there nearly a week. Tess called him several times a day and he'd spoken with his family. To his family, he was living a lie. Yes, he liked his job at the restaurant. Yes, he was earning good money and big tips. Yes, he decided to enroll in winter classes at LSU. Yes, he was doing great. Yes, yes, yes, yes, yes, he'd lied.

Nicholas sank down on the largest rock that had sucked the little kid in and laid his chin on his chest. He thought of all the heart to heart talks his dad had given him and his brother over the years. All the love they'd shown him in a house with little money and less education. He'd wanted his sons to go to college and Nicholas was smart enough to earn scholarships to do it. His parents had tears in their eyes when he'd won and again when he left to pursue his dream. Energy Conservation was something he'd talked with his dad about a lot…before he died last year. His breath caught. He rose to head back to the cottage. What to do!!???

As he stepped up on the porch, he was stunned to see Anna standing at the sliding door watching him.

"Hi, Nicholas." She saw him look beyond her shoulder and shook her head. "No, it's just me." She opened the door and he rubbed his feet with the towel just outside the door, ever careful to keep the sand on the beach where it belonged and not inside the beautiful cottage.

"I didn't expect you," he said, curious.

"Tess wants to come here to you. I told her to wait a day; I'd come first and make it look like she was coming to spend time with me. That way, it will look normal." Her eyes slid toward him, noting the angular lines in his handsome, dark face. "If you can manage my bag, I'll clean up and treat you to a wonderful dinner at the Bay House. Can your ribs handle it? We can walk down through the sand…it's my favorite path." She saw him smile uncertainly and head outside the double doors that framed the stone entryway.

She watched him from the window and saw his shoulders slump, his pace slow. It wasn't the same Nicholas that Tess brought home months earlier. Something had to give. She agreed Tess should be with him. Holding off Cole and Sam's search for him was getting on her nerves so badly she had to think of something and she hoped coming to *Mirafleures* was the answer.

Later, sitting at her favorite table by the window, she stared at the ocean as it beat against the sand in wild laps and beautiful shades of blue. She watched seagulls swoop and dip, the smaller birds scrounging for feasts in the sand, all the while the water ebbed and flowed. Violin music and flickering lights said dusk was upon them. Swirling her wine glass, she watched Nicholas play with his scallops, sip his draft beer. She waited. She knew he was unsure where to begin, so she left it to him.

"You know you probably saved my life, Anna."

She nodded, sipped more wine.

"You haven't asked me what happened and I am grateful but I need to tell you everything or I'll split. Tess knows a little, but not all of it. I think she's kept the important stuff to herself.

Anna nodded again. As he began to tell her how it all began so many months ago, she made murmurs, soft sounds that urged him to continue. He spoke about his father, his brother, their financial history, his wrestling scholarship, his acceptance at LSU, his parent's proud tears and he spoke about Tess. Then, there was his father's death and the need for less money for Nicholas and more money for his mother. Even with a scholarship, it didn't pay for everything. He and his brother helped her. She wanted him to graduate; his parent's strongest wish. She was so proud of him, he didn't dare drop out and it would break his own heart if he did. He was almost there but money was a problem. A powerful man found out his dilemma and offered him a way out.

Anna's eyes were moist as she listened to him bare his soul.

"Michael and I became friends. He told me he'd been stupidly blackmailed into stealing. Michael asked why I agreed to DAL's offer. Although I hated the idea, the promise of a college education numbed my ethics gene. The old man promised nobody would get hurt. I agreed to the bizarre arrangement only until I could graduate. It was my last year at university and shortly before I met Tess. I hated every minute of it; the job, the old man and the young kid, Andreas." Nicholas' facial muscles sagged a little. "I didn't hate him enough to want him dead though. If you hadn't seen him on television that morning, I'd probably also be six feet under by now."

Anna waved her empty glass toward Sarah, who brought more wine and a beer with a curious question on her face. "Thanks, Sarah."

Nicholas continued. "When the Man with a Story program began, DAL got so angry we were all even more afraid of him than usual. He's mean, nasty...quite a bastard. When I refused to rob your house, DAL told me he would be very sorry if Danny got hurt when he was riding his bike to and from work..." Nicholas fought tears.

"Danny?" She paused and lined up her utensils next to her plate.

"My brother," he whispered. "DAL knew where my family lived; he threatened to hurt my brother."

"Oh my God," she said in a horrified voice that was oddly gentle.

He looked at her, his dark eyes flashing. "So, I drove my car into the driveway, we took your Hummels, your beautiful tapestry and some other things...DAL keeps most of this stuff for himself I think. He is a maniac, wants more and more... I hated myself but didn't know what to do. I am so sorry, Anna. So, so sorry." His voice begged forgiveness.

She reached over and closed her fist over his hand. "Go on..."

"Well, when that didn't stop Sam but inflamed him to dig deeper to connect the theater patrons with the burglaries, DAL went so crazy he stomped and yelled like a child. Michael and I just kept our mouths shut.

Andreas laughed. The kid always laughed, like he got a high on the burglaries and everything DAL asked us to do. He's sure as hell not laughing now….." He lifted the beer and swallowed it jerkily before continuing.

Anna's fingers tapped the foot of her glass but didn't say a word.

"After that happened, DAL told us to meet him at one o'clock in the empty building by the theater where he always pays us. I don't know who owns it, but the old man has a key. There was just me, Michael and DAL. I don't know where Andreas was. We could always hear his motorcycle from a couple blocks away, so I knew he wasn't around. We'd already argued in front of the building about kidnapping Tess. The old man yelled at us and walked around to the alley entrance. We walked into a big room from the front. I remember looking up at a broken window, worrying about what job was waiting for us next…when I heard Tess's name again."

Anna looked up quickly and gripped the stem of her glass.

"I nearly stopped breathing while we listened to his great scheme. He wanted us to kidnap her. I told him he could go screw himself, I wasn't doing it. Well that went over like poop in a punchbowl. He started beating me, kicked me when I was on the floor… I practically crawled out while he gave Michael instructions. The plan was to leave Andreas with Tess tied up and send another note to Sam while he was on the air….I managed to get out and across the street to my old friend, Jimmy, at the deli so I could warn Tess. You know the rest…." He tipped the bottle of beer and drank the last drop. His eyes clung to her.

She blew out a long breath, sipped her wine and closed her eyes. "So now it makes sense. But when Michael noticed it was me instead of Tess, he didn't give me away. When Andreas was outside smoking a cigarette, Michael untied me and changed the plan. After he hauled Andreas away with him, I waited ten minutes like he instructed before running like hell. Then I called Cole to come get me and we raced to the television station.

"You called Cole Nites? Why call a lawyer?" He was confused but she didn't answer him.

"We told Sam to expect the note and to pretend it was nothing, and that we'd look for Tess. We didn't know until three hours later that you'd been beaten and were in the hospital with her at your side." She finished in a rush of words. "Then Andreas was killed and you are here...One thing I don't understand...two actually. It still doesn't make sense that Michael would want to kill Cris because she told Rainy Nites about his part in the burglaries. It seems so radical...and this DAL, the old man. What's his last name?" She looked earnestly at Nicholas as he shook his head.

"I honestly don't know but I heard Michael call him Darrin once. I asked Michael about it but he wouldn't tell me."

The evening was emotionally exhausting as they slogged their way back to the cottage in the sand. She needed to think about what Nicholas said and would probably head back to Lark Point the next afternoon. She wanted to make sure people knew she'd gone to her cottage so Tess could have a good excuse to join her mother.

As Nicholas was admitting his stupid choices to Anna with the Pacific Ocean as company, Tess was cradling a bowl of popcorn in her lap back in Lark Point. The women sat around a large, round stuffed ottoman in the glassed-in porch while classical music flowed into the room at Rainy's house. Tess's long black hair was pulled back into a pony tail and her wide blue eyes shifted between Cris and Rainy as they related a recent trip to Alaska during one of Rainy's insurance investigations.

Tess was amazed to see how animated the women were telling about the adventure they had on the ferry. It sounded like a great job Rainy had besides all the galas she planned for corporations around the city. She saw Cris smile at Rainy that lasted a little longer than Tess could understand.

When Cris looked up to see Tess's curious face, she got flustered and pushed popcorn into her mouth. And then she scooted the bowl over for Tess to add more to her little bowl.

Cole was in the adjoining room, huddled over files with a law book opened on the table before him. His own small bowl of popcorn was within reach and wayward kernels littered papers in one corner. While only half listening, he prepared his brief for the judge.

Laughter caught his attention and his ears perked up when he heard Cris ask Tess about Nicholas. His hand stalled above the popcorn bowl, his ears straining to eavesdrop over the music.

"Nobody knows where Nicholas is, Tess. I'll bet you do…where did he go after he got hurt?" Cris's voice was insistent. She wrapped a red curl around her finger and waited for Tess to answer. "He might be able to help Cole with my case, Tess. He must know that, doesn't he? I mean the guy who beat him up must be the same guy Michael told me about and I saw them together in the room of that building. What gives?"

Rainy knew the boy could help Cris. She slowly chewed her popcorn, reached for her wine glass and curiously watched Tess become nervous, thoughtful. Rainy's breasts stretched across her knit blouse and she pulled it down over her soft belly unconsciously. She was sure Tess knew where Nicholas was and wondered why it was a secret.

"Well, he was hurt badly. He had broken ribs, his lip, shoulder and hip all had stitches. His mom wanted him to come home, so that's where he went. I don't think it's such a big secret. Since I don't know exactly where his mother lives, I didn't really have any information to give. The police questioned him at St. Elizabeth's Hospital when I was there. Nick doesn't really know much though. He said he didn't know the old man's name, just called him Dal. I asked him what his last name was but he didn't know. If Michael knew, he didn't tell Nick. A simple phone call should get him," she finished with anxiety in her voice.

Cole's eyes narrowed. He'd already spoken to Nicholas' mother. She said he'd gone to stay with a friend who had a job waiting for him. Where? *Another damned question that didn't add up.* He ran a thumb over his beard as if it was a genie's bottle and decided he needed a trim.

"Well why is everyone in a snit if he's at his mother's? They could interview him there, couldn't they?" Cris turned to Rainy with a question on her face. "If he was part of the gang, wouldn't the police have brought him in? There must have been a reason he was beaten up. It really doesn't make sense to me, but nothing does lately," she pouted.

Rainy looked at her and rubbed her shoulder. Tess noticed something was a little odd between the women but focused, instead, on how her heart raced, hoping her lie sounded steady.

"I'm going to visit Mom at the cottage in Ashby tomorrow," she continued. "Her book is nearly finished so, she needed a break. I think she'll be there a week or so. I thought I'd go visit, run on the beach, get sand between my toes…. I love it there and the seafood is to die for. I'm leaving about nine so I can miss the morning commuters, so I'll be gone awhile. I start classes at LSU in January, so I might work through the holidays at the Bay House. The owners are friends of mom's since forever and Sarah told me she could fit me into the staff." She placed the bowl of popcorn on the cushion between them and took a deep breath before wiping the butter off her mouth with a tissue and stuffing it into her pocket.

Cris was surprised at her change of plans since she'd planned to help her study through November and December. Not wanting to put her friend on the spot, she set aside her questions for later.

"Thanks, Rainy. This was fun and I am so glad we had a visit, Cris. I've been worried about you and Mom sends her best too. We're glad you put off returning to your apartment for a few days. After the funeral, it was good to know you weren't going to be alone there." She jumped up to leave. Her stomach was still clenched tight and she rubbed it as if a knot had grown out of too much popcorn.

"Bye Cole," she said from the hallway.

"Have a nice drive to the beach tomorrow, Tess," he said after her, trying to keep his mind from racing back to the last time he'd been at the cottage holding her mother in his arms. Fighting visions of the bubbling hot tub, the bed, the sand, the woman…he replayed Tess's conversation, hearing the quake in her voice as she explained about her trip. Odd, that.

The detectives held the motor vehicle list in their hands and mapped out their strategy before punching in the first address on the GPS. Marveling at the electronic equipment, they remembered how, back in the day, a CB took priority in the police cruiser with a well-fingered map. Now, cell phones and GPS devices were the norm; many folks couldn't remember not having them. Children didn't even know what a CB was.

The first two names were in the outskirts of Lark Point, fancy houses on hills adorned with elaborate landscaping. The drive between town and the gated community made them wonder where all the money came from. Maybe it was the perps, they joked. The first address had a small tricycle in the driveway, a cat asleep under its wheel. They knocked on the door and a housekeeper answered before a young woman about thirty came to the door. Her husband was thirty five. No white hair.

The second address was a house with columns along the front, two-story surrounded by another yard straight out of a Home and Gardens

Magazine. The owners were in their forties and invited them in. The detectives saw a family photo, asked questions. No white hair there. Again, they asked one another as they drove out of the clanging gates, where does the money come from for this generation?

After they left the fourth house, it was lunch time; after they left house five and six it was dinner time. Five houses, five silver Mercedes and no white-headed owners. The sixth Mercedes was listed under a corporation that appeared buried in paperwork. They weren't happy when they returned to the station and neither was Charlie Royce.

"Who owns this corporation? Never heard of the company. The report shows it's a local company. Why all the secrecy? It doesn't make sense…or maybe it does…..Maybe this is our guy." He scratched his eyebrow and studied the detectives.

The investigators looked at Charlie for direction.

"City Hall."

Fifteen minutes later, the detectives stood at the counter and flipped through pages of the public tax records for local corporations. They noticed the corporation was listed as a sub-entity for a firm in Hong Kong. What the hell? Clyde Mark's finger traced down a list of seven corporations all held in Hong Kong.

He looked at Ted. "This is a pretty small town for so many corporations to find their way here under this umbrella, don't you think?"

Ted asked the clerk to print out the page.

"Let's see what addresses are listed for each one. I think we found something and it will probably lead us to our man." The detective scanned the following pages for the Hong Kong affiliates and his brow furrowed. Each page showed a corporation name and a post office box address. He was mumbling when Ted brought him the print out and he pointed to the last page.

"Seven local corporation affiliates all with post office boxes? Isn't it a law that a street address must be listed? How are taxes paid? What do the corporations manufacture? Do they sell services instead? Something definitely stinks here. We need a print out of more than just the corporation names."

Ted glanced at the page on the screen and narrowed his eyes. "Wait, that one looks different than the others. This says a stock corporation is a for-profit corporation which has shareholders (stockholders), each of whom receives a portion of the ownership of the corporation through shares of stock. These shares may receive a return on their investment in the form of dividends. Shares are used for voting on matters of corporate policy or to elect directors, at the corporation's annual meeting and at other meetings of the corporation."

"So, we find the director's listing."

Ted continued to read the fine print on the last page. If one person owns one share of stock more than any other person, that individual is said to have "controlling interest" in the corporation. Corporations may also be non-stock, and a corporation may switch back and forth between stock and non-stock status. An example is if the corporation was designated as a "stock" corporation in its Articles of Incorporation, and it initially issued 1000 shares of stock at $1 a share.

"What a bunch of gobbledygoop."

Ted snickered. "Is that a word, Clyde?"

"It is now. This says there's only one share holder for all the corporations. And get this, this last page shows an address and if my memory holds, it's that brick building where the kid was shot near the railroad station. Let's take all this back to Charlie. I think we found our man. Anyone who owns all the shares in seven affiliates so well hidden and the corporation is in Hong Kong makes my truth meter question why.

The papers were strewn across Charlie's desk and his detectives waited for his reaction. They had nearly fallen over one another getting back to the station and seeing Charlie's face afterward was worth the effort.

"Okay, go find him." He was losing sleep, had trouble eating and his wife was ready to toss him out on his ear. The case was making him crazy. He knew Sam Berg was going through the same thing but at least Charlie had a woman at home who cared about tossing him out.

He grimly shook his head. He had to find the kid and the Mercedes. He'd called Alonzo's mother only to be told he was working all winter to save tuition money for his final term. Where? She wasn't sure. She'd ask him next time he called. The Mercedes? Who the hell knew? How could you lose a silver Mercedes? If the DMV showed six and five were accounted for, they'd find the corporate car. He headed for the coffee pot. It was going to be another long day until dark.

The judge agreed to meet with Cole and the district attorney at one o'clock. Lyn Corelli wasn't happy. Cole was delighted. The judge was known to be fair and receptive to logic.

Cole was shuffling papers when Darrin walked into his office just before lunch. "Looks like you're heading out, Cole. Any plans for lunch?" Darrin studied his partner shrewdly. Something was in the air and he wasn't privy to it. Yet.

"Sorry, Darrin, I'm off to see Judge McPherson."

"Oh?"

"I'm requesting a Pre-Trial Hearing on the Crissman case; the DA doesn't have enough evidence for trial. María Crissman shouldn't have been arrested at all and I think McPherson will agree after I outline my points. Lyn Corelli can go to hell.

"Cole, the woman used her martial arts to overpower the guy, a man she lived with and slept with. Maybe she didn't like the way he parted his hair. She's an actress, isn't she?" Darrin ticked off his own points with his fingers, intent on rattling Cole.

Cole didn't like hearing the actress bit again. "Darrin, Mallory had a handgun. The bullet was found in the wall of her dressing room!" He gripped his briefcase and walked past Darrin. "I plan to push that one fact alone down Corelli's throat and I want the judge to see me do it."

Darrin watched Cole walk away, sniffed agitatedly and returned to his own office. Maybe he should call the judge, call in a favor. He pursed his lips. No, he knew he couldn't do that; Cole was his partner after all. There'd be too many questions. He closed his door and stared at nothing. Maybe he should retire and leave Lark Point.... just walk away. But he wasn't ready to give up the golden goose the town continued to provide him. Maybe lay low for awhile, change tactics. Stop using others to do what he did best; the thrill was just too sweet to quit.

He unlocked his desk drawer and pulled out three sets of contracts, each listing different corporation names. Slyly, he pulled the gold stickers from other contracts lying on his desk and transferred them to the hidden legal papers inside his drawer. He signed *Addison Lucas* on each page beside the new stickers and pushed them back into the drawer. His key made a snapping sound as he locked it.

He would take them across town later. Paying old Luther White to record the contracts instead of Steven made perfect sense. He didn't ask questions like Steven did. It was difficult staying ahead of his partner and that paralegal of his. That girl could sniff out a rabbit from a cave. In fact, she could also talk the head off one. Darrin chuckled at the vision.

Steven Mape's specialty was corporate law. Since the 2008 slump, he'd filed bankruptcy for several construction companies, often without receiving a penny. His paralegal efficiently checked City Hall records afterward looking for names of their past bankruptcy clients. If any of those clients tried to slide under the wire within five years with a new corporation name for the same industry, she would blow the whistle. And then Lucas, Nites and Mapes would finally receive the earned fees from their work on the old bankruptcy bill.

Darrin's convoluted paperwork had hidden his corporations for years, but he was never too lackadaisical, avoiding any errors that might raise a red flag. Here again, he enjoyed the subterfuge. And breaking the law. He smiled at the irony. He protected his own lawlessness at the same time he took cases for clients who did the same thing. Only they got caught. He didn't intend to land in that group, so he had to muzzle Cole, subdue the redhead and find Nico.

He glanced at his locked drawer and thought of the secreted contracts. They would hide his involvement when the old buildings were torn down and his deal with the governor went through. He laughed aloud at how easy it had been. Pass a little money and a weakness for cash changed their entire outlook on zoning and building projects.

But he had to put this other messy project to bed first. Visions of a dead actress, an accident of course, spun through his head along with finding Nico and putting an end to that young man's college dreams. He'd find him, by God, and then the third problem would disappear. He could almost taste the thrill of playing the governor.

Proud of his ingenuity, he yanked out his bottom desk drawer, removed the flask and raised it to his lips.

NINETEEN

Cole and the district attorney were ushered into Judge McPherson's office at one o'clock sharp. He had just finished his lunch and tossed a smashed paper bag into the wastebasket beside his desk. His glasses rode on the bridge of his nose as he eyed a cookie sitting on the paper napkin next to his phone.

Nodding to the attorneys, he took a deep breath and clasped his hands on the desk. The case of Michael Mallory's death was clearly outlined inside the file for the State of California vs. María Crissman. He'd read every page. "Cole, what do you have in mind? This is a bit irregular."

At one thirty, Lyn Corelli angrily left the judge's office and her spiked heels could be heard clicking across the marble floors like a jack hammer. She'd kept civility in her voice because she knew better than to alienate the judge but it was obvious she'd reached a melting point.

Cole stared after her and reached for his briefcase. Trying to keep the grin off his face, he barely restrained his own emotions when he said, "Thank you, Judge."

"She didn't like that, Cole. I hope your client is ready because Corelli is definitely ready to rock and roll on this one. I'll have my clerk call you with the date and time when it's coordinated with Corelli's office. I have an Alaskan fishing trip planned and my plane leaves in four days. If you can show me a valid argument and answer the questions floating around inside this file," he said as he tapped it with his finger, "and the DA does not give me anything beyond what she just outlined, then you can relax and I can go get my fish."

Cole shook his head, smiled at the judge and let himself out.

By four o'clock, they had a date in three days. Cris would be in court at nine o'clock Thursday morning. He picked up his papers, iPad and briefcase before calling Tim, his paralegal, and asked him to continue researching precedents for his case. He was going home.

Rainy kissed Cris, promising her they'd soon be in the land of Plumeria, Bird of Paradise and palm trees. When Cris slid her arms around Rainy's neck, they nearly missed the sound of a key in the front door. "I can hardly wait to put this behind me and learn the hula........"

"Cole's home," Rainy whispered urgently.

Cris sat at the table while Rainy busied herself at the kitchen counter. "Cole, you're home early." She looked at him expectantly.

"Good news. We have the hearing in front of the judge Thursday morning at nine, Cris. He's willing to listen to us. The DA must show concrete evidence to prove you did not kill Michael in self defense. If she cannot do that, your charges will be dropped."

Cris flinched over the words about killing Michael. It still seemed surreal; she felt hot and shakily asked, "What do I need to do, Cole?"

"We need to get to work. Rainy, please make us some coffee? We may be at this awhile. And food too? I'm starving."

Heaving a sigh of relief, she rushed for snacks, made coffee and brought a tray to the round glass table before the bay window. There were papers, files, pencils and clenched stomachs and coffee, coffee and more coffee. Cole was ready and he would be sure Cris was also.

The next morning, Anna sat in the back of Starbucks nursing her latte while tapping on her laptop. She was so intent on reading the last few lines; she didn't realize she had company until he sat down across from her. Looking up swiftly, her heart leapt and a thrill of anticipation crawled up her spine.

Cole's soft grey eyes twinkled. He placed his coffee along with two breakfast sandwiches beside her laptop. "I doubt you've eaten yet, so here's one of my favorite sandwiches, hot from the oven filled with bacon, Parmesan frittata, and aged Gouda cheese on an artisan roll." He grinned and took a sip of his steaming coffee. "I know you're busy writing but when I saw you back here, I thought I'd died and gone to heaven."

"Cole, you really have a way with words."

"I hope so," he said, vibrating with new life. "The judge agreed to a Pre-Trial Hearing. I have two days to prepare. I had Cris up past midnight last night. If only I could find Nicholas. It might be the icing on the cake. We'd have more artillery for the judge and possibly nail the old bastard who started this damn gang, causing one death and probably committing the other one." He bit into his sandwich, crunched into the bacon and briefly moaned as the food hit his belly.

Anna caught her breath before slowly lifting her sandwich from its warm cocoon of parchment paper. The aroma was almost as delicious as the tasty inside. She looked at Cole and inched it toward her mouth.

He saw something flicker far back in her eyes.

"This is delicious. Thank you. You're right; I have been struggling with this legal chapter and forgot to eat. It seems like so long ago that I asked you for help with it…...." Her eyes turned warm and she lifted her latte.

Cole's voice dropped, "…the night we met…yes and then magic," he whispered and watched her cheeks flush. He reached across to still her hand as it tapped on the table. "Are you nervous, Anna?"

She shrugged to hide her confusion, started to say something but took another bite of her sandwich instead. Her face clouded.

"Anna, what is it?" He squeezed the fingers she had clenched around her cup. "Can you attend the hearing Thursday morning? You may hear most of what you're looking for and it would be nice knowing you were in the room with me."

Anna stared a moment before nodding. She'd made a decision and her determination was like a rock inside her. As she finished her sandwich and sipped her latte, her mind cleared. She needed to make a call, put gas in her car and …. Her foot tapped and her chest hurt.

He saw expressions flit across her features like a YouTube video. He finished his sandwich, looked at his watch and knew his time was gone. "I have to meet a client in a few minutes. God, it was good running into you…Thursday morning, nine, Judge McPherson's court." He slid off the chair, touched his lips with a finger and waved it toward her.

Her features slipped from uneasiness to warmth in seconds. She closed her laptop, never taking her eyes off of him as he left.

Why would Nicholas Alonzo's name put her on edge? Cole couldn't settle his head around Anna's nervousness. And last night, listening to Tess made his mind prick. Could both women know where he is? The logical place for him to hide would be......... He quickly pulled his BMW over to the curb, pulled out his cell phone and called his secretary, Christina. He filled his gas tank and turned up his radio. He had a place in mind and he didn't need a map to get there

Tess looked into Nicholas' eyes. Her soft, fragrant strands of hair brushed across his cheek. "Are you tired? Not too tired, I mean, are your ribs still too sore?" The tip of her tongue grazed his lower lip.

A jolt of pleasure coursed through Nick's body. "Never too tired and at this moment, I don't think I have any ribs," he whispered, and wrapped his arms around her.

Later, instead of lunch, Tess and Nicholas shared toast slathered with Marmalade while sipping coffee on the deck. The slight breeze and the sound of the ocean waves were distinctly hypnotic as they wrapped their jackets tightly around each other. Seagulls nearly collided with one another during their feeding time, salt was in the air and they had a pile of seashells in a stack beside the door.

When Tess grabbed the last bite, Nicholas laughed and grabbed at her but she slipped away and ran toward the beach, zigzagging to the water's edge. The sand was wet and seaweed slid around her feet when the tide rushed back toward the ocean, freezing her ankles.

He caught her from behind, sliding his arms around to rest on her belly; she made room for his kisses by tilting her head slightly.

"Mmmm, you still taste like Marmalade," she told him once she'd drawn a breath after his tender, lingering kiss.

"And you smell like roses," he responded, letting his head rest for a moment against her soft neck. "You know I have to make some decisions, don't you Tess?" He spoke above the crashing breakers and snuggled, glad she didn't move away or answer him.

She waited for him to speak of it; she'd known it was coming. Ever since she'd arrived, it was written all over his face, in his sighs, in his kisses, his lovemaking. He wasn't a man to loll around when something so important kicked him in the gut. That was just one of the reasons why she loved him. He'd finally told her the full story.

Turning around to face him, she held his face in her hands and kissed him slowly, tenderly. Her black hair was loose and whipped around their faces in the wind. "I do and I've been waiting for you to tell me your plan. I knew you'd tell me when you were ready." She whispered his name and kissed him, drawing him back to dry sand where they sat, kicking broken shells and watching the gulls dip and swoon.

"Maybe I can help Cris. I can't sit here like a frightened woman..." He laughed when he saw her face. "....ah...wrong analogy....how about like a chicken- shit weakling? I'm frightened of the old man. My body still hurts. I can't believe I ran after you through this shifting sand.......but you're so easy to follow."

She laughed into the wind.

"The guy must be a rich big shot. He drives a Mercedes but keeps an old van locked in that brick building next to the theater. I'm sure the police have found it by now since Cris told them that's where she saw me get knocked around. I don't know where she hid. I didn't see her at all and I don't think Michael did either. He and DAL were busy talking about grabbing you when I got out of there. If he'd seen her, DAL would have hurt her. No doubt in my mind. Michael would have spit nickels, not stood there like he did when the guy hit me. It would've been a different story if it was his girl DAL wanted to rough up. When he told me to kidnap you........I saw red..." Sighing heavily, he put his arm around her and she leaned into him.

"I want to call Cole Nites. Let's do it now, huh? I want to get it over with and hopefully, he can put me in protective custody so DAL can't get to me. God, that guy is nasty." He shivered.

She held his hand tightly all the way back to the cottage.

They were both clearly disappointed to learn Cole was out of the office all day. His secretary wouldn't give out Cole's cell number but promised to tell him that Nicholas wanted to find him.

Christina could barely control her excitement when she called Cole to give him the message and Nicholas Alonzo's cell phone number. "Cole! You'll never guess who just called to talk to you....Nicholas Alonzo!" She'd scribbled his name on her tablet but repeated his cell number from memory.

"I could kiss you!" Cole grinned and swung over to a pull-off area to scribble down the number, wondering if his guess was right about where he'd gone.

His secretary smiled. She knew this case held a special place for her boss since the defendant was his wife's friend. Wondering if the guy knew a Pre-Trial Hearing for María Crissman was set for Thursday made her curious but she stashed the thought and moved on to other case files.

In Ashby, the phone rang within minutes. Nicholas and Tess stared at one another, not recognizing the number on caller ID but they both knew who it must be.

Nicholas answered quietly. "Hello?"

"Nicholas?" Cole's voice boomed across the room.

"Yes, sir."

"Can I venture a guess that you're in Ashby with Tess?" Cole's mind had been clicking since he left Anna. Where would he hide out? And he'd bet Tess was with him. No wonder Anna was nervous........why didn't she tell him?

"Yes, I am. We're at........."

Cole sighed knowingly. "........*Mirafleures*, right?"

Tess was stunned and Nicholas equally so. "Yes, how did you know? Oh, God, if you know then DAL might....."

"Slow down, Nicholas. I'm only an hour away. I guessed it when I ran into Anna earlier today and she was nervous when I mentioned wanting to find you. The timing is perfect. Are you willing to answer my questions and help with Cris's defense?"

"That's why I called you. I'm not hiding anymore. Tess and I will be waiting for you."

"Good, because there's a hearing on Thursday. With you as a witness, I believe the judge will listen more seriously. On my way, hope there's coffee?" He stepped on the accelerator and the little car held the road like a champ. His heartbeat was racing. Straightening to relieve the ache in his shoulders, he decided he wouldn't tell anyone about the meeting, not Sam, not the police. This was his witness and he didn't want the DA or anyone else to get wind of it.

A few minutes after Christina talked to Cole, Darrin walked by Cole's office and peeked in, scowling to see it empty. "Where's Cole?"

She clenched her jaw. "He's out for the day, Mr. Lucas, but you can reach him on his cell phone. She didn't like the look on his face or his hands fisting near her desk. She moved a file to cover her notepad and decided if Cole wanted anyone to know about Nicholas Alonzo, he would tell people himself, even the great Mr. Lucas.

Darrin squeezed his fists tightly and studied her a moment before angrily calling over his shoulder to send a paralegal to him.

She watched him leave. She might tell the paralegal and she might not. There was a menace surrounding the man she didn't like and she wasn't his lackey. She'd earned her stripes and being Cole's legal secretary didn't oblige her to be Darrin Lucas's gofer.

Anna was sure she'd made the right decision to bring Nicholas home. Thursday's hearing was important and he just might swing the judge's decision. She trusted Cole's judgment and remembered the distress etched on his face when he mentioned needing Nicholas as his witness.

She had every intention to be in that courtroom, not only for her research but for Cole. It seemed important to him and..... There was something warm and enchanting about the man. Her slim fingers wrapped themselves around her steering wheel as the Audi sped over the mountain road toward Ashby. She loved driving to *Mirafleures*, especially now as her mind conjured steamy memories. Cole had worn those sexy jeans at the cottage that night and when he bent down....

Her thoughts crackled through the noise of her daily life. She thought of Julia Cameron's book, *The Artists Way* about making changes when you can't imagine what's on the other side. She said *"leap and the net will appear"* which excited Anna and frightened her in equal measure. She turned on KLOK and hummed along with the tunes she knew so well, rolled down the window and felt a cold breeze whip her hair as if she was doing cartwheels.

Nicholas explained his part in the fiasco from the beginning as Cole took notes and shook his head in exasperation. Whoever Dal was needed his ass kicked and tossed in jail. It wasn't hard to see that

Nicholas was afraid of the guy and had been for some time. After the way he'd been beaten, he wasn't surprised but it sounded like the fear stemmed from previous encounters. Months of thefts and neither Cris nor Tess were aware of the events? The guys must have been good at hiding their feelings and working their crazy stunts. Throw in the young Andreas and the old man must have laughed himself stupid at how easy it was to intimidate kids who needed money. He rolled his eyes a little, wondering at the ease the old guy had with the plan. Not only intimidate the boys but threaten those they loved to keep them in line. He was astounded to hear he'd broken Andreas' arm to make a point too. Getting his hands on the guy was nearly as important now as saving Cris.

"Is there anything else you need before we leave, Cole?"

"I think I have everything and if not, I will know where Charlie stashes you. Are you okay with all this, Tess? I know you and your mother thought you were doing the right thing and you probably were. But I'm relieved, elated actually, that I heard from you, Nick. The timeliness couldn't have been better with Cris's hearing Thursday.

Tess poured more coffee and placed some fruit on the table among the papers already taking up most of the area. Nicholas reached for her hand and she sat down as they each contemplated what the next couple of days would bring.

Cole was anxious to get back to Lark Point. He was going directly to Anna before he went home. Maybe it wasn't the right thing to do but he'd be damned if he couldn't talk to her about meeting with Nicholas. It sounded like she'd gone to a lot of trouble to whisk him away from there and send him into hiding. And he had an axe to grind about her not trusting him. He took a deep breath and snapped his briefcase closed.

When Anna pulled into *Mirafleures'* driveway, she didn't notice the BMW parked off the side of the road. Gathering her bag of groceries and purse, she walked past the browning flowers and tapped on the door a second before walking through it. The scene on the other side of the door turned her face to chalk.

Three faces turned to Anna, equally surprised. Cole started to rise but before he said a word, she stalked over to him.

"You followed me! Were you trying to trick me into telling you where Nicholas was hiding? Have you been working this neat little piece of investigation into your file, hoping to trip me up? Cole, I trusted you.......how could you?" Anna noticed Tess staring at her, Nicholas sitting with his mouth open and Cole's face turning dark.

"Anna, how could I follow you when I am already here?" He reached toward her, devilishly handsome and stupidly logical.

"I came to get Nicholas for your hearing. He wanted to talk with you but we were afraid of this Dal character because we think he killed Andreas and thought Nicholas might be next...so he's been hiding here and............." She marched into the bedroom and slammed the door.

Tess looked at Cole as if seeing him for the first time; sure his wide-eyed innocent look was a smoke screen. Well, well. She turned to Nicholas. "Ah, Nick...we better get back to town."

Nicholas was still wondering what happened.

"What time do you want Nicholas to arrive and where do we hide out until you send someone for him? It would just be his luck to have Dal, whoever he is, learning about the hearing. He might try to actually kill Nicholas this time."

Nick found his words. "I'll be fine, Tess. Let me handle it now. You and your mother have helped give me healing time. Now, let's go kick butt. The judge needs to know Michael's part in the burglaries and Cole has promised they'll be easy on me because I'm coming forward. Maybe they'll put me in that witness program if they don't find him?" He looked at Cole.

"I'm going to call Charlie Royce on our way back to town and have you set up in a hotel room nobody knows about. Sorry, Tess, but it really should be a place well away from everyone he knows. Someone might follow you and..." He glanced toward the bedroom door. His thick hair tapered neatly to his collar and he slid his finger to loosen the tie, all the while never taking his eyes off the hallway.

Tess didn't miss his interest and stood calculating. "So you are taking Nicholas back to town? I'll follow Mom back home later," she said as uncertainty crept into her expression. She planned to open more than just a door when the men left and she wanted them on their way.

Nicholas stuffed his clothes into a bag.

Tess hugged him goodbye before turning to Cole with a measured look and nodded, smiling suddenly. "Goodbye, Cole...I'll see you in court."

Cole recognized her mother's twitching mouth and grinned. "Okay, I'll be in touch but you probably won't see either of us until court. I hope your mom.......''" He thought he masked his turmoil but Tess noticed, saw his eyes darting toward the doorway as he left.

She didn't answer him as she showed them out.

"Okay, Mother, they're gone. You can come out now." Tess tried to keep her words from sounding like they'd been playing hide and seek.

The door opened. Anna slipped out with a determined set to her jaw. Acting as if she'd just arrived, she walked into the kitchen, made herself a cup of green tea in the microwave and sat down.

"Okay then.....let's have it, shall we?" Tess studied Anna. "You were mighty touchy when you came in. You should've been glad Nicholas called Cole to talk about helping Cris....."

Anna's head snapped around. "Nicholas called Cole? I thought......"

"Yes, we all heard what you thought, Mom. I think Cole still feels your fist in his gut. He is a mighty handsome man, just noticed that today. Those deep gray eyes, gorgeous tanned face, hooded brow, distinguished salt and pepper hair and that short beard...with that tiny patch of white...yes, quite handsome actually..." She watched her mother out of the corner of her eye.

Anna froze a beat before a smile found its way to her mouth.

"Gotcha!" Tess grinned. "Now you want to tell me what is really going on between you and the good lawyer? He was way too interested in your closed door and your face is way too flushed. Does it mean you think he's handsome too....just a little bit?" she wheedled.

"It's complicated but before I say another word, I want to tell you I have always been true and loyal to your father. I have never looked at another man in our entire life together....not until I already knew divorce was the end of our story. I am telling you this not in my defense but because I don't think I need to or want to."

Tess stared at her.

"Do you have any idea what the last few months have been like for me, Tess? I tried to talk with you about it but you wouldn't listen and then when you did, I was too overwhelmed. And then the time I spent in France opened my head to life as it should be. And then Michael kidnapped me, Nicholas was beat to holy shit and Cris was thrown in jail for killing Michael. Your dad has finally faced the fact our marriage is over and my book is nearly finished. I wondered if it would ever be done because I couldn't stop editing, editing, editing. And then hiding Nicholas trying to keep him safe, making sure you stayed on track, keeping my head on straight and….."

"Mom, slow down already….."

Anna took a deep breath. "I'm telling you all this because I love you and……..and I love Cole." Her eyes held a gleam that no makeup could improve. "And he loves me…he is getting his life together as soon as the trial or whatever… is over for Cris. He and his wife have not been happy for so long he can't remember when he ever was. I am not a marriage breaker and neither is he. That's all I'm going to say."

"That's *all* you're going to say, Mom? I've never heard anyone encapsulate six months of craziness into a tight thirty seconds before…but guess that's because you're the writer and I'm not? Holy Moses." Tess was speechless.

Anna's face cleared as if a great burden had fallen off her shoulders and a spurt of laughter escaped. "Now let's go to the Bay House. We need to celebrate all kinds of things. Let's put the groceries away. You put the tapenade and cheese in the fridge and grab your windbreaker." She put down her empty cup of tea and began a whirlwind of activity in the kitchen.

Tess was still a bit dumbfounded as she rehashed her mother's words in her head, while acutely feeling Nicholas' absence. Life could be so crazy and just a few months ago all she worried about was getting an A in her classes. But with Nicholas' advent into her life and her parents crashing their marriage into bits, she wondered if those were really marbles bumping around among the mind chatter.

"Ready?" Anna locked the glass door and led her daughter off the deck into the wet sand courtesy of the recent rain storm. The wind picked up and sent their hair blowing in all directions but they trudged down the beach arm in arm anyway.

Sarah raised her eyebrows when she saw the women slip off their shoes at the beachside door and trudge inside out of the wind. Her girls were finally laughing. She yanked off her apron, grabbed menus and motioned to Jeff to bring wine, dipping oil, a baguette and a small plate of pimiento-stuffed green olives. She wasn't missing the party this time.

"Ok, what gives?"

Anna grinned at Tess.

Tess shook her head and a chuckle slipped out.

"Well, ladies?"

Still shivering, Anna and Tess settled down into their chairs and wiggled the sand loose from between their toes.

Jeff poured three glasses of wine and arranged the food on the table, giving Sarah a thumbs-up look before heading back to the kitchen.

"Here's a toast to the good lawyer, Mom." Tess chuckled.

"Here's to an Energy Conservation degree, Tess." Anna grinned.

Sarah's face looked blank.

Tess began to talk about Nicholas and Anna's voice rose above her to relate the story about Cris, Michael and Andreas, the kidnapping.

Their words fell over one another. "And he's been snug in the cottage for a few days and then….."

"This is a joke, right?" Sarah's eyes grew round as she tried to make sense. "It's really a new story Anna is writing, right?" She stared at both women and shook her head.

Tess and Anna raised their eyebrows over the rims of their wineglasses and shook their heads back and forth.

Laughter bubbled among the women and the olives disappeared.

TWENTY

The buzzer sounded and Deputy Aurore Gulle snapped to attention. "All rise," she intoned loudly.

Judge Jason McPherson's black robe caught on his doorknob momentarily as he entered the courtroom. The attorneys with María Crissman stood at the front tables. The courtroom crowd appeared eager for the preliminary proceedings to begin. He nodded toward the group. They sat down and he tapped his gavel. "The court will hear State of California vs. María Christina Crissman. The District Attorney and defense attorney are here to discuss the case to decide if it should proceed to trial or if it can be resolved without a trial. They will each argue their pre-trial motions. Let the record show the defendant and her counsels are present."

He looked at Cole. "Are you ready to proceed, Mr. Nites?"

The judge noticed that although Lyn Corelli typically sent an assistant DA to these hearings, today she basked in her power, tossed her thick hair over her ear with a slim finger and tapped the file before her. The judge looked at Cole Nites, his red-headed client and Cole's second. They all nodded agreement.

"As you both know, Pre-Trial Hearings are a precursor to a full trial or they open the possibility of resolving a case without a trial. This court will hear Mr. Nites clarify his findings. Our District Attorney, Ms. Corelli, has the burden of showing evidence of a crime beyond a reasonable doubt against murder as self defense. There will be no opening statements by either side, but instead, victims and witnesses will speak from the witness stand. Since, obviously, the victim is Michael Mallory and he cannot attend, Mr. Nites has assured the court he will call a witness who will stand in his stead."

Lyn Corelli turned to Cole with a probing query. She had agreed to the irregularity but hadn't heard of the witness. She didn't like it. Highly irregular indeed. She started to object but decided to let him bury himself. Her case was a slam dunk with the use of Taekwon-Do. The woman smiled briefly, showing nothing of her annoyance. Gathering her pad and glancing down at her questions, she'd wait and then pounce.

Cris heard thunder in her ears as she walked toward the witness stand with all eyes on her. It should have been easy with her theater experience, but today, she didn't know her lines and there was no curtain to hide behind. Swallowing hard, she turned around to see Rainy sitting beside Chuck and several others. The officer held up a Bible and she placed her right hand on top of it as she'd seen on television. A bubble of misplaced humor erupted behind her eyes. Television indeed.

"Do you swear to tell the truth, nothing but the truth, oh help me God?"

"I do." Cris's voice was low.

The judge said, "Thank you, you may be seated. Could you please state your name for the court?"

"María Christina Crissman."

The judge looked at the DA, who stood and walked slowly toward Cris. "Ms. Crissman, will you explain your relationship with the deceased, Michael Mallory?"

Cris held the sides of the chair seat with both hands. "We were roommates for two years. He had his life and I had mine. Our lives rarely crossed except during work hours and sometimes before and after our shows. It was a strange relationship, really, but we were happy the way it worked until we became intimate in the last few months……." Cris met her accusing eyes without flinching.

"Ms. Crissman, were there any witnesses to your alleged argument with Mr. Mallory the day of his death?"

"It was more than an argument……" she insisted.

"Just answer my question please."

"No, there were just the two of us. My friend had just left."

"May I ask which friend that was?"

Cris looked across the room toward Rainy. "Lauraine Nites."

The district attorney spun around to look at Rainy, where she sat beside Chuck Champion, the owner of the Artists Repertory Theater. "Did Ms. Nites see Mr. Mallory enter your dressing room before she left?"

"Objection, hearsay on the part of the witness," Cole said, raising his hand.

"Sustained."

Lyn Corelli paused a moment before staring at Cris. "A relationship such as yours, Ms. Crissman…. your explanation about that day leaves me with questions. Tell me, did you love Michael Mallory?"

"Objection your honor, that is irrelevant," Cole hammered.

"Objection overruled. Answer the question please."

Cris looked at Cole and then back at the woman in front of her. "Yes, I loved Michael in a special way," she said quietly. She bit her lip slightly and glanced at Rainy.

Rainy smiled encouragingly and nodded her head slightly.

"It seems hard to believe, Ms. Crissman, that your lover would try to kill you just because you told a friend you thought he was involved in several burglaries…"

Cris cut in, her voice raising an octave. "He did!"

"You haven't given the court a good reason why you think……"

"Objection, your honor. It is not Ms. Crissman's job to prove why the victim tried to kill her, but to try to prove she was saving herself from his doing so." Cole's voice boomed toward the bench.

"Sustained. Strike the question from the record." He leaned his chin on his hand, his elbow against the edge of his desk. "Proceed."

"Tell me, for the record, what Michael Mallory's state of mind was in when he entered your dressing room the afternoon of November 12th?"

Cris's brow was thoughtful a moment. Cole nodded at her. "He was angry, shaking with anger. His voice was low, controlled, menacing. I hadn't realized he was outside the….."

"And Ms. Crissman, what was your first reaction? Was this something you saw often in your lover?" she said with a slight sneer in her voice, cutting her off.

"I was shocked…scared…and no, it was very unlike Michael. He was usually laughing and loving. He was never like that before." She looked at Rainy again quickly before bringing her attention back to the district attorney and dug her fingers into her thigh.

"So, you are saying that on that particular day, Michael Mallory was not himself. Something happened between your lunch date and six o'clock that changed a loving man into a would-be killer and I think you know what that was!" Lyn Corelli hissed at Cris and placed her hands on the railing in front of her.

Cole jumped up. "Objection, your honor, she's badgering my client!" He bit down on his lip and ground his teeth.

"Sustained. Is this line of questioning leading somewhere, Ms. Corelli or are you simply trying to force the defendant into hysteria on the stand?" the judge asked humorlessly. "Get to the point, madam." He glared at her as she stood rigidly in a smooth-fitting navy suit with a turquoise blouse that dipped a little lower than was professionally acceptable. His stare pinned her to the floor.

"Forgive me, your honor. I'm trying to prove to the court that Ms. Crissman is withholding vital information from this court. I feel it!" Her voice rose an octave as she tried to make her point while remaining calm.

"Well, Ms. Corelli, please resume your questioning in a manner that pleases this court with facts, not feelings, or I will reprimand you from this court until nine o'clock tomorrow morning."

Cole smiled behind his hand, his eyes half closed.

Rainy sat frozen, unable to breathe clearly. Her chest hurt as if a vise was clamped around her lungs. Holding a fisted hand to the place where her heart beat didn't loosen the knot. The tightness in her throat promised to escape in a wild cry for Cris's fear and distress. Taking a deep breath, she wrapped her jeweled fingers around her black Gucci bag.

Anna and Tess sat across the aisle and watched and listened with complete interest. Anna was bewildered every time Cris glanced at Rainy as if her friend held the answers. Staring at the back of Cole's head, willing him to meet her eyes, Anna sat riveted by the onslaught of the district attorney's questions.

Cris sat unmoving. The words hammered across her brain echoing loudly like a litany; I can't tell them. I can't tell them... I can't tell......

"Tell me, Ms. Crissman....."

Cris's head jerked toward the threatening prosecutor as her words mirrored her frightening thoughts. Afraid she'd actually spoken the words aloud, she glanced around like a rabbit in a cage, locked in, dark, with no escape.

Cole kept his own counsel as a warning voice whispered in his head. A tumble of confused thoughts came back from the first interview at the police station the day Michael died. He tapped his legal pad and exhaled slowly, listening intently to the DA's next question.

"Was your lover angry about something besides your betrayal regarding his alleged burglary connection? What else added to his anger that day?" She retorted with both hands on her hips.

Cris lowered her eyes. She couldn't tell. She couldn't tell, her mind spun in circles. "I don't know." She shook her curly head hopelessly.

"He changed from lover to killer in a few hours and you don't know why? Isn't it true that you followed him into a building, hid inside a closet and witnessed Mr. Mallory meeting with two other men? Was this meeting a secret? Could he have been angry that you didn't trust him? Were you angry he might have been hiding something from you?"

"One question at a time, Ms. Corelli. Let the girl catch her breath." The judge jabbed his finger on his desktop and stared at her.

The silence in the chamber lay heavy in the room.

"Again, Ms. Crissman. Do you have any idea why this loving man would turn into your would-be killer in the space of a few hours?"

Cris shook her head and her eyes filled with sparkling tears.

"Answer out loud please."

"Objection. My client has already answered that question plainly for the court, your honor." Cole's gut hurt. He ran his hand over his slight beard and he sat down again.

"Sustained. May I remind you, Ms. Corelli....."

"Yes, your honor," she said stiffly. Continuing, her voice abused Cris's conscious mind and blurred her thoughts. "Did you hear the victim on the phone talking to anyone during lunch?" She smiled benignly at Cris, trying to knock her off guard.

"Yes, all the cast and I saw him on the phone twice. We couldn't hear his conversation. He seemed fine when he came back to eat pizza with all of us. I didn't ask him who he was talking to..." Cris noticed Cole watching her closely. She placed her shaking hand on the railing. She ached to stand up and run screaming, but instead, she turned back to the woman in front of her.

"And Ms. Crissman, after you left your hiding place and called Ms. Nites…..how long was Ms. Nites with you? You mentioned that you were alone when Michael Mallory stormed into your dressing room." She continued innocently before finishing with, "and why betray your lover to her and not the police? Why not ask Mr. Mallory first if your guess was true before telling your friend? Where was your loyalty, Ms. Crissman?"

Cole started to jump up but the judge pursed his lips, waiting for Cris to answer.

A thread of hysteria was back in her voice, "Rainy was with me about twenty minutes maybe. I don't remember. She was going to call the insurance company where she investigated the thefts. I was afraid for Michael. I didn't know what happened to him or Nico after I sneaked out of there. I didn't want to call the police yet."

The district attorney walked slowly back to her table, tapped the file and glanced at the audience before looking at Cole. Her expression grew hard and thoughtful. Anna saw Cole stare back at the woman, and wondered what he was thinking.

"Later, Ms. Crissman, before he crashed into your dressing room, did you hear anyone else outside your door?"

"No, there was nobody around. We made sure…..." She winced when the woman snapped her head around.

"You made sure of what?"

Cris sat mute.

Rainy felt faint.

Cole sat rooted to his chair.

"My friend, Rainy Nites, was with me. I told you already. I didn't want anyone to hear me tell her….we made sure we were alone," she finished lamely. I told her about Michael's fight with Nico. I heard them talking about the burglaries. I told Rainy….because she worked at the insurance company. She was trying to solve the thefts…He must have heard me because as soon as Rainy left…that's when Michael came in……came at me." Her eyes filled with tears.

"So, at noon the victim was loving, laughing and normal, eating pizza with everyone. You allegedly saw a fight between three men and your friend arrived after you called her and you remained alone. Then, you threw your boyfriend under the bus….." Lyn Corelli continued, nodded a faux apology to Cole as he started to raise his hand. "Then a crazed lover attacked you and there was a fight to his death. Do I have the timeline, correct, Ms. Crissman?" She gave her a final brutal stare.

Cris fought through the cobwebs of her living nightmare and looked up, disoriented. "Yes."

Cole's fingers thumped quietly on the manila folder atop the oak library table, his mind racing. *What in hell was she getting at?* He glanced at his assistant meeting raised eyebrows.

"Tell me, Ms. Crissman, about the conversation you heard between Michael Mallory and the person he called Nico when you followed them into the building by the theater."

"Well, Michael said 'Nico, we have to shut him up' and Nico yelled, 'not Tess!' Michael said, 'sorry Nico, DAL ordered it. Then Nico yelled at Michael and said, 'let's stop stealing for him then…' Michael got real mad and called Nico a damned, crazy spik.'

Lyn Corelli's eyes narrowed at the ethnic slur. She'd been called that and worse because of her name but it never got easier to hear. "And then?"

Cris thought back to the day of the argument, "I remember hearing Michael yelling at him that he wouldn't let them quit. He said things like, 'you don't cross DAL and he wants Berg to shut his mouth. Nico said he wouldn't do it.' Cris stopped a moment.

"Go on, Ms. Crissman."

"Well, then Michael said he was sorry and promised Nico everything would be okay and to just hang loose or something like that. I was scared. Then somebody else came into the room from a back door. I could barely see through the crack from the closet I hid in. It was the older man with white hair I'd seen them arguing with earlier in front of the building. I heard a loud slap and scuffling. Nico was moaning. The old man knocked him down and kicked him. By then, I knew they were talking about the burglaries for sure." She studiously avoided looking at Rainy.

"Dal, Michael and Nico? Those were the names?"

"Yes, but I recognized Nicholas. Michael always called him Nico when he talked to me about his friend. I knew Nicholas was also Michael's friend, my friend's boyfriend. I'd never heard him called Nico so I didn't know they were the same guy until I saw him that day."

"Okay…why didn't you try to call Michael after you left the building instead of your girlfriend?"

"I was afraid."

"But you told the court he was a loving guy. You're dancing around my questions. Why all the secrets?"

"Objection!" Cole stood, bent over his table and glared at the DA, before looking at Cris a moment.

"Sustained."

"He was a thief and a liar," Cris exclaimed.

"So you told your good friend, Rainy Nites, without confronting him first. It's just odd you didn't first confront Mr. Mallory."

Cris looked quickly at Cole before answering.

"Because I knew Rainy was hired by the Metro Assurance Company to investigate the thefts. I already told you that."

"Why not tell the police first?"

"I don't know….. I said I was afraid for Michael."

"Who is Dal?"

"I don't know."

"Objection!" Cole stood up, his chair scraping the polished wood floor, his arm raised in a fist. "Badgering." He saw Anna on the bench behind him just before he turned to sit down again and felt a heavy rock slide away.

"Sustained."

"No more questions your honor."

"Mr. Nites." the judge said simply.

"Thank you, your honor." Cole gave what he hoped was an encouraging smile and led Cris through a maze of prepared questions. He threaded her through the relationship with Michael, the Repertory Theater, Rainy's part in the day of his death, her indecision about who to tell about the conversation she heard in the old building and the subsequent beating she witnessed.

Cris began to relax. She tried not to look at Rainy too often but each time she did, Cole noticed and his eyes came up to study her face.

"Tell me, Ms. Crissman, in your own words, exactly what happened from the moment Lauraine Nites left your dressing room that day." He smiled at her, quieting his thumping heart while trying to pinpoint his unease.

"I barely heard Rainy close the outer door. It's loud, so we usually know when someone comes in or goes out. All of a sudden, there was movement in the mirror…I was sitting at my makeup table and I saw him coming into the room behind me. He looked strange and started asking me questions that made me realize he'd heard my conversation with Rainy. He was angry and pushed me and then slapped my face hard. I was stunned. And then he had a gun pointed at me so I kicked it out of his hand. The gun went off. I don't know if he meant to shoot me but the bullet was real and since I am a Black Belt, trained in self defense, I defended myself. He went down but his head crashed into the corner of my makeup table and he didn't get up." Her voice was a whisper and her lips trembled.

"Is there anything else you would like to tell the court?" he asked quietly, trying to keep the judge riveted on her.

Cris sunk into the witness chair. "No, it was just poetic justice." she answered, relieved. She darted a quick look in Rainy's direction.

Puzzlement filled Cole's eyes.

"Poetic justice?" He asked sharply.

Her green eyes suddenly filled with panic and an intense pleading of remorse crossed her face.

"What was poetic justice, Cris?"

"He didn't want to learn Taekwon-Do because he said he could defend himself without it so he refused to attend my classes and……."

"And…..?" He waited for her to continue.

"I can't tell……." When the whispered words escaped her lips, her trembling hand flew to cover her mouth. She felt the room sway and heat climbed into her face as she stared at Cole.

Cole shuddered, now very sure he'd missed something important and suddenly remembered what nagged at him. Poetic justice, Cole repeated the words in his head slowly and gazed penetratingly at Cris.

Their eyes locked.

The words attacked his memory like a falcon's talon on a leather glove. He heard the phone message in his own kitchen. *"It's poetic justice, darling."* My God, he thought. It was Cris. Cris and Rainy. The panties, the envelopes; M, the initials stood for María. Hell. It sucked the wind out of him as he thought back over the snippets of conversation that Rainy and Cris shared over the past few years in his presence. His eyes held an instant of iciness and he swung around swiftly to look straight into his wife's white, pinched face.

She met his liquid eyes with a start before quickly glancing down at her tightly entwined hands. When she looked up again, she heard him talking to the judge.

"I'd like to approach the bench, your honor," he said as he beckoned Lyn Corelli to join him. She looked confused a moment, and then joined him with a furrowed brow.

Judge McPherson's eyes narrowed, his back ramrod straight.

"There's a new twist to this case. May we please meet in your chambers, sir?" Cole's gut wrenched, still stunned. With his new revelation and Nicholas due to testify, his hope at the possibility of dropped charges fought in tandem with his emotions.

Ten minutes later, the judge slammed the glazed wooden gavel. Everyone was quiet, waiting.

Cris stared straight ahead.

Rainy stared at Cole.

Cole remained mute.

"This court is recessed until two o'clock. Please use this three hour break to rest and prepare for the remainder of the hearing. You may step down, Ms. Crissman." The judge watched her leave the chair, his eyes thoughtful, a little sad.

The bailiff rose. The courtroom began to empty. Cole's hands shook. He shoved his hands into his navy suit pocket to hide them and with all the strength he could muster, walked swiftly out of the courtroom feeling the taste of ashes in his mouth. His assistant grabbed his briefcase, shoved papers inside along with the legal pads. While struggling to understand Cole's behavior, he was also curious about the meeting in the judge's chambers.

Rainy moved toward Cole but he walked straight through the doorway without glancing left or right. Like a well-trained robot, he walked away with Cris's innocent, yet damning, words still in his head. *Was I out to lunch? It was right in front of my damned face.* Cole's lips compressed tightly. His teeth cut through the sensitive skin as he continued along the wide staircase leaving everyone behind.

Anna watched Cole leave in a daze. *What actually happened?* Whispering voices surrounded her as she watched Cris lean heavily against Rainy, saw them embrace. She stared at their faces. Questions cleared and light dawned.

"It's all right, honey," Rainy told Cris as she led her out of the room. "It couldn't be helped. Cole will work it all out for you, I know that and you must too." Rainy's encouraging words came from hope more than sureness. Suddenly, she wasn't sure of anything and gripped her bag until her hand turned numb.

"I'm so sorry, Rainy, but I think he knows about us somehow..."

"How could he guess, Cris? Don't be silly," Rainy murmured, rubbing Cris's back and pulling her along the marble steps leading out to the street. Rainy's head was spinning. "We were so careful." Just imagining Cole knowing about their relationship made her pause but her head swam with possibilities. People bustled around them and they were swept along, unaware they were being watched.

The shock of discovery hit Anna full force. She felt sick and quietly left, numbed with surprise. She turned quickly toward Tess.

"I have to find Cole..." Her face was pale and her breath came in a gasp as she pushed herself along with the crowd.

"Okay, Mom, I'll meet you back here before two." Tess's brow creased as she watched her mother move quickly with her hair wildly off kilter as she skimmed down the steps into the cold, brisk wind.

Anna walked briskly and headed toward Cole's office building.

Sam gathered his cameraman close and called Trudy to his side. He knew he'd seen something in the court room but he was damned if he could figure out what it was. Now that he knew Nicholas was involved, he would have a hell of a story but wasn't budging from the Court House until he got his answers after listening to the hearing in its entirety. He was sure Cole Nites would have Nicholas tell his story to the judge, but Sam knew he'd have his own story either way.

He'd been surprised when Tess called him the evening before to promise him an exclusive interview with Nicholas whether he was in or out of jail. Sam had been shocked. Jail? After nearly an hour's conversation, the story clenched his gut and the adventure of journalism spiked his emotions. His mind was already creating a script from Cris's explanation, the courtroom conversations, the haze of questions and Nicholas Alonzo's part in so much of it. The kid was nearly killed trying to save his daughter. Sam's insides skipped a beat.

Trudy squeezed between the crowd and Mitch, his cameraman. Her smile radiated excitement. She enjoyed the experience of trailing after him, learning the ropes, and liking the man. She wrapped her scarf tighter around her neck and stuffed the ends into her coat front. "What do you think, Sam?"

He smiled down at her and grinned. "It is going to be story time and Elliott will be happy to hear what we come up with on this one. As soon as Cole finishes and we know if there will be a trial or not, we will be ready and beat out the Democrat, hands down. With Mitch videotaping me from the steps, it will be a winner either way. It's all coming together."

Trudy sucked at her bottom lip. "I sure hope she doesn't have to go to trial. It doesn't seem fair when the guy had a gun and tried to…"

Sam looked at her quickly. "Trudy, please keep those feelings to yourself. We must always try to show unbiased opinions. That's one of the most important things to remember when we go on the air and while we are discussing situations like this when others are listening. You must remember that, right?"

She looked down, chastised, but she didn't change her opinion. "Yes, got it. I know you're right. That's why I'm following you like a shadow…I want to learn what the audience needs to hear and say it like the journalist I want to become."

Sam nodded and turned to look at the crowd milling around them. "Mitch, did you get footage of Cris leaving the Court House?"

"Yes, sure did…she was wrapped around her friend, Rainy Nites but I got a good face shot."

Trudy beamed up at Sam and gave him a high five.

"Who's up for hamburgers and a beer?"

His companions looked at their watches. Mitch stashed his camera strap over his shoulder. It was pause time now, but they'd be ready for the remainder of the day on a full stomach.

TWENTY ONE

He was alone inside his office in the Pittock Blocks Building just where she knew he would be. He stared out the window at the pollutant-rich haze trapped between the taller buildings that added to the misery of the air. Its oppressiveness matched his mood.

Christina sat at a desk outside his door, her brow creased with worry. When she saw Anna moving toward Cole's doorway, she put a hand up to stop her.

"Please don't stop me," Anna whispered, eyes begging.

The young woman was unsure how to handle the situation but remembering the look on Cole's face when he returned from court still burned in her memory. She was about to override any qualms about allowing the woman in when her decision was quickly taken out of her hands. She saw Anna slip into Cole's office, quietly clicking the wooden door closed.

His outstretched hands rested on his desk pad while his glazed, grey eyes stared toward the city outside the large plate-glass windows.

She entered quietly and stood behind his chair. Smelling his aftershave, Anna idly wondered again where he shaved when he had such a perfectly shaped beard. She placed her hands on each of his shoulders and pulled his head towards her.

He inhaled her lavender scent but couldn't move. .

Her hands lifted to touch his face, feeling the prickles of hair when she brushed his jaw with her fingers. One hand on each side of his face, the ends of her fingers moving along his neck, she placed her chin on the top of his head.

He groaned softly and covered her hands with his own while leaning his head to rest in her softness, knowing it was Anna from her soft touch and scent. His eyes closed and his lips relaxed into his not-quite full smile.

"Arianna. I'm tired of twisting in the wind too."

"Mmmmmmmmm?" she answered, suppressing a sigh.

"Let me love you."

"With pleasure," she whispered, raising her fine, arched brows.

"Let it be our turn. I was always afraid to love because every time I loved someone, I lost them. This time it feels different. Maybe this time luck will be with me."

"It is." She couldn't miss the musky smell of him as he leaned into her breasts.

"I don't want to just touch the moment, Anna. I want to……."

"……I know," she whispered again, tears lacing her voice.

Cole swung around and pulled Anna onto his lap, buried his head into her soft neck and breathed a kiss where he touched his lips to her aching breast.

She kissed the top of his head and leaned into him.

"Cole, you remade me."

"No, you give me too much credit. You didn't have to be remade. This Anna was always there, inside the old Anna. You just had to be encouraged to…to grow and bloom."

"It was damned hard …. even when you want to change more than anything in this world. Old habits are…….."

"……hard to break?"

"All this time, Cole….I've been looking for the music."

"You are my music."

Anna's eyes dipped to his lips, saw them crinkle into the warm smile she loved. When he looked up, his grey eyes were filled with a curious, deep longing; first he kissed the tip of her nose, then her eyes, and, finally, he satisfyingly kissed her soft mouth while she slipped her hands inside an opening in his shirt to touch his skin. She couldn't recall a time when she'd felt more certain about what she was doing.

As she kissed away Cole's shock, she unlocked his soul.

~

The gavel rose and fell in a thunderous echo.

Cole was slightly surprised to notice Darrin in the hallway after he'd spoken with Cris in the anteroom at 1:30. He'd said something to Cole about watching the master at work. Cole had laughed shortly, wondering about the iron in the older man's voice.

What really surprised him was the conversation he had a few minutes ago with Charlie Royce. Again, it was right in front of his face. Two shocks in one day left him not just a little overwhelmed.

Cris knew what was coming but still flinched under Cole's gaze. He'd said her testimony this afternoon might avoid the need to put Nicholas on the stand. When he'd guessed she had a lover but hadn't said who that lover might be, she was hopeful they were still in the closet. Mixed feelings surged within her.

"Ms. Crissman, would you please tell the court the real reason why Michael Mallory was incensed with a killing anger on the afternoon of November 12th?"

She swallowed hard. "Michael found out I had another lover," she said without hesitation and not just a little relief.

All eyes clung to Cris's face and caught each word as if they were pearls slipping out of an oyster shell.

Sam heard her statement as he eased his way next to Anna and Tess. When he sat down, he patted Tess on the shoulder.

Anna nodded stiffly but her attention was on Cole, praying he could get through the rest of the hearing without faltering.

Darrin Lucas sat at the end of the row by the wall. His face was red and blotchy; the starch in his collar allowing him only a small breathing space. With narrowed eyes, he stared at Cole's back and Cris's pale face beyond.

Rainy sat erect, her eyes also staring into the back of her husband's head, her porcelain nails cutting into the palms of her hand. Nervous, sweat dripped between her large breasts. She hungered for the end of the chaos.

Cris did not take her eyes off Cole as he'd instructed her sternly. She wasn't to look at anyone in the audience, just look at him. Period.

"Ms. Crissman, who your lover is isn't relevant to this case. However, I want to remind you that you are still under oath. Please try to remember the conversation between Michael Mallory and Nico. You mentioned someone named Dal and Andreas. Don't you agree that Dal is an odd name?"

"Yes, I wondered if maybe it stood for someone's name or a short last name....or a nickname."

"Think back, please. Were there any other names mentioned? Either when you saw the old man leave your apartment from the hallway stairs or when he came into the building next to the theater and beat up the young man we now know was Nicholas Alonzo."

Cris sighed deeply before placing her palms to her temples and closed her eyes.

"Take your time, Ms. Crissman," the judge said firmly, kindly.

The courtroom audience sat hushed.

Sam slid to the edge of his seat, watching the scene unfold before him. He glanced quickly at Anna, who was staring with unwavering eyes.

Cris's eyes snapped open. "Oh!" Her face filled with fear, remembering the threatening voice on the end of the phone line. She ignored Cole's instruction and scanned the audience; her breath caught when she locked eyes with the malevolence of Darrin Addison Lucas.

Cole turned slowly and caught Darrin's menacing stare. He stumbled slightly and caught the security guard's eye as they'd planned before he entered the courtroom. A flicker of an eyelid was the barest indication that any message had been sent or received.

Seconds ticked by.

Again, Cole turned to Cris. "Ms. Crissman?"

"Yes," she whispered. "It was Darrin I heard Michael call him. That's him," She pointed to the man at the end of the row as a breathless feeling of triumph flooded through her.

A clatter in the back of the courtroom drew everyone's swift attention as they stared at a white-haired man fighting his way past Anna and Sam's bench, which was completely filled with spectators. He carried his bulk as fast as he could, but stumbled when Sam's right foot tripped him, pulling him into the crowd.

"Damn you, you glory-hunting son of a bitch," he snarled.

The security guard snapped metal rings around Darrin's wrists behind his back and led him out of the courtroom. He was still yelling at the round-eyed television newsman. Before the door closed behind him, he yelled, "I want to make a deal, Cole."

Darrin Lucas didn't hear Cole's steely response, "I'm not in the market."

The gavel pounded. "May we have order in the court?"

Sam Berg's smile glittered, his mind already whipping out the story in his head. He had his big guy, the runner of the game. The big fish. He couldn't wait to get back to work. Adrenaline rushed through his system. This would mean he would have no weekend. It meant overtime and headaches, cold meals and stale coffee. He was in his element. There was nothing quite like it.

A shiver rippled through Cris as she teetered on the threshold of uncertainty; but calmed by Rainy's love from across the room.

The DA stood before the judge. "The reason we are here today is to show substantial proof that María Crissman did, indeed, murder her lover, Michael Mallory. Her use of Taekwon-Do inadvertently caused his untimely death. No matter that she betrayed him twofold; once to her friend because of an alleged damning conversation and second, infidelity with another man. With her experience in martial arts, we know she could have stopped his threats without his death. I think we have cause for a trial and the charge of second degree murder stands from our office. Thank you." Lyn Corelli stared at Cris and took her seat.

Cris sagged next to Cole, her hands resting quietly in her lap, eyes on the oak table. She watched Cole's fingers drum the table quietly during the district attorney's statement. Then they suddenly stopped.

"Counselor?" The judge looked at Cole expectantly.

"If it pleases the court, I would now like to call my only witness, who I believe will give credence to Ms. Crissman's story and invalidate the district attorney's stance." He stood to meet the judge's glance.

He looked at the clock. "Please call your witness, Mr. Nites."

Cole nodded to the guard at the back of the room and within moments, Nicholas walked up the aisle, pushed open the swinging gate and proceeded to the witness stand. Everyone stared at him. At nearly six feet tall, his dark hair and serious demeanor caught the judge's attention as he promised to tell the truth, nothing but the truth or help me God and sat down to face Cole.

Please tell the court your full name."

"Nicholas Cristobal Alonzo."

Nicholas told his story again without a pause. He saw Tess's smile and that was all he needed to get through the dissertation. His chest was tight but his mind was clear; he couldn't hide anymore or steal anymore and he focused on Cole, promising to tell all.

The judge looked at the district attorney questioningly.

She huffed and made a face that resembled a monkey who just ate a sour pickle. "No questions, your honor." She slapped her pen on the table and closed her file.

Cole turned slowly toward the judge, his face calm. "Your honor, we have a young woman, a Black Belt in Taekwon-Do. A young woman who is independent, intelligent, a professional actress who was frightened senseless. Her lover slams into her dressing room brandishing a gun, shouting obscenities and threatens her with death. Her knowledge of martial arts did not lead to Michael Mallory's death by María Crissman's hands or feet. She was a good woman who panicked, pent up with fear. She smelled death in that room on November 12th of this year, possibly her own. She cowered in fear until her fighting spirit surfaced along with her gutsy character that overrode those fears. She wanted to live! No matter what reason the victim had in his head, she wanted to live! She kicked and fought against imminent death in that dressing room with a man she had loved. She is unfortunate rather than guilty. I beg the court to deem this action a death by self defense and drop the charges, avoiding a lengthy trial. Thank you." Cole abruptly turned and walked back to his chair. His fingers tapped distractedly on his knee.

"God, I can't stand the suspense," Sam whispered.

"Shhhhhhh," Anna responded through pursed lips.

There was a yawning pause in the courtroom as the judge studied his notes. With the raising of his hand, both lawyers approached him.

"Mr. Nites.....Ms. Corelli. This court sees no physical evidence to convince me that Ms. Crissman is responsible for Michael Mallory's death for any reason other than self defense. There was no premeditation and it appears her knowledge of martial arts was not used to kill but to save her own life. I see no implied malice or voluntary manslaughter in this case.

This court, therefore, is going to save Lark Point the cost of a trial and she is free to go."

Lyn Corelli nodded woodenly and walked back to her table.

Cole stole a look at the judge whose hand movements clearly showed he was holding a fishing pole, challenging Cole to acknowledge it. His mouth twitched and Judge McPherson banged the gavel. "This court is adjourned," he said loudly.

The bailiff called everyone to rise and the judge stepped off the dais and out of the room.

Cris began to cry as Cole gave her the news that only he and the district attorney was privy to in front of the judge. She reached to hug him but he kept busy pushing papers into his briefcase. "You're free, Cris," he said low. He looked at her and smiled into her tear-stained face as a smile wavered across her features.

"Cole, I don't know how to thank you," Cris spoke in a suffocated whisper as hope slowly rekindled.

"You have already helped me more than you'll ever know...," Cole said. "More than you'll ever know," he repeated. "It was just poetic justice, actually." His words had an odd inflection and he stood.

Rainy's hand touched his arm. He looked at her, feeling indifferent, no longer angry. "Thank you so much, Cole," she said, her cornflower blue eyes shimmering, "for setting Cris free."

A chill black silence surrounded them. "Call a divorce attorney, Rainy.....you're free too," he said calmly and walked away from them.

Rainy stared after him, mouth agape, chest heaving. Standing stock still, her face flushed with embarrassment, she abruptly threw her arms around a trembling, vibrant Cris while her thoughts scattered..

Tears were still flowing as Cris let Rainy lead her past flashing lights, television cameras and away from panic, into freedom once again. Real freedom, it seemed.

"Cris! Rainy! Wait....." Sam Berg's voice was lost in the crowd as he fought his way toward them with his camera man in tow. Behind him, came a crush of newsmen who had been lying in wait at the entrance to the Court House who'd dogged Cris and Rainy all the way to the entrance earlier. Anna had disappeared once again, but he knew their time was over. It was a turning point for everyone.

He stood beside the television camera waiting for the red light to stop blinking, anxious and giddy to tell Lark Point about the judge's ruling and beating the Lark Point Democrat with the story. Trudy Knox handed him his microphone and helped pin it to his collar. Her eyes lifted to his and a blush crept into her cheeks. He lifted his hand to help her and covered it for longer than necessary. The red light blinked quickly, she ducked out of the way and he was Man with the Story once again.

Tess went with Nicholas and Charlie Royce to make a statement, both still unsure whether he would be arrested for his part in the burglaries. Cole hoped, but couldn't promise, his coming forward would make a difference. When they'd told Sam he'd have the exclusive on the story regardless of the outcome, her father said "hope for the best, expect the worst and settle for whatever falls in between." She knew he would be there for both of them.

Darrin Lucas was cooling his heels at the county jail screaming for an attorney, making a mental list of people who owed him so he could pull in their marks. He had a sick feeling Cole wouldn't show up and of course, Steven Mapes was a corporate attorney, so he pinned his hopes on one of the associate attorneys. He was the damned boss, for Gods sake, he knew someone would show up and he'd walk free. He expected to be out on bail soon. Nobody would believe a man of his caliber was actually guilty of any real crimes. Nobody would believe a silly actress and a college kid....would they?

Anna scanned the human wave of spectators as she fled the courtroom in search of Cole. Weak with emotion, she glared at the Channel 14 cameras blocking her way, hoping to avoid Sam.

She felt relieved, free. It was as if life had suddenly come back into focus. Crisp air filled her lungs and joy inflated her soul as she swung her arms and walked down the sidewalk to her Audi parked near the South Park Blocks. *"Tess is okay. Sam's is too really...and me? Yes, I am!"*

Wind blew. Horns honked. Broken thoughts ran rampant through her mind. She would ask Cole to defend Nicholas, call Laura in New York about her book.... She laughed aloud thinking about researching a court case, finding the lawyer, finishing her book with what she learned and above all, she knew she would remember yesterday, plan today and anticipate tomorrow.

There was a crowd surrounding her car when she reached the corner. Inching forward, a gurgle of laughter broke loose amid the people hovering around her. Dancing briskly in the slight breeze was a bright yellow balloon tied to her side mirror emblazoned with SMILE TIL YOUR FACE HURTS. Anna's face was pink as she pulled a small white card between her fingers and looked inside while the crowd watched and egged her on. She smiled, wondering when he could have found the balloon or the time to put it there. The pricking at the back of her eyes told her tears were coming whether she wanted them to or not. Brushing them away, she read the words that finally spelled out the music.

> Dear Anna — — .
> Look beyond the words....
> Is there the remotest
> possibility you might be
> interested in marrying an
> aging attorney who didn't
> know what life had to offer
> until he met you?
> Miraflenras by 8 o'clock?
> Cole

Hugging the card, she tugged at the balloon's twine but it held tight, twisting in the wind. Smiling at the irony, she raised her hand to the crowd, jumped into her yellow Audi and drove away from Lark Point toward the man who began untangling her beside a baby grand piano.

The End

If you would like to sign up for my blog or Facebook Author page to receive updates on my new releases, giveaways or general nonsense from time to time, please send me an email at plumeriapress@gmail.com and I'll add you to the list. I promise to never share your personal information with anyone. And if you would please leave me a review on Amazon or Goodreads, it would be the icing on my cake!

Thank you!

Patricia

www.patriciabbsteele.com/blog

www.facebook.com/patriciabbsteele

www.amazon.com/author/patriciasteele

Twitter @RuizSteele